"I loved this book. Heartwarming and wonderful . . . Elizabeth Grayson captures the American West and makes it her own."
—Maggie Osborne, author of
The Promise of Jenny Jones

"Do you want to see the drawing?" She held out the sketchbook, inviting him, challenging him to have a look.

Baird's hand wavered as he reached for the pad of paper. "You've made me look like some knight errant riding off to do battle against all odds."

But she had drawn him as he was, more kind than inconsiderate, more caring than insensitive. Less of a rakehell, and so much more of a man. She had portrayed both his vulnerability and his strength, the paradox she'd found in him. The things that drew her to him, to the man he was becoming more each day.

"It's the way I see you." She trailed her fingertips along his jaw, leaving a dark smudge in her wake: a curl of carbon that tracked from the corner of his eye to the corner of his lips. "I'm afraid I've put a mark on you," she apologized.

Baird caught her wrist and held her still. "What you've done is put *your* mark on me."

Ardith stood there staring at him. He had left his mark on her, too. Because of him her life had changed. Because of him she had discovered the best and worst about herself. Because of him she'd realized what she wanted her life to become.

She wanted him to mark her again. Now. To-night . . .

To Elaine —

COLOR
OF THE
WIND

Hope it rewards the

Elizabeth Grayson

Elizabeth Grayson

BANTAM BOOKS

NEW YORK · TORONTO · LONDON · SYDNEY · AUCKLAND

COLOR OF THE WIND

PUBLISHING HISTORY
A Bantam Book / May 1999

ISBN 0-553-58010-8

Published simultaneously in the United States and Canada

Bantam Books are published by Bantam Books, a division of Random
House, Inc. Its trademark, consisting of the words "Bantam Books" and the
portrayal of a rooster, is Registered in U.S. Patent and Trademark Office
and in other countries. Marca Registrada. Bantam Books, 1540 Broadway,
New York, New York 10036.

PRINTED IN THE UNITED STATES OF AMERICA

OPM   10 9 8 7 6 5 4 3 2 1

To my nieces
Courtney Lynn and Jacqualyn Elizabeth
Who were my inspiration for this novel.

ACKNOWLEDGMENTS

*B*ecause a great deal more goes into putting a book together than a story, characters, and endless revision, there are a great many people to thank for their interest and expertise.

On the research front, I am obliged to Charles Brown at the St. Louis Mercantile Library Association for leading me to just the right book at just the right moment. Also to Sally Hawkes, for her ability to ferret out the odd bits of information I don't know how I'd find otherwise. Her insight into the vagaries of British marital law is one of the things that made this story work. And special thanks for her friendship.

On the art front, I deeply appreciate the insight watercolorist Jane Mason gave me into the way my characters would deal with this medium. I also owe a big thank-you to Joyce Schiller of the Reynolda House Museum in Winston-Salem for talking me through some of the ideas I used to create the heroine for this novel.

John Villeneuve has once again offered his expertise on frontier weaponry.

If I managed to write convincingly about horses, which I fervently hope I did, it was due to the guidance of these four ladies: Linda Madl, Ginny Schweiss, Kayla Westra, and most especially Tami Hoag. These were very dangerous waters for a confirmed city girl to navigate, and if there are errors in the sections of the novel that deal with horse breaking or horse behavior, they are my own and not for lack of good advice from these four.

Eileen Dreyer gets a gold star and special accolade for her insight and her patience and for listening to me whine. The Divas deserve my thanks for support above and beyond the call. Also there are the friendships that mean so much: Carolyn Villeneuve, Libby Beach, Eleanor Alexander, Renée Witmer, Debbie Pickel, Debbie Dyrks-Norris, Johann Stallings, and so many others.

My special appreciation goes to my new editor, Stephanie Kip, for her inspired insight, and to my agent, Meg Ruley, for helping me to find my way to a safe harbor once again.

And thank you to my husband, Tom, who supports me through fair wind and foul. Being able to share this with you makes it all worthwhile.

He that hath wife and children hath given hostages to fortune; for they are impediments to great enterprises, either of virtue or mischief.

FRANCIS BACON

PROLOGUE

*O*nly her sister's deathbed request could have wrung this promise from her. Ardith Merritt tightened her grip on her nephew's hand, bustling him and her other two charges across the lobby of Boston's busy train station. She had never set eyes on any of the children until a fortnight before, but now that Ariel's death had left them motherless, they were her responsibility—at least until she delivered them to the wilds of the Wyoming Territory. *And to their father.*

Ardith grimaced at the thought and pulled six-year-old Khyber Northcross through the gate. "It's this way, children," she admonished them and glanced back to where Khy's fifteen-year-old sister China and his eleven-year-old brother Durban were trailing along behind.

Out on the platform the coal smoke from half a dozen trains boiled upward to fog the grimy glass of the train shed roof. The engines huffed and wheezed, spewing steam. Bells clanged, metal shrieked against metal, and conductors called out destinations.

Ardith sliced through the crowds and confusion like the

prow of a ship through a choppy sea. She paused only when she reached the train that would take them on the initial leg of their journey west.

The moment they paused, China struck a pose, adjusting the wide grosgrain bow of her bonnet that exactly matched the blue of her eyes. Durban scuffed his feet and scowled with exaggerated impatience. Khyber wiggled his fingers in Ardith's grasp, trying to slip away to go exploring.

She tightened her hold on him and pushed up on her toes, looking for the gentleman who'd been kind enough to see them off. Ardith spotted him immediately. Broad across the shoulders and half a head taller than most of the people around him, Gavin Rawlinson wended his way through the crush on the platform.

Ardith's chest constricted at the sight of him, and she let go of Khyber's hand to adjust the brim of her maroon felt hat. Gavin spotted her at the foot of the steps and flashed a smile. A flush of pleasure warmed Ardith's cold-reddened cheeks.

Silly old maid! she admonished herself, but gave her hat an extra little tilt, anyway.

It was certainly good of Gavin to bring them to the station, and a good deal more than most publishers would do.

"Here are the claim checks for the children's trunks," Rawlinson said, and extended four shiny brass and leather tags. Ardith took them, relishing the brush of Gavin's fingertips even through the fabric of his gloves and hers. "Are you sure there wasn't anything you wanted me to check for you?"

"I have everything I need in this one valise," Ardith answered, patting her voluminous carpetbag. "It's not as if I'll be gone for long. Once we reach the Rock Creek station, I'll turn the children over to their father and board the next train home."

"You don't even want to see the ranch your brother-in-law is managing?" Gavin asked her.

Ardith shook her head, though it was not so much the ranch she was loath to see.

"Visiting the wild west doesn't hold any fascination for me," she lied and affected a delicate shudder. "I much prefer to sit in a comfortable chair drawn up to the fire and *read* about the frontier."

"I'm glad to hear that," Gavin answered, smiling again. And though she knew it was foolish, Ardith allowed herself to imagine his reasons for wanting her here in Boston were personal.

He dashed the notion with his next words. "We need to get the newest 'Auntie Ardith' book printed up as soon as you finish the paintings, since all the others have sold so well."

Ardith had been surprised and pleased that the children's stories she'd written and illustrated had been received with such enthusiasm. She was even more pleased that her words and her paintings of the imaginary community of woodland animals had inadvertently brought her into Gavin Rawlinson's sphere.

He was breathtakingly handsome standing there before her, a few strands of his chestnut-brown hair fluttering in the April wind and his golden eyes crinkling at the corners. She liked the drape of his silky mustache, the cut of his gray wool frock coat and pinstriped trousers. She liked his ivory-handled walking stick and the subtle tilt of his high top hat. He was exactly the kind of man she'd hoped she would find when she was younger—but never had.

"O-o-oh! Aunt Ardith," China gasped, standing with one kid-gloved hand pressed to her flawless cheek. "Just look where Khy's gotten off to!"

Ardith whirled around, realizing suddenly that while she was talking to Gavin, she'd relinquished her grip on the six-year-old. She didn't know how any child could disappear as quickly as Khy did, or get into so much trouble. This time she found he had scaled the towering pile of coal in the coal car.

"Khyber Northcross!" she gasped. "Whatever are you doing up there?"

"I'm king of the hill," he crowed, bracing his hands on his hips, his smile as broad and as dangerous as a pirate's.

And so like his father's.

Ardith strode toward him. "Young man," she demanded, "you climb down from there this instant! I simply won't tolerate—"

But before she could finish, the concussion of cars being coupled to the end of the train sent the force shuddering toward the engine. Khy lurched and flailed his arms, fighting for balance. Coal skittered beneath his feet, and he disappeared behind the side of the car in a puff of dust.

Ardith stepped closer in alarm. "Khyber! Khyber, are you hurt, child?"

"No, ma'am," came the muffled answer.

Ardith hitched up her narrow skirt, preparing to climb the ladder to the coal car to retrieve the boy.

"I'll get him," Gavin offered.

Ardith shook her head, appalled that a man like Gavin Rawlinson should have to dirty his hands on her account. But before she could say a word, the engineer appeared, steadying a child smudged head to toe with black.

"This yours, ma'am?" he drawled.

"No," Ardith answered before she thought. "Yes," she amended. "He's—he's my nephew."

"Well, it appears your nephew will need a bit of washing up," the man observed, assisting the boy down the iron ladder to the ground.

"Indeed he will," she agreed. "I thank you for your help, sir."

Once Khy reached the platform, she gingerly gripped

his collar at the scruff of his neck. It was about the only place that wasn't soiled.

"Oh, Khy!" she admonished him. "Can't you stay clean and out of trouble for even a few minutes?"

Khyber grinned as if being grimy and naughty were laudable accomplishments. He waggled his hands in his sister's face.

"Stop that!" Ardith ordered, tightening her hold and feeling the coal dust grit even through the fabric of her gloves.

"Don't you touch me, Khy!" China squealed and fled up the steps into the sleeping carriage.

Khy reached for his brother instead.

Durban froze him with a glance. "What would mother say?" he asked with cool disdain.

At the mention of his mother Khy burst into tears.

"Durban!" Ardith admonished him, and she thought she saw a flicker of regret cross the older boy's face.

Gavin didn't give him so much as a moment to apologize. He caught Durban by the elbow and maneuvered him up the steps so he could follow his sister inside.

"Oh my dear!" Ardith breathed in exasperation and fished a tatted-lace handkerchief out of her reticule. It was ruined the moment she tucked the delicate square into Khyber's hand.

"Get on the train," she instructed, wondering how she was going to manage these next few days. "And don't touch anything—*and I mean anything*—until I get there to help you wash up."

Sniffing and snuffling and wiping his nose on her pristine handkerchief, Khyber disappeared into the sleeper car.

Climbing onto the bottom step Ardith turned back to Gavin, meaning to thank him and bid him good-bye. He was fighting a smile—and standing so close that she could smell the sweet, smoky scent of sandalwood that clung to his clothes and skin. She could see the razor-fresh turn of his cheek and wondered what it would be like to test its smoothness with her lips. The air fluttered for a moment beneath her breastbone, before she let it out on a sigh.

These were such silly notions for a woman like her to be having. A plain woman. A woman noted for her mind and not her beauty. A woman four years older than the man she fancied.

Then Gavin's gaze shifted from where Khyber had disappeared to her. "Are you sure, Ardith, that you'll be all right traveling alone with those three? I'd feel so much better about you going all that way if you had a maid or someone with you."

"I'll be fine," she assured him, though she, too, was wishing she had some other adult to depend on.

But who might that have been? When Ariel died, the governess who had accompanied her and the children from England had demanded passage back to Bristol. After her uncle's many kindnesses, Ardith dared not ask him to disrupt his lecture schedule to accompany her. And if their long-time housekeeper in Concord thought Boston was at the edge of the earth, what would she make of Wyoming?

Ardith forced herself to smile at Gavin. "All I have to do is get the children through these next five days. Their father will be at Rock Creek station to claim them. Certainly I can keep them together and out of trouble for that long." Yet the words rang hollow in her ears.

Gavin laughed softly, down deep in his chest. "Of course you can; you're 'Auntie Ardith.' You know all about children, don't you?"

Before she could deny it, the bell on the engine clanged and billows of steam wheezed out around the wheels.

" 'Board!" the conductor called out. "All aboard!"

Gavin smiled and handed her the wicker hamper he'd been carrying.

"What's all this?"

"Just some sandwiches and things I thought might make your journey a little easier."

Ardith smiled back, touched by his concern. "Thank you, Gavin."

He reached out and caught her free hand. "Have a good trip, Ardith dear. I'll see you when you get back. I imagine you'll have some very diverting tales to tell me."

Ardith nodded her head. Now that the moment was upon her, she didn't want to take the children to Wyoming. She wanted to stay here, finish the book Gavin was so eager to have from her, and bask in the warmth of this man's smile. It was soft and intimate enough to keep her warm all winter.

Regret gathered in her chest, and she tried to conjure up some appropriate parting words. Just then the train began to move.

As it did, Gavin let go of her hand. She could feel the imprint of his fingers and resisted the urge to press that warmth to her cheek.

The train pulled out. The space of a yard opened between them, three yards, ten. Ardith waved. Gavin smiled and waved back.

Though she knew she was a fool, Ardith savored the moment, wishing there was more to it than there was. Still, she shamelessly indulged herself, standing there a moment longer than was necessary, clutching her valise in one hand and the hamper in the other. Then she turned and climbed the steps.

Once inside she trundled down the aisle of the sleeper car and saw that her charges were settled in seats halfway back. China had turned around, and was smiling and chatting most engagingly with the man in the seat behind her. Durban had his nose jammed in a book. Beside him Khyber sat waiting, long white tear streaks scored through the soot on his face.

Ardith sighed, the pleasant glow of Gavin's good-bye evaporating.

Only the promise to the sister she thought she'd lost long ago could have brought her to this, to chaperoning these three motherless waifs as far as Wyoming—and to confronting their father after all these years.

ONE

So this is exile. Baird Northcross shifted on the seat of the rumbling farm wagon and stared toward a cluster of hardscrabble buildings nestled into the base of the mountains. This dung-heap of a ranch was a full five thousand miles from the leather and tobacco scent of his club in St. James, from the taste of aged brandy and saucy kisses from Drury Lane's opera dancers, from cold fogs off the Thames and the warmth of coal fires burning in London's most fashionable drawing rooms. He'd been exiled to this godforsaken wilderness because his family was quit of him, because his cousin Bram had paid with his life for trusting Baird to act quickly and shoot straight.

Baird's chest tightened as he remembered. He had barely returned from Burma when his uncle, Earl Northam, had summoned him to his London townhouse. But beyond expressing his profound regret at having been responsible for his cousin's death, Baird had had nothing at all to say for himself.

His uncle had skewered him with cold blue eyes, eyes

whose unusual cobalt color was known as the "Northcross Stamp."

"You're thirty-nine, nephew," the earl had begun, "and in all your years of living you've done nothing but seek your pleasure. You've squandered every opportunity the family has given you and every penny of your wife's inheritance on these harebrained expeditions."

Baird had defended himself. "They're for the Royal Geographical Society, sir."

His uncle went on as if he hadn't heard. "It's high time you stopped all that trundling around and accepted some responsibility."

"For Ariel's property in Northumberland, you mean?" Baird asked hopefully, knowing that even at the isolated manor he could find his own diversions.

"No." His uncle's mouth had narrowed with satisfaction. "I have something else in mind entirely."

And this had been it.

Baird tightened his grip on the seat, as the man beside him contrived to ease the wagon over the deep, frozen ruts that passed for a road.

"That 'ere's the Sugar Creek outfit," the driver volunteered unnecessarily. They were the first words he had spoken since they'd headed out at dawn. Baird had given up asking questions about the ranch two days before.

"I gathered as much."

He couldn't help wondering if this fellow had any idea why he was here—or what they called men like him back in England. Men who'd made a scandal of their lives, who'd been censured by their families. Men who'd been sent as far away from London as possible. They were called remittance men—sons of the aristocracy who'd been given an allowance to pave their way to perdition. *Or a job managing a cattle ranch two hundred miles from nowhere.*

Baird had been exiled, plain and simple. But his uncle

hadn't counted on him contriving a way to undermine the sentence he'd been given. No one had. Before he left England, Baird had booked passage to Wyoming for Ariel and the children. They'd be here in less than a month, and then he'd see how long this exile lasted. How long could his uncle hold out against Arthur Merritt's pleas that his daughter and grandchildren be saved from this godforsaken place? And his son-in-law with them—or so Baird hoped.

As the wagon jolted across the wind-battered grassland, Baird began to make out the details of the outpost. The house was larger and far more substantial than he expected. There was a barn around back, several paddocks, and a string of two or three other buildings whose use he could not immediately identify. All of them were roughhewn, made of peeled logs that had weathered to a soft gray-brown in the scant three years the ranch had been in operation.

As the driver shortened up the reins to make the turn that would take them into the yard, Baird caught his arm.

"Stop here," he ordered.

The man blinked. "We unload supplies 'round back."

Baird stiffened; three centuries of Northcross arrogance were evident in the eyebrow he cocked in the ranch hand's direction. "I will arrive by the front door of my new home," Baird informed him, "and be greeted properly."

The fellow shrugged and pulled the team to a stamping halt. Baird jumped down from the wagon seat, his muscles stiff from the hours he'd spent hunched and hanging on for dear life.

"Unload my trunks with the other goods," he instructed and strode toward the door, wondering why the servants hadn't already hustled out to greet him.

When no one had appeared by the time he'd crossed the front porch, Baird stepped up to the door and rapped sharply with the knob of his walking stick.

There was no answer.

He banged his stick again and waited.

Still, no one came.

He tried the latch. The door opened soundlessly until a gust of wind tore the handle from his grasp, banging the wide wooden panel back on its hinges. The sound echoed through the house like a cannonade.

Baird grabbed for the door and closed out the wintry wind. It was little warmer inside. No fire had been laid in either of the wide, stone fireplaces that stood at each end of the long main room. The curtainless windows were etched with frost. The servants would hear about their negligence in not having a fire blazing on the hearth and hot water steaming in preparation for his arrival. Even on safari in Africa and high in the mountains above the Khyber Pass bearers had seen to such necessities.

Putting his irritation aside, Baird strode to the center of the room. So, this was to be his home for the foreseeable future.

At one end a long pine table stood before the hearth. At the other a cluster of heavy furniture flanked the opposite fireplace. The floors were rough-sawed and scrubbed almost white. A few woven rugs broke the uneven expanse. Hunting trophies adorned the walls, several brace of elk and moose antlers, and a buffalo head, its cold glassy gaze fixed on him.

At each end of the main room were doors that must open into the bed chambers. Stairs leading to the enclosed loft above the parlor area climbed the near wall. The place reminded Baird of a hunting box he'd visited in Austria years before.

For all that the floor was freshly swept and the furniture dusted, there was not a soul around.

"Hullo," he called out. "Your master has arrived. Come out and make him welcome."

Still no one came.

Baird shifted on his feet, inexplicable uneasiness pinching his belly. The wind moaning around the corners of the house and his own breathing were the only sounds in that cavernous room. The solitude enforced by those miles of unbroken prairie suddenly bore down on him.

So this is exile, Baird thought again and shivered in spite of himself.

"*Hullo?*"

Baird heard the voice behind him and spun around, scowling his displeasure at the man and woman who came toward him from the back of the house. "It's about time someone came to attend me," he admonished them. "I'm Baird Northcross, your new master."

The tall man ambled nearer; his gray eyes settled deeply into the pockets of wrinkles in his face. "Well, Mr. Northcross," he said. "I expect I do work for you, but out here there's not a man who calls another his master."

Baird raised one eyebrow in disdain. Never did a servant correct his betters.

"I'm Buck Johnson," the man went on. "Before he left for England last fall, Mr. Wycliffe renewed my contract as foreman for another year. This here is my wife, Myra. She cooks for the hands."

Baird spared a glance for the broad, doughy woman who stood nearly as tall as her husband.

"You're not my butler, then?" Baird asked, shifting his gaze back to the older man.

The woman gave a snort of laughter, quickly muffling it behind her hand.

Baird bristled, a flush creeping up his neck. He wasn't accustomed to being laughed at by spoon-wielding hags.

Buck Johnson's mouth tweaked just a little beneath his salt and pepper mustache. "I don't suppose this is the kind of outfit you're used to, Mr. Northcross. We run cows here, not house parties. There aren't any servants, though Myra has showed a couple of the Indian women what she expects when it comes to dusting and washing the floors."

Baird took a moment to wonder how Ariel was going to manage without servants to attend her. He supposed he'd have to get a telegram off to her somehow apprising her of the situation and suggesting she hire servants in Boston to see to their needs while they were here.

"What about my meals?" he asked.

"You're welcome to take breakfast and supper with the hands," Myra invited him. "The mess is out around back. It doesn't much pay to cook a noon meal when so many of the men are gone all day."

It was almost as if these people expected him to adjust his day to accommodate the needs of the men who worked for him.

"I see," Baird answered, but he didn't mean to leave it at that. Once he had established his position here, these people would do as he saw fit. He'd seen how well that practice worked in British possessions across the world, and there was no time like the present to impress upon them that he had every intention of having things his own way.

"I would like for you, Mr. Johnson, to escort me on a tour of the property—this afternoon, if possible. I want to become acquainted with the acreage and see how the stock has fared over the winter months when there's been no company representative to oversee things."

Johnson narrowed his eyes as if he were watching everything from way back inside himself. "If that's what you want."

"Indeed it is. Have my trunks brought in," Baird continued, "and have someone unpack my riding clothes."

"Shall I make up the bedroom upstairs?" Mrs. Johnson asked.

"Is that the master bedchamber?" When she nodded, Baird added, "I want fires laid and lit immediately. I'd like a basin of hot water brought in to me as soon as possible, a bath prepared for when I return from my ride, and dinner tonight on a tray."

"In case you need them, Mr. Wycliffe kept the company ledgers in the bottom drawer of the desk over yonder," Johnson volunteered.

"Well, then," Baird went on. "Perhaps I'll look them over after dinner. Oh, and I'd also like a decanter of your very best whiskey."

Johnson and his wife exchanged a lingering glance. "Very well, Mr. Northcross," Johnson answered. "We'll do what we can."

As the couple turned to go, Baird couldn't help reflecting on just how well his first meeting with the ranch foreman and his wife had gone.

*M*ore than an hour later, Baird emerged from the back of the ranch house and crossed the yard toward the low log barn. Though the fires in the house had been lit, he'd had to carry his own trunks up to his room and rummage through them to find his melton hunting jacket, jodhpurs, boots, and black top hat.

A fair number of ranch hands were gathered out by the main paddock. Buck Johnson came toward him as he approached.

"You about settled in, Mr. Northcross?"

Baird decided not to mention the matter of the trunks. "I've a bit more to do, Mr. Johnson, but I want to see what I can of the ranch while we have daylight."

"I thought you'd want to meet the hands so I called together as many of them as I could find," Johnson explained. "This here's Frank Barnes. He's about as good at wrangling horses as any man I've ever seen."

The Negro cowhand bobbed his head.

"Next is Jeff Mason. He helped bring the first of the company's cattle up from Texas. Willy Martin knows the range 'round here as well as anyone. And Lem Spivey . . ."

Baird acknowledged them all, though he had no intention of being here long enough to get to know the men who worked for him. Only "Bear" Burton and Matt Hastings made much of an impression, the former because he lived up to his name, and the latter because he seemed too young to be doing a cowboy's work.

Once Johnson had finished, the men stood waiting, their mouths drawn tight at the corners and their eyes bright. Did they expect him to address them, Baird wondered, the way his uncle did his retainers when he arrived at one of his country estates?

Baird cleared his throat. "I'm pleased to be in America, and I hope that during my tenure you'll work hard to make this ranch as profitable as possible for our investors back in London."

Baird sensed a reaction among the men, but before he could gauge what it was, Johnson was opening the paddock gate. "We've got a horse all saddled up for you, Mr. Northcross," he said.

Inside the fence a bay and a buttermilk stood tacked and ready. The buttermilk whickered when he saw Johnson.

Baird moved gingerly toward the bay, gathering up its reins, giving the gelding a chance to catch his scent. He'd been riding since before he could walk and knew how to approach an unfamiliar mount.

The bay snuffled and shook his head.

Baird gave the gelding a minute to settle, then reached out to stroke his neck. His eyes rolled and his muscles shimmied beneath Baird's hand, but the bay stood his ground. Baird could sense that the cowboys perched on the fence were judging him by how he treated this animal.

Ignoring them, he kept his touch firm and his voice gentle. "You're a fine, strong brute, now aren't you?" he cajoled, sliding his hand under the gelding's throat latch. "You'd like to be friends, but it's just too soon to trust me."

Baird stepped in close to check the saddle girth, and the pony danced. Baird gathered up more of the reins in his left hand while he stroked with his right.

After riding with English tack, this western saddle seemed monstrous, cumbersome. The horn and cantel were too tall, the stirrups boxy and awkward. Even for a seasoned rider it would take some getting used to.

Beside him, Johnson mounted his buttermilk with practiced grace. Baird would have liked a bit more time with the bay, but he turned his stirrup and tucked his foot into the toe box. As he swung into the saddle, his mount abruptly shied. Baird fought to find his seat and gripped hard with his knees, searching for the off side stirrup. The gelding hopped twice to the right, kicked up his heels, and sent Baird sailing.

He landed hard. The frozen earth was like rock beneath him. Baird rolled to his feet, aware that the men along the fence were hooting with laughter. Hot color seeped up his throat. He had meant to make a more impressive start than this.

Without sparing a glance for anyone, Baird scooped up his hat and set out to catch his horse. It was tripping around the paddock, ears back and reins trailing. Baird spread his arms, shifting right and left and right again, forcing the animal back into the fence. He lunged for the reins and managed to snag them as the horse broke past him.

He took his time winning back the gelding's confidence, soothing it with barely intelligible words, stroking its muzzle, working back to its neck and shoulder.

Except for the shuffle of several more hands arriving, the men along the fence were expectant and silent. Baird let them wait until the bay had lost a few of its misgivings. Cautiously he eased his foot into the stirrup.

The gelding bucked as soon as Baird hit leather, kicking up its heels twice before it gave a twisting hop to the left that unseated him again.

The ground slammed him harder on the second landing. His shoulder pulsed pain down his arm, and he'd twisted his knee. Then above the good-natured ripple of the cowboys' laughter, came the sound of a single man clapping his hands in sarcastic applause.

Baird wheeled toward the cowhands just in time to recognize grins of sly complicity pass from man to man. But before he had time to think what those smiles might mean, he recognized the man at the end of the fence.

It was Cullen McKay.

Baird sucked in a gasp of surprise, his belly tightening. The last time he'd seen Cullen was across a gaming table at White's the year before Baird's younger son was born. He had been spending a few days in London while he waited for the Indiaman he'd booked passage on to load cargo.

McKay had lurched to his feet as Baird raked in the last of his markers. "God'am son-of-a-bish," he'd proclaimed. "B' now, I should know better than t' cross paths with the likes o' him. He's played me false since we was boys t'gether at Harrow, played me false more ways than I can count. And played me false again tonight."

Someone at the table had leaped to his defense. "You're not implying that Mr. Northcross is cheating, are you, sir?"

"What he's implying," Baird had broken in, "is that he

can no more accept responsibility for his actions now than he could when he was fourteen."

McKay had lunged and two of his cronies had swarmed over him. With a smirk of contempt, Baird had watched them wrestle McKay toward the door.

But Cullen was the one smirking now—and at Baird's expense.

The cowhands sensed the animosity between the two men and their laughter gave way to wary silence.

Baird ambled nearer, taking time to study McKay, the lean, wind-bronzed planes of the other man's face; the confident set of his shoulders; the loathing in his bright blue eyes. Nothing had changed in these last years except the essence of the men themselves.

Dressed in fringed and beaded buckskins and a deep, broad-brimmed hat, Cullen McKay seemed to have become a part of this. Part of this life, part of this land.

"Well, well, Mr. Baird Northcross. Whatever in the world has brought you here?" McKay taunted.

Shame glowed like a live coal in the center of Baird's chest, its heat pulsing outward until he couldn't breathe. These *cowboys* didn't know he'd been exiled here, but Cullen did. They wouldn't realize what he was, but Cullen knew what name to call him: failure, outcast. Remittance man.

It didn't matter that Cullen might have been sent here for the same reasons he had. Not when Baird had always considered himself so far above his uncle's bastard son.

Though feverish color burned in his face, Baird kept his tone level and gave what credence he could to the lie. "I agreed to oversee the family's holdings in the ranch this year."

"Really?" McKay exclaimed on a gust of derisive laughter. "What an incredible stroke of good fortune!"

"Good fortune?" Baird flushed hotter, the butt of some joke he didn't understand. "And how is that?"

"I manage the Double T, over that ridge to the south," McKay drawled. "My investors have been trying for some time to buy the Sugar Creek's cattle and water rights. So far your uncle and his board of directors have refused all offers. But after you've managed this place for a season or two, they'll be happy to sell—probably for pennies on the dollar."

Baird hadn't considered what his uncle and his backers would expect of him in financial terms. He hadn't acknowledged the responsibility that came with this place. He hadn't acknowledged anything but the disgrace. And his resentment.

Now, faced with Cullen McKay, his taunts, and his evident success, Baird would be forced to acknowledge why he was here in Wyoming.

"I wouldn't count my chickens before they've hatched, McKay," Baird shot back. "If you've learned to run a cattle ranch, any monkey can!"

"And you think you're that sort of monkey, do you, Northcross?" Cullen gave a snort of laughter. "With you here, my job is a good deal easier. I can scarcely wait to write my backers and tell them you've come to manage the Sugar Creek this season. Baird Northcross, indeed." He pushed away from the fence. "A man who can't so much as keep his seat on a western saddle."

As if to demonstrate his own facility, McKay turned and sprang onto his horse. The two cowboys who'd ridden in with him did the same.

Baird watched them go, furious with McKay and disgraced in front of his own hands.

There wasn't a sound in the paddock after McKay and his men left, nothing except the ceaseless chatter of the wind through the winter-dry grass. Baird, who'd traveled far and wide, had never felt so displaced, so very much a stranger.

With an effort he turned to where the gelding stood.

The horse's head was bowed, his reins trailing on the ground.

"What's his name?" he asked, suddenly needing to make some connection in this alien world. "Does this horse have a name?"

"Dandy," someone called out, and the irony was not lost on Baird.

"Well, old Dandy," he crooned, as he moved nearer. "Are you going to let me ride you this time?"

The bay rolled his eyes and shifted his feet.

Baird gathered up the reins and stroked the gelding's rough winter coat. "Does no one curry you, fellow?" The horse snorted. "Will you let me groom you later?"

As he waited, working his hand up the big bay's chest and toward his shoulders, Baird became aware of a hum in the air, a focused awareness from the men gathered along the fence. He could feel the heat of it against his back, a certain discomfort emanating from the assembled ranch hands.

He glanced over his shoulder as he reached to grip the saddle horn, but something in the cowboys' faces gave him pause. Baird turned and looked at them directly.

One ducked his head; several turned their eyes away.

Baird looked toward Buck Johnson, seeking something in those deep, watchful eyes. Johnson studied him hard, then gave the ghost of a smile.

Acting half on intuition, Baird slowly loosened Dandy's cinch and ran his hand along the shallow curve of the horse's back.

"Easy, boy," he whispered as the bay began to dance. "Easy, Dandy."

He probed deeper, beneath the saddle, not sure what he was looking for until he found it. Something pointed and sharp was wedged between the saddle blanket and Dandy's coat. He pulled the blanket free and worked a long, wicked-looking thorn out of the thick, woven fabric.

Baird stood there in stunned surprise. The thorn had been stuck in that blanket deliberately. His hands began to shake as he looked from the thorn, to the gelding, to the men along the fence.

This time the cowboys stared back without flinching, acknowledging what they'd done. These men had dared to test him. These—*hirelings*—had challenged his horsemanship, his skill, his very right to be here. They'd humiliated him in front of Cullen McKay. He ought to fire the lot of them, tell them to clear out their belongings and leave the ranch.

And what would that accomplish?

He sensed Johnson's eyes on him, sensed him waiting to see what Baird would do.

He looked down at the thorn again, all spiny and black—and then he laughed. Deep, rich peals of hilarity, that spiraled upward in the cold air. Booms of mirth that made Dandy shy and left Baird gasping.

Along the fence, the cowboys spat and slapped each other on the back, chuckling among themselves. They raised their eyebrows and shrugged as if to say this boss was an Englishman who might bear watching.

The men were grinning by the time Baird caught his breath enough to unsaddle Dandy. He went through the tack carefully, smoothing the blanket before settling the saddle over it, double-checking the girth to be sure it was tight. This time when Baird swung up onto the big bay, he settled back in the saddle like a granny into a rocking chair.

Johnson's mustache quirked at one corner and he nudged his buttermilk toward the gate. "You 'bout ready for your tour now, Mr. Northcross?" he inquired.

Baird nodded. "Oh yes, Mr. Johnson, I believe I am."

• • • •

"*It* certainly isn't England," Baird mumbled half to himself as he stared out across what seemed like an endless expanse of prairie land.

Beside him Buck Johnson shifted in his saddle. "Did you expect it to be?" They had paused in their tour of the ranch at the base of a high stony ridge that ran off to the south. Baird shrugged, not sure what he'd expected—not England's manicured countryside, not its saturated shades of green and gold, not the scent of boxwood or the trill of meadowlarks.

But he hadn't anticipated anything like this, either. He scanned the miles of yellowed grassland to where it met the thick gray fleece of the winter sky. He sensed the mountains hunched in ridges at his back, felt the raw wind and the solitude.

This place was different from anywhere he'd ever been—the steamy jungles of Burma, the towering peaks of the Khyber Pass, the teaming African savannah. This land, this Wyoming, was like a feral half-grown child, one who would never tolerate a master. That spoke to something inside of Baird.

"How much of this belongs to the ranch?" he asked, glad that the sudden tightness in his throat hadn't tainted his voice.

Johnson shook his head. "All of it," he said. "None of it."

Baird turned to look at him. With his hat pulled low and his sheepskin collar turned up around his ears, Johnson's cheeks shone red in his weathered face.

"What do you mean?"

The older man's mouth narrowed, drawing his mustache down over his lower lip. "Didn't anyone tell you how this works?"

Baird remembered the portfolio of papers his uncle had had delivered to his father-in-law's house the day before he left London. He hadn't so much as glanced at them, not once on the voyage, not once on the train.

"No," he answered.

Johnson drew breath as if he were reluctant to explain to someone who didn't give a damn about the ranch and who would leave at the end of the summer—if not before. But Baird continued to stare, not giving him any choice.

"This ranch," Johnson began, "and most of the cattle ranches from here to Mexico, count on something called free range. That means that the cattle graze on the land that no one claims, land that belongs to the United States government."

"You mean the Greater British Cattle Company doesn't own any of this?" he asked incredulously.

"The company bought range rights when they invested in the herd so they'd be sure to have access to water."

"Down along Sugar Creek, you mean?" When Johnson nodded, Baird went on. "And the rest of this is good grazing land?"

It seemed hard to believe, as trampled and yellowed and weather-beaten as the landscape looked.

Johnson's eyes began to shine. "It's the best the Lord could provide. Come spring that bay of yours will be chest deep in grama grass, as green and sweet as honey. The beeves thrive on it, and as it dries, it blows in the wind like waves of gold. For cattlemen, it's every bit as precious."

Baird nodded in acknowledgment. If what Johnson said was true, whoever came up with this investment was a genius. "So we buy cows cheap, fatten them on this free grass, and sell them for a profit."

"That's the way it's supposed to work," Johnson allowed. " 'Course, it's not always as simple as that."

Baird turned a deaf ear to the older man's qualification. This wasn't an investor's gamble; it was a sure thing. Maybe he should unearth that portfolio from his baggage and see if he could figure out just how successful the enterprise had been these past three years. It must be fool-proof, he thought, for his uncle to entrust the ranch to him. Something even he couldn't mismanage. He felt both suddenly better, and infinitely worse, about his exile to the wilds of America.

Baird shortened up his gelding's reins. "I'd like to see the rest of it."

Johnson led him higher up the ridge, into the foothills of what he told Baird were the Big Horn Mountains. With each loop of the trail, the view became more spectacular, a rolling carpet of land stretched to where the horizon blurred with the haze of approaching dark. Baird tried to fill his eyes with it and failed, tried to understand his place in the scope of such country as this and failed a second time.

" 'Bout time we started back," Johnson finally suggested. "Myra'll have supper ready."

Baird was cold and the idea of a meal, a warm fire, and a tumbler of whiskey appealed to him. Still, he was reluctant to leave this new place that had begun to work its wiles on him.

Buck Johnson led the way down the ridge, circling to the north and taking a different trail, one that shadowed the creek's meandering course. They had been riding for some time through a cluster of pines and the deepening dusk when Johnson pulled up short. He signaled Baird to stop and slid the rifle from his saddle holster.

Baird instinctively reached for the Winchester that hung to the right of his own saddle and peered ahead. There were half a dozen deer grazing in the meadow at the far side of the creek, standing motionless and nearly invisible against the brindle-brown grass.

"We'll just get one of these to take home to Myra," Johnson said under his breath as he raised his rifle. He carefully sighted down the barrel and fired. The boom reverberated from the sides of the creek bed and the deer scattered, springing away swift and graceful.

All the deer ran.

Johnson swore softly. He'd missed his shot.

In a single motion Baird knocked the rifle to his shoulder, and barely taking time to aim, pulled the trigger. He caught one of the deer in mid-flight. The animal stiffened, lost its grace, and dropped like a stone. It lay twisted and broken halfway up the slope on the far side of the stream.

Baird lowered the rifle from his shoulder and realized his hands were shaking. His chest was tight and he sucked in one long breath and then another. He was dizzy, feverish and sweating as if it were high summer instead of twenty degrees.

Johnson swiveled around in his saddle and stared at him in surprise. If he noticed any of what Baird was feeling, he gave no sign of it. "Nice shot, Mr. Northcross," he said. "You're quite a marksman."

Baird stifled the urge to mop his brow on the sleeve of his riding jacket. "Yes," was all he said.

Two

Ardith's troubles with the children began their very first night on the train. She was just snuggling down into her Pullman berth when Khy peered at her from the bed above. Even in the dim light that filtered through the privacy curtains, Ardith could see that he'd been crying.

"What's the matter?" she murmured, mindful of the other sleepers only a curtain away.

"I—I . . ." His lip began to quiver.

"What is it, Khy?"

He climbed down into her narrow berth. "I wet the bed," he whispered back.

She stared at him, appalled. Did boys his age still do that? "Why—why on earth didn't you get up and use the gentlemen's privy?"

Two big tears rolled down Khy's cheeks. "I—I don't know. I didn't mean to do it."

Ardith heaved a sigh. "Of course you didn't." She reached for her wrapper and pulled it on. "I guess I should go ask the porter for fresh sheets and see—"

Khy's eyes went wide in a face still faintly smudged

with coal dust. "Oh, no, Aunt Ardith! You mustn't tell anyone!"

The way he ducked his head and the quaver in his voice made something shift uncomfortably in Ardith's chest. Instead of acknowledging it, she pursed her lips and clambered past the boy into the aisle.

A tall Negro porter swayed toward her. "Is there something you need, ma'am?"

Feeling her own face heat with embarrassment, Ardith explained the problem.

"That happens sometimes," the man soothed her. "Traveling upsets children's schedules. Sometimes they don't wake up. Sometimes they're just too shy to climb out of their beds to do what they need to do."

Ardith swallowed hard. This porter—this stranger—was showing her nephew more concern and understanding than *she* had been able to muster on his behalf.

"I—I thank you for your kindness," she murmured.

After Ardith had located a clean pair of drawers for Khy and helped the porter strip the upper bed, she ducked back inside the curtains. Khy was wedged into the farthest corner of her berth, curled in upon himself as if he wanted to disappear.

"Are you better now?" she asked him.

He sniffed and nodded.

Ardith eased onto the bed and wondered what to do with him. The mattress on the upper berth was soaked, and the porter said there were no unoccupied berths anywhere on the train.

"Well, Khy, I—I think you should sleep with me tonight," she began, trying to sound more matter-of-fact about the arrangement than she felt.

"You do?" His eyes went round again.

"I think you were lonely up there by yourself," she went on, seizing on the first thing that came into her head. "I—I think in a strange place it helps to have some-one close at hand."

He ducked his head, his shoulders hunching. "You won't tell Durban, will you?" She could hear the tears still in his voice. "He'd call me baby for—well—you know."

The weight inside her shifted again, and Ardith didn't have the faintest idea how to make things better.

Oh, dear, but I'll be glad to get these children to Wyoming! she thought before she mustered a smile to reassure him.

"I won't tell Durban anything. But I do want you to lie down here beside me, but on the aisle, so that if you need to get up, you can. And I want you to wake me so I can walk you to the privy. Is that all right?"

"Yes." It was a small word, spoken with grave uncer-tainty.

Ardith helped him climb past her in the swaying berth and then put her own back to the wall of windows. Khy settled down on his side facing away and lying there stiff as a stick, as if he wasn't sure she could give him the comfort he needed.

Ardith wasn't sure either, but she had to try. "It's all right," she murmured and tentatively put her palm against his back. When he didn't flinch away, she curled it around his shoulder.

In all her life Ardith had never slept with anyone, not even as a child. It made her profoundly aware of Khy's heat radiating against her chest and thighs. His soft, ruf-fled breathing seemed loud in the silence. She wasn't sure she even liked having someone so close, yet she let him nestle nearer.

His tousled hair brushed her throat. His faintly musty little-boy scent filled her nostrils. She shifted her palm to the center of his chest, inscribing a warm, protective arc with the curve of her arm.

Just when Ardith was beginning to think Khy had fallen asleep, he turned to her. "Aunt Ardith?"

"Yes?"

"Why did our mama go away from us?"

The catch in Khy's voice tore at her. She'd expected the children to ask her that a few weeks back, and she had practiced some proper Christian platitudes she'd hoped would satisfy them. She'd been heartily relieved when none of them had wanted her to explain their mother's death.

Now, lying with Khy's vulnerable flesh pressed close against her own, Ardith knew she couldn't ease his misery with those cold, dead words.

"Oh, Khy," she murmured, hugging him tight. "I don't know why your mama went away. I know she loved you and China and Durban. I know she wanted to stay with you, and that she cried when she asked me to take you to your father."

Ardith remembered the feverish glitter in Ariel's eyes as she'd demanded that promise, and Ardith was ashamed that the words that would release her sister and give her peace had stuck to her own lips like bits of cotton wool.

She heard Khy sniffle and she pressed her cheek into his hair. "Don't doubt for a moment how much your mama loved you," she whispered. "She would have stayed here with you if she could."

Ardith lay barely breathing, waiting for some sign that what she'd said had helped. Finally, Khy sighed and the tension seemed to leave his curled body.

*T*he children asked Ardith no more questions about their mother during the next two days, but there were a myriad of others. How did trains get across rivers before there were bridges? Why did apples have skins you could eat and oranges didn't? How do cows make milk? There would be plenty more today, Ardith surmised, because they were going to explore Chicago.

She originally had intended simply to change stations in Chicago and press directly on toward Omaha. But traveling with these three was like being corked up in a jug of fermenting cider, and they needed a day out of the swaying cars to expend that pent-up energy.

After securing a suite of rooms at the Palmer House, Ardith and the children explored the city, visiting the lakefront, going to museums and shops. When she finally collected their key from the desk clerk just before five o'clock, she had to admit the day had gone far better than she'd dared to expect.

But as she trailed the children across the lobby, that sense of well-being evaporated. Ardith began to notice how the women paused in their conversations to stare at China, that men looked up from their newspapers, their eyes alight. The girl shone like a comet searing its way across the sky. And suddenly Ardith felt like she had when she was a child; like a dull, dun-gray shadow trailing in her sister's glittering wake.

She came up behind the children where they were waiting for the elevator, just in time to hear a man addressing China. "Do you suppose, Miss Northcross, that I might meet you here in the lobby later? I'd like to hear more about this ranch your papa's managing."

The way the man was leering at her niece sent ripples of alarm along Ardith's nerves. "She most certainly may not meet you, sir!" Ardith spoke up before China could answer. "And it's completely inappropriate for you to be proposing such a meeting to any lady, much less a girl of my niece's tender years."

"Oh, Aunt Ardith!" China gasped, her cheeks flushing the color of cherries. "Please!"

"How old *is* she?" the man asked, turning a scowl on her.

"She's fifteen," Ardith answered and watched with a pinch of satisfaction as the man hastily backed away.

"Be assured ma'am, I meant no offense," he mumbled.

Just then the elevator arrived, and Ardith hustled everyone into the car. They had barely risen beyond the level of the lobby when China burst into tears.

"Oh, Aunt Ardith! How could you embarrass me so?" she accused with a sniff. "I was only chatting with that gentleman. He meant no harm, and I'm old enough to take care of myself!"

The man's oily smile had hinted at something far less innocent, something Ardith was loath to discuss with her outraged niece. "You're just like your mother," she hissed instead.

China's tear-bright eyes widened. "My mother was a great and beautiful lady. I would be proud to be like her."

"Your mother was a flirt," Ardith pronounced and heard China gasp.

Remorse for her hasty words grabbed Ardith hard. How could she have said such a thing to Ariel's own daughter—especially in the wake of her mother's death? How could she malign her sister's memory?

"I'm sorry, China." Ardith reached out, needing to apologize and cursing her lack of delicacy in dealing with her temperamental niece. "It's just that I don't want to see you hurt."

China sniffed and chose to ignore her. Once inside their suite, she flung herself into a chair to sulk.

Ungrateful chit! Ardith thought, aggravated by the girl in spite of herself. When she'd promised Ariel to see the children to their father, it had never occurred to her that her responsibilities might include the role of duenna.

But then, why not? China had been blessed by the same kind of fairy who had waved her wand over her mother. Ariel had discovered the power her beauty gave her when she was little more than a child and had used it without a qualm.

Beauty was not something to which Ardith had ever

aspired. How could she be beautiful when her hair was mud-brown and her eyes were the color of agates? When she far more resembled an Amazon than a sylph? Ardith had accepted long ago that there was no sense wanting things she could not have: things like beauty, or a father who adored her, or marriage to a man who set feminine hearts aflutter.

Instead Ardith had devoted herself to being astute and dependable, the kind of woman her Uncle Franklin found so useful. Yet even in Concord, she had suffered for her plainness. Men with whom she'd been discussing Plato would look up to follow Dulcy, their sweet-faced parlor maid, with their eyes; or take note of ravishing Cecily Mayhope's entrance into the room. They were small defections, but each of them was a reminder of a larger one—the scandalous defection that had sent Ardith fleeing England for America.

China had yet to understand the power her beauty would give her over some men's hearts, or the responsibility that wondrous gift required. It was something Ariel had never learned; she had never tried to sheathe her claws. And though the scars Ardith bore had long since faded to white, there were nights when she lay alone in her narrow bed and cursed all she had forfeited to her sister's loveliness.

Pushing memories of Ariel to the back of her mind, Ardith took out the Ned Buntline novel she'd bought this afternoon and began to read aloud. It was one of what her uncle referred to as "ten-penny dreadfuls," but the children had seemed to enjoy the book she'd read them on the train, and they seemed as eager to hear this new yarn as they had the last.

The western novels were Ardith's secret vice, tales of men who wore guns on their hips and fought for justice and honor. Of course, no one else in Concord read such sensational tripe, but Buntline's stories were colorful and fast-paced. There was an allure in the way he portrayed the west that Ardith found irresistible.

Truth to tell, her reading material had played no small part in her decision to take her niece and nephews to their father. She might well have stayed on in the Wyoming Territory—the setting for many of the books—if not for her loathsome brother-in-law. Being civil while she dealt with Baird over the matter of Ariel's death and the children's future would tax her almost beyond bearing. To stay longer would mean accepting Baird Northcross's hospitality, and she utterly refused to do that.

Once they reached Wyoming, she would relinquish the children's welfare to their father and climb aboard the first train she could find that was headed east, rejoicing at having discharged her responsibility to her sister, her sister's children—and their father.

"*D*urban! Come away from there, Durban. You're not having another of those meat pies are you?"

Ardith felt as if she'd been trying to herd feathers through the warren of waiting rooms, baggage areas, newspaper stands, and food vendors on the platform of the Omaha station. The overnight trip from Chicago had been uneventful, but she had just barely had time between trains to recheck their baggage and telegraph Baird that his children would be arriving at Rock Creek this evening. And now Durban was dawdling.

Leaving Khy in China's care, Ardith stalked toward the pie vendor. She saw the flash of wariness in the vendor's face as she bore down on him, and for once she was pleased that she cut such an intimidating figure. "How many pies have you sold this young man?" she demanded.

"I sold him five," the old man answered, drawing back into the folds of his coat as if it were a turtle's shell.

One look at the man's grimy clothes and hands convinced Ardith she wouldn't eat anything he sold her. But by now she'd learned that eleven-year-olds weren't nearly so discerning.

"Five pies?" she echoed.

"I was hungry," Durban defended himself.

Ardith shook her head and put her hand on Durban's shoulder. She steered him back toward the spot where China and Khyber were waiting, and together the four of them hauled their baggage up the steps of the first-class car.

Before they were five miles out of Omaha, Khy was tipped upside-down in his seat, and China was complaining she was bored. Durban watched through half-closed eyes as Ardith took out the Buntline book she'd begun to read them the night before.

"Chapter Five," she said, struggling to keep the print in focus on the swaying train. "The Midnight Raid."

The children were immediately caught up in the story of Will Stanton, who had been steadily losing the cattle in his herd to rustlers. Having determined who the culprits were, Will was setting out to confront them.

She was halfway through the chapter when Durban interrupted her. "Aunt Ardith?"

The boy was bent nearly double in his seat, his face slick with sweat and faintly gray. Ardith's heart slammed to a stop against her breastbone.

"I think I'm going to be sick," he said, his mouth gone slack.

"Not now!" Khy protested. "I want to find out what happens!"

Ardith had no such compunctions. She tossed the book to China and leaped to her feet, hustling Durban toward the gentlemen's washroom at the end of the car. Two or three men were waiting for their turn at the privy, but she pushed past them without so much as an apology. The man washing his hands at the sink squawked in protest at a woman bursting into this male sanctuary, but Ardith was too busy maneuvering Durban to his knees in front of the commode to take much notice.

The boy was horribly ill, shivering and choking up everything he'd eaten since breakfast. "I'm sorry," he whispered. His knuckles shone white as he clung to the wooden seat of the commode. "I'm so sorry."

"It's all right, Durban."

"I didn't mean to be so much trouble," he murmured and, with a shiver, was sick again.

He looked so defenseless crumpled there on the floor, not a prickly boy but a helpless child. Ardith bent above him, gnawing at her lower lip in sheer frustration. Her palms itched with the need to touch him, to hold him, but she didn't have any idea how.

"It's all right," she finally said and reached across to steady his head.

Even after the worst of the nausea had passed, Durban hunched over the commode as if moving would take more energy than he could muster. He began to cry.

It was the very last thing in the world Ardith had expected. Durban was usually so aloof and self-contained, so stubborn and defiant.

Ardith tasted tears of her own in the back of her throat. If ever a child needed comforting, Durban did. He was ill and alone, except for her. His mother was dead, and there was no one in the world for him to depend on. *There was no one but her for any of these babies to depend on.*

Ardith longed to hunker down and wrap her arms around the sobbing boy, but something about the way he curled in upon himself held her back.

Desperate to do something, Ardith pumped water into the sink and sacrificed another of her lacy handkerchiefs. She handed Durban the square of dampened linen and supervised as he mopped his face and throat.

A modicum of his color was returning and the tracks of

his tears were fading when Durban finally struggled to his feet. "I—I think you were right about the pies," he allowed.

Hearing him admit that should have given Ardith a twinge of satisfaction. She felt responsible instead, totally ineffective at protecting the children, stewing in regret. She should have done better.

She brushed back a few limp strands of his sweat-slicked hair, straightened his collar, and patted his rumpled clothes into place. She might have done more if she hadn't suddenly realized how tall he was and how rigidly he was holding himself.

"Are you feeling better?" she asked, knowing there was nothing she could do to prevent him from withdrawing again, from becoming that aloof, sullen Durban Northcross. She could see it happening before her eyes.

"I think I'd like to sleep for a while, if that's all right."

"You're not going to be sick again?" she asked, her hands still fluttering over him.

He shook his head. "I don't think so."

Ardith followed Durban out of the washroom and back to his seat. "You just rest," she told him and snugged the wooly folds of her shawl around his shoulders.

He hunkered down in his seat and nestled his head into the crook of China's shoulder. Wrinkling her nose with distaste, his sister grudgingly let him.

Ardith stood over them feeling useless, inept. Left out somehow. Instead of resuming her seat, Ardith wheeled toward the front of the car.

She stepped out onto the open platform and wrapped her hands around the railing. She let the wind and cold beat over her. She was shaking inside, not so much from Durban's bout of illness, but from what those minutes in the gentlemen's privy had made her realize. How terrible she was at dealing with these children. How utterly lacking she was in humanity.

She should have known enough to get down on her knees beside Durban and hold him. She should have known what to say to Khy about his mother. She should have been able to put her own feelings of inadequacy aside and ease China through her first encounter with a man's less-than-noble attentions.

She was only beginning to realize how desperately fragile these babies were in the wake of their mother's death. They had been abandoned, deprived of their stability, stranded four thousand miles from their home with a woman they barely knew. With a woman who wanted nothing more than to shunt them off to their father and didn't even know enough to hide her feelings.

Like most women who'd never had children of their own, Ardith had always wondered what kind of a mother she might have been. She'd told herself she'd be warm and tender and caring, but in these last few days she'd proved she wasn't strong enough or compassionate enough to give these children the kind of safety and security they cried out for.

She was without the most fundamental maternal instincts. She was more given to ideas and theories and stories in books. She was more concerned with herself than providing the stability these children needed. Knowing that shamed her, tormented her—made her feel as if she was only half the woman she should have been.

Well, at least when they reached the Rock Creek station they'd have their father. No matter what had passed between Baird and her years before, no matter what she thought of how he'd treated her sister, these children were his. He'd know what to do with them, how to comfort them, how to protect them.

She would be able to give the children up to someone who loved them. She would discharge the promise she'd made to Ariel, and knowing the children were safe, she could climb on the train bound for Massachusetts. Once she was back in Concord, once she was immersed in her world of books and painting and lectures, she'd be able to ignore the terrible inadequacy she'd discovered in herself and take comfort in the cold, inevitable fact that she would never have children of her own.

THREE

Ardith glowered at the balding telegraph operator who stood behind his grill at the Rock Creek station. "What do you mean Baird Northcross isn't here? I telegraphed him this morning advising him that his daughter and sons would be arriving on this evening's train."

The man nodded and peeked at her from under the curve of his green eyeshade. "Yes, ma'am, you did. I see here Charlie took down the message neat as you please."

"You mean the message hasn't been delivered to Mr. Northcross's ranch?"

"To his ranch?" The telegrapher looked at her in surprise. "No, ma'am. Our job's to transcribe and send messages, not see they get delivered. And the Sugar Creek's a full two hundred miles from here."

Ardith stared at him. The ranch Baird Northcross was running was two hundred miles from a telegraph line? Two hundred miles from any semblance of civilization? Had Ariel had any idea what she was getting into when she agreed to spend the spring and summer in Wyoming with her husband?

Obviously not, Ardith thought. Ariel had always abhorred rustication.

"Well, then," Ardith continued, shifting her attention back to the telegraph operator. "Just how can I get word to Mr. Northcross that his children are here?"

"The fastest way's to take it yourself," the man suggested.

A trip across miles of open country in the last wheeze of winter wasn't part of Ardith's plan. "Isn't there someone I could send?"

The clerk shrugged. "You might ask at the hotel or the saloon and see if there's someone headed up that way." Just then the telegraph receiver began to clatter, drawing the man back to his duties.

Ardith turned and stomped across the station's waiting room, furious at Baird Northcross for living so far from the station, furious at herself for not sending the message sooner.

The children were waiting on the platform in the quickly gathering dusk. China perched primly on one of the trunks. Durban still looked pale and wilty even though he had slept most of the afternoon. Khyber was racing from one end of the station's boardwalk to the other whooping like an Indian savage.

"Is Papa coming?" China asked above the din.

"It seems as if your father never got the telegram I sent him," Ardith answered, peering toward where Rock Creek's unimpressive cluster of buildings hunched together in the twilight. "The ranch is some distance from here, and we're going to have to get someone to take us."

"How long will it take to get there?" Durban wanted to know.

"Several days, I should think." Ardith took a bracing breath and in spite of their predicament, liked the crisp taste of the prairie wind. "Our first priority is to find rooms for the night. We'll have a good sleep and figure out the rest in the morning."

Unfortunately, accommodations at the rickety building that passed itself off as a hotel were far more suited to tired cowboys than to a New England lady and her charges.

"We're staying here?" China asked incredulously when she saw the small, dim room with its sagging bed and graying linens.

Ardith's reaction might have been the same if she hadn't been wrestling with their baggage and trying to keep Khy from bolting down the hall. When she did have time to notice, she concluded it was probably the best room they were likely to find, and set to making up pallets on the floor where the boys could sleep. When she was done, she gathered up her coat and reticule.

"You're not leaving me alone with the two of them, are you?" China gasped.

Ardith swallowed a surge of irritation. "I need to find someone who'll take us to your father's ranch," she explained as patiently as she could. "And there's no one to keep an eye on the boys while I'm gone but you."

"Mother would never have expected me to look after them," the girl complained, her azalea-pink lips puckered mutinously.

Your mother would never have gotten as far as this without a maid, a governess, and a battery of footmen. Just what arrangements Baird might have made to convey his wife and the children to the ranch Ardith could only guess.

"Just keep the door locked while I'm gone," Ardith instructed. "I *can* count on you to do this, China, can't I?"

The girl grimaced, shrugged and finally nodded.

Promising the children she would return with something for supper, Ardith went downstairs. She was consulting with the desk clerk about how they might reach the Sugar Creek Ranch when a man came in from the street.

"This is the very fellow I was telling you about, ma'am," the clerk said by way of introduction.

Ardith turned to a tall, sandy-haired man dressed in a pale buckskin shirt stitched thick with beads and a pair of tight, fringed trousers. He sported an impressive blond mustache and wore a six gun on his hip. *A real cowboy,* Ardith thought with a start of delight.

But her hopes were dashed a moment later when she heard the sharp, clipped articulation of English public school speech. "May I be of service to you, ma'am?" he asked, doffing his hat.

"Mr. McKay?" she began. "Please allow me to introduce myself. My name is Ardith Merritt. I am escorting my niece and nephews to their father at the Sugar Creek Ranch."

The man's sun-bleached eyebrows angled upward in surprise. "Do you mean Baird Northcross's children?"

"Do you know Mr. Northcross?"

McKay hesitated, then nodded. "Mr. Northcross and I were at Harrow together. I saw him shortly after he arrived at the ranch. But I was under the impression that his wife was to accompany the children west."

"Regrettably, my sister passed away while she was visiting me in Massachusetts," she volunteered cautiously.

His face drew taut with sympathy. "I'm sorry to hear that. Though I never had the pleasure of meeting her myself, Mrs. Northcross was reputed to be a lady of great beauty."

Ardith experienced a familiar stir of resentment. "Indeed she was," she answered shortly.

"Does Mr. Northcross know what's happened? I haven't heard . . ."

"This isn't something one wants to put in a telegram." Ardith had wanted to tell Baird about Ariel herself, to see the expression in his eyes and gauge his feelings. If there was a touch of vindictiveness in that—well, Ardith had a right to be vindictive where Baird Northcross was concerned.

"I did telegraph him asking him to meet the children's train," she went on, "but unfortunately the message was never delivered."

McKay nodded solicitously. "Communication is difficult out here sometimes."

"Which brings me to what I was discussing with Mr. Norton." Ardith gestured toward the clerk. "The children and I need passage to the ranch, and I understand you live out that way."

"On the property just to the south."

"Then I was wondering if you would be willing to take us to the Sugar Creek on your way home. I'd be more than willing to pay you for your services."

McKay looked her up and down. "It's a rough trip, Miss Merritt," he answered. "And all I have is my horse and the supply wagon I brought into town."

"If there's not a carriage I can let, we'll make do, Mr. McKay. It's imperative I get these children to their father."

McKay stroked his mustache, and Ardith saw some dark emotion skim the plane of his eyes. "If you're sure that's what you want, Miss Merritt," he said after a moment, "I will be happy to escort you."

At about three o'clock in the morning, Ardith realized who Cullen McKay was. She hadn't been able to sleep— not with the voices booming up the stairwell and the thud of boot heels moving past their door. When the rhythmic squeak of a bed frame began in the room next door, she all but bolted to her feet. Yet perhaps it was the enthusiastic tempo the headboard beat against the wall that helped her make the association between men, their illicit passions, and Cullen McKay.

Because unless she was very much mistaken, McKay was Baird's uncle's by-blow, his child by the notorious actress who for years had been Earl Northam's mistress. If Ardith remembered the story correctly, the boy had been given every advantage—a privileged childhood, an education at the best schools, an *entré* to society. *Every advantage, except his father's name.*

On the heels of realization came the certainty that if she remembered him, McKay would remember her. He was Baird's cousin, after all, and in the closed world of English society scandals as ignoble as hers were whispered about for decades.

As Ardith stood at the window staring down into the deserted western street, suffocating heat pressed against her chest. *This* was why she'd left England sixteen years before—so she would never have to face the sly glances, the smug smiles, the searing humiliation of meeting people who *knew*.

Still, what choice did she have but to continue her association with McKay? She and the children needed passage to the Sugar Creek Ranch, and from what the desk clerk said, McKay was the most dependable companion they were likely to find. What she needed to do was prevent McKay from making some reference to her unspeakable shame in front of the children. It would never do for them to learn that their father had jilted her—that he and their mother had run away to Gretna Green the very day Ardith was to have become Baird Northcross's bride.

The sun was just cresting the horizon when their party assembled at the livery stable the next morning. In the midst of the preparations for leaving, Ardith gestured to

Cullen McKay. "I'd like a word with you in private, if I may."

Leaving the children with the ostler, she led the way out into the gray, wintry dawn. As McKay stood over her, his sandy hair and the fringe of his buckskin clothing fluttering in the April wind, Ardith recognized the Northcross stamp on him, the resemblance exhaustion had made her miss the evening before. Now that she knew who he was, it was evident in the shape and color of his eyes, and the cut of his features.

The Northcrosses were most often dark like Baird, but the mingling of other traits sometimes mitigated that Norman-French heritage. Certainly that had happened in Baird's own children. China was blonde, like Ariel. Durban was fair-skinned and sandy-haired, more closely resembling Cullen McKay than his own father. Only in Khy did the Northcross traits run true.

Ignoring the feverish flush of humiliation creeping upward from her diaphragm, Ardith raised her head. "I realized last night who you are." The words were almost an accusation.

McKay's mouth quirked at one corner. "Phillip Northcross's bastard, you mean?"

Ardith nodded, hearing the bitterness in his voice. "And I expect you know who I am, too."

He lowered his chin in acknowledgment. "Truth to tell, Miss Merritt, I'm amazed you've come all this way for Baird Northcross's sake."

"This has nothing to do with Baird Northcross," Ardith felt compelled to clarify. "My sister's last request was that I see her children safely to their father."

"And you're making a noble effort to do that."

Ardith felt the heat in her cheeks intensify. "There is nothing noble about it. The children have lost their mother. They're alone and confused. They need to be protected. Because of that, I'd just as soon they didn't know—" She hesitated and looked away, enmity for Baird all but choking her. "—what passed between their father and me when we were young."

When McKay didn't immediately respond, she raised her gaze to his. "May I count on your discretion in this, Mr. McKay?"

Cullen looked at her long and hard, then nodded. "What kind of gentleman would I be if I disclosed a lady's secrets?"

Any further discussion they might have had was cut short by the ostler leading the team and carriage Ardith had hired out of the barn.

"Are you sure you can handle that horse and buggy by yourself?" McKay asked her, acknowledging the children's arrival by changing the subject.

Ardith let out her breath. "Of course I can. I've been driving my uncle to his lectures for years."

McKay turned to where his own heavily loaded wagon stood, a white-stockinged roan tied to the back. "Would you like to ride my horse, son?" he called to Durban where he was dallying in the stable doorway.

The boy shook his head. "I don't like horses," he announced.

Baird Northcross's son not like horses? It was the first Ardith had heard of it. Riding had always been his father's passion, and she couldn't imagine Baird would have missed the opportunity to pass his love of good horseflesh on to his son.

"I'll ride your horse for you," Khy offered, shifting from foot to foot.

McKay ignored the younger child. "Would you like to ride in the wagon with me, Durban?"

The boy glanced to where his sister was already ensconced in the rear seat of the carriage. "All right," he answered.

"I want to ride Mr. McKay's horse," Khy complained.

"I can ride. Papa had the stable master at Heatherleigh teach me."

Stranger and stranger, Ardith thought as she turned to Khy. "I'd feel so much safer on a trip as long as this if you were here in the buggy with me," she said, taking a moment to smooth down his hair. "Would you mind riding with me too much?"

Khy looked wistfully across at McKay's leggy roan, then up at her. "Not if you need me to protect you, Aunt Ardith."

The ostler hefted Khy onto the front seat of the carriage and helped Ardith clamber up beside him.

"Are we ready?" McKay called back from his own wagon.

Ardith waved in confirmation and snapped the reins over her horses' backs.

"*D*oesn't anyone live out here?" China asked staring out at the prairie. "We've been traveling three days, and all we've seen are deer and antelope—and grass. We've seen *lots* of grass. Is this what it's going to be like at Papa's ranch?"

Ardith looked up from where she was bent over the fire frying hog-back and beans for their noon meal. Dark smudges marred the delicate skin beneath her niece's eyes. Her nose and cheeks were red from the cold. Ardith cringed with remorse at having dragged this child and her brothers all the way out here. Nor could she think of a single thing to say to reassure her.

None of the reading Ardith had done had prepared her for the vastness of this place, either. Not one of her precious books had hinted at how big the west was, how empty and overwhelming. She felt lost in this endless scrub country, buffeted by the wind, crushed by the weight of the sky. And the only shelter they'd had was at the tumbled-down road ranches where they'd stopped to sleep.

"Cullen says we'll get to Papa's ranch tomorrow," Khy piped up. "Won't he be glad to see us?"

Khy was the only one of the four of them whose spirits were as high as when they'd begun, though all three children had done well, considering the hardships.

"I'm certainly eager to see Papa," China agreed. "I've missed him so much!"

"We'll have to tell him about Mother," Durban reminded them, casting a pall on his brother and sister's momentary pleasure.

"We'll all tell him," Ardith spoke up, reaching to catch China's hand. "We'll do it together."

"You'll feel better about coming all this way," Cullen advised them, "once we start to see mountains this afternoon."

"Are they big mountains?" Khy wanted to know.

"Some of the biggest," Cullen assured him.

He was telling the truth. They had barely gotten underway when the southern peaks knuckled up on the western horizon. By mid-afternoon they had grown into towering, snow-capped giants that shimmered in the sunlight like chips of ice.

They sheltered that night on a ranch owned by men McKay knew well, and supper turned into an affable affair seasoned with stories and laughter. Once everyone else had gone to bed, Ardith and Cullen sat up finishing the coffee.

"When we reach the Sugar Creek tomorrow," McKay began, "is your brother-in-law likely to welcome you?"

Ardith shielded her doubt behind the rim of her tin cup. "I imagine he will tolerate me for a little while—long enough for me to explain about Ariel and see the children settled."

"Then you'll leave, drive all the way back to Rock Creek?"

She became aware of the intensity of McKay's blue eyes, the assessment in them, the attentiveness. It was how most men here in the west looked at females—a perusal that fell somewhere between blind admiration and asking to check her teeth. She supposed women as plain as she was ought to be flattered by such blatant interest. Ardith found it restrictive and uncomfortable instead, like wearing a fabulous gown that didn't quite fit.

"My life is back in Massachusetts," she answered him. "I have my duties as my uncle's assistant, and books to write."

McKay's eyebrows rose with interest. "Books? What kind of books?"

"I write and illustrate books for children. I'm known as 'Auntie Ardith' to the younger set."

"I've heard of 'Auntie Ardith!'" McKay's smile broadened. "Is it lucrative, your writing?"

Cullen McKay wasn't the first man to show an interest in Ardith's money. The five thousand pounds a year from her mother's estate had made her both a tolerable dancing partner and a magnet for younger sons the year she came out. Nor did anyone need to explain that beyond her "settled nature" and her "maturity," it was her income that made an old family like the Northcrosses consider her an appropriate match for one of their own.

"The writing gives me pin money," she demurred, deliberately downplaying earnings which had mounted steadily with every book. "But how is it you came to be raising cattle in Wyoming, Mr. McKay?"

Cullen seemed unaware that she had deliberately changed the subject. "I came to America some years ago to seek my fortune. The Close brothers began a farming operation in Iowa to teach agricultural methods to men who would eventually inherit or manage land in England."

"An interesting concept," Ardith observed. "Did you find their instructions useful?"

"They taught me a good deal about ranching," he told her. "More than your brother-in-law will ever know."

"You don't think Baird will do well out here?"

The light in his eyes might have been malicious. "I think he'll have failed miserably with the Sugar Creek before the year is out."

Ardith's stomach pitched, and she tightened her grip around her cup. Though she had every reason to wish Baird Northcross to perdition, she wanted him settled enough to take time with Khy, cosset his daughter, and get to know his older son. She might well be expecting more from Baird than he was capable of giving. But how else could she go back east and leave those children here with him?

Ardith tucked her concerns about her niece and nephews away and climbed to her feet. "Since tomorrow looks like another long day, I'd better turn in."

Cullen rose and smiled at her. "Sleep well, Miss Merritt," he said.

Sleep well, indeed, Ardith thought as she made her way into the bedroom they'd been given. There wasn't much chance of her sleeping tonight. Not when Cullen had called up the devil in Northcross's guise. Not when she'd be facing the man himself tomorrow.

But then, Baird had been dogging her footsteps from the moment she'd given Ariel her promise. He'd been hovering in the shadows of the parlor when she told the children their mother was dead. He was hiding at the back of the car when they boarded the train. He was here tonight, God help her, a terrifying presence lurking just beyond the confines of the bed she shared with China.

She didn't sleep, and once the ranch house had fallen

silent, Ardith eased from the crackling dried-grass mattress. She crept back out to the hearth so she could confront the specter of the children's father in her own way.

In the faint waver of the firelight she envisioned Baird Northcross as he'd been sixteen years before. Tall and lithe as a carriage whip. Graceful, wide-shouldered, black-haired, with the broad sculpted face of a fallen angel and eyes—

Dear God! His eyes had all but consumed her as he'd come toward her across her stepmother's ornate gothic sitting room the first time they met. Those eyes had gleamed, reckless and alive, in a face sun-bronzed by a recent expedition to Africa. Baird's exploits on safari with the Royal Geographical Society had given him the cachet of an adventurer, a worldliness that made other young men of her acquaintance pale by comparison.

No wonder she'd wanted him.

Yet even as her father and Earl Northam had been negotiating the marriage contract, Ardith had known she was not the only woman to dream of cupping the breadth of Baird's jaw in her two hands or kissing that sensual mouth. She wasn't the first to want to stand sheltered by his height and breadth, to bear his name and children. To seek approval in his smile.

Nor was she the last—as it turned out.

When she'd come to Massachusetts, she had done her best to wall off her feelings for Baird, to put away the past. Even at nineteen she'd been wise enough to know that no one could build a productive life harboring the kind of enmity she bore him.

Yet tomorrow she would look into his face again. How would she speak civilly to him, without the old feelings of betrayal and resentment overwhelming her? Could she act wisely to ensure the children's welfare, when what she wanted was to tear him apart with her bare hands?

Ardith shivered and drew her shawl more closely

around her, terrified by what was at stake. Not just for the children but for herself. Would she have to sacrifice her pride a second time to keep her promise to her sister?

She closed her eyes against the sudden burn of tears and wished with all her heart that she was home. She needed the solitude in her uncle's garden, the comfort of her worktable with its mugs of brushes and tubes of paint. She longed for the bustling streets in downtown Boston and to see Gavin. She so desperately needed the glow in Gavin's eyes, the touch of his hand, his sly wit and tender smile to remind her of who it was she had become. To remind her that Ardith Merritt was no longer a woman to be scorned and cast aside.

But before she could go back to all that was familiar and safe, she had to confront Baird Northcross. And here in the midnight silence of a house in the wilds of Wyoming, she tried to muster her courage to face the devil one last time.

FOUR

"*Is* that Papa's ranch?" Khy demanded, lurching to his feet in the jolting carriage. Tightening her grip on the reins and reaching out to steady her nephew, Ardith nodded.

"Oh, Aunt Ardith," China breathed with evident relief. "It's so much nicer than the other places we've stayed!"

Ardith might have agreed if she'd been able to suck a breath past the burr of apprehension lodged in her throat. As they rumbled closer to the cluster of buildings at the base of the mountains she could see that the main house was rustic and handsome, its log walls thick enough to withstand both the howling cold of a prairie winter and the relentless beat of summer sun. Cullen McKay pulled his wagon to a stop in the ranch house yard, and Ardith drew up behind him.

"Do you think there's anyone here?" she called out.

Just then the door of the house snapped open and a tall, deeply sun-brown man dressed in jodhpurs, boots, and a white collarless shirt came bounding across the porch.

Ardith froze, her fingers knotting around the reins. *It's Baird.*

Her heartbeat staggered, then surged inside her, beating harder and harder. Spangles of cold danced through her veins. This was the man who'd had a letter delivered the morning of their wedding to tell her he'd run off with her sister. This was the man who had shamed her so horribly that she'd fled England for America. This was the man who was supposed to have been her husband.

He looks the same, she found herself thinking. Every bit as vivid, every bit as arrogant. And so damned beautiful.

"Papa!" Khy cried out and burst into tears. Before Ardith could think to grab the boy or offer him comfort, he had flung himself out of the carriage and was racing toward his father.

Something about the way Baird caught Khy up in his arms, as much in self-defense as real affection, made Ardith catch her breath. As she sought to make some sense of the impression, China jumped out of the carriage and followed Khy.

"Oh, Papa! We've missed you so!" she gasped and also set to weeping.

Ardith never dreamed the children would cry the moment they saw their father. They'd been so eager, so excited . . .

She'd also imagined she'd have a moment to explain about Ariel before Baird greeted his family. But Khy and China had just scattered that intention like matchsticks.

All at once, Ardith realized Durban had made no move toward Baird. He stood beside McKay's wagon instead, his back straight, his head tilted defiantly.

A frisson of uneasiness shot down Ardith's back.

Baird's eyes skimmed over to his son. "Hello, boy," he said, then glanced past him to Cullen McKay.

"Sir," Durban acknowledged.

Something about the way the child stood caught between McKay, who looked enough like him to be his father, and Baird, the man who was, sent queasiness skipping through Ardith again.

Then Baird raised his gaze to where Ardith sat on the carriage seat. She felt herself flush as his eyes moved over her. They were all fire and ice, all shivery blue intensity—just as she remembered.

Then Baird's brows narrowed and his expression darkened. She wasn't Ariel. Ardith's gravest fault had always been that she wasn't Ariel.

Determined to face him head-on, Ardith looped the reins across the dashboard and leaped down from the carriage.

"Hello, Baird," she said, glad that her low, frosty tone didn't reveal the turmoil bubbling inside her.

Judging from his expression, Baird didn't have the faintest idea who she was. This man had wooed her and scorned her. He had turned her life inside out, made her into a far different woman than she'd ever intended to be. He'd sent her from her home to a new life in America. *And he didn't even recognize her.*

Rage blazed through her chest like a comet. It roared in her ears and stained her face with heat. She'd vowed to keep a hold on her emotions for the children's sake, but the feelings that swept through her were too raw, too overpowering.

She stepped toward him, taut and quivering, anger singing through her veins. "I know it's been years, Baird, but surely you haven't forgotten me."

"Ardith?" he breathed then, blinking in confusion. "Whatever are you doing here? Where's Ariel?"

Ardith paused, savoring the moment, suddenly avid to see his reaction. "I'm afraid I have some very sad news," she began.

"Oh, Papa!" Fresh tears spilled down China's porcelain cheeks. "It's the most tragic thing!"

Fear flashed across Baird's sharply cut features.

"M-M-Mama died!" Khyber sobbed, tightening his hold on his father.

Baird let out his breath in a low, sharp groan. He looked to Ardith for confirmation.

A hot, sweet bolt of satisfaction flashed through her at the pain and disbelief in his eyes. She inclined her head, suddenly ashamed that she was taking such pleasure in his anguish.

Baird staggered back a step, his face gone slack. China threw her arms around him and hung on tight. Khy's sobs grew louder. Baird stared past them, not seeming to hear them, not seeming to see them.

Then, as Ardith watched, he carefully disentangled himself from his weeping daughter and lowered Khy to the ground.

Her mouth went dry with shock and outrage. Why, he isn't even going to try to comfort those children! *He doesn't have any better idea how to do that than I do!*

Instead of attending to China and Khy, Baird bore down on her. "What happened to Ariel?" he demanded.

Cullen McKay stepped protectively between them. "It's not as if any of this is Ardith's fault."

"Get out of my way," Northcross said with a snarl and pushed past McKay.

Ardith steeled herself to confront him, raising her head, feeling her cheeks burn with fresh emotion.

"*Is* Ariel really dead?" he demanded.

"Yes," she confirmed.

"Goddamnit, Ardith, tell me what happened."

Ardith had honed the words as if they were a blade, whetting the edges until they gleamed, until she was sure that when she wielded them they would slice down to the core of him. But as she opened her mouth to speak, she became aware of the children weeping only a few feet away.

She wasn't the kind of person who could deliberately destroy a man, was she? Especially in front of his children. Yet the temptation was fierce, a long-banked fire burst into flame. He'd earned this; he deserved it.

Still, she hesitated. Then she deliberately blunted the thrust, fumbling for other words, less damning words. "I—I think it's best that we discuss this later."

"Later? Why?"

He might not care what the children heard, but Ardith did. She didn't want them hurt by something that was strictly between their father and her.

"We need to get everyone settled," she replied, glancing toward her niece and nephews. "I'll be glad to answer your questions later. *In private.*"

The reason for her reluctance seemed to penetrate Baird's rancor. His shoulders shifted, losing a bit of their rigidity. "But why are you here?"

She swallowed hard, his ingratitude one more mark against him in the tally she was keeping. "I'm here because Ariel asked me to bring the children to Wyoming. It was her last request."

Baird's eyebrows angled down over the bridge of his nose. "You were with her when she died? I didn't know she meant to see you on her way through Boston."

Was it possible Baird didn't know she and Ariel had made their peace some years before, that they'd been corresponding? But then, he'd been gallivanting from one end of the world to the other. How much could he have known about Ariel's life?

"Ariel came to my uncle's home in Concord when she fell ill," Ardith explained, stepping forward to gather Khy up and dry his tears. She slid a comforting arm around China's waist.

"Hell, Northcross," Cullen McKay broke in. "Let the woman alone. She's gone to substantial difficulty to bring your children here to you. Show a little appreciation."

Baird scowled and turned back toward the house.

"Papa?" China asked, leaving the shelter of Ardith's embrace and taking his arm. "Papa, is this really going to be our new home?"

Baird looked down at his daughter as if he was not certain where she'd come from. Then, as if returning to himself, he nodded and led them across the narrow, covered porch. "Perhaps until fall."

Once inside Ardith was charmed by the rustic grace of the structure—the peeled log walls and mammoth stone fireplaces; the beamed roof and acres of scrubbed pine floor specked with bright, zigzag-patterned rugs. It smelled resinous and warm and welcoming, like fresh-cut lumber and baking bread.

They'd had no more than a minute or two to admire the house when a broad, wind-burned woman came bustling from somewhere out back. "Has your family arrived safe and sound, Mr. Northcross?"

Baird turned abruptly. "This is Myra Johnson, my cook," he said in a cursory introduction. "Her husband is foreman here at the ranch."

"Good to have you," Myra said, her gaze sliding over each of the children and coming to rest on Ardith. She gave the slightest of nods, as if she liked what she saw.

"You all must be hungry," she continued. "By the time we get you settled, I'll be serving supper. Now, Mrs. Northcross, I'll have one of the hands bring your bags up to Mr. Northcross's room so you can—"

"This is *not* Mrs. Northcross!" Baird all but barked. "My wife is dead."

Myra Johnson's broad face puckered up like a drawstring pouch as she turned to Baird. "I'm so sorry for your loss, sir. And that these poor lambs have been left without a mother before they're half grown."

Khyber gave a teary sniff. China leaned closer to her father as if she hoped to absorb his warmth. Durban bowed his head, and Ardith saw Cullen McKay lay a hand across the boy's sagging shoulders.

Baird was obviously not accustomed to having demands of such an intimate nature made on him and shifted away from his daughter.

Ardith watched his withdrawal, a frown pinching hard at the corners of her mouth.

Then she spoke, breaking the spell of melancholy. "I'm Mrs. Northcross's half-sister, Ardith Merritt. Mrs. Northcross passed away at my home in Massachusetts some weeks ago. Now, did you say, Mrs. Johnson, that you have rooms prepared for us?"

"Sure enough, Miss Merritt." Myra Johnson said with a nod. "We'll put you in the room to the right of the fireplace, and the young lady to the left."

"Mr. Northcross's daughter is China," Ardith picked up the introductions Baird had not thought to make. "His older son is Durban, and this is Khyber." She tightened her arms around her nephew. "But we all call him Khy."

Myra nodded again. "Then we'll put the boys together in the room under the stairs—if that's all right with you, Mr. Northcross?"

Baird shrugged, staring at the floor. "Whatever makes sense, Mrs. Johnson."

"And perhaps Mr. McKay will be willing to spend the night in the bunkhouse."

"May I stay in the bunkhouse, too, Papa?" Khy begged, wriggling to be let down. "Durban and I stayed in a bunkhouse with Mr. McKay on our way here and—"

"I'm afraid Mr. McKay won't be accepting your hospitality," Cullen put in before Khy could continue. "If I hurry, I can make it back to the Double T before nightfall. They need these supplies as soon as I can get them there."

Baird hesitated, then nodded to the other man. "I appreciate your delivering my children to me safely, Mc-Kay."

"It was all *any gentleman* would do, Northcross."

Ardith had sensed the animosity between the two men out in the yard, but she'd been too distracted by her own concerns to give it more than a passing thought. Now she wondered at the cause of it.

"I want to add my thanks, Mr. McKay," Ardith said with considerably more warmth. "We might never have found the ranch if it weren't for you."

"It was my pleasure to escort you, Miss Merritt. I hope you and the children have a lovely visit."

"I'm sure the children will enjoy their stay, though as you know, I won't be here long."

"A pity," McKay answered as he made his way to the door. "You would have made a pleasant addition to our society."

As McKay's wagon rumbled away, Baird straightened and shifted on his feet. "Perhaps I should go see about getting your baggage unloaded."

"Can I come, Papa?" Khyber asked, trailing after him. Baird made it out the door before Khy caught up.

Durban glared after his father. "He's *never* been able to stand being around us for long."

Wondering if what Durban said was true, Ardith herded the children toward their rooms. As she got them settled she couldn't help wondering if there wasn't going to be a good deal more to keeping her promise to Ariel than she'd ever anticipated.

Ariel was dead—his porcelain doll of a wife was shattered and gone.

After a noisy, difficult meal with the children, Baird finally had a chance to ease himself into one of the chairs before the fire and pour a glass of whiskey. God knows, he needed it. He needed time to absorb the news of Ariel's death, to turn it over in his mind, to contend with his bewilderment and loss.

Ariel had certainly seemed well enough when he'd left her. She'd been curled in their magnificent, silk-draped bed at her father's London townhouse, her face flushed and soft with sleep. The ivory curve of her throat and the arch of one bare shoulder had been limned by the first pale light of dawn.

He wished now that he'd awakened her to say good-bye, but he hadn't wanted to argue with her. Ariel had had every right to be angry. He was leaving for America a mere fortnight after he'd returned from Burma and asking her to follow him halfway around the world. So he'd bent above her and brushed her brow with a kiss. He'd stroked her cheek, breathed the mingled scents of rosewater and last night's champagne. He'd gone downstairs and hailed a cab to the train station, never dreaming he had seen his wife for the very last time.

Baird drank down the whiskey in his glass. Had Ariel been ill and afraid to tell him? he wondered. Had she contracted some disease aboard the ship? Had there been some kind of accident? What was it Ardith had refused to discuss in front of the children?

Baird frowned and filled his glass a second time.

Ardith. Dour, bitter Ardith. How could anyone have changed so much? Once he'd admired her as a plain but touchingly eager girl; now she'd become a woman as dry and brittle as stale bread. She stood taller and more robust than he remembered, but she was straight as a carpenter's rule and every bit as rigid. Her eyes, when she'd looked at him out there in the yard, had been bright with fury, then hard with a resolve that was single-minded enough to send a shudder running through any man.

It must be living in New England that had changed her so, Baird told himself. Spending years shut up in her un-

cle's library and being part of a community that valued
rumination more than reality would wring any woman
dry.

But she had learned to be resourceful; he'd give her
that. Without his help, without a governess for the children, and without a proper escort, Ardith had managed to
get the children to the ranch. She'd arranged their trans-
portation, found McKay, driven a carriage four full days
across miles of wind-blown countryside. And once they'd
finished their dinner, she'd swept the children off to bed.

Gotten them out from under his feet—thank God.

A man couldn't properly toast his dead wife with a
parcel of children watching him. All during supper, he'd
seen the unanswerable questions in their eyes, seen them
wanting things from him that he had no idea how to give.

It wasn't that he meant to deny them, he just had no
damned experience being a father. He'd been at the back
of beyond when each of them was born—as their names
pointed out. He'd been farther away still while they were
learning to walk and talk and cipher. That had been his
choice he supposed, and he didn't regret it.

He'd never even considered that he should learn to dry
his children's tears and wipe their noses. He'd hired people to do that. Now that Ariel was dead, he didn't want to
face the implications of the children's arrival here or acknowledge the effect their mother's death was bound to
have on them.

Let Ardith handle it, he thought and tipped the bottle
above his glass.

Just then the very woman he'd been considering
emerged from the door to the boys' bedchamber. He felt
more than saw her enter the room, a prickle of premonition moving up his backbone, the wave of her contempt
washing over him.

She crossed the floorboards with deliberate strides and
stopped when the toes of her shoes were a precise six

inches from where his booted feet were stretched out and crossed at the ankles. From her hem to her hairpins, it was obvious what she thought of him and that she was preparing to share her opinions.

Baird didn't give her a chance. "Are the children tucked up tight and fast asleep?"

"Indeed they are," Ardith answered crisply. "You might have come in to bid them good-night."

"I might have—except that I had things I wanted to do."

His flippancy brought angry color to her cheeks. "And what might they have been?"

Baird raised his brimming glass and took a deep, satisfying swallow. "The first was drinking a toast to my dear wife. Would you care to join me?"

Ardith fluttered like a quail just flushed from cover. "No! Of course not! I never touch ardent spirits."

"Not even for Ariel's sake?" he cajoled. The whiskey was beginning to blur the edges of his regret, and Baird was glad. His marriage to Ariel hadn't turned out the way either of them wanted, but he mourned her anyway. "Come along, Ardith. Do join me in a drink to the most gloriously beautiful and infuriating woman a man could ever hope to possess."

He hadn't meant for her to hear the throb of emotion in his voice, but he could tell she had.

"Good God!" she exclaimed. "You really did love her, didn't you?"

Ardith settled herself on a footstool not three feet away and stared at Baird as if he were some specimen pinned to a mounting board. He took a long pull of whiskey, embalming himself to endure her scrutiny.

"Of course I loved her," he admitted, wishing his voice weren't so raw, that his regrets weren't so evident. "Ariel was my grand passion, and I was hers. I thought you understood that."

At least, he had convinced himself Ardith understood.

He and Ariel had been smitten the moment they met at his and Ardith's betrothal party. They had been stealing kisses on the balcony before the evening was over. They'd met at a hotel for a private dinner a week later and adjourned to the bedchamber before dessert. Their love had been forbidden, secret, out of control. For those first few weeks it had been like existing inside a living flame. They'd been too wrapped up in each other to spare a thought for anyone else. Especially Ardith.

"If you loved Ariel so much," Ardith demanded, "why did you abandon her for months at a time?"

Why indeed? Baird took another swallow and thought about his wife. For all that he had cared for her, she hadn't met his needs, nor had he met hers. After the wildness and the passion had burned out, their flame had flickered to an ember.

That was why his clearest memories of these last years were not of his wife and family, but of the rustling grass on the savannah, the bitter cold dawn in the mountains at the top of the world, the scent of saffron and curry rising from a cauldron of steaming rice. Memories of the chase and the danger. Ariel had never been part of that, part of what kept the blood pumping in his veins and his reflexes sharp. She'd never understood that it was the traveling and the hunting and the adventure that gave his life a purpose—however hollow, however vague.

"I was offered opportunities I couldn't refuse," he finally answered, then continued with a shrug. "And sometimes grand passions don't wear well."

It was a more honest answer than he'd given anyone in years. Ardith, with her resolute mouth and uncompromising eyes, seemed to demand that of him, as well as a modicum of introspection. Now what he wanted was to be answered in kind.

Baird took a shaky, whiskey-flavored breath and asked, "What happened to Ariel? How did she die?"

Ardith pinioned him with her gaze. He could see the anticipation in her eyes. "Ariel died of a miscarriage. She bled to death."

Baird thought he had prepared himself for her answer, but the words slammed into him, tore through him. He remembered just how eagerly he and Ariel had come together when he returned from Burma. He'd needed succor and forgiveness after what had happened to Bram. What Ariel had offered was diversion, and he'd tried to convince himself it was enough.

Even as they were making love, he'd known it was dangerous. Ariel had suffered miscarriages twice since Khy was born and nearly died with each of them. Yet since she'd invited him to her bed, Baird assumed she'd taken precautions. These were modern times and modern women knew about such things. But apparently Ariel either hadn't known or hadn't done what was necessary.

Now Baird was forced to acknowledge that his baser nature had killed his wife. The whiskey soured in his belly, and he wasn't deep enough in his cups to ignore the searing heat of responsibility.

"So did Ariel curse me with her last breath?"

Shock at his cynicism flickered across Ardith's features, but she refused to back down.

"She must have forgiven you," she answered. "The last thing Ariel said was for me to bring the children to you."

"Didn't her parents—your father—have anything to say on the matter? I would have expected him to demand that you send the children to England."

"He did." Ardith's face was expressionless.

"And you chose to bring them here to me?"

She glanced away, tight-lipped and scowling. "I promised Ariel."

"Well, you've discharged your duty most admirably."

Baird lifted his glass and toasted her. He meant the words as a dismissal. He wanted her to leave him alone so he could go to hell in his own way.

Ardith refused to budge. Instead she stared at him with even greater intensity. "Now that the children are here, what do you mean to do with them?" she asked.

"Do with them?"

China and Durban and Khy had been looked after by an endless string of nannies and governesses and tutors, like all the children of their class. Ariel was supposed to have brought a governess to the ranch to see to the children's lessons while they were here. That Ardith had arrived without one presented a problem Baird had no idea how to resolve.

"I want to know who's going to look after the children while you are—" Ardith hesitated. "What is is you do here?"

Baird pushed up a little straighter in his chair. "I'm running the ranch."

"Really? And just what does that entail?"

He was a little too fuddled to give her a comprehensive answer. He'd been ignoring the ledgers and voluminous correspondence from London in favor of riding out with Buck Johnson every day to oversee the herd. He was good at that, and being out on the land was very satisfying, though it didn't sound like much.

"Looking after the cows," he fumbled. "Preparing to take the steers to market. That's what ranchers *do*."

"So you *will* have time to spend with the children, then."

Baird scowled. "Why are you so concerned?"

"Because if you can spare someone to accompany me as far as Rock Creek, I mean to leave as soon as possible," she answered. "But I can't do that unless I'm sure the children are provided for. You don't need me to stay on, do you?"

"Good God! No!" Baird snapped at her. "We'll do without you—somehow."

"How exactly?"

"Well, we . . . I think the children should . . . Um . . ." Baird blinked at her. He didn't have the faintest idea how to provide for the children. He didn't even have the faintest idea what "looking after them" meant.

Ardith matched his scowl and pushed to her feet. "I can see we'd better discuss this tomorrow when your head is clearer."

He looked up at her, a little ashamed that he'd drunk enough for her to notice. "Very well, then," he answered, trying to regain his dignity. "We'll discuss this in the morning."

She started toward her room, then paused and looked back at him. "You disappointed her, you know," she said.

"Who?"

"Ariel. She'd hoped for so much more from you."

Baird wasn't sure how Ardith knew that and was mortified that she did.

"I shouldn't be surprised if she was disappointed," he acknowledged, instinctively tugging the shroud of his past mistakes around him. "Disappointing people has always been my special gift."

Ardith's eyes went hard. "Don't disappoint the children, Baird," she warned him. "Don't waste the love they feel for you. It's far too precious."

Without another word she moved beyond the arc of firelight. He heard the door to her room close behind her.

"I won't disappoint them deliberately," he promised.

Taking a deep breath, he set his empty glass aside and heaved to his feet. It was only a few yards to the door and the porch that ran along the back of the house. Baird shivered as he stepped outside, but he braced his hands against the railing and waited for the cold to clear his head.

He could feel the foothills rolling up behind the house, see the shadowy ridge of mountains rising toward the sky. There was something about this place with all its grandeur and wildness that spoke to him. Just standing here in the thick of the night, a speck of a man amidst such vastness, soothed him.

After talking to Ardith he needed soothing. She had ripped into him in her sly, superior way. She had forced him to see how much of a bastard he was, and just how good he was at wasting other people's lives. His negligence in Burma had cost Bram everything, and now he had Ariel on his conscience, too.

He flexed his shoulders and looked up at the sky. All his life he'd been running from responsibilities, dusting them from his palms like so much dirt. But Ardith wasn't the kind of woman who'd let him get away with that—especially when it came to his children.

Baird hurt just looking at them. China was so bright and fine and fragile that he could crush her with a word. Durban wore his hatred like a badge. Khy barrelled through the world needing someone to protect him. Baird wasn't the kind of man to do that.

He wasn't careful enough or patient enough or wise enough to raise these children. He knew he'd given them life. He knew he should accept responsibility for their welfare, but he didn't know how to be their father. And God knows, he'd made so many mistakes.

Yet the children belonged to him now—only to him—and that thought scared the hell out of him.

Khyber looked up from his breakfast. "So, Papa, what's a half-sister?"

Baird scowled down the length of the pine table at his younger son. "What do you need to know that for?"

"Well," the boy began. "Yesterday Aunt Ardith told Mrs. Johnson she was Mama's half-sister, but Aunt Ardith doesn't seem like half of anything to me."

Baird took a swig of his coffee and wished there was someone else to answer Khy's question. He wasn't feeling his best this morning, though if he *had* been trampled by wild horses, he didn't remember it. Nor was discussing family matters his long suit.

"Half-sisters," Baird began, "have one parent the same and one parent different."

Khy blinked at him, not the least bit enlightened.

Durban looked up from dabbing jam onto one of Myra Johnson's feather-light biscuits. "What Aunt Ardith meant is that she and mother have the same father but different mothers."

Something about the precision of the boy's explanation made Baird's teeth itch.

"Can people *do* that?" Khy demanded, clearly horrified.

"Obviously they can," Baird answered. "When Aunt Ardith's mother died, your Grandfather Arthur married your Grandmama Sarah. They are your mother's parents."

Khy's eyes widened with understanding, then clouded with tears. "You aren't going to marry someone else now that Mama's dead, are you?"

Baird choked on his coffee. He then hastened to answer his son. "I certainly don't plan to."

"Don't plan to what?" Ardith asked, emerging from the bedroom where she'd been plaiting China's hair.

Baird preferred that Ardith not be privy to this particular conversation and spoke up before either of the boys could answer. "I don't have any plans at all," he assured her.

China bussed Baird's cheek and swooped into the place beside him.

"Since you don't have plans," Ardith said, settling down across the table, "you should be able to show us the ranch."

Baird glared at her over the rim of his cup. He didn't want to show them the ranch. He didn't want Ardith and the children dogging his footsteps. He wasn't ready to reveal his feelings about the ranch to anyone. "I don't think that would be a good idea."

"Oh, Papa, why not?" China cajoled. "I'd love to see the ranch!"

"It's cold out," he hedged. "It looks like snow." *And I don't want to have to look after you.*

"We've been traveling across open country for four days," Ardith pointed out. "A little cold isn't likely to hurt us."

"Oh, Papa, please!" Khy piped up. "Please, show us the horses and the cows."

Ardith spooned sugar into her coffee with studied nonchalance. She'd known damn well he'd have no choice about showing them the ranch if she mentioned it in front of the children.

"Some of these are special cows, too," Durban put in around a bite of biscuit. "They're a mix between Texas Longhorns and Herefords brought from England."

Baird stared at his elder son. *He* had been at the ranch a full week before he's discovered that. "How did you—"

"I went out to the corral this morning. Mr. Johnson told me," Durban volunteered, looking smug.

"Well, if you want to tour the ranch you'll have to ride," he warned them, "and there's only one lady's saddle with the tack."

"That will do us well enough," Ardith assured him. "China can use the sidesaddle. I ride astride now and then, though it always causes a sensation in Concord."

Baird registered his opinion with a raise of his eyebrows. "I can just imagine!" Still feeling thwarted, he pushed to his feet. "Come out to the barn once you've finished breakfast."

Khy was at his heels before he reached the door. Durban came straggling out to the corral a few minutes later. By then Baird had ordered a gentle, white-stockinged roan for China and had a leggy buckskin named Primrose tacked up for Ardith. He'd resigned himself to taking Khy up on Dandy with him since the horses at the ranch were too unpredictable for a six-year-old.

He came to where Durban was perched on the corral fence watching the ponies run. "Is there a horse you particularly fancy for yourself, son?"

"Oh, I won't be going with you," the boy replied.

"And why is that?" He had expected the boy to be as eager to see the ranch as the others.

"I don't ride."

Baird turned to look at his son. "What do you mean you don't ride?"

"I don't ride," Durban enunciated, as if Baird's hearing were defective.

"But I left specific instructions with the stable master at Heatherleigh to teach you."

Durban gave one of his contemptuous shrugs. "I never learned."

Baird stared at the boy in disbelief. Horses were the only thing he'd cared about when he was growing up. They'd been his sustenance during terms at school. How could his son not share that interest? How could Durban defy his forebears, men who'd hunted with Henry VIII and charged to their deaths at Balaclava?

"I don't like riding," Durban declared. "And I don't think I care to see any more of the ranch!" He jumped down from the fence and darted past Ardith and China on his way to the house.

Ardith sized up the situation in a glance. "What did you do to upset him?"

"Did you know that Durban doesn't ride?" Baird demanded.

Ardith nodded as if it were a matter of no consequence. "All Northcrosses ride!"

"Ariel never rode," Ardith reminded him. "Perhaps Durban takes after her."

Damn the boy, Baird seethed, disappointment and incredulity chewing at his insides. And damn Ardith for defending him.

He clung to his exasperation until everyone had mounted up, until they had turned to the wide, rolling fields that lay off to the south. Only when the plains and sky opened in all their splendor before him could Baird put his frustration with Durban aside.

He led his little party south along the base of a towering ridge and up a trail that rose and rose. They dismounted when they reached a broad, flat clearing at the top of the first rocky crest, then stood with the snow-capped Big Horns at their backs and the expanse of the Powder River Valley falling away before them.

"It's so big," China said in a very small voice.

"So vast," Ardith echoed, her tone tinged with awe.

Baird smiled with pride, as if he'd had something to do with creating all of this.

When he glanced across at his sister-in-law, he saw that she was standing with her head high and her face turned into the wind. Tendrils of her tightly pinned hair had unfurled and were fluttering against cheeks scoured red by the cold. Her pale eyes glowed as if she were as touched and exhilarated by the primal scope of this land as he was.

"I can breathe out here," she whispered in astonishment.

Baird shivered with recognition. He had been stirred by

the same stark, unexpected beauty; had sensed the echoing harmony of earth and sky. He had tasted freedom in the wind.

He saw the transformation in Ardith's face and suddenly wished he hadn't brought her here. He didn't want his own fierce enchantment with this place diluted by Ardith's appreciation. He didn't want to share it, didn't want to feel kinship with her, especially when they'd all but declared themselves enemies the night before.

As he turned away, leaving Ardith and his daughter to contemplate the vastness of the Wyoming prairie, Baird realized Khy was no longer beside him.

"Khy?" he murmured and wheeled around. "Khy?"

The boy was nowhere in sight.

Concern wiped the exhilaration from Ardith's face. Something in her expression made Baird's heartbeat pick up speed.

"Where did he go?" he demanded. "How could he have disappeared so quickly?"

"Oh, Papa!" China answered with a hint of exasperation. "Khy heads off exploring all the time."

Ardith cupped her hands to her mouth. "Khy!" she shouted. "Khyber Northcross, can you hear me? Where are you, child?"

All they could hear was the roaring of the wind.

Baird turned on Ardith. "If you knew he might run off like this, why didn't you keep an eye on him?"

"You're his father," she snapped back. "Why didn't you?"

"Khy! Khy!" The rising note of anxiety in his daughter's voice reminded Baird their first priority was finding his son.

He strode toward the edge of the clearing. Beyond a scattering of rocks and some twisted pines, the cliff side dropped away. He hadn't realized how high they'd climbed until he stared down at the cluster of aspens a hundred feet below.

"Khyber Northcross," he shouted, trying to ignore the way his stomach dipped. "You come back here this instant!"

"He won't just come," China offered with a modicum of authority. "Not until he's ready."

Baird swore under his breath. "Well, we can't just stand here and wait. Too much could happen."

He chose not to elaborate. The precipitous drop was the obvious danger, but there were animals a boy could encounter in the woods. He could break a leg in this treacherous terrain, or lose his way in the trees. It was also beginning to snow.

"We need to find him," he declared and began giving orders. "Ardith, take the trail up the south side of the ridge behind us. I'll move around to the north and meet you on top."

"Let me help," China offered.

"I want you to stay with the horses."

The girl drooped in disappointment. "I want to do something important!"

"That is important, China. We'll be in real trouble if the horses wander off. And besides, I'm leaving my pistol here with you," he said, slipping the gun from the holster at his hip.

"Baird," Ardith said in a warning tone.

"If Khy comes back," he went on to spite her, "I want you to fire a single shot."

"Baird!"

"Do you know how to do that?"

China shook her head, fear replacing the eagerness in those wide blue eyes.

"I don't think that's wise—" Ardith warned him.

Baird turned on her. "Just what the hell do you know about finding someone in the woods?"

"Not much," she admitted without backing down. "But I do know that children have no business around firearms."

"We need a way to signal if Khy comes back, or if either of us finds him. I'll show China what she needs to know."

Ardith curled her fingers around the girl's arm. "Do you really think you can do this, China?"

"I'll be careful," the girl promised.

With a reluctant nod, Ardith turned and started up the trail she'd been assigned to search. Once he was sure China understood how to cock, aim the pistol, and pull the trigger, Baird scrambled up the opposite one.

He swept quickly through banks of cedars and pines, calling Khy's name. The snow was falling more steadily when he came out of the trees, and all he could think about was his son being lost up here. Khy wouldn't last the night if a storm closed in.

When the trail branched, Baird set off to the right, wondering if a child Khy's age could have come this far. Still, he knew how distances disappeared in curiosity over a bird's abandoned nest, a scurrying animal, or a rock that seemed to be streaked with gold. He walked a good distance and was looping back when the report of a pistol boomed through the hills.

The tightness that had been building in Baird's chest drained away. "Thank God!" he murmured and retraced his steps.

Ardith came skidding down the path on the far side of the clearing just as he reached it himself. He took one look around and his relief abruptly evaporated. The children were nowhere in sight.

"Where have they got off to now?" he demanded, though Ardith clearly had no more idea where China and Khyber were than he did.

"Oh, Baird," she gasped. "Do you think something could have happened to them both?"

He snatched the pistol from the rock and felt the barrel. It was still hot. "They can't have gone far."

"Khy? China?" Ardith shouted, and the tremor in her voice set something inside Baird quivering.

He added his voice to hers. "China! Khy!"

"Here, Papa!"

Baird spun around just in time to see Khy and China round a boulder at the lip of the ridge. Ardith ran toward them and snatched Khy up in her arms.

China grinned and scrambled the last few steps, sending a trickle of stones skittering down the trail and into the trees at the base of the cliff.

Anxiety sparked up a firestorm in Baird's chest. "Where the hell have you been?"

China lost her smile. "Khy dropped the whistle Mrs. Johnson gave him onto that ledge," she explained, pointing, "and went down after it. But once he got down there, he couldn't get back. All I did was go after him."

Baird stalked past her to the head of the trail. God above! His children had been on a path that clung to the face of the cliff like cobwebs to a dusty wall. His stomach pitched and his knees nearly went out from under him.

He turned to his daughter, breathing hard. "I don't *ever* want you doing something so foolish again," he told her savagely. "I don't *ever* want you taking that kind of chance."

"But I rescued him!" she shouted. "I fired off that beastly gun just like you said, and then I went and brought him back!"

Baird's heart was beating like he'd run a footrace, and his hands were shaking. He couldn't seem to rein in his temper.

"Baird, for God's sake," Ardith admonished him, lifting Khy against her hip. "She did well. Khy's all right. It's fine now."

But it wasn't fine. Khy shouldn't have gotten away from them. His daughter should never have been dancing along the edge of that cliff. Baird shivered, not able to let it go.

Ushering the children toward their mounts, Ardith glanced back and must have read his expression.

"Baird," she spoke sharply. "Baird!" Not trusting his voice, he acknowledged her with a jerk of his head. "That snow you were so worried about seems to have started."

Flakes the size of silver dollars were drifting around them, and the mountains that had been so visible half an hour before were disappearing in veils of white.

Baird swallowed his anger like a bitter tonic. "We've got to get out of here," he agreed. "Buck says when a storm rolls out of those mountains, it can last for days."

He went to help his daughter mount her gelding, but China shrugged away. "I can manage on my own," she sniffed and clambered into the sidesaddle unassisted.

Baird didn't argue. The wind had changed direction and was howling down from the peaks. Cold pierced his jacket like talons. He grabbed up Dandy's reins and looked for Khy.

The boy was already mounted on Ardith's horse, wrapped up tight in Ardith's arms.

"Damned children are nothing but trouble," he muttered under his breath and swung into the saddle.

Sugar Creek Ranch
April 15th, 1882

Mr. Gavin Rawlinson
Publisher—Rawlinson Books
305 Oak Street
Boston, Massachusetts

Dear Gavin,

Due to circumstances beyond my control, it is necessary for me to stay on in Wyoming for a time. Having spoken with the children's father at length about his plans, I am reluctant to leave them here with him. Though facilities are considerably more luxurious than I expected, no provision has been made for someone to look after China and the boys. To be perfectly fair, Mr. Northcross believed that Miss White was going to continue in her position as governess and accompany my sister and the children west. If I pack up and leave the ranch as I intended, the children will be quite without supervision. However, Baird and I have managed to come to an agreement where the children are concerned. I mean to stay on until after the roundup, sometime in mid-June.

What kind of delays this will cause in your publication of "Abigail Goose Goes to Town," I cannot say. I don't see any reason why I can't work on the manuscript while I am here. To that end, could you please ship me the art supplies I will need to complete my sketches? A separate list is enclosed.

I hate to trouble you with this, Gavin, but I know these materials are available in Boston, and it is easier for you to send them on to me directly than to wait for Uncle Franklin to finish his latest essay and pack up my paints. I needn't tell you that he's brilliant, but not of a particularly practical turn of mind. Besides, I imagine he is already considerably put out that I will not be returning to Concord to accompany him on his round of spring lectures.

In closing, I must say that our journey here was uneventful, for the most part. I would so like to thank you for seeing us off at the station and for your foresight in providing the hamper of foodstuffs. They proved to be our salvation on the train. Your suggestion that we spend a night in Chicago was little more than a stroke of genius.

Since the ranch is quite remote, it is useless to try to reach me by telegraph. Send the supplies and any other correspondence in care of Baird Northcross, Sugar Creek Ranch, Rock Creek, Wyoming Territory. Sooner or later one of the cowboys will ride into town to pick them up.

I am most rustically yours,
Ardith Merritt

P.S. Gavin—Could you also send me the newest ten-penny dreadfuls from the book stalls there in Boston? You know the kind I like. Thanks so much, A.

FIVE

The art supplies from Gavin arrived three weeks later. As Ardith unpacked them at the long pine table before the fire, she could not have been more pleased with his selection. Everything fit snugly into a handsome, wooden paint box. Gleaming metal tubes of pigment and an assortment of brushes lay in a carved walnut tray. Beneath it nestled a small ivory pallet for mixing colors, two pewter flasks for carrying water, and a tiny ceramic bowl. Gavin had also included a drawing board, several pads of good rag paper, a parcel of books, and a letter that delighted Ardith more than anything else.

April 29th, 1882

My dear Ardith,

How I regret that your brother-in-law's inattention to his children's needs is detaining you in Wyoming. I am not sure how all of us will manage while you are gone. I am, however, sending on the things you asked me to get, including a supply of ten-penny dreadfuls that should hold you well into next winter. But then, it sounds as if your duties will not keep you in the wilds as long as that. Do let me know about your progress with your book and the situation with the children.

I am ever your obedient servant,

Gavin

"Oh Gavin," Ardith breathed and smiled to herself. "You dear old thing!"

China glanced up from examining the elegant tin of candy that had come from Arthur Merritt with the rest of the mail. He'd sent Durban dominoes and put in a troop of bright tin soldiers for Khy, but there wasn't a word of greeting for Ardith herself.

"Gavin?" the girl asked, clearly intrigued. "Are those from Mr. Rawlinson? The man who saw us off at the railway station?"

"Yes," Ardith answered.

The way she said that single word must have betrayed more about her feelings for her publisher than Ardith intended, because China's regard immediately sharpened. "Why, Aunt Ardith, do you have a *tendre* for Mr. Rawlinson?"

Ardith felt the color seep into her cheeks. "Heavens, child! He's my *publisher*." Unbidden, Ardith remembered the way Gavin's golden eyes had glowed when he'd said good-bye to her in Boston. She could almost feel the intimate warmth of his fingers clasping hers.

"Still, he's a handsome man, your Mr. Rawlinson."

"He's not *my* Mr. Rawlinson," she corrected her niece. "What Gavin and I have is a business relationship."

Ardith was not able to gauge how much of the denial the girl believed because just then Baird, Durban, and Khy came slamming in from the back of the house.

"—can't think when I've seen anyone take such a foolish chance!" he was admonishing one of the boys. Ardith didn't have to question which.

Though they'd been at the ranch three full weeks, Baird had yet to grasp that he needed to be particularly vigilant when it came to his younger son. But then, in spite of the arrangement they'd made, Baird had spent precious little time with the children.

The late-season blizzard that blew in the day they'd toured the ranch had given him an excuse to ride out with the hands as they drove the cattle down onto the flats. Then, when the weather cleared and the chinooks swept down the mountains to melt the drifts, he'd stayed away rescuing cows from the bog-holes that developed in every arroyo and around every stream.

In truth, Ardith was more than a little surprised by Baird's commitment to the Sugar Creek. Though he never seemed to find time to look at the ledgers or answer the mounting pile of correspondence, Baird was in the saddle from dawn to dark. He only returned to the house to wolf down supper, swallow a tumbler of whiskey, and fall into bed.

In fact, it was unusual for the boys to be with their father at this time of day, but the hands had brought the saddle band into the corral this morning, and with it a score of mustangs. Apparently Khy had gotten closer to the wild horses than he should.

"You could have been trampled!" Baird had Khy by the scruff of the neck. "You could have been killed!"

"Those horses didn't look half so big from the top of the fence," the boy admitted.

Baird turned on Durban. "And why didn't you keep an eye on your brother?"

Ardith set Gavin's note aside and rose to Durban's defense. "You're their father. Why weren't *you* looking after them?"

Baird turned to her, the ruddy flush in his face deepening. "I thought we agreed that *you* were going to see to the children until I got back from the roundup."

"What we agreed," Ardith clarified in a tone guaranteed to set Baird Northcross's teeth on edge, "was that I would stay on until you got to know your children better. You'll never do that unless you spend time with them."

The long and rancorous negotiation several nights after Ardith arrived had led to this agreement and an uneasy peace. Though to her way of thinking, Baird was already shirking his responsibilities.

"Well, just so you know," Baird went on, "I'm going to be busy all afternoon. Buck hired some fancy bronc peeler to ride the mustangs we need to break."

I've read about this, Ardith thought, her head swimming with scenes from her ten-penny dreadfuls: of a sunny corral, of a brawny bronco buster, of a sleek-skinned mustang jumping and bucking.

"I thought the children might like to watch." Baird slid her a sidelong glance as if he sensed how much the horse-breaking intrigued her. "But I'll be too busy to keep an eye on them. Now if *you* were willing to do that . . ."

"Mr. Johnson says bronco busting's really something to see," Durban put in.

"Oh, Aunt Ardith, please!" China cajoled. "You will go with us to the corral so we can watch?"

"I'll be good," Khy promised.

Ardith knew Baird was manipulating her, using the children to win his way. It didn't help that she could see the twitch at the corner of his mouth as he waited for her capitulation.

Damn him, she thought. Though his underhandedness rankled her, Ardith wanted to be out at that corral when one of the mustangs bolted in. She wanted to feel her pulse race as the rider swung onto its back, wanted to hear the cheers and taste the dust kicked up by the churning hooves.

She'd make him accept his responsibilities for the children one way or the other, she vowed—just not today.

"China, find our hats and shawls," she ordered, scowling at Baird. "Durban, get a jacket; it's not warm enough for you to be outside in your shirtsleeves. Khy—" She pinioned the six-year-old with her gaze and waited until those wide blue eyes were locked with hers. "—I want your word that you'll stay where we put you and not wander off."

"I will," the younger boy answered, giving a promise she knew he *meant* to keep.

Once Ardith had skewered her hat in place with a long, bone-tipped hat pin and flapped her shawl around her shoulders, she ushered the children out the door.

With something that looked suspiciously like a smirk on his face, Baird stepped back to let them pass.

When they reached the big round corral behind the barn, Baird saw that the dirt had been turned, plowed up as if they meant to plant instead of trample it. A bridle and a coil of rawhide rope hung on the snubbing post in the center of the paddock. A saddle with its stirrups tied up was thrown over the fence on the far side of the enclosure.

The bronc peeler Johnson had hired stood nearby. He was a tall, rail-thin man named John Burroughs, who had a cocksure way of holding himself that made him look like he was sauntering even when he was standing still. Baird hoped that confidence was justified—especially since he was paying Burroughs eight dollars a head to saddle-break the mustangs.

After shaking Burroughs's hand and exchanging a few words with Buck Johnson, Baird went back to where

Ardith and the children were perched on the fence. He glanced across at them as he took his place. China's mouth was bowed in a *moue* of impatience, eager for the excitement to begin. Durban's carefully schooled indifference had slipped a little. Ardith had Khy nestled into the crook of her elbow, as if mere proximity could keep him out of trouble.

For a moment Baird studied his sister-in-law, surprised by the anticipation in her eyes. He never expected someone so straight-laced and Boston-proper to like it here, never thought she could adapt to this rough and ready life, or make friends among these simple, plain-spoken people.

And he never imagined that the land would speak with the same beguiling voice to Ardith as it did to him.

God knows, she wasn't at all the Ardith he had expected his guileless nineteen-year-old English fiancée to become. She had developed backbone over the years, and passion and an iron will. She'd come to expect too much from people—damn her. More than they were prepared to give, more kindness and concern and patience than they had. More tenderness and wisdom.

It wasn't as if he could be the kind of father she wanted him to be to his children. It wasn't as if he were capable of changing, and he didn't like looking up and finding her there, waiting for him to become the man she thought he should be.

Though he wished she was anywhere but here on the Sugar Creek, he didn't have the faintest idea how he'd manage without her. If she weren't seeing to the children's needs, he wouldn't be able to ride out at sunrise and stumble home in the dark, too tired to think. He'd have to acknowledge the longing in his children's eyes, face their need for things he couldn't even begin to fathom. When she left he'd have to provide for these children somehow, and he just didn't know—

The first mustang burst into the corral, and Baird let

his concerns about the children dissolve in a rush of exhilaration. He edged forward, watching the horse skip in nervous circles around the corral. It blew and snorted, its muscles rolling beneath its dun-gray coat. The animal's fear was instinctive and palpable.

Baird gripped the top rail of the fence, his heart thudding heavily.

Burroughs ambled over to the snubbing post and shook out his rope. With a single flick of his wrist he played out a broad, sinuous loop and made an overhand toss. It dropped unerringly around the mustang's neck. Then Burroughs wrapped his end around the snubbing post and waited for the horse to run out the slack. When it did, the loop pulled taut, all but jerking the pony off its feet.

The mustang stumbled and fought the line, backpedaling, pulling the noose tighter. It trumpeted, shook its head and jerked back, half-rising in fear.

Baird's hold on the fence rail tightened.

Burroughs worked hand over hand up the rope, approaching the terrified animal. While the mustang's eyes were riveted on the bronco buster, another roper rushed in to snag the mustang's forefeet with a second line.

The pony staggered, all but crashing to his knees, then it stood there hobbled, helpless and quivering. Its eyes were wide; its ears lay back. Its sides bellowed in an out.

Burroughs crept forward.

Slowly now, Baird found himself advising. Ease toward him. Let him settle.

Burroughs yanked the neck rope tighter. The horse heaved and blew.

"Don't rush him," Baird warned under his breath.

This time Burroughs seemed to heed him. The buster waited until the horse had quieted, then pushed in close and slid a bridle up the pony's muzzle.

The mustang tossed its head, fighting the leather bands and metal bit. Burroughs stayed with him and pushed the snaffle into the pony's mouth. He buckled the straps to keep the bridle in place then gathered in the reins.

In spite of the hobble and the bronco buster's grip, the horse heaved back on its haunches and tried to rise. Burroughs stepped out of the way and jerked the reins. He hauled the animal down again.

Baird shifted uncomfortably. Though he understood the mixture of determination and discipline it took to break a horse, he knew it took patience and kindness, too.

In the center of the corral, Burroughs dragged hard on the pony's reins, fighting it to a standstill. He threw a blanket over the horse's back, then dropped the saddle on top of it.

The mustang shied and shook, trying to dislodge the weight of the saddle as if it were an enemy on his back. But before he could manage it, the peeler stepped in close and drew up the cinch. The horse shied, fighting to get away. Burroughs dragged on the reins, determined to control it.

"He's going to ruin that pony," Baird muttered angrily.

When Buck had explained how things were done out here, he'd assured Baird that Burroughs was one of the most efficient horse breakers in the territory. But it was hard to watch this, hard to sit still.

Out in the corral both Burroughs and the mustang seemed to be catching their breath. Burroughs took off his hump-crowned Stetson and wiped his brow with his handkerchief. The horse stood quivering. Once he'd resettled his hat, the peeler gave a last tug on the cinch, pulled free the rope that bound up the stirrups, and jumped into the saddle.

At the same moment, the second cowboy loosed the hobbles.

With Burroughs's additional weight on its back, the mustang snorted and heaved. He hopped twice to the right, kicked up his heels, and twisted sideways.

A whoop swelled through the men gathered around the corral.

Baird turned in surprise when he heard Durban yelling as loud as everyone else. The child's spontaneity tweaked the corners of Baird's mouth. Maybe there *was* a boy tucked up inside his son, after all.

That smile died on his lips when Baird turned back and saw Burroughs had pulled a quirt from his belt and begun to use it.

Though one horseman didn't interfere with the way another man handled his animals, Baird's blood ran cold. He tried to tell himself this was Burroughs's job, Burroughs's ride, but his instincts clamored for him to intervene.

Out in the corral the pony rolled its eyes and plunged to the left. It made three stiff-legged hops around the ring. Burroughs slashed with his quirt on every one of them.

China's fingers closed over Baird's, squeezing hard. He glanced across and read the distress on his daughter's face. Khy's eyes were wide as dinner plates and filled with tears.

The ranch hands howled in appreciation of the peeler's seat.

Each time Burroughs slashed it, the gray horse screamed.

Then Baird saw blood streaming down the mustang's flank. He was off the fence before he could think.

Burroughs and the pony made a series of stiff-legged jumps across the corral. At the far end, the horse gave a violent heave that sent the peeler sailing.

Baird bore down on the man as he was clambering to his feet. "Get out of here, you son of a bitch!" he shouted. "I won't have my horses mistreated!"

Burroughs turned, acknowledged Baird, and pushed back his hat with a flick of his thumb. "An' just what exactly do you know about breaking mustangs, Mr. Northcross?"

Baird felt heat come up in his face and hung on to his temper by his fingertips. "I know enough not to beat them bloody. I know enough not to drag on their mouths. I know that a perfectly good mount can be ruined if it's mistreated the first time it's handled."

"What's the matter here?" Buck Johnson arrived from the far side of the corral, a little out of breath.

Baird became suddenly aware of the Sugar Creek cowhands sitting along the fence, watching him, judging him. *Probably thinking he had no business interfering.*

He held his ground. "I won't have my animals treated with such brutality."

Burroughs snuffed and spat. "I been breakin' horses for fifteen years, and nobody's ever questioned me."

"I'm questioning you now."

"Mr. Northcross," Buck broke in, his expression conciliatory. "The animals we rounded up aren't like the horses you're used to in England. Those horses have been handled since they were colts."

"This is the best way to break in mustangs," Burroughs assured him.

"Not at my ranch."

"A little discipline's good for a bronc. It builds character."

Baird's face went hotter; his shoulders flexed.

"Just how would you break the horses if you had the chance?" Buck Johnson asked reasonably.

Baird swallowed hard. He needed to give his foreman a serious answer. "I'd gentle them first. I'd win their trust before I expected them to tolerate a saddle."

Burroughs snorted with derision. "And spend all summer doin' it."

"We need ten mustangs green-broke for the roundup," Johnson reminded Baird. "That's only three weeks away."

"If this bothers you, Mr. Northcross," Burroughs

sneered, "why don't you head on back to the house and let me get on with the job you hired me for?"

Baird swung at Burroughs. He landed a punch that sent the peeler staggering.

Grinding out a curse, Burroughs righted himself. He battered Baird with a roundhouse punch that knocked him sideways.

Baird shook off the blow and raised both fists. He had occasionally boxed in gentlemanly contests in England, but he'd also brawled his way through some of the most disreputable stews on earth. He could take this bastard.

As if to prove Baird wrong, Burroughs slammed his fist into Baird's ribs. He grunted and sucked in breath. He lunged at the peeler. They crashed sideways and went down.

They thrashed in the dirt, gouging and kicking. Burroughs landed a knuckler that sent Baird's head snapping back. Baird pounded his fist into the other man's belly.

In spite of the hands hollering encouragement, Buck Johnson and Lem Spivey managed to drag the two of them apart.

Baird twisted out of Spivey's hold and stood there panting. Burroughs's nose looked mashed to one side, and he was weaving on his feet. Baird's jaw throbbed and his lower lip seemed twice its usual size.

He hadn't felt this good in weeks.

Then he realized where he was and what he'd done. He'd been brawling in front of his children. He'd been behaving like a ruffian. Mortification scoured his face and throat. It took everything he had to turn to where his family was seated on the fence. He did his best to prepare himself for the shock and condemnation in their eyes.

The boys' faces were bright with excitement instead. China's hands were clasped across her chest, and her expression was almost worshipful—as if he had done something heroic.

A flush of victory sluiced through him, tingling beneath his skin. His children understood. They hadn't wanted to see the horse mistreated, either.

Then he realized that staid, proper Ardith was sitting there, too. Doubtless his behavior confirmed every reprehensible thing she'd ever thought of him. He steeled himself to look at her.

Unaccountably, she was smiling. If he hadn't known better, he might have thought there was pride shining in her eyes, that he could see a begrudging kind of respect.

He immediately discounted that and turned toward where the peeler was shaking off Johnson's grip.

Burroughs wiped a smear of blood from his cheek. "You keep your goddamned horses, Northcross. They're a mangy lot. I'm going to find me a boss who likes what I do."

"You do that," he advised and indicated the direction of the corral gate with a lift of his chin.

Burroughs limped over and gathered up his gear. Once the bronco buster had gone, Baird turned to Buck Johnson.

A frown had settled deep into the foreman's weathered face. "Well, now," the old wrangler said, as if he were scolding an errant schoolboy, "that there was a damn fool piece of business."

Baird flushed. He was far too familiar with the sound of censure not to recognize it in Johnson's tone. Still, he'd done what he thought was right.

"And since Burroughs has up and quit," Johnson went on, "just where in hell are we going to get the horses we need for the roundup? Who's going to break these mustangs?"

Baird thought for a moment. "I guess I am."

•   •   •

*A*rdith sat at the table before the fire, her pen poised over the half-written letter. Trying to recount to Gavin what had transpired these last three weeks was proving to be far more of a challenge than she'd ever imagined. She frowned, shook her head, then dipped her pen and tried again.

After the bronc peeler left, Baird took over training the horses. Though he'd been renowned for his horseman-ship in England, I couldn't imagine that he'd know how to break wild mustangs.

His first order confirmed my worst fears. Baird had the horses penned up in twos and threes and directed that they not be given so much as a mouthful of hay without his permission.

"You just can't stop feeding them," Frank Barnes, the horse-wrangler, had argued. "Wild ponies graze all the time. You can't shut them up in a corral without hay."

Baird refused to compromise. "Then they'll learn what I intend them to."

"That we're gonna starve 'em to death unless they let us ride 'em?" Lem Spivey snapped.

The children and I pleaded with their father not to mistreat the mustangs.

"What you're doing is inhumane," she had protested.

"Please, Papa!" Khy begged. "Please don't hurt the po-nies!"

Baird just looked at her and the children. "I promise all of you, I won't let these horses be harmed in any way."

Contrary to our worst fears, the mustangs were fed often, but only a little at a time. Within a few days they began to anticipate the arrival of their feed—and the

*people who brought it. They began to tolerate the sound
and scent, and occasionally even the touch of humans.
When one of the ponies showed signs of gentling, the
cowhands would turn it into the corral to start its
training with Baird.*

Ardith and the children had been there when the first
mustang came bolting into the ring. It had bucked and
snorted and kicked up its heels. It had run flat out, its
hooves beating up hazy puffs of dust, its mane and tail
flying.

Ardith found her fingers itching for her pencils and
sketch book as she watched. She wanted to capture the
sinuous play of the pony's muscles, the grace of its movements, the irrepressible spirit of this wild and beautiful
creature.

Her heart twisted with the knowledge that whatever
Baird did today would change this horse, tame it, con-
strain it. And Ardith knew far too much about constraint.

But Baird didn't seem eager to do that. He positioned
himself in the center of the ring and let the mustang run.
He kept turning and turning as if he couldn't take his eyes
away from the pony, either, as if he appreciated both its
beauty and its spirit.

Once the mustang had run off its pent-up energy,
Baird gave a high-pitched whistle and swung the rope that
had been hanging lax in his hand. The black pony snorted
and sprinted in the opposite direction around the ring,
bucking once and running another full circuit before it
slowed. Baird stepped in close, turned it back again, and
sent it running. He turned it half a dozen times in the
next few minutes.

"What does he want it to do?" China asked in a
whisper.

Ardith shook her head. Then slowly she came to understand that all Baird wanted was for the horse to acknowl-

edge him, to turn toward him instead of away. It was a simple enough demand, but one the mustang kept refusing.

Baird asked and asked again. His eyes never left the pony. He turned toward it and then partially away, his body constantly in motion. It was as if he and this horse were dancing some mysterious dance, carrying on some wordless communication that was subtle, yet filled with meaning.

Ardith's chest went tight just watching them.

Though his movements were minute and spare, Ardith recognized the intensity in Baird, a focus she had never imagined he could sustain. There was calm and consistency in every gesture, as if Baird were drawing strength from some deep well inside himself.

This was not the Baird Northcross Ardith knew. This man was gentler, surer, more compassionate. A man of determination and will. A shiver of recognition moved up Ardith's back. This was the man his children needed.

Ardith instinctively opened her arms, bracketing the children who were poised beside her on the fence rails. As she did, she wasn't sure if she meant to protect them or reassure herself of her own connection to them.

Out in the corral Baird's body flexed as he worked with the horse, his every muscle taut with concentration, his balance and coordination flawless in the churned-up yard. Ardith couldn't tear her eyes away from the unconscious grace of his movements, from the breadth of his back and shoulders, the length of his legs. He seemed heroic standing alone against this untamed beast, unaccountably compelling. So different—and yet so much the same—as the man who'd lived inside her head for all these years.

Baird kept the pony loping until its sides were bellowing and the labored *chuff* of its breathing came loud on the cool spring breeze.

"Is he hurting the horse?" Durban wanted to know.

"I don't think so," Ardith whispered back, almost as breathless as the pony in the ring.

Ardith sensed when the horse began to respond to the movement of Baird's hands and the shift of his weight even before she consciously recognized the proof of it. When Baird signaled this time, the black turned toward him instead of away and warily approached.

A thrill moved through her, something sentient and innate, an understanding that went deeper than conscious thought.

Baird let the pony stand and catch his breath. The mustang watched Baird with wide, dark eyes.

Ardith stood as silent as the others gathered around the ring, recognizing the spell this man was casting and wanting to see if his sorcery worked.

Baird stepped to the right. The horse pivoted in his direction. He shifted left, and the pony turned its head. He moved right again, and the pony looked away.

Baird whistled and waved, sending the mustang running. Giving him back his freedom.

This time when Baird turned it, the black came toward him and paused. It stood warily, one hoof raised, ready for flight. Baird let it rest.

As they both stood motionless near the center of the ring, Ardith became aware that Baird was murmuring, cajoling. His voice was low and melodious, yet he wasn't quite singing. Whatever it was, it awakened an answering vibration in Ardith's chest, as if she were attuned to this man in some strange way. As if she'd become part of him, part of this strange, unexpected gentling.

He raised his hand toward the horse, slowly, tentatively. The mustang's eyes widened. Its nostrils flared, but it stood its ground.

Baird shifted his weight, stepping nearer, his palm outstretched.

Ardith's heart thudded in her ears. Her body went taut with anticipation.

Baird continued that warm, wordless lulling until it hung in the air like some kind of ancient music. He reached for the black pony's muzzle.

Ardith shivered, awaiting the stroke almost as if he were reaching for her. She sensed how her flesh would quiver under the caress of those long, sun-darkened fingers, how her skin would warm beneath his hand.

But she also recognized the danger in that fine, brave gesture. Would this mustang allow Baird in so close? Would it strike out in fear?

Just before the pony shied, Baird turned and walked away.

Ardith's heart constricted with disappointment, then leaped with fear. Surely Baird knew it was mad to turn his back on an unbroken horse. Surely he realized the danger, especially with a horse as wild as this.

Ardith's gaze flickered to the cowboys arrayed along the fence. Disbelief froze all of their faces. Buck Johnson raised his hand to the gate, ready to intervene.

The mustang shook its head and snorted.

A shout poised on her lips.

Baird never broke stride.

The mustang blew, shook its head, and fell into step behind him.

Ardith felt her knees tremble.

Baird turned slowly, and this time when he raised his hand, the pony sniffed at him. It rolled its eyes and shifted its ears. Baird stepped in close, speaking in those low, faintly musical tones. He rubbed the mustang's muzzle and neck, its face and ears.

Ardith was exhilarated, breathless with unexpected pleasure. She felt flushed, as if she had witnessed something extraordinary, some mythic feat she wanted very much to understand. How could the man she knew have done this? Was there more to Baird than she'd been able to see?

She looked around and saw the same amazement in the cowhands' faces. Buck Johnson was shaking his head. Lem Spivey scrubbed at his whiskery chin as if he were supremely perplexed. Matt Hastings was wearing a one-cornered smile.

"Has he tamed the horse?" Khy asked her, never turning his eyes from his father.

"Of course he has," China answered fervently. "And he did it without using his whip or his spurs."

It shook Ardith's perceptions to admit that Baird had done something far more significant than calming a frightened animal or bending it to his will. He had kept his promise. Without brutality, without domination, he had won the pony's cooperation.

Before Ardith could think the concept through, Baird turned the horse away with a swish of his rope and made it run.

In the course of the afternoon he demanded more and more of the mustang. When it did what he wanted he rewarded the pony with a scratch and a few soft words. When it balked, he sent it sprinting away.

Ardith and the children never strayed from the corral, compelled to stay by Baird Northcross's conjury, by the gentleness and unexpected power of this man. Even the hands ignored their duties around the ranch, and just this once Buck Johnson let them.

By the end of the day the pony was wearing a hackamore and following after Baird like a well-trained dog.

When he came into the house for the night, Ardith crossed to where he'd stopped by the sideboard to pour himself a whiskey. She could smell the freshness of the wind on him and the pungent musk of horses.

"How did you learn to do that?"

He poured three fingers of amber-brown liquor into a

glass and jammed the cork back into the bottle before he glanced in her direction. She caught the flicker of new life behind his eyes.

"Old Ben, the stable master at my uncle's estate," he finally said, "was known for being able to train the most recalcitrant animals. He believed that you could teach a horse anything if you could get his attention and overcome his fear."

Ardith wanted him to make more of what he'd done than that. She needed him to tell her the trick he'd used to gain the animal's trust so she could explain away the magic. *She wanted a reason for being so affected by what she'd seen.*

He'd made it seem simple instead, and that simplicity unsettled her. It made her a little less sure of him. And far less sure of herself.

That uncertainty brought a challenge to her lips. "Do you think the horses you're breaking will be ready in time for the roundup?"

Baird set down his glass and turned to her. His intensity washed over her like the bright beam of a lantern. He looked her over from the knob of her tightly bound hair to the toes of her high-laced boots.

She realized how close he was to her. He gave off a strange, bone-melting warmth; waves of energy that played havoc with her breathing, her thinking. She trembled a little before the breadth of him, the lithe, leashed strength in his torso and legs. Her nerves clamored with a need for her to step away, but she managed to hold her ground.

"Are—are the horses going to be ready for the roundup?" She repeated the question, hoping to regain control of the situation, of herself. And of him.

A shadow passed over his face. "I don't know," he said, and took his drink out onto the porch.

Something about the set of his chin as he turned away

and the rigidity of the lines around his mouth had sent a quiver of regret through her. She didn't like the part of herself that wanted him to fail at this.

Baird has his own rather unorthodox methods of training, yet he seems to be able to make the horses want to do whatever he asks. It is really quite remarkable.

The second lesson with the mustangs was meant to quell their fear and prepare them to be ridden. Once again Ardith felt drawn to watch the training. She was down at the corral minding the children when the same black pony loped into the ring.

As before, Baird kept it moving until it had run off all its restlessness. When he signaled it to approach, the pony lowered its head and shifted its ears. It was docile, ready to be scratched and petted—and taught.

This *is* magic, she admitted, newly shaken by the discovery. It was the very same enchantment that drew the children to their father. It was the same mysterious force that had drawn the shy, eager girl Ardith had been so long ago.

She remembered how Baird had led her out to dance the first waltz at their betrothal ball. Unaccustomed to being the center of attention, she'd been pale and quaking until he squeezed her hand.

"To hell with them, Ardith," he'd whispered. "You're dancing with me, dancing only for me."

He'd slid his hand around her waist, and she'd felt his warmth and energy seep into her. When the music had begun, they'd spun across the floor, and she *had* danced only for him, basking in the light of approval in those fierce blue eyes.

When she thought back she realized Baird had charmed her that night, beguiled her just as he was charming this pony today. He had beguiled her and made her believe in herself, made her believe he cared for her. Then he had betrayed her as cruelly as any man could.

As she stood watching Baird work with this pony, feeling shivers of his magnetism reverberate deep in her flesh, Ardith began to wonder if there wasn't danger here—a very personal kind of danger. She thought what had passed between them years before had made her immune to Baird. Yet she found herself responding to him now in ways that frightened her. She didn't want to believe she could be so weak, yet there was something about this new Baird that made her strangely susceptible.

Fear gathered in her chest and rose hot beneath her skin. She wanted to run, to flee as this pony had fled, before Baird's charm and power coerced her.

Still, he could only use that power against her if she let him. She might not understand how the sorcery worked, but in these last years, she'd learned to protect herself. She could use that knowledge to protect the children, if it came to that.

Ardith took a shaky breath and shaded her eyes with her hand. Out in the corral, Baird continued his work with the pony.

He rubbed his coiled rope against the pony's neck and chest, pausing just before the pony shied, giving it time to collect itself. He brushed the rope on its withers and legs, its back and flanks. He exchanged the rope for a folded saddle blanket. By the end of the day the little black mustang was trotting around the ring with a saddle cinched firmly in place.

You would find it hard to believe what Baird has managed to accomplish with those mustangs. Within a day or two of their first lesson, he had a saddle on each of them.

Even then he worked gradually, testing his weight on each of the stirrups, easing slowly into the saddle. Once the horses had accepted him as a rider, he began to put the ponies through their paces.

By the time Baird and the men set out for the roundup ground this morning, he had managed to turn all the mustangs into perfectly acceptable saddle horses.

Ardith paused and smiled at the memory.

The scene was like something from one of my ten-penny dreadfuls. The cowboys rode out driving the horses that would make up the saddle band. The chuck wagon rattled along behind, clattering and clanging. They will be gone the best part of six weeks, and after that I shall be able to come home.

Though I am tremendously impressed with what Baird has been able to accomplish with the horses, I can't help wishing he was spending half as much time with China and the boys. They need his attention far more than these horses do. The children are all mopey now that he's gone. While they are not easy youngsters to manage, I think we will get on tolerably well until he returns.

Just then Durban came dragging in from somewhere out back. In spite of his animosity toward his father, he seemed as dispirited as China and Khy by Baird's absence.

The boy came to where she was sitting and stood over her. "Aunt Ardith," he began.

She was surprised by the taut line of his mouth. The reticence that had been less evident these last weeks had returned. "What is it, Durban?" she asked him.

"I was wondering—" He lowered his gaze. "—if while Papa is gone . . ."

He paused and fidgeted. Durban almost never fidgeted.

"Yes?" Ardith asked, intrigued.

". . . if while Papa is gone you could teach me something about riding."

Ardith did her best to keep her mouth from popping open in astonishment. "I'll be happy to teach you," she assured him. "Shall we have our first lesson this afternoon?"

Durban ducked his head. "All right," he answered and spun on his heel.

With a slow, half-smile Ardith watched him go.

I am enjoying my time in the west, dear Gavin, far more than I ever expected. Perhaps now that the horses are broken and everyone has gone off to the roundup, I'll have a chance to finish the illustrations I have been promising you. Please be patient with me, and take care of yourself while I am here.

> *My fondest regards,*
> *Ardith*

As an afterthought, she took up her pen and sketched a horse and rider at the bottom of the page. In the drawing the rider was waving, just as Baird had waved to the four of them this morning before he'd ridden out of sight.

SIX

They met up with the men from six other ranches at the roundup ground on Crazy Woman Creek. As they rode in, Baird estimated that there must be nearly a hundred men and six or eight times as many horses milling around a cluster of a half-a-dozen wagons. The cattle themselves were not yet much in evidence. Only a score of cows and their calves were confined in a makeshift corral.

As the hands from the Sugar Creek drew rein, a tall man hailed them from the center of the encampment.

"That's Thornton Watkins," Buck Johnson murmured as he and Baird rode closer. "He's the captain in charge of this division."

The man striding toward them was tall and seemed as broad as an oxbow across the shoulders. The hair that flowed from beneath his battered hat was iron gray and frothed like breakers against his collar. A grin broke across his wind-worn features as he came closer. "You look like winter sat hard on you this year, old man," Watkins hooted in greeting.

Johnson dismounted, grinning back. "I hear the Devil

came to take your soul, but he decided you were too damn ornery to invite to hell."

Watkins and Buck thumped each other soundly on the back. When they were done, Watkins gave a nod in Baird's direction. "Who's the pup?"

It was years past the time when anyone should have referred to Baird as a pup.

"Baird Northcross," Johnson informed him. "This year's manager."

"Fresh from London, is he?" Watkins asked.

"Not all that fresh," Baird spoke up.

Watkins leveled a measuring, black-eyed gaze on Baird. "Last year's manager—Warner? Wycliffe?—some such name, only stayed through one day of roundup. You going to be here longer than that?"

"We'll have to see."

"I expect he will," Johnson volunteered, voicing a faith in Baird's abilities that took Baird by surprise.

"Well then, Northcross, come along with us and have a cup of coffee. I'll introduce you to the others."

Baird dismounted and followed them toward the fire. He recognized some of the men who were gathered around it. He'd hunted with the Frewen brothers at a country estate in the Midlands several years before, and he knew Horace Plunkett from evenings at White's. He acknowledged his introduction to each of them with a nod of his head.

Cullen McKay stood off to one side. "My, my, Cousin Baird," he murmured when they came face to face. "I wasn't sure you'd last out here as long as this. Tell me, how are your children and lovely sister-in-law getting on?"

"Well enough, I suppose," Baird answered levelly. Since he and McKay would be living in each other's pockets for the next six weeks, it seemed irresponsible to take offense at the first thing the man said.

Watkins continued with the introductions. Baird shook

hands with Tom Mathews, a ranch hand who'd started his own small spread off to the east; with Mayfield Jennings, a former Texas ranger with polished manners and callused palms; with a good many other men.

After a day of wrestling, horse races, and foolery, everyone gathered near Watkins's wagon so the captain could lay out his plans. "Our district runs from Sayles Creek to the Middle Branch of Crazy Woman Creek, and from the Powder River to the face of the Big Horns. I think it's best if we cover the country from east to west, starting tomorrow with Mathews's range."

Watkins scrawled a map in the dirt indicating the wagons' main line of travel. He showed how men would fan out to the north and south, and where they would turn back.

"This over here," he pointed to the southeastern section of his rough map, "is all pretty broken countryside, so we'll need to scour every dip and every hollow looking for beeves. Once you find them, relay them back toward where the wagons will be set up for nooning. Then we'll see about getting the animals branded.

"Buck," Watkins went on, "I want you to take men from the '76 and the Sugar Creek and ride north. Mathews, you head down south. Put your best men and circle horses on the perimeter, and turn the others back a few at a time to ride the gullies and the draws. Everyone know what we're doing?"

There was a mumble of assent and the meeting broke up.

As Baird and Buck ambled back toward the Sugar Creek's wagon for supper, the older man spoke. "I want you riding the outside sweep with me tomorrow. I'll show you what to do and let you try it yourself in a day or two."

Baird shrugged uncomfortably. "Perhaps you should have one of the more experienced men accompany you," he suggested.

The older man glanced at him. "I wouldn't have asked you if I didn't think you could keep up. You got a lot to learn about ranching, boy, but you already know how to bounce your butt in a saddle."

Baird was unaccountably warmed by the older man's words. Perhaps he was going to prove useful in this enterprise after all. He carried that warmth around with him as they sat by the campfire eating supper, and as the men swapped stories of other roundups. He carried it until he headed down to the creek to wash up for the night.

Cullen McKay crested the top of the bank not two minutes later. Baird bristled a little as the other man approached, but he tried to tell himself it was coincidence that had brought them both here at the same time.

Cullen's first words disabused the notion. "I thought you'd like to know, I recently got a letter from Chuffy Culverson."

"Oh?" Baird crouched to dip his bandanna in water still icy with winter runoff, trying to call up some memory of the boy they must both have known at Harrow.

"Chuffy's in London for the Season," McKay went on, "and he says everyone's talking about Cousin Bram's death."

Baird's belly pitched, going as cold as the water running over his hands. "Cousin Bram?" he managed to murmur.

McKay ambled closer. "No one seems to know exactly how he died. They said he'd gone off hunting somewhere."

Baird didn't want to talk about Bram's death, much less recount it for McKay. Still, he felt compelled to answer. "In Burma. He was hunting in Burma."

"Ah yes, Burma," McKay confirmed. "Do you know what happened?"

Visions of Bram sprawled torn and bloody on the matted grass swam through Baird's head. He could smell the gunpowder and hear the bearers wailing.

The bandanna he'd been wringing slipped between his fingers and fell into the creek. Retrieving it gave Baird a moment to regain control of himself. His lungs burned as he sucked in a ragged breath and used it to give credence to the lie. "A tiger got him."

"A tiger you say? Oh, poor devil!" McKay grimaced, though his gaze was avid.

"Yes." Shivers radiated along Baird's ribs. To hide the way his hands were shaking, he wiped his face and neck with the dripping bandanna. He couldn't let McKay see how much the questions about Bram unsettled him.

He found himself longing for a good deep dose of Irish whiskey, and he concentrated on how it would burn in his throat and warm his chest, on how drinking enough would banish memories of Burma and lull him to sleep. But there'd be no strong spirits tonight; all Watkins allowed on his drives was medicinal whiskey.

As if suddenly reminded where they were, Baird became aware of men on the far side of the rise bidding each other good night. He noticed the thump and splinter of someone chopping wood for tomorrow's fire and heard the distant lowing of cattle.

Those sounds drowned out the conspicuous thudding of his own heart and gave Baird the impetus he needed to push to his feet. "I hear Watkins gets us up pretty damned early, so if you've no other news, I believe I'll search out my bedroll."

The other man watched him speculatively. "Indeed, Cousin, we both must prepare for tomorrow. And please pass my condolences on to Cousin Bram's *legitimate* relations when you have the chance."

Baird collected his bedding from the camp wagon, spread it on the ground, and lay for a very long time staring up at the sky. He felt wrapped in its endless expanse; enfolded in profound, dimensionless blackness.

Was this what death was like? An infinity of endless night, a world without substance or form? A vast, oppressive emptiness? Was this where Bram had gone? And his poor Ariel?

Ariel. He shifted amid his blankets and closed his eyes. The vision of her might as well have been painted on his eyelids. The way she'd smiled at him when they'd first met began it. The brush of their hands when he asked her to dance had set off sparks. The force between them had been like gravity, like the pull of the earth on the moon. The first kiss they shared had sealed their fate.

Baird blinked and stared into the dark. It had been so good at the beginning, all feverish heat and expectation, all hope and need and possibilities. But he and Ariel had never been able to build a life on the intensity that had drawn them together. She'd wanted swishing silk dresses, champagne suppers, and dancing until the sky blushed bright with dawn. He'd needed reckless gallops with the wind in his face, far-flung places, and adventures. Neither of them had known how to find the common ground that might have enabled the love that had drawn them together to fulfill its promise. In the end, only embers of the magic remained, embers that had kindled that last night in London.

They'd gone to dinner at Antire House. It had been a pleasant evening until their host inquired about the hunting in Burma. Baird had managed to hold himself together long enough to frame an answer, long enough to finish dinner and voice their regrets. They'd been back at Arthur Merritt's townhouse by half past ten.

Ariel had removed her garnet necklace and matching earrings and dropped them onto her dressing table before she turned to him. "I was quite enjoying myself at the marquis's," she complained. "Why did you make me leave so early?"

Baird hesitated and studied his wife, then decided not to lie to her. "Antire asked me about Burma, and I didn't want to talk about Bram."

He needed to tell someone the whole of it, someone who wouldn't censure him for Bram's death. Not that he didn't deserve it.

He crossed the bedchamber to where Ariel was standing, a shimmering tower of claret-colored velvet and silky skin. He stood for a moment, looking down into that beautiful face. He didn't know if his wife would spurn him or offer consolation once she learned the truth, but he had to find a way to ease his anguish.

"Ariel," he whispered, fighting for control of the memories, for the courage to speak. "I—I need to tell you . . ."

For an instant, dread flickered across those pale, perfect features, then she gave him her most coquettish smile. She slid her cool, soft hand between the studs at the front of his evening shirt and pressed her fingers against him.

"You don't have to tell me anything," she whispered. Rising on tiptoe she'd claimed his mouth.

The embers left between them had burst into flame. He'd made love to his wife like a man possessed, and those moments of frustration and frenzy had left Ariel carrying his child. They'd made him fully and irrefutably responsible for his wife's death.

Baird shifted in his bedroll and focused on the vast, black void of the western sky. Wherever Ariel was, she'd taken the last scraps of his youth and idealism away with her, the finer parts of himself. He felt old, disheartened, drunk down to the dregs.

How had he and Ariel managed to squander the love they'd felt for each other? Baird's throat ached with regret. His chest heaved. His vision blurred, smudging the stars that swirled off into the endless night. Why was he still here when Ariel was gone? Why had God spared him when she and Bram had been struck down?

He was the one who was unworthy.

He swiped at his eyes with the back of one hand, and by degrees the world around him reasserted itself. A breath of breeze rustled the grass around his bed. An earthy coolness crept along his skin. A salting of stars winked into focus high above. He could hear the wickering of horses and the snort of a sleeper a few feet away.

Intensely aware of the sharp, crisp air in his lungs and the throb of life around him, Baird finally closed his eyes.

The very next instant someone was shaking him awake. In a blink the sky had gone from velvet black to pearlescent gray. He heard groans from the men around him, felt the morning damp, and smelled the tang of frying bacon. He rolled to his feet and tied up his bedding.

"You riding out with me, Mr. Northcross?" Buck Johnson hollered from the far side of the campfire.

"Be right there," Baird answered back.

As daylight banded the horizon with red and gold, they caught and saddled their circle horses. They rode out with more than a score of men into a country where grasses swayed restlessly and cycles of rainstorm and drought had nibbled finger-like draws into the gray-brown soil.

As they traveled, Buck sent men off in twos and threes, until only the pair of them was left, galloping their horses across the prairie. The rising sun limned each blade of grass with gold. The wind carried the tang of sage. They drew rein on a rise above the Powder River, and Baird reveled in the way its surface swam with slivers of coppery light.

There was something in this land that fed his soul. He'd known it the first time he'd ridden out with Buck, the first time he'd seen all this from the top of the ridge. That affinity had grown during the long, raw days of early

spring when he'd given himself over to the glorious simplicity of this work; of this place. He'd found peace in the
incalculable scope of the plains, security in the folds of the
mountains, welcome in the silence. And to think he'd
argued with his uncle about coming here.

This country offered a man a future he could grasp and
hold, a tangible connection to work and life and the en-
during power of nature. It could convince a man new
beginnings were possible, and he found himself longing
for a chance to make himself part of something larger and
more lasting than himself.

Beside Baird, Buck Johnson shifted in the saddle.
When he spoke it was clear his thoughts had been running
a very different course.

"There used to be buffalo out here," he began in a
voice gone low with something that sounded suspiciously
like regret. "So many the plains were black with them.
You ever see a buffalo on the hoof, boy?"

Baird shook his head.

"They're magnificent animals, a thousand pounds of
muscle on the hoof. The Cheyenne and the Sioux thought
the buffalo would keep their people clothed and fed for
centuries."

"What happened to them?"

Johnson shook his head. "Men came west. Hunters like
me working for the railroad or the army. We shot as many
buffalo as we could, stripped them of their hides, and left
their carcasses to rot in the sun."

Baird could not imagine such carnage here—especially
not this morning when life seemed so bright and new. It
was like the sun was being born on that horizon, and the
earth was quickening beneath its amber glow. He felt its
warmth on his skin, felt its soothing heat sink into him.

Still, Baird knew he must acknowledge Johnson's
words, especially when he seemed to be seeking some sort
of absolution. "Why did you do it?"

Buck's eyes were dark as if he were seeing other days. "The government wanted it done, and all this seemed so limitless. None of us believed we could make a difference—but we did. What we're doing today is making a difference."

Baird couldn't bear the thought that this could change. He needed to know there would always be wide, swaying grasslands that rolled like the sea; rough-faced mountains to claw at the sky; rivers shimmering in the sun like the Powder was shimmering this morning. He needed the nourishment they gave him far too much to think they could one day be gone.

Buck snuffled and gave a self-effacing shrug. The blunt, practical ranch foreman Baird was coming to know so well reasserted himself. "Seems like I done more than enough jawing for one day," he said. "We got beeves to chase. You take the far side of the creek and push any beeves you find downstream."

Baird nodded, nudged his horse down the slope, and as he crossed a meandering trickle of nut-brown water, he caught sight of half a dozen cows grazing down the draw. With a whoop and a wave of his rope, he lit out after them. In the space of the next few hours, Baird learned that cattle were the most contrary beasts he'd ever encountered. They moved only when and where they chose and hid in the most inaccessible nooks they could find. It took every bit of his horsemanship to stay on Dandy's back as they picked their way along the ridges and chased down strays in the streambeds between them. An hour before noon, Baird brought his animals down to where one of the '76's hands was holding a herd.

"If there are more beeves out there, they've taken up residence with the prairie dogs," Baird greeted the man with a laugh. He was sweat-stained and saddle sore and breathless. His shoulders ached from swinging his rope, and his throat was raw with shouting. But never in his life had he felt more satisfied.

The other cowboy grinned in answer. "Then let's get the last of these dogies back to the wagons. Watkins will be wanting to brand the calves before we've had so much as a bite of beans."

An hour later, when he rode into camp, Baird saw Buck Johnson look up from his plate and nudge Thornton Watkins. Watkins raised his eyebrows in acknowledgment and gave Baird a grin.

It was as sweet a moment of approval as Baird had ever known.

*T*hey could smell the branding a full mile off.

"What *is* that stench?" China demanded, wrinkling her nose.

Ardith pulled in the team that drew the lumbering farm wagon and sniffed discerningly, recognizing the smell she'd only read about. "It's singed hair and hide, dust, and cow dung. And men who haven't bathed in several weeks."

"How barbaric!" China said with a huff and adjusted her parasol to better shade herself from the pounding sun.

The wagon jounced into a rut, and Ardith glanced over her shoulder at the boys riding in the back. "Everyone all right?" she called out. "Nothing shifted, did it?"

The wagon was packed to the racks with provisions: flour, canned goods, dried apples and beans, bacon and salt pork, and a full dozen loaves of Myra's fresh-baked bread.

"We're fine," Durban answered. "Are we there yet?"

"Here comes your father riding out to greet us."

From somewhere in the maelstrom of smoke and mooing and dust, Baird cantered toward them. Ardith slowed the wagon and watched him approach.

Baird had always ridden well, but today he and his horse moved with a unity of purpose that brought his horsemanship very near to poetry. The way he came at them, silhouetted against drifts of gold and gray, made Ardith want to paint him. She wanted to capture that dauntless freedom, the compelling arrogance of a man in tune with this raw, unfettered world. The power in that image sent chills up her back.

"Papa!" Khyber shouted as Baird drew rein beside the wagon.

Baird reached to grab the boy, who was teetering on the edge of one of the crates, and lifted him effortlessly into his saddle. Though it had been Buck who'd invited them to watch the branding when he'd stopped to visit Myra, Baird seemed genuinely glad to see them.

A broad grin split his face, showing white against his sun-darkened skin and the sooty stubble that smudged his chin and cheeks. His hat was battered and dusty. His clothes were creased to the shape of his body, as if he'd ridden and eaten and slept in them. And perhaps he had.

Still, the roughness suited him somehow, suited him in a way that sent a surprising warmth seeping into Ardith's belly. It was a treacherous warmth, a completely unacceptable warmth.

"Buck says things have been going well with the children."

Baird's greeting startled her from her thoughts. Had he asked about China and the boys, or had Johnson volunteered the information?

"Yes, they have." Ardith began enumerating the goings-on, judiciously deleting the less than perfect moments she'd had with the children. "China has discovered Myra's cache of Dickens's novels."

"I'm reading *Oliver Twist*," the girl spoke up, "and quite enjoying it."

"I jumped into the hay pile from the top of the barn," Khy crowed.

"And were very lucky not to have broken your neck," Ardith reminded him severely.

Baird turned to his elder son. "And what have you been about?"

Ardith waited, hoping Durban would tell his father about the riding lessons, the hours he'd spent cantering around the corral on Myra's gentle roan.

"Oh, this and that," the older boy said with a shrug.

Baird's smile dimmed, and Ardith spoke to cover the awkwardness. "Well, I have finished the paintings for my new book and shipped them off to Boston."

"Have you now?" Baird asked her. "And have you begun work on another?"

Before she could answer a loud bawling came from the direction of the branding fire.

Baird turned to look. "I guess they're taking a part of that calf he doesn't want to lose."

Ardith bit her lip and waited for the question, knowing it was inevitable. It was China who asked it. "And what part is that, Papa?"

Baird suddenly realized what he'd alluded to, and to whom. His eyes widened. Fierce, fiery red swept up his jaw.

Ardith fought a gust of delighted laughter and let him stew in mortified silence until she was good and ready to rescue him. "They take off an animal's horns," she interceded, "isn't that right, Baird? So it can't hurt itself or the other cattle."

The color in his face intensified. He didn't like her helping him. "They take its horns," he finally agreed, a scowl rolling across his face like storm clouds. "Now if you just pull up beside the chuck wagon there on the left," he directed Ardith, "our cook, Jubal Devereau, will see that everything gets unloaded. And for godsake, China, do close up that parasol. It'll spook the cattle!"

With a flick of his wrist, Baird turned his mount back toward the noise and the smoke.

Still chuckling to herself, Ardith followed.

She and China and Durban found Baird and Khy at the branding fire a few minutes later. The activity around it was both frenetic and meticulously orchestrated. Several men on cutting horses rode into the snarl of milling cattle. Each selected a calf that needed branding, nudged it toward the edge of the herd, and eased it out. To keep the calf from doubling back, the cowboys had to ride hard and fast.

Ardith had read about their horsemanship: charging one way and sprinting back, standing, staring, whirling, and back-pedaling. She had never expected there would be such strategy in every move, such concentration and cooperation between a man and his mount.

"These cutting horses are specially trained," Ardith offered, curling one hand around Durban's shoulder. "The men watch for colts that are intuitive and intelligent, then give them special instruction. See how that rider is guiding his pony by shifting his weight and pressing with his knees? He hardly touches the reins."

"Do you think I could learn to do that?" he asked, his voice shaded with awe.

"I don't see why not," she encouraged him.

As if afraid to contemplate the hours of work such mastery would take, Durban shifted his gaze toward the fire. "Why are they using those metal rods to burn the cattle?"

Baird came up behind them. "That's how we know whose cows are whose. Each ranch has its own particular mark."

It was the first straightforward exchange Ardith could ever remember hearing between father and son.

"What does our mark look like, Papa?" China asked him.

Baird squatted down and drew an interlocking S and C in the dust. "That's our brand."

"They heat the branding irons in the fire and use them to singe off the hair," Ardith continued.

"Does it hurt?" Khy wanted to know.

As if in answer, the calf by the fire bawled piteously as one of the men stamped the gray-hot iron onto its rump.

"I guess it does!" Durban said with a laugh.

Just beyond the fire the calf's mother snorted with impatience and pawed the dirt.

"Look how worried she is about her baby!" China exclaimed.

"The cows get downright ornery sometimes," Baird confirmed.

"Wouldn't you be upset if someone was hurting your child?" Ardith asked him.

Baird turned away instead of answering, watching as the men hefted the calf to its feet and sent it loping toward its mother. "See, he's fine now, and none the worse for his experience."

Just then Buck came striding toward them. "Jubal said you'd arrived," he greeted them. "Have you been showing Miss Merritt and the children how all this works?"

"Ardith already seems to have considerable knowledge where roundups are concerned," Baird answered.

"From reading western novels," she put in.

"There's not much more to show them," he went on, "just how we keep the cattle from the ranches separated so they can be driven back to their home range."

"Well, then," Buck said, "I guess it's time we put the lot of them to work."

Baird shook his head to warn Johnson off, but the foreman ignored him. "Willis Roberts had to ride down to the

'76 this afternoon, so I thought we'd ask Miss Merritt to keep the tallybook."

"I'd be happy to help. Just show me what to do."

Buck motioned a young cowboy toward them, and Ardith recognized him as one of the hands from the Sugar Creek. "Maybe Miss China can work with Matt Hastings here, cooling down the horses as the riders bring them in."

The young man doffed his Stetson, revealing a broad, pleasant face and thick blondish hair creased flat by his hat.

"Ma'am," Hastings acknowledged Ardith. "Miss Northcross." A flush rose from his collar to his hairline.

Ardith pressed her hand to her lips to hide a smile. China had made another conquest.

"I'd be happy to work with Mr. Hastings," the girl replied, suddenly looking a little flushed herself.

"What about the boys?" Baird protested. "If we're all busy, who will watch—"

"That's why I'm giving *them* one of the most important jobs of all," Buck said with a smile. He turned to Khy and Durban. "You young fellows can tend the water bucket, can't you—keep it filled, carry cool drinks to the riders when they stop by?"

"Sure we can," Khy agreed.

Buck glanced at Baird. "And since you're working the branding fire this afternoon, I figured between you and Jubal at the chuck wagon, we could keep a pretty good eye on them."

When it appeared that Baird might balk, Ardith spoke up. "I'll be there, too. Between us we can keep them out of mischief."

With a nod, Buck Johnson took the boys and sent the rest of them about their tasks. Baird headed for the fire. Ardith gathered up the book and pencil and settled herself on a keg not far from where they were branding the animals.

The tallybook was easy enough to keep, and she divided her attention between it and the boys, who were ferrying a dipper and bucket back and forth between the cook wagon and the cowboys bringing in calves. Carving cattle was dusty, thirsty work, and the riders kept the two boys busy.

When the pace around the fire slowed, Ardith found her gaze straying to where Baird was working with the other men. She couldn't help noticing how the muscles of his shoulders and back rippled beneath his shirt, and what an advantage those long legs gave him when it came to wrestling cattle to the ground. Baird held the struggling animals with relative ease, making her realize how capable he was, how attuned to the sheer physicality of this work, how at home in the company of these rough-hewn men.

Watching him, she sensed some of the same intensity she'd seen when he was breaking the mustangs. The same focus and strength and energy. Glimmers of something fine and undefinable. And it surprised her all over again, warmed her somehow.

After a particularly long and busy stretch of counting and scribbling, Ardith looked up to make sure she knew where everyone was. Khy was perched on the seat of the cook wagon, eating a slice of pie out of his hand and listening to some story Jubal Devereau was telling him. China and Matt Hastings were leaning against the fence of the makeshift corral, their shoulders aligned but not quite touching. The girl had taken off her hat and was peering up at Matt from beneath a drape of sun-bright hair. He was giving her a soft, one-cornered smile and was clearly besotted.

Durban stood off by the Double T's chuck wagon with Cullen McKay. Something about the friendship that had sprung up between them on the way from Rock Creek made Ardith uneasy. Had McKay deliberately befriended the boy to strike out at Baird, or had Durban sought Cullen this afternoon because he sensed it would antagonize his father? Either way, seeing the two of them together brushed cold tingles along the back of Ardith's neck.

Just then, Baird and Buck Johnson converged on her. "How's the count coming along?" Buck wanted to know.

"Well enough, I think," she answered. "I have some preliminary totals."

"Mind if we have a look?"

Ardith handed over the book, pointing to the column for the Sugar Creek.

"Well?" Baird asked, and Ardith thought she heard both impatience and a hint of uneasiness in his voice.

Johnson's mouth drew tight beneath his mustache. "The count's lower than we'd expected here, too."

"Godamnit!" Baird breathed. "I was hoping we'd make up the shortfall once we got on our own range."

"You mean you don't have as many cattle as you thought?" Ardith asked him.

"The size of a herd is supposed to double every third year," Baird explained. "We're falling a good deal short of that."

"Even counting the calves born this spring, we're coming in with a lower number of beeves than we counted last fall," Johnson answered. "I can't rightly comprehend that, either. This wasn't all that bad a winter."

"Perhaps our animals drifted south," Baird suggested, squinting down along the face of the Big Horns. "Perhaps we'll find the ones we're missing when we do the Double T and the '76."

Buck Johnson's eyes warmed with concern as he looked at Baird. "What's your quota for shipment this fall, son?"

Baird shifted uncomfortably. "I'm a little behind on

my correspondence from London. I'm not sure what they expect."

Johnson must have known from the mound of papers on the desk at the ranch that Baird hadn't so much as looked at the letters. Or the ledgers, either, as far as Ardith knew.

Still, Buck allowed him the lie. "Well, last year Mr. Wycliffe drove eighteen hundred head to market in Cheyenne and sold them for nearly eighty thousand dollars. I doubt they'll expect anything less from you."

The lines around Baird's mouth deepened. "And how far short of being able to do that are we?"

"Well, if you're right about those cows drifting south," Johnson conceded, "we might just make it."

The idea that Baird might fail at this shouldn't have made Ardith go hollow inside. But then, her concern was for the children, not Baird himself. The children had just lost their mother, their home, their stability. If Baird were successful in running the ranch it would begin to give some of that back. And after seeing how hard he worked, Ardith had to admit, she didn't want to see Baird thwarted, either.

All of them looked up from the tallybook as three cutters rode in, each dragging a calf to be branded.

"Sugar Creek," the first cutter shouted and everyone sprang into action.

One of the cowboys flanked the calf, tossed it, and sat on its head, earmarking it in the bargain. A second immobilized its hindquarters, while a third snipped off its scrotum. Baird pulled a Sugar Creek iron out of the fire and held it to the little fellow's hip. The calf bellowed loud and long as Ardith made a mark in her tallybook.

"Looks like we've got about four dozen more to brand," Jeff Mason reported as he dragged another calf up to the fire.

Once the branding crew had taken it off his hands,

Mason motioned to Durban and Khy. "You boys still delivering water?" he called to them.

"We sure are!" Khy jumped down from his perch on the seat of the chuck wagon and grabbed up the dipper. He started toward Mason at a run, leaving Durban to heft the bucket and follow him.

The younger boy's path took him between the calf at the fire and its mother, standing bellowing and splay-footed at the edge of the herd. The heifer took exception to the boy's intrusion, snorted once, and lowered its head.

Ardith caught the movement from the corner of her eye and shouted a warning. Baird turned in time to see what was happening and bolted toward his younger son.

But Durban was closest. He shoved Khy aside as the heifer charged, then swung the pail of water. It smacked the cow in the nose and bought Durban the second or two he needed to shield his brother's body with his own.

The cow snorted and butted the bucket out of the way, her hooves dancing over the huddled children.

Ardith ran toward the boys, her heart in her throat.

Baird reached them first. He stumbled to his knees and grabbed Durban's shoulder. "Durban! Damnit, Durban! Are you all right?"

Ardith skidded to a stop just behind him.

Durban shrugged off his father's hand, slowly pushed to his elbows, then fell back to his knees. "I'm fine," he said.

Khy lay beneath him, curled in the dust.

Ardith's hands went cold as she searched for signs of life in the younger boy. Then she realized his shoulders were quaking, and tears were streaking down his dusty cheeks. Baird drew Khy's small, quivering body into his arms.

"I didn't mean to m-m-make that cow so m-m-mad," the boy whimpered.

Baird drew him closer, his big, work-gloved hands

moving over his son, soothing and assessing. "Are you hurt, boy?" he asked his son softly. "Are you hurt?"

Ardith realized his voice was shaking.

Khy snuffled back his tears. "No. I don't think so."

Baird's shoulders sagged; his back lost its rigidity. He rose, stood the boy on his feet, then swiped at Khy's tears with the rough leather thumbs of his gloves.

Ardith curled her hand around Durban's elbow, and eased him closer. "Did that cow kick you?"

The older boy shook his head. "Her hoof grazed my shoulder is all."

She turned him around and saw that blood was spreading down the back of Durban's shirt. Her mouth was suddenly hot and cottony, but she managed to keep her voice level. "I think Durban needs some tending."

As if sensing that there was trouble, cowboys had come from all directions. China and Matt had run over from the corral. Thornton Watkins's horse skidded to a halt, and the captain leaped out of the saddle.

"What's going on here?" he demanded.

"The boys got between a heifer and her calf," Baird explained as Ardith eased Durban toward the Sugar Creek's chuck wagon.

Jubal Devereau had already pulled out the box of medical supplies by the time Durban was settled on an upturned keg. Ardith helped him out of his shirt, revealing a deep, bloody gash curved like a sickle around his shoulder blade. Her stomach pitched at the sight of it.

Watkins and Devereau stood over the boy consulting. "It's not serious," Watkins pronounced, "but it's going to need stitching. You want to do that, ma'am?"

The idea of pushing a needle through anyone's flesh—much less Durban's—made Ardith's lunch back up in her throat. "Crewelwork is *my* specialty," she joked weakly.

"Then I'll take care of it," Watkins said. "That all right, boy?"

Durban managed a feeble smile. "Sure."

"Ah, Watkins is an old hand at this," one of the cowboys assured him. "It won't hurt more than stubbing your toe."

"Hell," a short, grizzled cowman volunteered, "he stitched me last year from knee to groin, and I never felt so much as a twinge."

"Yeah, Jake," someone else put in, "but you drunk down half of Watkins's medicinal whiskey before he even got out his needle and thread!"

The cowboys hooted with laughter.

Durban did his best to join in. "I guess I'll be all right then," he agreed and glanced at his father for confirmation.

That lingering look between Durban and his father was the first hopeful sign Ardith had seen yet.

Until Baird inexplicably turned and walked away.

What in the name of God was Baird doing? How could he rebuff his son when the boy needed him?

"You'll be fine, boy," Ardith heard Buck Johnson murmur as she stalked in the direction Baird had gone. She found him on the far side of one of the chuck wagons, standing with his hand braced against its side and his head bowed low.

"Just what in bloody hell are you doing?" she demanded, her voice raw with fury. "How could you walk away from your son when he finally turned to you?"

Baird's head jerked up. He seemed shaken and pale beneath the stubble of that days' old beard. There was confusion in the depths of those bright blue eyes.

"I just couldn't stay there and watch Watkins stitch Durban up," he admitted, his breathing catching a little. "I didn't think something like this could bother me—but it does."

He'd just discovered his vulnerability where the children were concerned. Ardith experienced an unexpected twinge of sympathy, but refused to indulge it.

She stepped in close instead, all but spitting the words in his face. "It doesn't matter how you feel. It's time you started thinking of those children instead of yourself. And Durban needs you."

He blinked at her. "Durban needs me?"

"Of course he needs you," she answered. "You're his father. He needs you to tell him how strong and brave you think he is, how clever and resourceful. Don't you realize what that boy did, how much he risked by going after his brother?"

"I know what he did—"

"He needs you to stand beside him, Baird, while Watkins stitches him up. And when it's over, he needs you to compliment him on how well he did."

She could see flickers of understanding in him. "You be a father to your son, Baird Northcross," she whispered fiercely. "You be a father to him—it's what he needs more than anything!"

Baird let out a long, shivery sigh. He swallowed hard and nodded.

Finally.

On the strength of that nod he brushed past her and paused by the rear wheel of the wagon. Though she could not see his face, she imagined that he was battling his own fears, gathering his fortitude. He scrubbed his mouth with the back of one hand; blew a long, uneven breath; squared his shoulders; and rounded the corner of the wagon.

Once he was gone, Ardith sagged back against the side of the wagon, her knees quivering. She was a little amazed that she'd stood up to Baird. But seeing him walk away when Durban needed him had unleashed such powerful feelings in her, such ferocious protectiveness for this brave but fragile boy, such unbridled fury. *Such overwhelming love.*

The realization of how much she had come to care for these children made her go weak and warm inside, frightened and fierce. It made her want to gather them up and hold them; made her want to assure them that no matter what happened, they would always have her to hold on to, that they would have her to care for them no matter what their father did.

She hadn't known she had the capacity to love so hard or want to give so much. Still, this wasn't the time to dwell on what she'd just discovered about herself, or the glimmers of concern for the children she'd seen in Baird. Durban needed her now every bit as much as he needed his father. She did her best to pull herself together and went back to where the cowhands had gathered around her gallant boy.

They got through the stitching somehow. Baird held Durban's shoulders still while Watkins worked. Ardith bit her own lips raw waiting for it to be over. Though a few tears slipped down Durban's waxen cheeks, he never uttered so much as a murmur of complaint.

When the older man had finished his needlework and bound the wound, the cowboys clustered around Durban claiming him in their own way.

"You're a game one," one of the '76 cowboys assured him.

"If push come to shove, I sure wouldn't mind having you riding with me," another mumbled approvingly.

"When you're a little older, boy, you'll be able to impress the women with that fine scar," Jeff Mason put in.

"You did well," Baird murmured, and to Ardith's ears his voice seemed deeper, warmer than usual. She looked up, waiting for him to go on, to tell Durban how proud he was of him, how brave he'd been to rescue his brother.

Baird didn't say any of that. He stood turning his hat in his hands, while Durban waited.

Cullen McKay spoke up instead. "Durban, my boy!

I'm so gratified to know a fine young man as brave as you. Do you realize you saved your brother's life? It took courage to stand your ground when that cow charged. I can think of grown men who wouldn't have handled the situation any better."

Durban seemed to bloom in the light of Cullen's praise. His eyes brightened; a slow smile transformed his face.

Baird turned away, and Ardith wished with all her heart that he had fought Cullen McKay for his son's favor. This was what Durban needed, this attention and approval of grown men after living sheltered so long as her sister's child.

Before she could think of a way to intercede, Buck approached her. "The wagon's all hitched up. I thought after this you and the children might want to head back."

"I think that's wise," Ardith agreed. Durban wouldn't admit it, but his wound must hurt. Myra would have potions and poultices at the house to ease his discomfort.

"He's quite a boy, our Durban," Johnson observed. "Quiet, but with lots going on underneath. He's like his father in that."

"Like Baird?" Ardith echoed. Could Buck see more in Baird than she could?

The older man nodded. "At least you won't be missing much. We're mostly done branding. I know you were planning to drive on to tonight's encampment and stay to supper, but maybe it's just as well you're heading home in the daylight. You will tell Myra I miss her, won't you?"

Ardith smiled. The warm relationship between Myra and her husband delighted Ardith in a way she couldn't quite explain. "I surely will."

"And Mr. Northcross said to tell you he'd ride back with you, to see you got home safe."

"Good," Ardith said, strangely gratified by Baird's deci-

sion. She bid Buck good-bye and headed off to gather up
the children.

Sugar Creek Ranch
June 15, 1882

Dear Gavin,

*The roundup was wonderful—even more exciting than
I had expected—though on the surface it seemed like
chaos. The cattle bawl ceaselessly. The smoke from the
branding fire stings your eyes, and your throat gets raw
from breathing dust. The men are constantly busy in a
dozen different activities, most of which involve hard
riding or hard work. I was tremendously impressed by
the way the seasoned hands maneuver their horses in
among the cattle, how they select the one they want,
and separate it from the rest of the herd. Doing that
entails some of the most daring horsemanship I have
ever seen. Though the enterprise seems wildly uncoordi-
nated, the afternoon we visited, they branded over four
hundred calves. I can't say it is the most efficient way to
count the cattle, or brand them, or doctor them, but it
is colorful and exotic. And far more enervating than
anything I have ever done in my life.*

*Of course the visit the children and I paid to the
roundup encampment was not without incident. What
event that involves these children is? Khy got charged by
a cow, and Durban jumped in to save him. In the
process Durban sustained a nasty gash, which, I'm
pleased to say, is already looking better. He is a brave
lad, and it concerns me that his father seems unwilling
to acknowledge it. But that is another topic entirely, one
I will not burden you with today.*

*I do so wish, Gavin, that you could have been here
and gone to the roundup with us. You would have been*

as fascinated as I was by the rough poetry of the riding, the pagan ritual to the branding, and the sheer beauty of this aspect of this land. Since you were not able to accompany us, I have tried to capture a bit of the spectacle in the painting at the top of this page and the vignettes at the bottom. I hope they give you a flavor of what we saw. It was undoubtedly one of the most fascinating experiences I've ever had.

Now, on an entirely different topic—I have begun writing the text for my next book. How do you feel about me giving Harland Hedgehog his own story? Please let me know before I go on to start the illustrations.

I look forward to hearing from you soon.

Fondly,
Ardith

SEVEN

*C*hina burst into the ranch house, her face flushed and her hair flying. "Aunt Ardith," she demanded, throwing herself into the chair opposite where Ardith was painting at the long pine table. "Have you ever been in love?"

Ardith made a blot in the middle of the illustration she'd been working on and stared up at her niece. She was stunned by the bluntness of the question—had she ever been in love?—and overwhelmed by its implications. *Had Ardith been in love with this child's father?*

The heat of a blush surged upward scorching her neck and cheeks. How was she to answer her niece?

Was she to say that she'd been fascinated by the bold adventurer who'd become her fiancé, that she'd been flattered by Baird's attention? Could she tell China that she'd been infatuated, irresistibly drawn to the man whose defection had broken her trust so completely that it was only now—sixteen years later—that she even dared to be attracted to another man?

"No," Ardith answered. "I've never been in love. Have you?"

"I don't know." The girl lowered her gaze, shading her eyes with her long, gold-tipped lashes. "I think I am."

China had spent the morning with Matt Hastings and had about her a glow that went well beyond the one from her fresh sunburn. Ardith hadn't felt that flush in years, but she knew what it was: a sense of excitement and delight and anticipation. When Baird had come calling all those years ago, Ardith had felt like this, like a flower budding, about to burst into bloom.

"What makes you think you are in love?" Ardith asked warily, knowing she was wading in beyond her depth.

China shrugged a little and looked away. "I think about Matt Hastings all the time. We have fun when we're together. He makes me feel so good, as if I'm smart and not just pretty. He says he'd rather be with me than anyone. And when he kisses me—"

"Matt's kissed you?" Baird would be apoplectic when he heard that. He was just back from the roundup and now this!

China's already flushed cheeks went the color of geraniums. "Well, yes, he has. But only twice. And when he does I get this funny, dizzy feeling in my stomach."

Ardith knew the feeling.

"Is that love, Aunt Ardith?"

Dear God, how was she to know? It was on the tip of her tongue to tell her niece what she knew she should—that nice young women didn't kiss men. That *nice* young women's stomachs didn't buzz with excitement. That it was wrong, scandalous to feel such things.

But then Ardith was too forthright to fob her niece off with that lie. She knew how it felt for a man to curl his hands around your shoulders, for him to draw you close. She remembered what it was like to look up into a man's face, smell the tang that clung to his freshly shaven cheeks, and lose yourself in his eyes. She'd experienced the soft, anticipatory mingling of breath, the brush of his mouth.

The strange, sweet hum in your blood and the warmth seeping through you. *Was that love?*

"It might be love," Ardith conceded, feeling flushed and shaken and like she was groping in the dark, "but, China dear, love is so much more than kissing. It's common interests and common dreams. It's wanting to make a life with someone, to start a family. And you're only fifteen . . ."

China shot to her feet, transformed in an instant from a questioning child to an outraged young woman. "I knew you'd say that," she accused. "I knew you'd tell me I was too young to be in love. And now you'll feel duty bound to inform Father that I've been kissing Matt."

Ardith frowned, strangely reluctant to forfeit her niece's trust. "I won't tell him," she bargained, "if you promise—"

"Promise what?"

Ardith's mind spun. What had Ariel told her daughter about relations between men and women? Did Ardith have either the gumption—or the expertise—to discuss such intensely intimate things with her niece?

"I want you to promise me that you won't go off alone with Matt," she bargained, buying time. "That you won't allow Matt to kiss you."

"But I like it when he kisses me."

Ardith nodded. "I imagine you do. But if I'm to refrain from discussing what you've told me with your father, I need some assurances."

China pursed her mouth and thought that over. "All right," she agreed. "I'll do as you ask, but I can't say I'll like it."

Ardith gave a wry twist to her lips. "Welcome to adulthood."

China cast her a resentful glance, then turned toward the kitchen. "I finished reading *A Christmas Carol* last night. I'm going to see what other books Myra has in her collection."

Ardith watched China flounce away, wondering if what she'd done was right. She could hardly sanction a romance between this child and one of the ranch hands. The girl was far too young, for one thing, and an earl's grandniece for another. But Matt was a nice young man, who clearly held China in high regard. And for all her tender years, China had a sense about men.

She's like her mother in that, Ardith thought, remembering the way men had been drawn to her sister, and how Ariel had managed and maneuvered them. China was capable of that, but she had also been tempered by her parents' marriage. She would be more wary of love than her mother had been. And now that Ardith knew about China and Matt, she could keep an eye on them.

Officially, of course, her agreement with Baird to stay and take care of the children had ended three nights before, when he and the rest of the hands had come home from the roundup. She should be leaving for Massachusetts any day. But she could see that Baird was nowhere near ready to handle China and the boys on his own, and she no longer minded staying for the children's sake.

Or for her own. She liked Wyoming, liked the space and the freedom. This house was so different from the one in Concord. It was busy and noisy and filled with life. There was turmoil every day, and Ardith had come to thrive on it.

Nor had Baird said anything to her about leaving. She supposed she should resent him taking advantage of her, but she couldn't quite manage that.

Late that afternoon, just as Ardith was putting the finishing touches on the first illustration for the book on Harland Hedgehog, Baird came in from somewhere out back. As he crossed the room, she saw him glance in toward the desk where the pile of correspondence from London had grown to gargantuan proportions.

"You're going to have to go through that sooner or later," she warned him.

Baird stopped beside her with a jingle of spurs. "I know," he admitted with a sigh. "But when I do, they're going to want to know the number of cattle here on the ranch and how many I'll be taking to market. They're going to ask about finances, and I can't make heads or tails of those ledgers. If they wanted reports, they should have sent a goddamned clerk."

The force of his frustration buffeted her. "Why *did* they send you here?" she asked him.

He shrugged, his shoulders bunching. "My uncle sent me to Wyoming because he didn't know what else to do with me."

It was the truth; Ardith could see that. But there was more to it, much more. She caught the creep of shadows at the backs of his eyes; his defensiveness rose like a barricade between them. She wasn't sure she should question him too closely, but she had to do something to make things better.

"I've kept Uncle Franklin's household accounts for years," she offered. "I can show you what you need to know about the ledgers."

Before he could refuse, she crossed the room and snatched up one of the big, leather-bound volumes. She brought it back to the table and opened to the page dated "October 1881."

"If you want to know how many cattle the Sugar Creek had at the end of last season," she said skimming her finger down the columns of figures, "add this up."

"Ardith—" Baird warned her.

She handed him one of her sketching pencils and a scrap of paper. "Use this for your figuring." She began to read.

Baird dutifully copied down half a dozen figures—the number of bulls, cows, heifers, steers, calves, and weanlings.

"How many is that altogether?" she asked when he was done.

He hunched over the paper at the end of the table, mumbling to himself and scratching at the page. Though she couldn't see his face, she could see that he was squeezing the life out of the pencil.

Ardith couldn't imagine what the problem was; a boy Durban's age should have been able to do the sum. She reached for the paper. "I'll add that up if you like."

He batted her hand away. "I'll—I'll get this figured out if you'll just be patient."

Another full minute passed. Two minutes. Five. Ardith counted every tick of the mantel clock. Baird's ears got redder and redder.

She offered again. "I told you I'd be happy to—"

Baird shook his head and then with a vile imprecation, hurled the pencil across the room. He crumpled the paper in his fist and stood there, breathing hard.

Ardith stared at him, at the angry line of his mouth and the resignation in his eyes. She held out her hand. "Let me see."

Baird didn't move.

"I want to see," she said, more forcefully, and curled her fingers around his fist. *Maybe if I see, I can figure out what's happened here.*

She pried at his fingers, as if they were children and he was playing keep-away. But she knew he wasn't doing this to vex her; he was hiding something.

"Baird, please," she whispered.

With a vivid curse, he gave up the scrap of paper and turned away.

Ardith smoothed out the creases and looked down at what he'd written. Somehow he'd got it all wrong. She'd read off that they had "nine hundred thirty-seven wean-lings," and Baird had written it as "three hundred ninety-seven." He'd completely reversed the numbers of heifers, as well, and the addition on the first column of figures was incorrect, throwing off everything else.

When she looked up, he stood with his head dropped low, like a child who'd been shamed and stood in the corner. She reached for him instinctively, wanting to pat and console him the way she did Khy.

He shied away. "Showing me how to do the ledgers won't do a damn bit of good," he told her. "My father might well have been able to calculate the apogee of the moon, but I'm a hopeless blunderer when it comes to numbers."

Now that he'd reminded her, Ardith recalled that when her father and the earl had been arranging their betrothal, Northam had suggested that Ardith control their finances. He'd laughed and said that Baird couldn't add up two and two—but no one had taken him literally.

"Very well then," she began again, determined to make this right for him. "If I needed your help with something, do you think we could arrange an exchange of services?"

"What do you mean?"

She could hear the suspicion in his tone and plowed ahead. "I've been giving Durban riding lessons."

His head came up. "Have you really?"

"I've taught him as best I can," she continued, "but I think he would benefit from having a more experienced teacher. If I promised to bring the ledgers up to date and keep them current, would you take Durban's lessons in hand?"

The brightness in his face dimmed. "Do you think the boy will agree to taking lessons from me?"

Ardith was gambling that Durban's growing fascination with horses would carry the two of them through the rough spots—and maybe if they spent time together, Baird would find a way to reach his son.

"I know he respects your horsemanship . . ." It wasn't really an answer, and both of them knew it.

"Well, if Durban agrees . . ." he hedged. ". . .I suppose you and I would both be getting something out of it."

"I'll talk to him tonight."

Baird leaned his hips against the edge of the table and slid a slow, sideways glance at her. "Now I don't suppose I could convince you to write the reports for London as well, could I?"

Ardith pursed her lips. Was Baird just bettering the bargain, or was there more he needed to tell her? "Is there some reason I should?"

It was a moment before he realized what she was asking and he immediately straightened. "No!" he assured her. "I can do them."

"Good, then the only reason I'd write those reports was if you were incapable of lifting a pen."

"I can't say that's likely," he said. And then he grinned. It was a quick, wry grin that rearranged his features and brought a spark of genuine appreciation to his eyes.

His smile was as intimate as if he'd reached out and skimmed his hand along her skin, as if he'd drawn her closer. A frisson of warmth moved through her; a soft, unsettling hum began in her veins.

She abruptly thought of China and her questions. How could Ardith give in to this dangerous awareness—especially now? Especially with Baird?

Just then Bear Burton came lumbering in from the back of the house. "This mail just come in from Rock Creek," the big man told them, spilling his armload of packages and wrappers and envelopes at the far end of the table. "Buck said you'd be wanting it right away."

The intensity between Baird and her dimmed, leaving

Ardith with a strangely hollow sense of relief. To cover her confusion, she headed to the pile of mail at the far end of the table.

"There's another package from my father for the children," she observed, "and three more letters from your uncle in London." Then, with a crow of delight, she pounced on a letter from Gavin.

"What's that?" he asked her.

"A letter from Gavin Rawlinson."

"Rawlinson?" The scowl on Baird's face made her wish she had been considerably less demonstrative.

"My publisher," she prodded him. "He saw the children and me off in Boston."

"Why is he writing to you?"

Something in his tone made Ardith bristle. "It could be business," she answered. "Or something more personal."

He snorted in disgust and turned toward the door.

"I thought you promised to take care of these letters from London," she nettled him. "This one's marked 'Urgent.'"

"It'll keep until you get those ledgers updated," he told her. He was gone with a rumble of boots, leaving Ardith alone to savor her letter from Gavin.

This isn't going to work, Baird thought and paused in the doorway of the barn to swipe his sweaty palms on the seat of his trousers. No matter how determined Ardith was that he and Durban settle their differences, a few riding lessons weren't going to mend the rift between them.

How was he to make peace when the boy's animosity was positively virulent—and completely justified? Baird had been an abysmal husband and father. He'd abandoned his wife and children at Heatherleigh for months at a time. Then, God knows, he'd arranged for them to traipse halfway around the world on a journey no woman in Ariel's condition should ever have made.

But since Baird had accepted Ardith's skill as a bookkeeper, he thought he should get on with the riding lessons he'd promised to give his son. Breathing a sigh, he adjusted the cant of his Stetson and stepped out of the barn into the afternoon sun.

After the dimness, the sky was such a bright, stunning shade of blue that Baird had to squint things into focus. When he did, he saw that Durban was already saddled up in the corral and talking to someone on the near side of the fence. At first Baird was pleased to see the boy was making friends here; then he realized the friend was Cullen McKay.

Baird swallowed down the swift, hot surge of anger. He didn't want McKay showing up on the Sugar Creek to see his son. He didn't like the way the boy looked up to McKay.

Just then Durban saw Baird coming, and eyes that had been alive with interest and amusement went flat. With that change the small, carefully budding kernel of hope Baird had been harboring shriveled away.

McKay assessed the situation at a glance; a smug smile crawled across his face. "Well, Northcross, here you are at last! Durban says he's been waiting for quite some time."

A second wash of heat swept up Baird's neck. Who was Cullen McKay to question him? He'd been busy in the barn, goddamnit, patching up one of the horses that had run into a fence. *And trying to shore up his courage.*

Baird jammed his hands into his pockets and tried to keep the irritation out of his voice. "And to what do we owe the honor of this visit, McKay?"

Cullen grinned, knowing he'd rankled Baird. "I came to issue an invitation. While one of our London stockholders is here, we've decided to host an evening of dancing."

People from London—just what Baird needed.

"Well, I'm sorry, McKay," Baird said, without even asking the time or date. "I'm not at all sure we'll be able to attend."

"Don't you think Aunt Ardith would want to go?" Durban broke in. "And China? China loves dancing."

In that moment, Baird almost wished his son to perdition. He didn't doubt how China would feel. Ariel had always loved parties, and China was her mother's daughter through and through. It was Ardith he wasn't sure about. He couldn't imagine her taking the same delight in primping and flirting and gossiping his wife had.

"When is it?" he asked, careful not to commit himself.

"On Saturday night," Cullen answered. "All the hands are invited, too. And our cook has asked that Myra make one of her special cakes. Will you come?"

Knowing that if everyone else was there their absence would be remarked upon, Baird surrendered. "I suppose we will."

Cullen grinned again, this time in satisfaction. He reached across the fence to shake Durban's hand. The smiles the two of them exchanged were warm, the connection between this man and his son was like a spike through Baird's heart.

"We'll look for you on Saturday," Cullen called as he mounted up.

Baird glared after him, then turned to Durban. "I want to let your Aunt Ardith know about this. Keep circling the paddock. I'll be right back."

He found Ardith where she spent most of her afternoons, sitting at the long pine table before the hearth writing or working on her sketches. She was so deep in thought that when he came into the house she didn't even stir.

Baird stood for a moment, watching her, noticing how the sun streaming in the windows set off sparks of copper in her dark hair. It traced the graceful curve of her throat and etched her strong, clean features with gold. It warmed her skin to the consistency of Devonshire cream, and made her lips look ripe and sweet as raspberries.

Ardith seemed younger and softer in this light, infinitely more appealing than he'd imagined she could be. The notion that he could find this strong-minded and difficult woman attractive unsettled Baird somehow. He cleared his throat, suddenly eager for her to notice he was there.

Ardith looked up and smiled. "Did Durban's riding lesson go well?"

He could hear the hopefulness in her voice and instantaneous contrition crushed down on him. "He's out there now. I need to get back to him. What I came to tell you was that Cullen McKay stopped by to invite us to a dance at the Double T Saturday night."

"Oh?" Interest flared in Ardith's eyes.

"One of Cullen's stockholders is here," he went on. "He's brought a party from London to hunt in the mountains."

"Oh." Her excitement dimmed the way an oil lamp did when you turned down the wick.

For an instant Baird was at a loss to explain her reaction. Then it dawned on him that she might have reasons of her own for dreading a confrontation with people from London, people who might once have been friends. He'd been dreading questions about Ariel or Bram. Now he wondered what kind of comments Ardith might be concerned about—especially if she arrived at the party with him.

"I suppose everyone else around here will be going," she offered hesitantly, a frown tugging at the corners of that raspberry-colored mouth.

He drew closer, not quite sure why he wanted to protect her. "That doesn't mean we need to," he said softly.

She shook her head. "No, it will be all right. Besides, I can't imagine that China would be happy staying home if everyone else was going." She gave a long shaky sigh that sounded like it was at least partly in resignation.

Then she glanced up at him and scowled severely. "You can manage to be civil to Cullen for an evening, can't you?"

The way she'd turned the mood of their conversation, surprised him, delighted him. He swallowed down a chuckle. "Oh, I suppose," he answered with a groan of great forbearance. "Though his impudence will certainly test my mettle."

Ardith laughed outright and picked up her pen. Baird grinned at her and shifted nearer.

"What is it you're working on?" he asked, remembering how intently she'd been scribbling when he came in.

"A letter to Gavin."

Gavin. Her publisher.

"What's that you've done around the edges?" he asked, trying to get a better look.

Ardith eased the sheet of stationery in his direction. "Just a few illustrations of things I've seen. I wrote describing the roundup, and Gavin wanted more details. Sometimes it's easier for me to paint things than explain them."

Baird bent nearer. The illustration at the top of the page showed the scene around the branding fire: two men holding a calf, someone—Baird himself judging by the clothes and stance—wielding a branding iron, and a woman—Ardith—minding the tallybook. On the left side a roper was riding down the page toward the calf he'd lassoed at the bottom.

Her paintings were skillfully done, accurate, colorful, and a little wry in their depiction of the events and characters. Still they caught this bit of life and froze it in time.

Baird liked that she'd made a memory that could never

fade. He found himself wishing this extraordinary letter was meant for him. He'd never received anything in the post that was so personal or so fascinating. But the salutation at the top of the page read, *"My Dearest Gavin."*

Something about the phrase made him bristle. He hadn't much liked the fuss Ardith made over the letter she'd received from Rawlinson the other day, and he didn't think it was right for her to be addressing her publisher as "her dearest" anything.

He shoved the paper back at her. "That doesn't look very businesslike," he observed. "Besides, if you're going to paint scenes of the ranch, why waste them on letters?"

A line came and went between her brows. "Are you saying I should be making actual paintings of things I see?"

Baird wasn't sure what he meant.

Ardith didn't wait for him to answer. Fresh color blossomed in her cheeks as the idea seemed to take root and grow. "I could do a few genre sketches, you know," she went on, half to herself. "Some lovely little landscapes. And portraits—maybe portraits of the hands. Oh, Baird, don't you think Frank Barnes would make a wonderful subject?"

Baird nodded, knowing Frank Barnes wouldn't thank him for agreeing with her.

"And Myra. I really must paint Myra." She looked up at him and smiled, a smile so warm and bright that Baird just stood and basked in it. "I love the idea of painting things here at the ranch!"

For a moment he thought she meant to throw her arms around him in appreciation, and he couldn't help a little start of anticipation. He wondered how she'd feel against him. Long-boned and solid, he figured. Womanly, soft. She'd definitely be soft. *He really enjoyed women who were soft.*

He was distinctly disappointed when Ardith didn't

make a move in his direction. She nibbled on the tip of her pen instead, lost in thought.

He shifted his feet to regain her attention.

"Oh," she said, looking up as if she'd forgotten he was there. "Shouldn't you be getting back to the corral? Isn't Durban waiting?"

"Right," he agreed gruffly, feeling dismissed. The encounter with Ardith had knocked him off balance somehow, as if something one of them had done or said had set the world a little out of kilter, a little awry. He didn't like the feeling one bit.

He headed for the corral. When he reached it, he saw that Durban's sulky frown was still firmly in place. For reasons Baird didn't care to examine too closely, the tension in his shoulders eased. He might not like the way things were with his son, but he never had to wonder where he stood.

Ardith picked her way up the trail that led into the foothills of the Big Horn Mountains, up to the ridge where Baird had taken them that first day. She'd been back here once or twice, but never alone, and never with her painting supplies.

Now, in the full bloom of summer, the grasslands of the Powder River Valley rolled away before her, lying thick and golden in the sun. It was a scene of primitive majesty that begged to be captured, immortalized.

Settling herself on a boulder a few yards back from the edge of the ridge, Ardith unpacked her brushes and paints, poured water into the ceramic bowl, and pinned a paper in place on her drawing board. She bent above it, laying down washes ripe with yellow and brown, thin translucent glazes that faded toward the rim of the vast horizon. She worked to mix a bright, fierce blue for the summer sky; struggled to show how the hot, cloudless expanse dominated the land beneath it. She used deeper colors to simulate shadows and added details to the painting as the washes dried. As hard as she worked, her efforts did not please her.

She set the paper aside and began again, struggling to give the scene context, scope. She sketched in the shapes of the boulders near at hand and framed the right edge of the painting with the bristly branches of the pines that grew along the edge of the cliff. Her nerves hummed as she worked; her face flushed with concentration. She recognized the feeling—the sense that she was one with the brushes and paints—but it had never been so strong before, so powerful. Yet as the painting progressed, Ardith could see that she'd failed again.

She pinned a third paper in place and focused her concentration.

"Myra said she thought you'd come up this way."

Ardith swung around at the sound of Baird's voice, startled half out of her skin. He was sitting his horse not ten feet behind her. How in the world had he gotten so close? she wondered. She almost always felt the prickle of his energy along her back when he came near her.

Baird dismounted and ambled toward her. "I'm not sure it's safe for you to be up here alone."

She waved one hand to indicate the burled handle of her Colt revolver poking out of her canvas bag of supplies. "I brought my pistol."

"Do you know how to use it?"

"I learned to use firearms at my father's knee," she said, and was proud of it, too.

When Ardith was ten, her father had decided that if his second wife was incapable of giving him the heir he so desperately wanted, he'd turn his older daughter into the son he'd never had. It was how Ardith had received her academic tutoring, instruction in shooting and driving and horsemanship. She'd turned herself inside out to please her father, but even her most diligent efforts could not compare with Ariel's more subtle artistry.

Baird hunkered down on his heels beside her and checked the load on the Colt. "While I'm duly impressed that you can handle this," he said giving the weapon back to her, "that isn't what I'm concerned about. You didn't hear me come up the trail behind you. You didn't even look up when Primrose whickered. You were oblivious to your surroundings, Ardith, and up here in the mountains, that's just plain dangerous."

Something about his concern warmed her, as if she belonged here at the ranch, and that made him responsible. "I'll be more careful next time," she promised. "What are you doing up here?"

He dropped down onto the rock beside her. "Buck and I were checking on the herd."

"Is everything all right?"

He shifted restlessly, removed and resettled his hat. "More of our cattle have gone missing."

She set down her brushes and stared at him. "How is that possible?"

"Buck thinks Indians drove the cattle off. Now that buffalo are so scarce, the Sioux take beeves when they need food."

"Are they allowed to do that?"

Baird shook his head. "The Army buys cattle for the Indians; those Army contracts are one of the things that make these ranches profitable. But sometimes cows aren't available—or the ones the army buys never reach the Indians. Buck says the Indians don't like accepting what the army gives them, either." Worry settled like dust in the fine lines around his eyes. "I wouldn't begrudge the Indians a few cows, except that if I'm to meet my quotas, I don't have any to spare."

The Sugar Creek had still been short of animals at the end of the roundup, with no explanation of how the projections about the growth of the herd had gone so far awry.

"What do you mean to do about it?"

Baird compressed his lips. "We're only a week from driving the herd up to the summer pastures. Buck and I thought we might put a regular crew up there to keep an eye on them."

"Isn't that how it's usually done?"

"Not as far as I understand. Most of the ranchers just let the beeves wander. The grass is lush and the animals stay within a day's walk of water."

"If you put a crew up in the high country, will it leave you shorthanded at the ranch?"

"A little. Nothing we can't manage."

Then, as if he wanted to set his concerns about the ranch aside for a little while, he leaned closer. "So how's the painting going?"

"Not all that well," she answered with some consternation. "Though who wouldn't be inspired by such beautiful country? It's as if the colors are more vivid here, as if life is more vivid."

She could tell by the light in his eyes he understood. He reached for one of the paintings and their hands brushed as he took it from her. She caught the smell of horses and sweat and honest work on him. She felt the press of his shoulder against her and was somehow comforted by his nearness.

He studied the paper in his hand and the one on the ground beside her. "Well, I'm no critic," he began, "but I think these are rather nice. It's the scope of the place you're missing."

Ardith nodded. "This land just goes on and on. There really are no boundaries."

He smiled in a way that made her realize he knew what that meant in her work—and in her life. But what could Baird Northcross possibly know about boundaries? He'd gone places and done things she could barely comprehend.

He glanced at the paintings again, and she could see the appreciation on his face. "Maybe it's something as simple as painting on a larger scale."

"I see what you mean," she murmured. Her scenes crowded the edges of the paper, as if the subject she'd tried to capture was just too big for the page. The strokes she'd used to commit her impressions to paper were small, precise. This was not the kind of country that could be captured in a finite way.

If she was going to do this world justice, she had to be free to paint with the sweep of her arm, the thrust of her body. She needed big canvases, brushes with size and authority, oil paints instead of watercolors so she could make the hues richer, bolder . . .

"Or maybe you should be painting smaller things." Baird's observation broke into her thoughts. "The pictures in your letter were wonderful. It made me wish you were sending them to me."

She heard something that sounded like wistfulness in his voice and then dismissed the notion as ridiculous. What would a man like Baird want with her sketches? They'd been jottings, a way to formalize her memories.

Maybe she needed to do the sketches in preparation for larger works. The possibilities pushed at her, tingling along her nerves; spreading a warm, heady flush beneath her skin.

She turned to Baird, and it was all she could do to keep from throwing her arms around his neck. "You're a genius, you know!"

He laughed at her. "What? Me?"

"You are!" she insisted and started gathering up her paints. "You've put your finger on exactly what's wrong with these paintings. And now that you have, I know what to do to fix them. When I get back to the house I'm going to write Gavin—"

"Gavin," Baird said with a scowl. He shoved to his feet.

"—so he can send me oils and canvases and bigger brushes."

"Maybe we can get what you need in Cheyenne," Baird offered, waiting for her to finish putting things away and then hefting the bag of supplies.

"In the meantime, I could be doing watercolor sketches of smaller things, like the house and the horses."

Baird led her to where their mounts were tethered among the pines and helped her tie her drawing board to the back of her saddle. She mounted up, and he handed her her bag of supplies.

She caught at his shoulder with one paint-smudged hand. "I want to thank you, Baird, for helping me see what the paintings need."

"I didn't do much, Ardith."

"I appreciate your opinions, nonetheless. And once I get in touch with Gavin . . ."

She saw his eyes darken, saw a shadow creep into his smile. "Well, I'm just glad I could help," was all he said.

EIGHT

The main house at the Double T blazed with lights, sending a warm, welcoming glow into the deepening twilight. As Baird guided the wagon nearer, Ardith could see that the place was grand by Wyoming standards. Tall, narrow windows ran the width of the clapboard facade. A corresponding set were tucked into the slope of a mansard roof. The wide porch that wrapped around three sides of the structure was already filled with guests.

"It looks like this is going to be quite a party," Ardith observed, hoping Baird couldn't hear the quaver in her voice.

"Buck says the house is built in the style of a club all the ranchers frequent in Cheyenne," Baird volunteered. He had been suspiciously silent most of the way to the ranch, and Ardith thought he might be as nervous about the evening as she was. "He says McKay's backers shipped rugs, wallpaper, and furniture all the way from New York."

"You English gentlemen do like your niceties."

"Yes, we do." Baird tipped a wry eyebrow in her direction as he guided the horses to a spot in the yard where a number of other wagons were clustered.

China and Matt Hastings cantered up as he set the brake. "I'm so excited I can hardly breathe," the girl confided, beaming at Ardith. This was China's first grown-up party, and she and Ardith had consulted for days over what she would wear.

Matt helped China dismount and stood gazing at her with an expression that hovered between profound respect and wanting to eat her up. Still, he was soft-spoken and mannerly, and Ardith liked him.

Baird jumped down and came around to help Ardith out of the wagon. She appreciated the courtesy but was uncomfortably aware of the breadth of his hands at her waist; of the sharp, clean scent of vetiver and cloves that clung to his freshly shaven cheeks.

Once Matt and China had handed their horses off to one of the wranglers and the men had unhitched the team, the four of them gathered up Myra's special chocolate cake and a towel-wrapped basket of yeast rolls and made their way toward the house.

Inside, they left the food with the Double T cook and moved into the hall where Cullen McKay was greeting his guests. He had dressed the dandy tonight. His bright double-breasted vest, striped trousers, and jay-blue coat stood in sharp contrast to Baird's all-black attire. Anyone looking at them might have thought Cullen a carnival barker and Baird a somber parson.

"I'm glad to see that the contingent from the Sugar Creek has arrived at last," Cullen welcomed them.

"Good evening, McKay," Baird greeted him formally.

"And, Miss Ardith, aren't you a positive vision?"

Ardith had dressed with particular care this evening, selecting a midnight blue gown, its skirt draped at the back with scallops of lace. She smiled in acknowledgment of his gallantry. "It's kind of you to say so, Mr. McKay."

"And, Miss China," he continued, directing her to a room at the top of the stairs, since she had brought her party dress in a carpetbag rather than arrive smelling of horses.

Once she was gone, Cullen McKay turned to the bluff, ruddy-faced gentleman beside him.

Ardith's mouth went dry as she waited for the introduction.

"Lord Melton, may I present Miss Ardith Merritt."

"Ardith Merritt?" Melton took her hand and blinked at her. "By God! The last time I saw you, you were barely out of pigtails. Where the devil have you been keeping yourself?"

"I came to America, my lord," Ardith answered, smiling a little now that she saw Cullen's guest was probably too much the gentleman to bring up her past.

"All the way to Wyoming? Imagine that! Save a dance for me, will you, my dear? I'd like to renew our acquaintance."

Cullen directed Melton's attention to Baird. "And this is Mr. Baird Northcross. He is managing the Sugar Creek Ranch for Northam and his partners. It's the property I told you about."

Melton reached for his monocle. "Northcross, eh? Was that your cousin Bram who was killed in Burma?"

Ardith noticed hot color seep into Baird's cheeks. "Yes, my lord, it was."

"Nasty business," Melton murmured in sympathy. "They say a tiger got him."

Baird's expression froze, his eyes glacial. "So I've heard."

Then abruptly he tightened a steely-fingered grip on Ardith's elbow and steered her past Melton and McKay. Once they were out of the crush, Ardith jerked away from him.

"Weren't you in Burma before you came here?"

"Yes."

"You didn't tell me about your cousin being killed."

"It must have slipped my mind."

Something stark and terrible in Baird's face kept Ardith from asking anything more, and just then, Buck and Myra Johnson joined them. Buck was flushed and jolly, and had evidently already visited the barrel of whiskey set up on the porch. Myra was clinging to his arm like a schoolgirl with her first beau.

"I don't suppose you know many of these folks, do you, Miss Ardith?" Buck asked her.

"I met a few of the men at the roundup. And my cousin kept company with one of the Frewen boys for a time," Ardith answered.

"Then you need to meet the women—not that there are lots of them out here. Myra will introduce you while I have a word with the boss—outside."

While the men went to smoke cheroots and sample the Double T's whiskey, Ardith and Myra ambled from room to room chatting. Ardith liked most of the ranchers' wives. Some were strong, blunt women like Myra. Others were eastern ladies, transplanted to the west and trying to set down roots. A few bore the tight, long-suffering expressions of women who wished they were anywhere else.

Ardith couldn't help noticing that even the plainest unmarried girls were knee-deep in men. She recalled the flattering, yet claustrophobic way Cullen had treated her when they'd first met. The men out here appreciated single women in a way they didn't back east, and Ardith couldn't help wondering how her life might have turned out if she'd come to Wyoming ten years sooner.

As soon as the little band began to tune up, everyone shuffled into the parlor. When they swung into a reel a few minutes later, the floor immediately filled with dancers.

Before too many sets had passed Cullen McKay appeared at Ardith's side. "Will you do me the honor of dancing with me, Miss Ardith?"

Just as she gave him her hand, the reel wound down and the musicians struck up a waltz.

"I'd rather waltz with you anyway," McKay offered gallantly and swept her up in his arms. They spun across the floor, his guiding hand strong against her back.

"How have the children settled in at the Sugar Creek?" he asked her once they'd made a circuit of the room.

"Khy loves the ranch," she began. "And China is finding her own diversions."

"I noticed that," McKay observed, glancing across at where Matt and China were dancing a fraction closer than would have been sanctioned in London.

What would Ariel think? Ardith found herself wondering. Would she approve of her daughter's first beau? Would she think China was too young to be passing time with a young man already out on his own?

"And how is Durban?"

Cullen's question drew Ardith from her musings. "Haven't you talked to him?"

"Once or twice," he hedged.

"I think he likes the ranch, though he will never admit it. I've tried to get Baird to teach him to ride, but the lessons invariably end with one or the other of them slamming into the house. So I'm trying to teach him myself."

"He's a fine lad, your Durban," McKay observed.

If only Baird thought so, she found herself wishing. If only he could show his approval now and then, there might be something between his son and him besides hostility.

"And how is Baird doing with his cattle?"

Ardith shrugged, her thoughts still occupied with Durban. "Baird's worried about meeting his quota come fall," she volunteered. "The count at the roundup was lower than he and Buck expected. Then, too, the Indians have been appropriating some of our cattle."

She glanced up and recognized the anticipation in Cullen's eyes. Her stomach fluttered as she realized that she'd said more than she intended to.

Before she could decide what to do, the music faded, and Cullen escorted her back to where Myra was chatting with several other women. Her misgivings about her easy confidences deepened when she saw McKay cross the room and murmur something to Lord Melton.

She was still worrying a good while later when Baird came and offered her his hand. "You will dance with me, won't you, Ardith?"

His invitation surprised her, even though she'd seen him stomping and elbow-swinging with Myra Johnson earlier. "Of course."

The fiddler struck up another waltz, and Baird slid his hand around her waist. Ardith had not waltzed with Baird since the night of their betrothal party, and the feel of his palm against her back, the muscular grace of his movements, the scent of his skin were oddly familiar even after all this time—and they stirred up memories.

Amazingly, not all of them were unpleasant. Ardith had delighted in the scores of wedding gifts that arrived at the townhouse, and the crisp, rustling gowns of her trousseau. She'd been proud to be seen on Baird's arm and enjoyed being the center of attention, just this once. But then Baird's letter had come and everything had changed for her.

Yet as sharp as those memories were, they'd been superseded by the memories she'd made in these last weeks: of Khy chasing Myra's chickens around the yard and Durban riding a horse for the very first time, of China bending close as she tried to learn to spin out tatted lace to trim her handkerchiefs. Ardith smiled a little thinking what pleasure she found in hearing Baird come into the house at night and knowing he'd made certain all was well.

Somehow she couldn't help wondering what it might have been like if there had been no Ariel to tempt him. What if she had become Baird Northcross's bride? What if they had come to Wyoming together? What if his children had been her children?

Longing crushed down on her, so intense it all but drove her to her knees right there on the dance floor.

She'd loved her sister. She truly had forgiven Ariel and grieved for her death. But these last weeks at the ranch had felt so right, like an alternative life Ardith might have lived if there had been no Ariel . . .

A scalding rush of shame replaced her longing, deep soul-scorching regret at even thinking such things. It wasn't as if she were wishing she could take her sister's place; that would have been bad enough. She was wishing Ariel had never lived, never burned with that quick, glorious radiance. Never given birth to the children Ardith loved so deeply.

She shivered with revulsion at the thoughts circling in her head. How could she have shared her childhood with Ariel and think such things? How could she live with herself now that she had thought them?

And why would she think them now, while she was dancing in Baird's arms? Why here in a room full of strangers, when such thoughts, such selfishness, was best indulged in solitude—if indulged at all? What kind of a woman was she?

The kind of woman who wanted so much more than she had. A voice Ardith recognized as her own echoed in her head and the insight frightened her half to death. She didn't want more, she told herself, and frantically shoved the thought away. She couldn't have more. She couldn't think of this now, couldn't think of it ever again. How would she live the life she had if she wished she were someone else?

"Ardith?" She became abruptly aware of Baird looking down at her, his expression intent. "Ardith, are you all right? You haven't heard a word I've said."

She straightened instinctively, aligning her hips and shoulders, lifting her chin. "I'm sorry. I must have been woolgathering."

"You had the most peculiar look on your face."

She shuddered at his solicitous tone. She couldn't let him be kind to her right now. She didn't deserve his kindness after what she'd been thinking.

"I'm fine, really." She raised her chin another notch and scrambled to find a diversion. The perfect one came into focus just beyond Baird's shoulder.

"I want you to ask China to dance."

"What? Ask her to dance?" he echoed. "Why?"

She nodded to where China and Matt were just coming in from the porch. He turned and followed her gaze, the lines of a frown nestling between his eyes as he looked at them.

"Do it because she's so beautiful tonight," Ardith whispered, suddenly desperate for him to agree to this. "Do it because you're her papa, and she won't be your little girl very much longer."

Do it because she's so like Ariel—and this is the one way I can appease her memory for myself.

Ardith saw the almost imperceptible softening at the corners of his mouth and recognized the dawning of a father's regret.

"All right," he agreed.

Ardith breathed easier after that, and somehow endured the rest of the waltz. She was heartily relieved when Baird left her with Myra and set out across the floor toward his daughter.

Ardith watched as Baird bowed with a flourish over

China's hand. The girl flushed and fluttered, then allowed her papa to lead her onto the dance floor.

They were beautiful together. His black hair and sun-darkened skin were the perfect foil for China's porcelain-pale beauty. His height and breadth complemented her slim, coltish figure and proud carriage. He held her gently, tenderly, as if she were spun from moonbeams.

China glowed beneath his regard. She ducked her head and smiled at him, flirting the way all little girls flirt with their papas, practicing at being women where they felt safe.

Ardith blinked back another surge of tears. She was so terribly grateful to Baird for giving his daughter that semblance of safety. She was so terribly grateful he'd given her this moment to set her own regrets to rest.

As Baird and China danced past, Myra leaned toward Ardith. "She takes after her mother, does she?" the older woman murmured.

Ardith nodded, unable to tear her eyes away. "She's the very image of my sister."

*T*he fight broke out at about quarter to one. At the swell of angry voices, Ardith glanced up from where she was settled in the dining room drinking coffee and resting her feet with a handful of other women.

Not surprisingly, the commotion came from out where the whiskey keg was set up on the porch.

As they listened, boots scuffled across the floor. Wood creaked and crackled as the baluster gave way. Bodies oofed onto the ground beyond it. The chorus of masculine shouts rose to a clamor.

"Wouldn't be a proper party without a fistfight," Myra observed and pushed herself to her feet to go watch. "Wonder what the young bucks found to fight about this time?"

But it wasn't young bucks fighting. It was Baird North-cross and Cullen McKay.

At the edge of the yard they were circling each other, their fists raised. Their clothes were dusty and disheveled. Blood was trickling from the corner of Baird's mouth.

"What are they fighting about?" Ardith asked one of the hands from the '76.

"I don't rightly know, ma'am," he answered. "One minute they was having a drink friendly as you please. The next Mr. Northcross took a swing at Mr. McKay."

Ardith shook her head, more appalled than surprised. These two had been snarling at each other like mongrel dogs every chance they got.

Out on the lawn, Cullen swung at Baird. Baird jerked back and smacked his left into Cullen's chin.

The cowboys around Ardith groaned.

McKay staggered, then righted himself. He rushed at Baird and slammed his fist into the taller man's belly. Baird hunched into the blow, but grunted with the impact. By the way he wavered afterwards, Ardith knew the punch had landed hard.

The two Englishmen circled, rasping, sucking in air. They shifted sideways on the balls of their feet.

Ardith worried her lower lip as she watched them.

The crowd on the porch bawled instructions, wanting excitement, bloodshed, carnage.

Baird took their encouragement and waded in. He slammed a right into Cullen's jaw. The blond man hissed between his teeth and staggered back.

Baird waited, hovering, his eyes aflame.

Why was he so angry? Ardith wondered. He looked like he wanted to rip off Cullen's head.

McKay found his feet and plunged back into the fight.

Northcross covered up to protect himself. Cullen broke past Baird's guard and landed a punch that snapped his head around.

Ardith gasped, wringing her handkerchief. Why didn't someone break this up?

The crowd roared its approval, a loud guttural sound lubricated by liberal amounts of whiskey.

Baird stumbled back, the blood and sweat on his face glistening in the lantern light. He shook himself and came back swinging. He drove his fist into Cullen's belly and followed it with an uppercut.

The cowboys went wild.

McKay reeled back and sprawled in the dust.

Baird stepped over him.

Moreton Frewen pushed between them. "That's enough! I don't know what this was about, Northcross, but it's over now."

For a moment it looked as if Baird might take on Frewen, too. Then reason prevailed; his fierceness dimmed. He dropped his fists and stood there panting.

"Miss Merritt?" Frewen called out.

Ardith started, surprised to be summoned. Myra pushed her through the crowd to stand before the Englishman who'd made himself the referee.

"I think it's time you took Mr. Northcross home," Frewen advised her.

Ardith stiffened, angry that she'd been singled out.

"He's hardly my responsibility." Yet when Baird swiped at his bloody lip with the back of his hand, she flicked her lace-trimmed handkerchief in his direction. He took it with poor grace and wiped at his face, marking the delicate cloth with things Ardith knew would never come out in the wash.

"The party's over," Frewen announced to everyone else.

A few of the men helped Cullen to his feet. A few others returned to the whiskey barrel. But most of the crowd oozed back into the house to gather their things and say their goodnights.

"Now don't you worry about those empty dishes or China and Matt getting home all right," Myra assured them, coming to Ardith who was doing her best to disassociate herself from the battered man beside her. "Buck and I will see to that. You need to be bound up before you get in that wagon, Mr. Northcross?"

"No."

Myra lifted an eyebrow. "Well, Ardith, why don't you drive anyway. He's going to be sore enough in the morning without putting any extra strain on those ribs."

Ardith nodded her assent and took Baird by the elbow, as if he were Khy. "Engaging in fisticuffs" she admonished him. "Again."

"You don't know anything about it."

Buck had the team hitched when they reached the wagon.

Ardith didn't wait for Baird to help her into the box. She climbed over the wheel and heard him grunt as he pulled himself up on the opposite side.

"Don't you worry about the young'uns," Buck reassured her and gave one of the horses' rumps a pat. "Myra and I will take care of everything."

What Ardith wanted them to take care of was Baird. She thanked Buck anyway and pulled away. Except for his wheezy breathing, Baird sat beside her silent as a stone.

You fool! You goddamned fool! Baird hunched on the wagon seat trying to protect what was probably a broken rib. What in hell was he doing brawling like a stripling half his age?

He could tell by Ardith's frigid silence and her poker-straight back that she was even more appalled by his behavior than usual. Not that she didn't have a right to be.

He'd fought in front of China, too. After Frewen had stepped between McKay and him, he'd looked over and

seen her standing on the porch steps, her eyes wide with
shock. This fight wasn't like the fight he'd had with Burroughs. That had been a point of honor; the man was
mistreating his horses. This one had far less noble roots.
How could a daughter respect a father who behaved the
way he had?

He'd picked this fight because McKay had baited him,
asking how many cows he meant to take to Cheyenne,
asking about other things that were none of his goddamned business. And he'd reacted like a ten-year-old.
But how would Cullen know he was short of his quota?
Buck would never have said a word. Myra knew the straits
they were in and she wouldn't let on, either.

"Ardith?" Ardith had danced with McKay. He'd seen
them chattering like old friends.

"What?" She was staring straight ahead, concentrating
on following the wagon trace that lay like a shadow in a
landscape painted buttermilk-blue by the light of the
moon.

"Ardith, did you say something to Cullen McKay
about us not having enough cattle to meet our quota?"

She must have tightened her grip on the reins because
both horses snorted. "Is that what the fight was about?"

"He goaded me," Baird answered. At least he could tell
her that much. "He said the men who own the Double T
knew our profits were going to fall short of our London
shareholders' expectations, and that they meant to buy up
the ranch."

"And what did you say?"

Baird shrugged, wishing he could shift the responsibility for the fight to Cullen's shoulders. "I didn't say anything. I hit him."

Ardith must have felt the need to own up, too. "Well,
I—I might have mentioned that you—that you had lost
some cattle to the Indians. That you were—"

"Short cattle to meet my commitments?"

"I suppose."

The hot bite of betrayal burned in his throat.

"I said you were concerned is all," she offered defensively.

He shot her a withering glare. "What would make you tell him that? Why would you compromise both me and our efforts at the ranch?"

Her mouth narrowed, but she wouldn't look at him. "I didn't tell him to compromise you. And why does it matter what I told him? You don't give a damn about the Sugar Creek, do you?"

Baird shifted uncomfortably. He still wasn't sure how the ranch had become so important to him. It just had.

He'd be forty this fall, and in all those years he'd never once set his sights on things that didn't come easily. He'd always had a way with horses. Until Bram's death, he'd considered himself a superb hunter and an exceptional marksman. Both were skills he'd mastered without much effort.

Managing the ranch was hard—and he wanted to make a success of it anyway.

He didn't want to care about Buck and Myra and the hands, about ensuring their livelihood. He didn't want to care about meeting his commitments. If he let himself care, it would be agony when he failed.

All his life he'd walled himself off from people who expected things, people his failures could hurt: his mother, old Ben the stable master, Ariel. He'd tried to wall himself off from this, too. But the first time Buck had taken him into the mountains, he'd felt a connection to this land he couldn't deny. He'd seen the possibilities, and that promise had goaded him into wanting something—something he dared not name.

Baird compressed his lips, trying to hold back the admission. "I suppose the ranch *has* come to matter to me."

Ardith turned to look at him, and he wondered what

she saw. A worthless rake? A husband and father who abandoned his wife and family when it suited him? A man who for all his advantages, had never amounted to anything?

"Good!" she finally said.

"Good?" He glanced across at her. There was a slim, satisfied smile on her mouth, damn her.

"Everyone needs to care about something."

He did care about the ranch, and it scared him to death.

The children's expectations scared him even more. Khy looked at him as if he'd invented daylight. Durban's resentment might run deep, but the boy was learning to ride. And then there was China—with her shining eyes and impulsive embraces, making him into the hero he could never be.

And Ardith? What Ardith expected scared him more than anything else. Ardith expected him to be a man worthy of his children's love. How could he live with himself if he failed her—again?

He shifted on the seat, not wanting to think about any of it. He cast about for a diversion and found one.

"I say, Ardith, what the devil is going on between China and Matt Hastings?"

"Why do you ask?" Her voice held a note of suppressed amusement that made him turn and look at her more closely.

"They danced together several more times than was proper," he began and realized he sounded like a fusty, white-haired chaperon.

"I'm not sure London proprieties count out here," she observed mildly.

"When I caught them coming in from the porch, Matt looked like the cat that had lapped up all the cream."

He didn't say that China's hair seemed mussed and her lips were suspiciously rosy. He couldn't bring himself to put his misgivings into words. All he knew was that he wanted to lock his little girl away somewhere and strangle Matt Hastings outright.

"I'd say Matt's smitten," Ardith confirmed.

"How long has this been going on?"

Ardith glanced at him, a smile teasing the corners of her lips. "Since the roundup. Haven't you noticed them together?"

Good God! He hadn't noticed a thing! "She doesn't fancy herself in love with him, does she?"

Ardith hesitated.

His stomach balled, anticipating her answer.

"As a matter of fact, she does."

How could that be? He remembered the tiny dab of humanity Ariel had placed in his arms when he returned from the expedition to Cathay. He'd been clumsy, afraid to hold the child, afraid he'd make it cry. Then China had raised those bright blue eyes to his and something he'd never expected to feel had flickered to life. It stole through him, stronger than warmth or wonder or pride, a powerful emotion that turned him all quivery inside.

Now Ardith was telling him that his daughter, his baby girl, had fallen in love with somebody else. Pure, rich jealousy stabbed his heart.

"China's too young to be in love!"

"She doesn't think so."

"She's barely fifteen."

"She'll be sixteen just after the new year," Ardith reminded him, then paused. Her voice went softer, as if the words were hard for her. "She's only a few months younger than her mother was when you married her."

Baird realized with a sick twisting in his gut that it was true.

But Ariel had had a certain sophistication, an innate understanding of life and men and how society worked.

She'd possessed a nascent sensuality that had run raw between the two of them from the moment they met.

Something about the possessive way Matt's arm had been curled around China's shoulders when they came in from the porch sent a chill of recognition tingling along Baird's nerves. He'd seduced Ariel the very same way—on a porch in the moonlight with dance music floating around them. If Baird was honest with himself he would have to admit that Ariel had been as innocent, as newly flowered and fragile as China was tonight. *And as completely unready for marriage.*

Yet barely three weeks after he'd first taken Ariel in his arms, he had spirited her off to Gretna Green. Driven by their fierce physical attraction, Ariel's delight in being courted, and his own headstrong determination to defy his family and live his life as he saw fit, they had spoken their vows—a girl too young to be a wife and a man who had yet to prove he deserved one.

And tonight he was sitting beside the woman he and Ariel had betrayed to do that. Without a thought, they'd humiliated her. Ardith had been so shamed by what they'd done she'd fled England to maintain her self-respect.

Baird stole a look at her by the light of the waning moon. Ardith's lips were drawn together, and there was a fine, tight line between her brows.

Was she thinking about China and Matt? Or was she remembering how he and her sister had twisted all of their lives?

Ardith deserved to know how sorry he was for what they'd done to her. One day, if he ever managed to shore up his courage, he would have to tell her how ashamed he was. But not tonight.

Tonight he had to ensure that his daughter didn't make the same mistakes her parents had. "I don't want China spending so much time with Matt Hastings," he decreed, breaking the silence that had fallen between them.

Ardith turned the wagon onto the track that would take them toward home and glanced across at him. "And just how do you mean to keep them apart?"

He settled back against the seat and smiled to himself. For the first time since they'd left the Double T he felt like a man in control. "When we take the cattle up to the high country to graze," he told her, "I'll assign Matt to stay at the summer camp."

> *Rawlinson Books*
> *Boston, Massachusetts*
> *June 23rd, 1882*

My Very Dear Ardith,

I really must tell you how much I have enjoyed the paintings and drawings you have been doing in the margins of your letters. I was especially fond of the ones showing life around the Sugar Creek. They have given me a far clearer picture of where you are and what that part of the world is like than I would have had otherwise.

I hope you won't mind that I have shared the letters with my family. After taking Mother, my sisters, and my nieces and nephews to see a collection of Mr. Catlin's paintings at the museum, I felt compelled to read your letters' most colorful passages aloud. I passed the pages around so everyone could see the illustrations. I must say, all of them are quite in awe of your experiences. Mother says I must invite you to dinner once you return to Boston. I think she has taken a special delight in your travels and wants to hear your stories firsthand.

As I heard them exclaim over the sketches, I found myself wondering if there was some way to incorporate these new subjects into your books. These paintings have so much action, so much life that I believe other children would be as captivated by them as my nieces and nephews were. Perhaps we could begin another series of "Auntie Ardith" books, dealing not with your woodland creatures, but with life in the west. What do you think?

I am pleased to hear that "Harland Makes a Friend" is going so well. "Abigail Goose Goes to Town" will be printing next week, and I will forward copies to you as soon as they are ready. Your young readers have been asking in our bookstores for quite some time when "the next Auntie Ardith book" will be available. I need not tell you that bodes well for this book's success.

Let me say in closing that I find your recent letters only tantalizing sips of a friendship I am afraid I had taken too much for granted. I miss your visits to the offices, and the lunches we shared. That they encompassed not just discussions of business, but of politics and philosophy and theatre made them all the more enjoyable. I will miss seeing your face light with pleasure when you hold the first copies of "Abigail" in your hands, and I look forward to the day when circumstances in Wyoming allow you to return to us.

Until that day I am your very humble servant,

Gavin

Sugar Creek Ranch
July 3rd, 1882

My Dear Gavin,

I received the news that "Abigail Goose Goes to Town" is so near publication with wondrous delight. That it has a ready readership is very exciting indeed. The idea *of doing a series of stories set here in the west interests me, but at present I am so caught up in painting anything and everything I see that I am reluctant to narrow my focus to tales appropriate for my young readers. Still, I promise I will think on it.*

I am delighted that you and your family have enjoyed the descriptions and illustrations in my letters. As you can see, I have not painted in the margins of the pages of this missive, but am enclosing several of the full-page sketches I have been doing lately. The first is one of our Negro horse-wrangler, Frank Barnes. Mr. Barnes is very skilled and learned his trade as a slave on a plantation in Virginia before the War. The second picture is painted looking west from the house. I send it on to you so you will see that I am indeed spending my summer at the very foot of the Big Horn Mountains. The third is of Baird's prize bull. After many delays, he arrived at the end of last week to improve the quality of our breeding stock. I would not normally paint such an animal, but there was something so disdainful and dignified in his bearing that he reminded me of the old gentleman you and I so often saw taking a turn around town. Khyber has decided to call the bull "Randy," an appellation that never fails to send the cowhands into gales of laughter.

After resolving to broaden the range of subjects I have been painting, I also decided to try my hand with oil colors. Baird secured a set for me in Cheyenne, and I have begun to experiment. Working in oil is a good deal more difficult than painting with watercolor and gouache. I worry that I have not the skill to become proficient, but I am heartily convinced that only oils can provide the scope this landscape requires. Since I hope to work larger than I have been thus far, I was wondering if you could arrange to have a roll of stout canvas sent to me here, since my stay has been extended indefinitely. Please deduct the price of it and of the other supplies you have already sent from my upcoming royalties.

Let me say in response to your letter, dear Gavin, that I miss your company more than I can say. I hold our friendship in high esteem and greet the arrival of one of your letters with tremendous enthusiasm. It would be my pleasure to have dinner with you and your family when I return to Boston, but I am looking forward to simply chatting with you even more.

As I write this I realize that tomorrow is Independence Day, and I am reminded of the lovely time Uncle Franklin and I had last year attending the celebration with you on Boston Commons. Since "red coats" are in possession of the ranch, I doubt that much will be done to mark this nation's birth. Still, I resolve to sit out on the porch tomorrow night, pretend the stars are fireworks, and that you are there beside me enjoying them.

Your very dear friend,
Ardith

NINE

"So there you are!"

Baird tossed the forkful of hay he'd been turning and looked down from the loft to the floor below. Ardith was standing in the very middle of the barn with her chin jutting out and her arms braided across her chest.

"I've been right here most of the morning," he answered, evenly. "We've got to get this hay stored away before we can take the cattle up to summer pasture."

"That's exactly what I wanted to talk to you about!"

Baird braced the handle of the pitchfork against his chest and mopped the sweat from his forehead with his arm. "Storing hay?"

"Going up to summer pasture!" He could hear the frustration in her voice, and knew it went deeper than him deliberately misunderstanding her. "Myra says when you take the herd into the mountains, you intend to stay."

Baird nodded. "I told you we were putting an extra crew in the high country. Someone needs to be there to supervise them."

"Can't Buck do that instead of you?"

Baird fought a swell of irritation. What right did Ardith have to second-guess his decisions about the ranch?

"Is there a reason why he should?"

"I was thinking about the children," Ardith said. "Between breaking the horses and being away at the roundup, you haven't done much about holding up your part of our bargain."

It chaffed Baird that she would bring up their bargain now, when she'd voluntarily stayed on after the terms ran out. He was glad she'd stayed. Having Ardith here made it so much easier for him to keep his mind on his work.

"I'm the one going to the summer camp," he explained, "because Buck can keep the whole ranch functioning. All I'm good for is chasing cattle."

He hoped she'd let it go at that. But Ardith, being Ardith, had more to say. "What exactly will happen to the children while you're up there?"

Because he'd grown so used to having her here, he hadn't given much thought to the children. "I thought they'd stay at the house."

"And who did you expect to look after them?" She sounded reasonable enough, but he could see the glitter in her eyes.

"Since you've stayed on here, I thought you would."

One dark eyebrow snaked upward. "I've stayed on because you've had so little time with them. I stayed because I thought they needed me. Now I find you're going up to the mountains. What would you do if I were going home to Massachusetts?"

"You're not, are you?" Damn Ardith for making this more difficult than it needed to be.

"Not right now," she conceded. "But I will, and when I do, those children are going to have to depend on you for guidance and affection. I don't think you've done nearly enough to prepare yourself to accept that responsibility."

Baird scowled down at her. He figured he'd taken on about all the responsibility he could handle when he'd decided to try to make a go of the ranch. He'd have time to devote to the children once he sold his stock in Cheyenne.

Baird stabbed his pitchfork into a mound of hay and stepped to the edge of the loft. "You know how important summer grazing is. It's what fattens the stock for market. Since our margin is so small, we can't afford to lose so much as one damned cow. We have to make sure they don't stray. We have to keep them from getting sick, or hurt, or falling prey to God knows what other disasters! I can either go to your father with hat in hand this fall, looking for money to take care of the children, or drive enough steers to market to keep the Sugar Creek afloat."

"I understand about the cattle," she acknowledged, her jaw still set at an implacable angle. "But isn't the children's welfare infinitely more important? You're their father, Baird. You can't just hie off into the mountains for weeks at a time. With Ariel gone, they need you here with them. They need permanence, stability."

"Goddamnit, Ardith!" Baird shouted at her. "I can't be their stability right now. *You* be their stability!"

In the space of a heartbeat she went from defensive and angry to utterly still. His nerves sang with sudden tension. There was some inexplicable peril in that stillness.

"Is that really what you want?" she asked him.

He stared at her, instinctively wary. "What do you mean?"

She straightened one vertebrae at a time. Her head came up. The fierceness in her face might well have harkened back to Celtic queens or pagan goddesses. Yet when she spoke her voice was barely above a whisper. "Do you want me to take the children back to Concord?"

"No!" His answer came without an instant's consideration. As the word melted into the close, fecund silence of the barn, Baird scrambled to make sense of both her offer and his own impulsive refusal. What made her willing to take his children home with her now? Why hadn't she suggested it weeks ago? What could he possibly hope to gain by keeping China and the boys in Wyoming?

"No," he reiterated, utterly intractable.

He swung down out of the loft, landing lightly in front of her. "What I want is for you to stay. What I need is for you to see to the children's welfare while I'm up in the mountains."

She stared at him, and he wished he knew what was going on behind her eyes.

"I'll pay you if you like."

She recoiled from him. "Pay me?" she spat. "Pay me as if I were a governess? To tend my own sister's children?"

He wasn't sure why she was so incensed. "Please, Ardith, just look after them a little while longer—just until we get the herd to market, just until I know where I stand. Once I've sold the cattle, I'll be taking the children back to London with me, and you need never set eyes on us again."

Ardith's face suddenly went stark, her eyes haunted and hollow. She stood there seeming brittle enough to shatter.

"To London?" she breathed. "I—I didn't think about you taking them back to London."

Abruptly she turned away and dipped her head. Something about the way that gesture bared the soft, delicate hollow at the back of her neck made her seem unexpectedly vulnerable. Baird wanted to curl his hands around her shoulders and pull her close. Though for the life of him, he couldn't think why.

"Of course I'll be taking the children back to London," he went on. "Even remittance men aren't expected to brave the winters out here. And I certainly wouldn't expect that of the children."

He was supposed to return to England in triumph, give

glowing reports on profitability, and disperse the huge dividends the stockholders had come to expect. The thought of facing his uncle and his investors with the news that those dividends weren't all they'd hoped turned Baird cold inside. He wouldn't face that censure alone, either. He'd have the children to contend with, to consider, to protect.

Nor was he particularly anticipating the swarming streets, the stodgy halls of the Royal Geographical Society, or the press of bodies around the tables at White's. He wasn't looking forward to any of the things he usually missed when he was away from London.

Something about that realization made him itchy inside his own skin. Instead of dwelling on it, he turned his attention to the problem at hand—getting Ardith to watch over the children for a little while longer.

He stepped around her, wanting to plead his case head-on. He needed to read the expression in her eyes. "Please, Ardith," he cajoled and reached for her hand. "Can't you help me with this?"

Ardith backed away, resistance tightening the line of that already prim mouth. Baird couldn't imagine how those taut, pursed lips could once have reminded him of raspberries.

He jammed his hands into his pockets and pushed doggedly ahead. "You know why I have to stay at the summer camp. You know that the children will need supervision while I am gone. I was wrong not to ask you about this weeks ago, but I still need your help."

He searched her face for some hint that she was softening, and found that she was staring up at him no less intently. It was as if she were trying to discern what kind of man he was, if he could really be a father to his children. And Baird wasn't sure what to tell her.

Then her eyes shuttered, excluding him in a way that

made him feel as if once again he'd fallen short of her expectations.

"Very well then," she said briskly. "I'll see to the children while you're away."

Her acquiescence startled him. He hadn't seen capitulation in her face, or in the way she'd stood there facing him. He didn't know what he'd done to convince her. He needed to understand why she'd told him she'd stay.

Before he could press her, Lem Spivey and several of the other cowboys arrived with the hay wagon.

Ardith sprang away from him like a housemaid caught filching from her mistress's dressing table. Distress flickered across her face, and he realized she was no more pleased by the intrusion than he was.

At least he had the presence of mind to thank her. "I appreciate you agreeing to stay on with us. I'll rest easier knowing you're looking after the children while I'm in the high country."

"You're welcome," Ardith said, and without another word, she wheeled in the direction of the house.

He watched her go, misgivings pinching his belly. Something in the twitch of her skirts as she crossed the yard, something in the angle of her head made him think there was something wrong, something he should have realized. Maybe if he went after her . . .

"Boss? Mr. Northcross, sir?"

With a scowl, Baird shifted his attention from Ardith to where Lem Spivey was perched on the narrow seat of the hay wagon.

"You want to step aside, Mr. Northcross," Lem suggested, "so I can pull this buggy into the barn?"

Baird stepped back, and Lem eased the wagon past him. The other hands jumped down and began forking hay up into the loft.

Before he joined them, Baird glanced toward where Ardith was disappearing into the house. He couldn't shake the feeling there was more they needed to settle between them, but if he meant to drive the cattle to the high country anytime soon, they had to get this hay stowed away.

He looked one last time at the back door, then climbed the ladder to the loft and grabbed his pitchfork.

$\mathcal{T}$he summer camp lay in a wide, wildflower-studded meadow, embraced by humpbacked mountains, and crowned by a blazing sunset sky. Ardith fought to catch her breath at the stark, wild beauty of the place. Since they'd left the ranch house this afternoon, they'd trailed Buck Johnson and the shimmying supply wagon through the foothills of the Big Horn Mountains. They'd snaked up steep-sided canyons, across meandering streams, and past vistas that Ardith saw as subjects for future paintings.

She wanted to capture the bristle of the pines and the way the mountains mounded together at the rim of the horizon. To show how the trappings of human habitation were dwarfed by this primitive grandeur.

"Is this where Papa went?" Khy asked her, twisting around in Ardith's saddle. Though the boy's new pony was tied to the back of the wagon, both she and Buck had agreed there would be less chance of mishap if Khy made the trip with her.

Ardith tightened her arm across his chest as they approached the chuck wagon. "Won't your father be surprised that we've come visiting?"

Baird would indeed—especially when he discovered they meant to stay. Ardith was going to force him to spend time with these children if she had to chase him to the ends of the earth. Not only were Khyber and China dispirited after Baird left; even Durban had become mopey and silent.

Buck brought the wagon to a stop, and Ardith pulled Primrose up behind him.

"What're y'all doing here?" Jubal Devereau asked, dusting the flour from his hands as he came toward them. "I didn't 'spect to see anyone from the ranch for a good while yet. We only been up here two weeks."

Buck jumped down from the wagon seat. "Myra was afraid you hadn't brought enough coffee. And what kind of reputation would the Sugar Creek get if our cook ran out?"

"True 'nough," Jubal agreed. "I see you brung his lordship's family, too."

Ardith swung out of her saddle and helped Khy to the ground. "The children miss their father."

"Children do." Jubal nodded sagely. "An' it looks like Marse Baird's coming this way now."

Ardith's stomach dipped precipitously, and inside her riding gloves her hands went clammy. Explaining this visit to Baird wasn't going to be the easiest thing she'd ever done, but she was fortified by the knowledge that these children needed their father. She thought he might just need them, too, but he was too damned stubborn to admit it.

Baird did give a fine impression of a man who was glad to see his family. Once he'd dismounted, he hugged China off her feet and gathered Khy up in his opposite arm. It was only when he turned to Ardith that his face went stormy.

"Just what brought you all this way?" he demanded, glaring at her over his giggling children's heads.

Durban stepped up to defend her. "We've come to stay," he announced, his tone cool and belligerent, as if he were daring Baird to send them back to the ranch.

Baird lifted one eyebrow in acknowledgement of his son's challenge. "Have you really?"

"Aunt Ardith borrowed a tent and some cots from the commander at Fort McKinney," China confirmed.

"How resourceful of you, Ardith," Baird observed.

"Why, thank you," she answered, ignoring his sarcasm.

"We thought you might be lonely up here all by yourself," Khy put in.

"I do appreciate your concern," he assured his son, "but I've had Jubal and the other hands to keep me company. As glad as I am to see you, I think your Aunt Ardith and I have a few things to settle before you take up residence."

With a nod of his head, Baird indicated that they would discuss them on the far side of the cook wagon. Ardith led the way and tried to tell herself that it was the hours in the saddle that were making her knees so wobbly.

Once they were around the corner of the wagon, Baird leaned in close so their voices wouldn't carry. "Just what in bloody hell do you mean dragging my children all the way up this mountain?" he hissed at her. "What made you think you could just stroll into camp and announce you mean to stay?"

Ardith might have been dreading this moment, but she met Baird toe to toe for the sake of China and the boys. "For reasons I personally fail to comprehend, your children missed you. They've been sulking and sighing since the day you left!"

Even she had found herself waiting for him to come noisily into the house bringing the smell of sunshine and the hum of that boundless energy. She hated that the place seemed empty without him—though it wasn't as if she liked having him underfoot.

"You say the children missed me?" She heard surprise in his voice and the faintest tinge of pleasure.

"There's absolutely no accounting for their taste!"

He grinned at her, then abruptly ducked his head. "Did Durban miss me?"

As close as she was, she smelled the wariness on him and saw a sudden susceptibility in the line of his mouth. She waited for him to raise his gaze to hers, needing to confirm that regardless of what he said, she'd been right to bring the children here. When his deep blue eyes came up to hers, she felt the intensity of the contact all the way to her toes.

"Yes, even Durban missed you," she said gently. "I would have put up with the other children's moping and their moods if it weren't for that."

He retreated a little, needing a moment to let the notion settle. "Well, Durban or no," he began again, "you don't have any business being here. We sleep on the ground and wash in the creek. There aren't any sanitation facilities and precious little privacy. Nights are cold this high in the mountains, and dawns are colder."

"Major Vaughn lent me cots and a Sibley stove along with the tent," Ardith countered.

"That hardly makes this comparable to spending a fortnight at Claridge's."

"We're far more hardy than you give us credit for," she insisted. "Besides, it's for Durban's sake."

"Durban's or my own?" he mumbled.

Her fingers twitched with the need to reach out and reassure him, but she wasn't sure he'd meant for her to hear. If it had been anyone else, she wouldn't have hesitated to touch and soothe and sanction. But this was Baird, and there was a restraint between them she wasn't sure she wanted to breach.

She smiled up at him instead, her eyes soft, and her voice softer. "The children need to have some time with you. And we're going to have to stay a night or two in any case since Buck has some business he needs to go over with you. Why can't we just make the most of the time we have?"

Baird glanced back toward the golden ring of firelight

where his children were waiting. She saw his mouth pucker with wry resignation, and she was satisfied that he'd missed them, too.

"Well, I suppose we could," he conceded.

By the time they returned to the fire everyone was balancing plates of spicy stew in their laps and sopping up the gravy with Jubal's feather-light biscuits. Matt Hastings had joined the party and was sitting as close to China as could be deemed respectable. He'd sprouted a mustache since they'd been here and looked eager and shy and rather handsome. Snuggled close against his shoulder, China was smiling up at him, her face alight.

"Oh, damn," Baird muttered when he saw them together. "I forgot about that."

"About keeping Matt and China apart?" Ardith asked, ladling stew onto both their plates.

"Don't you think it's wise to keep them from spending too much time together?"

Ardith took a biscuit and a cup of coffee from Jubal. "I think Matt's gentleman enough not to take advantage of her."

"Then you hold men and their good nature in far higher esteem than I do," Baird prophesied darkly.

"And not a thing in this world to base it on."

Baird had the good grace to blush.

Ardith watched the young couple, feeling oddly envious of the pleasure they took in just being together. "What China and Matt feel for each other is pure and sweet—and very fleeting. Give them this time; let them enjoy each other. I promise to keep an eye on them."

Baird cast her a skeptical glance, then found them seats on a log by the fire. "If you're sure . . ." he muttered.

When everyone had finished their meal, the men hauled Ardith's tent and stove and cots out of the wagon. With a good deal of pounding and cussing and foolery, they managed to get the various pieces assembled. By the time the construction and bed-making was complete, Khy was drooping with weariness.

Ardith caught him to her and snuggled him close. She pressed a kiss into his hair and breathed his musky, little-boy scent. She held him longer than was strictly necessary, liking his weight against her, soaking in his warmth, closing her eyes against a sudden rush of tears. Since Baird had made it clear he was taking the children to London in the fall, every hug, every smile, every moment Ardith had with them was unbearably precious.

Once she'd had her fill of hugging him, she eased Khy toward the tent to tuck him in.

"I'll take him, Aunt Ardith," Durban offered. "I'm going to bed myself, and I don't mind helping him."

Ardith smiled her thanks and patted the older boy good-night. "Just make certain Khy takes off his shoes before he gets under the covers," she warned him.

"I will, Aunt Ardith," he called back as he steered Khy between the tent flaps.

Dark had fallen and the moon was up by the time the rest of them settled by the fire. Buck and Jeff Mason each lit a cheroot and set up the checkerboard. Jubal kept busy putting away the supper dishes. China and Matt wandered off somewhere, which left Baird and Ardith more or less alone together.

The silence between them lengthened, and at last Baird turned to look at her. "So, why are you really here?"

Ardith shifted uncomfortably, feeling a little undone by his question. "I told you why; the children missed you."

He sat there studying her, as if he were waiting for more.

Ardith didn't know what it was he wanted. "I thought they needed time with their father." *Since you're going to take them so far away, I have to be sure you care for them enough that you won't abandon them the way you abandoned Ariel.*

He shifted a handspan nearer, courting her confidences. "What you really wanted was to see the high country, wasn't it?"

Her cheeks warmed, and she wondered why he was so determined to misjudge her good intentions. Truth to tell, she *had* wanted to visit the mountains. "Well, I have been reading about this country for years," she admitted, "and I'm pleased I'm finally having a chance to see so much of it."

The smile that tweaked the corners of his mouth was almost conspiratorial. "This is your life's one great adventure, isn't it?"

Outrage streaked through her and detonated like a mortar beneath her breastbone. She sucked in her breath. *Her life's one great adventure, indeed!* Coming from a man who had trekked from one end of the earth to the other, that observation was unbearably patronizing.

"Don't I have a right to a little adventure?" Her voice was shaking as she pushed herself to her feet. "Do you think I live at the back of a shelf somewhere, stored away in a box with old books, lost eyeglasses, and worn out mittens? And even if I do, don't I deserve to get more of a look at the world than I can see from the window of my uncle's library?" Ardith heard the bitterness in the words, the resentment she'd spent years trying to deny.

"After the way you begged me to look after them, how dare you question my motives in bringing the children here, or insinuate that I have put my own interests ahead of their welfare!"

Baird stared, nonplussed by her outburst. "For God's sake, Ardith! I didn't mean—" He jumped up and caught her arm.

Both Buck and Jeff Mason came to their feet on the opposite side of the fire.

Their gallantry made Ardith feel immeasurably better, though it also brought the press of hot, unreasonable tears to the backs of her eyes. She shook free of Baird's grasp and spun in the direction of the tent. She heard him shout her name, but she refused him the civility of an answer.

Once safely beyond the blanket that divided her and China's side of the tent from the one her nephews occupied, Ardith stripped off her boots and shirt and skirt with trembling hands. After fighting her way out of her demi-corset, she crawled into her bed in her chemise and lay there shivering.

Dear God! What if Baird was right? What if this was all of real life she'd ever have? What if these few weeks were her only chance to see the world, taste adventure, embrace a family?

She thought she'd known herself. She thought she'd understood her place. She'd done her work and dreamed her dreams. And been content.

At least she'd told herself she was content.

But being here in the west had changed her. Coming to love these children had changed her. Facing up to Baird had changed her. And what was she to do with the woman she had become? How could she go back to her staid little life in Concord after this?

Ardith huddled on her cot and waited for an answer. She was still waiting when China tiptoed in a good while later.

"Are you all right?" the girl asked, her voice all concern and unexpected maturity.

Ardith closed her eyes and lied. "I'm fine."

"Papa was worried."

"He has no reason to be."

"That's good, I guess. Shall I blow out the lantern?"

Ardith nodded and shifted so she lay on her side facing away from her niece. Once the glow on the lantern had dimmed, Ardith made no effort to stop the flow of tears. It was acceptable, she supposed, for a woman of her considerable years to weep—as long as no one knew it, as long as she consigned her fear and longing and broken dreams to the hours of the dark.

*B*aird smelled the blood even before they found the cattle—eight of them dead at the base of the stream.

Seeing them, smelling them set everything spinning. His ears rang. Weakness ran down his arms and legs. He flung himself out of the saddle and stumbled to his knees. His throat burned with bile. He hunched over, retching.

"You all right?" Buck's voice reached him from far away. Baird didn't have breath to answer.

The metallic tang of blood stung his nostrils. His mouth went hot and wet. He shuddered and retched again.

He hung there shivering, cold to his bones. It shouldn't still be like this, should it? Was he ever going to stop remembering?

He heard Buck move up behind him, heard him hunker down in the tall grass. He felt the older man's hand close around his shoulder. It was strong and unexpectedly comforting. "You all right, son?"

Son. The word was as alien to him as the far side of the moon. He wondered if he'd ever heard it applied to himself. Having Buck say it warmed him some. It warmed him even more that this man was here with him.

Baird raised his head. He tried not to turn toward the cattle, but he couldn't help looking. He couldn't stop looking.

Sickness tore through him again. His stomach spasmed. He gagged and coughed and shuddered until there was nothing left. He was too damned shaky to push up from his hands and knees, but he had to know.

"What did this?" he asked and closed his eyes.

Tigers. Burmese tigers.

"Wolves," Buck answered. "A good big pack of them, I'd say."

Baird sucked in air. "Do wolves attack cattle?"

Tigers did. Tigers had come close to decimating the herd that belonged to the Burmese village where he and Bram had camped. That's why they'd gone out, two arrogant white hunters intent on saving the little town's livelihood—and they hadn't even been able to save themselves.

Buck squeezed Baird's shoulder and then let go. He climbed to his feet and stepped a little nearer the carnage.

"I've seen wolves hunt like this sometimes," Johnson said, half to himself, "though it's usually in the dead of winter when they have to band together to survive. They chase and hamstring an animal, so they can get to its throat."

Baird shivered and gagged again.

"Taking down this many animals isn't usual. Can't say I've ever seen the like of it myself."

Baird swallowed and pushed cautiously back on his haunches. This time he wasn't going to look. "How many are there?"

"Five steers, two cows and a calf."

He let out his breath. "Five steers. Five more we'll be short when it's time to take the herd to market."

Buck ambled back and stood over him. "You can't take losing cows like it's personal. Things happen on a ranch: animals drink alkaline water and die. They get sick or stray. Wolves or Indians get them."

"We can't afford to lose any more cattle," Baird insisted.

"You're doing all you can, son," Buck said. "Sometimes a man works like the devil and just don't get nowhere."

"That man's still failed." Failure was something he should be used to by now. God knows, it was as familiar to him as his own name. Why did failing matter so much this time?

"Well, there's not a whole lot more we can do here except send someone back to poison the carcasses." The foreman went and gathered up his horse's reins. "It surprises me, though. These're pretty much all mature, healthy animals. Most predators hunt the smallest and the weakest in a herd."

Baird climbed to his feet and finally looked at the cattle. Buck was right. Those five steers were ones he'd have been taking to Cheyenne come fall.

He swallowed both his bile and his disappointment. Like Buck said, there was nothing to be done. He managed to mount up, and together they picked their way back toward camp.

*I*t had been a most productive day, Ardith reflected as she knelt beside the mountain stream and washed out her brushes—a productive day that crowned several extremely productive weeks. She'd completed a number of sketches and a full dozen fine watercolor landscapes, paintings she'd work larger and in oils once she returned to Concord. The sprawl of these high meadows, the long vistas shimmering in the morning light, and the intimate little side valleys were proving inspiring enough to keep her painting for a decade.

"Are you ready to head back?" Ardith called, turning to where China was sprawled like a forest sprite on a carpet of wildflowers. The girl had done some sketching earlier in the day, but for all her other attributes, she had not one lick of artistic ability.

China closed the book she was reading—another from Myra's cache of Dickens—and rose gracefully, fluffing her skirts.

"It's lovely in the mountains, isn't it?" she asked as they made their way to where they had picketed their horses.

"Matt says he'd like to have a place of his own and live up here."

"He'd like it until the snow flies," Ardith prophesied, hanging her bag of supplies over the saddle horn and tying her drawing board to the back.

Because Baird had agreed they could stay on after Buck went back to the ranch, Ardith was dividing her time between painting and chaperoning her niece. Khy had taken to trailing around on his pony at his father's heels, and to everyone's delight, Durban had attached himself to Matt. He was becoming a proficient rider just trying to keep up with China's beau.

She and China had ridden more than halfway back to camp when Ardith noticed two mounted figures poised at the edge of a pine grove some distance ahead. She immediately recognized Durban as the slighter one. The shimmy of the fringe on the other man's shirt made her realize the other was Cullen McKay.

"What are you doing this far north?" she called to him as she and China nudged their mounts through the milling cattle.

"Ardith!" Cullen greeted her with a smile. "And Miss China. How good to see you! I came up looking for strays. The Double T beeves don't seem to mind boundaries the way the Sugar Creek's do. I found nearly twenty head grazing near here just last week."

"Is the Double T keeping a summer camp?" Ardith asked him.

"Nothing as elaborate as the Sugar Creek's," McKay answered, "but we do come up to check on things."

"And how did you find Durban in all this wilderness?"

"Just by chance," the boy answered, not meeting her eyes.

Durban's evasion set her hackles rising. But before Ardith could analyze her feelings, Cullen gestured to the painting supplies tied to her saddle. "I didn't know you painted anything besides the pictures in your books."

"Actually I've found a good deal to inspire me since I've come west," she told him. "This is beautiful country."

"I've heard Massachusetts is pretty, too."

"It is," Ardith agreed, "but tame compared to this. Gentle, well-tended, and thoroughly civilized."

He nodded as if he understood the distinction. "Will you miss the west when you head home?"

Regret grabbed at her, making her eyes burn with unshed tears. She thought she'd made her peace with leaving, but Cullen's question reminded her how soon she'd be boarding the train and watching all of this fall away behind her.

Ardith swallowed hard. "Of course I'll miss it. But I'll be at the ranch at least until Baird gets his steers to market."

"He's not lost any more of them?" Cullen asked, his eyes alight. "Is he going to be able to meet the quota the stockholders set for him?"

Ardith sensed McKay's excitement, as if he knew just how close the margins were. She glanced at Durban, wondering what he'd overheard—and what he'd passed on.

"I imagine Baird is doing well enough."

If Cullen was disappointed by her answer, he gave no sign of it. "Since you're headed back to camp, would you mind if the boy rode in with you? I need to head these beeves toward home."

The smile that flashed between Durban and Cullen McKay filled Ardith with concern. If only the boy felt this kind of affection for his father, she found herself thinking.

"We'd welcome his company," Ardith agreed and turned her horse toward the summer camp. "Are you coming, Durban?"

Khy was wrapped up in a blanket and sitting by the fire when they got back.

"Just what are you doing there, young man?" Ardith asked him as she handed Primrose off to one of the hands. "Why are you wearing a blanket?"

"My clothes got wet," Khy answered with some asperity.

"He went fishing in the creek," Baird explained, coming out of the tent.

Perhaps it was seeing Cullen McKay all done up like a frontier scout that made Ardith realize how at home Baird seemed in his work-worn trousers and well-washed shirt. He looked like the rest of the hands, rough, sun-browned, and a little unkempt—not at all the English gentleman.

Baird fit out here. In some odd way he'd been absorbed into this society of rugged men and demanding work. It struck her all at once that he was going to have every bit as much difficulty shoe-horning himself back into his life in England as she was accommodating herself to hers in Massachusetts.

Shaken by the insight, Ardith turned to Khy again and tried to catch up with the conversation. "Fishing?" she asked. "You went fishing in the creek? Isn't a creek where most folks fish?"

"I went fishing *in* the creek, Aunt Ardith," the child explained with exaggerated patience. "I didn't go fishing with a pole. I went fishing with *all* of me."

Ardith burst out laughing and glanced at Baird. "I had no idea you were being so literal!"

"It isn't funny!" Baird scolded her. "Matt Hastings had to pull him out."

"He was down there taking *a bath!*" Khy volunteered. "He's in love with China, you know? And he said he didn't want to sit with her tonight *smelling like cows.*"

Ardith laughed again with pure delight, and though

Baird might have been scowling at his son, she could see a twinkle in his eyes when he looked at her.

"Damnit, Ardith!" he protested. "I figured he was old enough to be off by himself for a little while."

"I'll warrant he's just like you were when you were young."

Baird gave a comical, bone-rattling shudder. "Heaven help us all if he takes after me! My father had to cane me regularly for my shortcomings. Sometimes he was so determined to change my wicked ways that I'd have to stand at meals for two days afterwards."

Ardith could believe Baird had earned his share of punishment, but the lightness of his words belied such severity.

"Your father hit you when you were bad?" Khy piped up, understanding more of the conversation than either of them had expected. "But, Papa, you never hit me."

Ardith saw the color leach out of Baird's face, saw the stark reality of his childhood dawn in his eyes.

Ardith smoothed Khy's hair and spoke the reassurance she could see Baird wasn't going to be able to give his son. "Of course your papa would never hit you, Khy."

Baird couldn't manage more than a shake of his head.

His silence and her own experiences with Baird's family made it easy enough for Ardith to imagine all the ways his father had tried to subdue his impetuous son, and why the Northcrosses had written Baird off long before he'd had a chance to prove himself. Small wonder Baird's opinion of himself was such a shallow, fragile thing.

Ardith tucked the unexpected insight away and looked down at her young charge. "Now, Khy, will you tell me please, what happened to your clothes?"

"Jubal's hung them out to dry."

"I looked in the tent," Baird said, still sounding gruff and a little shaken. "I couldn't find anything except a pair of trousers with the knees torn out."

Ardith exhaled sharply, giving her opinion of his efforts, then brushed past him on her way into the tent. As she did, she felt his hand slip around her wrist, felt his fingers tighten and release. That fleeting touch left the imprint of his warmth on her, the imprint of his thanks.

Once inside the tent she stood breathing hard and trying to see past the sheen of tears. How could this man—of all men—have come to matter to her, too?

Swallowing her tears, she crouched beside Khy's cot and pawed through his saddle bag. She gathered up a shirt and trousers and a pair of socks.

As she emerged from the tent, Frank Barnes was riding into camp with a couple of pack horses in tow. "Buck sent me up with a few more supplies and a packet of mail," Barnes announced as he dismounted. "And there's something here he figured Miss Ardith would want as soon as she could lay her hands on it."

"Oh, what?" she asked him, as eager as a child.

With a grin, he pulled a rectangular package out of his bag. It was postmarked "Boston."

With fingers that shook she slipped the knots and ripped aside the paper. "It's my new book," she crowed, holding up a copy for everyone to see. "It's *Abigail Goose Goes to Town*."

Baird was suddenly beside her, peering over her shoulder. "You wrote this?" he asked her.

"I told you I was 'Auntie Ardith.'" She handed him the book and watched with a burst of anxiety she hadn't felt since Gavin had reviewed her first sketches as Baird leafed through the pages. She saw him smile at the illustrations and the bits of story.

Baird looked up at her, his eyes shining with pleasure. "Why, Ardith, I had no idea how clever your books were. This is the first time I've ever seen one."

"But I sent copies to Ariel. Didn't she—"

"No." His gaze met hers, then slipped away. "I can't ever remember her showing me—"

Ardith's heart constricted. She'd thought Ariel would be proud of her.

"Well, you may have that copy, if you like," Ardith offered, then went hot and cold with mortification. Good Lord! What would a man like Baird do with a book for children?

He looked up from the pages, and those bright blue eyes held hers this time. They were shining with warmth and pride. "I'd like having this. Thank you."

A smile stole across his face, making Ardith's breath catch and her stomach dip queasily. The charm and intimacy of it dazzled her.

Khy shuffled toward them, still clutching the blanket around him. "May I have one, too?" he asked.

Ardith drew a quick, shivery breath to regain control of herself and gave Khy her second copy. "Of course you may. I wrote it for children right around your age. You'll have to let me know if you think they'll like it."

China appeared around the corner of the chuck wagon with Matt only half a step behind her. "Oh, Aunt Ardith, please! Might I have a copy of my own?"

There had been ten volumes of *Abigail Goose Goes to Town* inside the package. She handed a copy to her niece, then passed another across to Durban.

He ducked his head as if he was chagrined to be offered a book meant for children so much younger than he, but something about the way he cupped the volume in his two hands made Ardith think he was pleased to have it.

The cowboys gathering around the fire for the evening meal each wanted to examine a copy, and she passed out all but one. The men who didn't read exclaimed over the illustrations. The ones who could read passages aloud. Even Khy took a turn.

None of her previous books had received such a joyous

reception when they arrived at the house in Concord. She was not sure the people she'd lived with for sixteen years had so much as turned a page or read a syllable of what she'd written.

Now Matt and China sat with their heads together looking at the pictures. Jubal Devereau clutched a copy in one hand while he stirred the beans with the other. Baird gathered Khy on his lap so they could read together. Durban fell over laughing at one of the illustrations. Brawny, gruff-voiced men discussed Abigail's adventures as if they were the bard's own words.

Ardith had never seen anyone smile at her pictures or chuckle over her sly humor. She hadn't known that watching people read her work could warm her so, that it could give her such a feeling of belonging, of sharing herself. She clasped her own copy to her chest, knowing that no matter what she had written before or would write after this, the book about Abigail Goose would always be her favorite.

*A*rdith didn't get around to the letter Gavin had sent with the books until everyone else was in bed. She read with the bed-covers bunched around her ears against the chill and the lantern turned low.

> *Boston, Massachusetts*
> *July 17, 1882*

Dear Very Dear Ardith,

Enclosed please find ten copies of "Abigail Goose Goes to Town," your most recent publication from Rawlinson Books. I believe this is your finest effort to date. The text is wonderfully wry and the illustrations are so colorful and lively that it should come as no surprise that in the last three days we have sold nearly a thousand copies in our Boston bookstore alone! The other "Auntie Ardith" books are selling well, also. Two of them have gone back to press. Needless to say, your most humble publisher (me) is delighted with your success.

All this wonderful news has made me wish that you were here. I would love to overwhelm you with flowers and take you somewhere special for a celebratory supper. We might even toast your considerable accomplishments with a sip of champagne.

Ardith smiled, imagining herself seated across the table from Gavin. There would be the gleam of silver and crystal, a soft melody from a violin ensemble playing nearby, an attentive waiter bringing glasses.

Gavin would smile at her, his eyes that warm, deep amber. She imagined how a flush would rise in her face, as he raised his glass to her. "To you, my very dear Ardith," he would say.

Ardith squeezed her eyes shut to hold on to the fantasy, but it was almost immediately replaced by the reality of Khy nestled in Baird's lap as they read together. Of China and Matt poring over one of the slim volumes, of Durban and the grizzled cowboys laughing.

She blinked the memory away and turned up the lantern a bit.

Things here at the publishing company have gone on as you would expect. I did steal away to our place at the shore for several days, as the weather has been very fine. My nieces and nephews do so enjoy playing in the ocean. I took everyone out in the sailboat one afternoon, which left us all tired, a little waterlogged, and very sunburned.

As much as I enjoy spending time with my sisters' children, I am beginning to consider having a few of

*my own. Can you imagine, my dear Ardith, that I
would make a passable husband and father? Do you
think that there is a woman somewhere who might be
willing to take up with a gruff old bachelor like me?*

As a matter of fact, Ardith had given Gavin Rawlinson's qualifications as a husband and father a good deal of
thought. He'd proved himself responsible by taking over
the family business when he was only eighteen. He'd
looked after his widowed mother and six younger sisters.
He liked and understood children. He'd known enough
about children's needs to insist she book a sleeper and
overnight in Chicago on the trek to Wyoming. He'd been
considerate enough to provide a hamper of food for the
first leg of the trip.

Gavin wouldn't lack for women willing to share his life,
once he started courting. He was handsome, well-spoken
and rich—the answer to a maiden's prayer. Once she'd
imagined he was the answer to hers. She'd been smitten
with Gavin the moment they met and had indulged herself in fantasies of what things might have been like if
she'd been pretty and a few years younger. Of course,
those fantasies had come to naught. He had never noticed
her, never seen the way she looked at him, never considered her more than a friend. He had certainly never imagined her as part of his future. And now even Gavin was
becoming a part of a life that felt too staid, too confining.
Too tied to the dreams of a woman Ardith feared she
would never be again.

With a sigh, she went back to reading.

*Before I put this in the post, I do want to comment on
the watercolor sketches you sent with your last letter. I
was very taken with the one of the Negro cowhand. You
captured him so very well. I could see both the ravages
of slavery in his countenance, and the pride he must feel*

at being his own man. You have a talent for portraiture, my dear. One, I venture to say, that is only beginning to break free. Do send me more of your work when you can. I would also very much like to see your oil paintings when you feel you have perfected your technique.

Odd as it may seem, I find that the longer this visit to Wyoming lasts, the more your absence chafes at me, and I am most disturbed to learn that you are staying longer than you planned. I had not realized how much I cherished seeing you, or how much of a hardship your absence would become. I often find myself wondering what you would say about some play or lecture I've attended, or someone new who has joined our circle. I try to sustain myself with rereading your letters, but it is not the same as having you here.

Considering your fascination with the west, I know you must be enjoying your experiences. But do not forget that there are those of us in the east who wish you would conclude your business and come home. Count me as one of them.

                              Most affectionately,
                              Gavin

Ardith smiled and tucked the letter away. Bless Gavin for his faithful correspondence. She would have a good deal to tell him about these weeks in the summer camp—everything from what the country was like to how they had managed without the most basic facilities. She would write him first thing in the morning.

*W*here had that fool woman gone off to now? Baird had warned Ardith not to go sketching by herself. Buck had warned her, and Jubal had admonished her about it just this morning at breakfast. This wasn't like stealing away to paint the view from the ridge above the ranch. It was wild country up here. Ardith would do well to remember that.

Following her trail, Baird nudged Dandy up the course of a fast-flowing stream. Over the millennia it had scoured its way through solid rock to gouge a narrow, steep-sided valley that sliced deep into the heart of the towering peaks. Water hissed along its course in lace-trimmed swirls, and the air was so crisp and clear it burned your lungs to breathe it.

He leaned sideways in the saddle and studied the damp, scattered stones at the edge of the stream. Ardith had passed this way not long before, moving slowly, probably looking for something to paint. He had nearly reached the end of the jagged valley when he came upon her. She was settled half a dozen yards up the bank with her drawing board braced across her knees, and her art supplies arrayed around her.

She was hard at work and oblivious to his arrival, just like she'd been that day on the ridge. Primrose, her buttermilk pony, acknowledged him though, wickering once in greeting.

Baird squinted at the scene before him, trying to see it with an artist's eye. Aspens rustled in whispers of green and gold on the far side of the stream. The cliff face was stained dark where the stream trickled down from high above. A pristine pool lay at the base of the cliff holding up a mirror to the azure sky.

Yet even in the midst of all this splendor, Baird found his gaze drawn back to Ardith. She had changed so much, changed in a way that made it impossible for him to find even a wisp of the staid, reticent girl he'd known in London. The way she'd jumped down from the buggy and faced him that first day had made him realize how strong and stubborn she'd become. Now she seemed to have changed again, becoming calmer, softer, though no less determined that he accept his responsibilities where the children were concerned. Bringing them to the summer camp had proven that. Still, she expected no more of him than she did of herself.

Somehow it was holding her book in his hands, reading her words, and lingering over her illustrations that made him able to see the whole of her transformation. It made him realize how bright and fine she had become, how gentle and funny and caring. Half a world and half a lifetime from where they had begun, Ardith had become a hundred things he'd never once imagined she could be. For now, Baird was content simply to sit back in his saddle and watch her paint.

But when the cold, familiar tickle brushed the back of his neck, he knew better than to ignore it. He tensed and instinctively scanned the sun-dappled shadows of the aspen grove and the parchment-gray boulders to the left of the stream where Ardith was still hard at work.

Whatever this was, Ardith's pony sensed it, too. Primrose's nostrils flared, and his ears lay back. He shifted on his feet, his attention on the rocks above Ardith's head.

Baird squinted at the spill of boulders, too. At first all he could see were jumbled shapes, sunlit crowns and blue-gray shadows. Then something moved halfway up the slope.

The hair stirred along his arms. His mouth went dry. He reached for the rifle in the saddle holster and closed his hand around the stock.

A sinuous flicker of yellow came and went—a good deal closer to Ardith this time. He was just pulling the rifle free when the animal broke cover. Baird tensed and froze.

It was a tiger.

Scorching heat swept up his chest. His ears rang. He started to shake. Dandy sensed his agitation and shifted restively.

The cat stalked nearer, sinuous and lethal. A yellow head came into view. A tail switched and disappeared.

It was a mountain lion.

Ardith's pony huffed and blew, straining against the reins tied around the branch of a fallen tree.

Ardith kept working.

What the hell was wrong with her? Why didn't she sense the danger? He'd warned her . . .

Baird sucked in breath to shout and couldn't squeeze so much as a word up his throat.

Bram didn't have any warning, either.

Baird dragged the Winchester out of the saddle holster, his hands slick with sweat.

He had to save Bram.

He had to save Ardith.

Backpedaling, Primrose whinnied, frantically fighting his tether. Ardith looked up, blinking like a sleepwalker coming out of a trance.

She finally realized there was something wrong and shoved her drawing board aside. She had her pistol in her hand when she scrambled to her feet.

Behind her Primrose screamed, half rising on his haunches in fear. His tether snapped like a strand of thread. He bolted away, splashing up the stream. Dandy tried to follow, but Baird checked him hard.

The cat loomed on the rock not ten feet above Ardith's head.

The tiger appeared out of the trees.

Ardith lurched backward and raised her gun.

Baird jammed the rifle stock into his shoulder. He sighted down the barrel and fought to aim. Sweat stung his eyes. He couldn't draw a bead on the animal. He couldn't keep still.

"Goddamn you!" he whispered. "Goddamn you, shoot!"

He was shaking too hard to be sure of his aim. His

heartbeat throbbed in his throat. He knew he was failing Ardith, just as he'd failed Bram, but he couldn't pull the trigger.

The big cat jumped.

Ardith straightened like a duelist and fired. The report of the gunshot chattered up the canyon.

The lion yowled and landed hard, right where Ardith had been sitting moments before.

She screamed and backed away.

The cat fought its way to its feet and limped into the aspen grove.

Ardith watched him go, then teetered like a child's tower of blocks. Her knees gave way. She crumpled to the ground.

Baird shoved the rifle into his saddle holster and kicked Dandy up the streambed. He dismounted on the fly and dragged Ardith into his arms. "Ardith! For the love of God, Ardith! Are you all right?"

She moaned and shivered against him. Her fingers tightened on his shirtfront. "Did you see the mountain lion?" she gasped. Tears spilled down her face. "Did you see how big he was? He jumped at me from up in the rocks."

He wrapped her more tightly against him, dizzy with relief.

"I—I don't even know where he came from," she sobbed. "Primrose screamed and bolted. And when I looked—"

"I'm sorry."

"—the lion was on the rock above me." She burrowed into his shoulder, shivering.

"I'm sorry." His hands trembled as they moved over her, needing to touch her everywhere. "I'm sorry."

"I—I got the pistol out of my bag, but I was afraid—afraid I couldn't fire. Afraid I couldn't hit him even if I did. I—I didn't see him until he was right over my head."

She shuddered again. "It was just what you warned me about."

He had to tell her. After failing her like this he didn't have any choice. Oh God! He had to tell her all of it.

Baird dragged her closer, clinging to her as if she were the one offering consolation. Not even the solidity of her in his arms and knowing she was safe could quench the dread of what he had to say to her.

"Ardith," he said, clasping his hands around her arms, easing her from him so he could see her face. "Ardith."

She took a shuddery breath and nodded.

"I could see the cat stalking you," he breathed. He had to get the words out before he lost his courage. "I could see him."

Ardith shook her head. "You—you could? Why didn't you shoot him?" The question was inevitable. He'd been waiting for her to ask it. "Why didn't you call to me?"

Baird shoved to his feet and turned away. He didn't want to see the expression in her eyes when he told her the rest of it.

"Baird?" He hadn't heard her move, hadn't heard her climb to her feet and come to him. All at once she was just standing there, tears drying on her cheeks.

"I'm sorry, Ardith. I'm so sorry," he whispered.

"It's all right."

"No." He shook his head, the guilt and rage wound taut in him. His heart contracted with the unbearable weight of another failure. He didn't want to tell Ardith anything, but his weakness had earned her the right to hear the truth.

He stepped past her and moved a little farther down the stream. "Do you know why I didn't shoot him?"

"No." The frailty of her voice tore at him.

He forced the words up his throat. "You know when you asked me about my cousin Bram, the one who was killed last fall in Burma?"

He heard her come up close behind him. "Yes."

He was shaking with the effort of putting those memories into words. "Do you know how it happened?"

"Cullen said a tiger got him."

Bile rose in his throat. "That is what happened—in a way."

He'd only told the story twice—once through the blessed numbness of a whiskey haze to the Burmese authorities, then again stone-cold sober to his uncle. Still, the memories were so strong that once he began they'd suck him down like a leaf in a whirlpool.

"Bram and I were hunting together," he started slowly, "tracking a tiger that had been killing cattle."

The oppressive Burmese heat had sent sweat trickling down his face and ribs. Air the temperature of tea had caught and rasped in his throat as they made their way up the narrow valley. He remembered how the jungle hills had mounded in lush terraces of tangled growth on the right of the track, and that rocks the size of boxcars had been scattered to the left.

They had set out at daybreak, the two of them and a score of beaters, determined to rid the village of the tiger that had been attacking the herds. The beast had led them deeper and deeper into the jungle where the smell of earth and corruption came rancid in his nostrils. For miles there had been the droning cacophony of monkeys and birds in the trees, and Baird didn't know if it had been the sudden silence or the shiver of premonition sliding up his neck that warned him.

Panic kicked hard in his gut, just like it had that day last fall. His pulse jumped and his breathing accelerated.

"Bram was a dozen yards ahead of me," he said, his voice rasping in his ears. "He was down on his knees examining the tracks in the sand. He didn't see the tiger. I only caught a glimpse of it myself; it was poised on the branch above him. Just as it jumped, I pulled up my rifle and fired—"

Baird hesitated, fighting to say the words, the gunpowder sting still strong in his nostrils.

"But you missed." Ardith finished for him. She was trying to spare him the pain at having to say the words. "Oh, Baird. Surely every hunter misses." She touched his arm and the muscles jumped beneath her hand. "I know you blame yourself for what happened to Bram, but—"

Baird's head throbbed with the vividness of the memory, the colors shimmering before his eyes, the gunshot echoing. He had to tell her.

"I didn't miss exactly."

"Then what happened?"

He turned to her. He wanted to see her face when he told her the worst of it. He wanted to see the horror dawn in her eyes. He needed to punish himself by watching it.

"I shot Bram. I shot my cousin instead of the tiger."

She paled, her skin going translucent, as if he could hold her up to a light and see right through her.

"The tiger was on him a moment after, tearing out his throat, pulling him . . ."

His voice seemed to come from somewhere outside himself. He fought down a swell of nausea. The story didn't get any easier with the telling.

"Oh, Baird," she whispered, still looking up at him, stunned. "Oh, Baird."

"There was so much blood I didn't even know what I'd done until we got his body back to camp." No one had realized that his bullet had shattered Bram's skull until they'd begun to prepare his cousin's body for burial.

She reached for him but he shrugged away.

The sight of that blood-soaked grass, the miasma of heat and death, the muffling black weight of his own remorse rose through him every time he touched a gun, every time he closed his eyes.

"But it was an accident," she argued softly. "An accident. You didn't mean for it to happen the way it did."

He heard the throb of compassion in her voice, saw pity and understanding shining up at him from the rainwater-clear depths of her eyes. She lifted her paint-speckled hand and laid it at the center of his chest. Her touch seared like cautery. His nerves and muscles jumped, rippling with the agony of that simple contact. He closed his eyes, basking in the pain of it.

Then her warmth soaked into him, spread through him. It took every ounce of his will not to drag her into his arms and cling to her. But a man bore the burden of what he'd done. He didn't accept sanctuary unless he'd earned the right to it.

He turned away. "I was just too sure of myself," he insisted. "Just too damned—"

"Oh, Baird, no." She followed after him and spread her palm against his back. "All you did was make a mistake."

Though he knew he was weak, he ached for absolution. He was so tired of living with the specter of Bram's death, so tired of feeling empty inside. He closed his eyes, fighting the agony and the bliss of what she was offering. If he let himself believe her words, he might find a modicum of peace. But he didn't deserve that, did he?

"It was a mistake, Baird," she murmured. "All you were was human."

After how he'd shamed her, after everything he'd done to hurt her, how could Ardith be willing to offer him consolation? Why had she heard him out, when Ariel had lured him with her body rather than let him speak the truth? If even his own wife had refused to help, why would Ardith be willing to give him this? How could she be so generous to a man who'd nearly cost her her life this afternoon?

He drew himself up, again denying the comfort she was

offering. "I only told you about Bram because I wanted you to understand why I couldn't . . ."

She eased closer, leaning into him again as if she understood how much he needed the contact he would not allow himself.

"I know it took a great deal of courage for you to tell me this. I know you'd have sold your soul to spare Bram."

"I'd never missed," he insisted, his voice gone low. "Before that day I'd never missed."

She pressed her face into his shoulder. He could feel the imprint of her forehead, her nose and chin. Her breath condensed against his skin.

"You're only a man," she whispered, "a brave but fallible man. You can't expect more of yourself than that."

He stood with her pressed close against his back, her hand splayed against him, pressing and circling. Bit by bit her compassion seeped into him, staining him in some strange indelible way.

He let himself absorb her touch because he needed what she was offering so desperately. Because he wasn't sure he could live without it.

Gradually the memories of the jungle receded. He let himself lean into her. The contact soothed him, spreading deep, warming him all the way to his bones. He closed his eyes and let himself drift.

He felt safe with her in a way he couldn't ever remember feeling safe. Safe to be fallible, safe to be weak. Safe to be his wholly irredeemable self.

By slow degrees, Baird became aware of the spatter of water drizzling down the face of the cliff, the scent of pine and sage drifting in the wind. He let out his breath, feeling as if he'd been holding it for a very long time.

He straightened and turned to her. "Are you all right? Are you ready to go?"

She nodded and tried to smile. "Oh, I think I've done quite enough painting for today."

Only now could he see how fragile she was, the way her paint-stained hands were shaking. In spite of the incredible gift she'd given him, she was still overwhelmed by her encounter with the mountain lion.

With a murmur of reassurance, he bound her to him, giving her the bulwark of his body to lean on, creating the gossamer illusion of physical safety. It was all he had to give her, but it seemed enough.

At length, he settled her on one of the rocks and hunkered down on his knees to gather up the brushes and tubes of paint. He found the pistol where she'd dropped it and tucked it away.

Once he had tied everything to Dandy's saddle, he helped her mount. "Do you think Primrose is all right?" she asked.

"He's probably stopped to graze somewhere between here and camp. We'll pick him up on our way in."

He swung up behind her and pulled her back against his chest. He liked the way she nestled against him, liked that she trusted him. Liked the hum of awareness that seemed suddenly to resonate between them.

He moved his mouth to within an inch of her ear. "Thank you," he whispered.

He thought he heard a smile in her voice when she answered. "You're welcome."

TEN

Maybe Baird was right, Ardith reflected as she stomped in the direction of the creek. Maybe she'd made a mistake in bringing the children to visit at the summer camp. God knows they were a good deal harder to keep track of than cattle. Not ten minutes before, she'd looked up from the mending she and China had agreed to do for some of the hands, and realized Khy wasn't where he was supposed to be. Right after breakfast, Jubal had put Khy to work helping him mix and cut out biscuit dough. Now at mid-morning, the boy had disappeared.

She ranged along the edge of the stream, hoping she'd find him down here somewhere. She wasn't eager to tell Baird Khy had misplaced himself again. Baird had had quite enough to contend with these last three weeks: the cows they'd lost to wolves, the demands the children made on him, and her run-in with the mountain lion just yesterday.

Ardith shivered with the memory—not just of facing the big cat, but of what had come after. She could still hear the thick, ragged timbre of Baird's voice as he talked about Bram; see how his eyes had gone dark with self-loathing; feel him shiver as the memories took him. It had taken courage to tell her what he had, to trust her with his secrets. She only hoped he'd been able to find comfort in what she'd said, or in the closeness they'd shared—something that would help assuage the terrible responsibility he felt for his cousin's death.

Baird had seemed like his usual gruff self this morning, except that while he was explaining to Khy why mixing biscuits with Jubal was far more diverting than setting out poison for wolves, he'd winked at her. So perhaps he was feeling better after all.

She was on her way back from a fruitless search of the creek when she realized that Khy's pony was missing from the picket line. "Can Khy saddle that pony himself?" she asked Durban as she hurried into camp.

Durban looked up from where he was practicing with a rope. "Sure he can. Why?"

Ardith told him.

"I bet he went after Father. I heard Khy ask about riding with him just this morning."

"And I heard your father tell him no."

Durban gave her a superior grin. "Can you remember one time when someone telling him 'no' has stopped Khy from doing anything?"

"I guess I'll have to go after him," Ardith conceded. "Your father won't be happy if he finds out Khy has disobeyed again."

"Is it all right if I go with you?"

Ardith nodded and not five minutes later they were riding north. As they picked their way across a meadow filled with grazing cattle, Ardith turned to Durban. "It seems as if you've come to like it here."

Her nephew nodded. "Sure I do. Matt's been nice about letting me ride with him. He's teaching me how to carve cattle."

That such a blatantly western expression had crept into the English boy's speech, made Ardith smile. "How are you doing?"

"Not all that well. I keep falling off when the pony changes direction."

"You'll figure it out," she assured him. "Are you seeing much of Mr. McKay?"

Durban's shoulders hunched; he tucked in his elbows, as if he were protecting himself. "Mr. McKay has more time for me than Father does."

The hairs along her arms prickled with heightened awareness. "Just how much are you seeing of Mr. McKay?"

But the boy never answered. He was gesturing off to the west. "That's Father, isn't it? And it looks like he's leading Khy's pony."

"That can't be good," Ardith murmured and kicked Primrose forward. As she and Durban closed the distance between them, Ardith could see Baird was cradling Khy against him.

"What happened?" Ardith cried as they caught up.

"A rabbit ran across his path, and the pony bolted," Baird said, his face drawn with worry. "Khy went over backward."

"How come you let something like that happen?" Durban accused, glaring at his father.

"This isn't his fault," Ardith snapped at the boy. "How could anyone have prevented it?" She reached across to make her own assessment of Khy's condition. He was waxy and limp in his father's arms. His skin was damp.

"Has he been awake at all?" she asked him.

Baird's voice quavered a little as he answered. "He was awake when I first got to him. But, Ardith, he—he looked right at me and didn't know who I was."

She could tell by the turmoil in his eyes that Baird was scared to death. "When did he fall asleep?"

"Right after he chucked up his breakfast."

Ardith nodded as if she'd had experience with injured children and told Baird what he needed to hear. "Khy will be fine," she said, "but we need to get back to camp."

She sent Durban on ahead so Jubal could unpack the medical supplies. Then she reached across and lay her hand against her nephew's ashen cheek. Khy stirred in Baird's arms, blinked twice at his father, then threw up all down his pant leg.

"Where's my pony?" he whimpered, his voice high-pitched and petulant. Then his eyes drooped closed again.

"That isn't good, him dropping off like that, is it?" Baird asked her.

"I don't think it will hurt to let him sleep a little while," she answered, her own uncertainties nagging her. "Let's get back to camp."

Everything was ready when they arrived. Baird carried Khy into the tent and laid him carefully on his cot. Ardith went down on her knees beside it. Seeing Khy so quiet and still frightened her more than anything.

Jubal squatted down on the opposite side of the bed, and Ardith silently blessed him for being there. Many cooks picked up a little doctoring one place or another, but Jubal Devereau was more skilled than most. It was part of what made him so valuable to the Sugar Creek.

"Did the boy bump anything 'sides his head?" he asked.

"I didn't think to check," Baird answered, poised at the foot of the cot. The older children bobbed at his elbow.

Jubal's dark, bony hands moved over Khy, checking for broken bones and internal injuries. While he did that, Ardith stripped off Khy's clothes. She took a damp cloth from a basin of water beside the bed and began to wash him down.

"Are you awake, Khy?" she asked as she worked over him. "Can you hear me?" He squirmed a little as she washed his face. "Come on, Khy, open your eyes and talk to me."

The boy's lids fluttered. He stared up at her, his eyes unfocused and vacant. "Where's my pony?" he whined, his face losing color. "I want to ride my pony."

Ardith snatched up the slop bucket just in time and helped Khy use it. When he was done, she laid him back on the cot, wiped his mouth and smoothed his sweat-damp hair. He was restless, whimpering, only half conscious.

She sent Durban running for fresh water and wished she had something to keep Baird occupied. He hovered at the end of the bed like a hunting falcon tied to a perch, fluttering a little and then settling, restless but unable to leave.

Jubal finished his evaluation just as she was considering whether to take Khy back to the ranch. "My little brother back in Biloxi got knocked on the head one time," the cook recalled. "Mama just let him sleep a little, and woke him up. Let him sleep a little more and woke him again. He was sick a time or two, but by morning he was well again."

"The boy looks like hell," Baird said miserably, his eyes afire.

"So do you, Marse Northcross," Jubal said with a slow half-smile, "if you don't much mind me saying so."

That set Baird pacing back and forth between the end of the cot and the tent flaps.

"Are you sure that's all we can do?" Ardith asked. "He doesn't need a doctor?"

"Pretty soon you'll be missing all this peace and quiet," the cook assured her. " 'Sides, you won't make it back to the ranch 'fore nightfall, and you ain't likely to get a doctor to see him 'til midday tomorrow."

Jubal was right, of course, and there was no sense chancing even the lower trails in the dark.

She turned to where Baird had settled for a moment on one of the campstools. She touched his arm. "Jubal says Khy's going to be fine."

"Is he *sure*?"

"Now, Marse Northcross, I been seeing to sick cowboys for twenty years. This boy don't have nothing but a bump on the head. You going to drag him down the mountain to have some doctor tell you that?"

Baird leaned forward over his knees, trying to decide what was best.

"Baird, please. Khy's going to be fine," Ardith added, taking Jubal's word. "Go have a cup of coffee. Catch your breath. You did everything you could for him. Now let him rest."

"You will sit with him, won't you, Ardith?" he asked her, his eyes still clouded with doubt.

"I wouldn't be anywhere else." Baird's obvious concern for his son warmed her, eased her mind. Maybe everything between Baird and his children really would be all right.

"China," Ardith directed. "Would you take your father outside and see that he has a bite of dinner?"

China raised her delicate eyebrows in a way that made Ardith realize suddenly how grown up she'd become—and how capable she was of handling her father.

"Come on, Papa," she said, taking Baird's arm.

Jubal gave Ardith a wide, white grin as the two of them left the tent. "Miss China'll see to her papa," he assured her.

Ardith had to bite her lip to keep from grinning back.

"I'd best be going, too," he went on. "I can hear the men coming in wanting their dinner. You'll be fine 'til I get back. And here's Marse Durban with that water you been needing."

Ardith sat with Khy all afternoon, crooning to him when he was fussy and restless, holding his head when he was ill, wiping him down with cool cloths afterwards. He slept by fits and starts, whimpering, running with sweat, awakening glassy-eyed and disoriented, asking for his pony again and again.

Durban sat faithful as a guard dog, leaving Khy's side only to tend the buckets. China popped in and out, spelling Ardith when she needed air. Baird prowled around the camp like a wolf outside a henhouse, never quiet, never still.

Khy was lying inert after a particularly vicious spell of sickness, when Durban began to mumble to himself.

"What's that you're saying?" Ardith asked as she wiped Khy down.

Durban glanced at her, rubbing his palms along his thighs in agitation. "I was saying that this is all his fault."

"Whose fault?"

"Father's fault," Durban told her. "He wasn't watching out for Khy. He didn't want him tagging along. He doesn't have time for any of us unless it suits him!"

"That's not true," Ardith answered. "Your father cares a great deal for you. And how could this have been his fault? A rabbit spooked Khy's pony."

Durban shifted up on his knees, his face intent. "Of course it's his fault. If it weren't for him, we wouldn't be in Wyoming. I heard the servants at Heatherleigh talking. Uncle Phillip sent him here because he let Cousin Bram get killed. He didn't watch out for him, either."

For a moment all Ardith could do was stare at the boy. She'd known the anger was there, but his vehemence surprised her. Then she glanced up and realized Baird was standing frozen between the tent flaps.

Though she raised one hand to silence him, Durban went on. "And Mother's dead because of him, too. The doctor told you she shouldn't have been traveling, didn't he?"

Ardith couldn't tear her eyes away from Baird. He

stood like a prisoner at the dock hearing the judge pronounce his sentence, his face getting more and more bleak with every word.

"Mama didn't want to leave England," Durban finished, "but Father made her!"

Ardith held Baird's gaze and nodded, urging him to speak. He would never have a better chance to answer his son's accusations and set them to rest.

"If I'd known your mama wasn't well," Baird said softly, "I never would have asked her to come here. I would have insisted you stay in England where you'd all have been safe."

Durban's head jerked up and horror dawned across his features. He knew Baird had heard everything he had said. He shoved to his feet and bolted out of the tent, all but knocking his father aside.

Baird spun on his heel and followed. There was a shuffle of feet, the snort and blow of a horse being hastily mounted. "Don't you just go riding off," he shouted a moment later.

"I'll go to hell if it pleases me!"

Ardith heard the sound of retreating hoofbeats.

"Durban," Baird called after him. "Damn it, Durban, you come back!" There was no answer.

Baird burst back into the tent a moment later, his face ravaged, his eyes wild. He threw himself down on one of the campstools and put his head in his hands.

"He didn't mean what he said," Ardith tried to console him.

"Of course he meant it."

"He's had so much to contend with since we've been here."

Baird raked his hands through his hair. "Don't make excuses, Ardith. Everything Durban said is true. You know about Bram. What happened to Ariel is my fault, too. If I had known about her condition, I never would have asked her to come here. But I didn't know, and now she's dead because of it."

He looked at his younger son. "And now there's Khy . . ."

She curled her hand around Baird's wrist. His flesh was as feverish as his son's beneath her cool, damp fingers.

"Khy's going to be fine," she said as gently as she could. "This isn't your fault, either."

"How I wish I could believe you!" He shoved to his feet and stalked out of the tent.

Ardith stared after him, wanting to go to him, wanting to hold him as she'd held him the day before. She went as far as the head of the tent and looked out at where Baird had squatted down and was staring into the fire. Perhaps he had to battle these demons his own way because his most unrelenting and formidable enemy was himself.

She didn't know how long she had been standing there when she heard a small, bewildered voice behind her. "Aunt Ardith?"

She turned to the boy, instantly seeing the change in him. Khy's eyes were bright. Color had begun to return to his cheeks.

"My head hurts, Aunt Ardith," he sniffled, wrinkling his forehead in confusion. "How come my head hurts so much?"

Relief tumbled through her, making her laugh, bringing tears to her eyes. She crossed to his cot and cupped his small, sweet face between her hands. His skin was dry and cooler.

"Baird!" she shouted, testing the soft, vulnerable flesh of the boy's throat and chest. *"Baird!"*

"Aunt Ardith, what happened?" Khy asked more insistently.

"You fell off your pony," she soothed him, feeling his brow, smoothing his hair. "A rabbit spooked Little Paint.

He took off without you. You bumped your head. But Jubal says you'll be right as rain come morning."

The tent flaps swished as Baird burst inside. She could hear the rush of his breathing, sense the panic that had been simmering all afternoon was bubbling harder.

She looked back at him, at his furrowed brow and haunted eyes. "Khy's better," she said. "He's going to be fine now."

Baird crossed the tent and knelt beside his son's bed.

"Papa?" Khy reached out his hand.

As he took Khy's small, pale fingers gently in his own, Ardith saw that Baird's beautiful eyes were bright with tears.

*A*rdith didn't realize Durban hadn't returned to camp until she left Khy in China's care to get a bite of supper. That Durban had ridden off angry with Baird and had stayed out so long worried her. That dusk settled so quickly here in the mountains added to her concerns. She wandered to the edge of the encampment and stood staring out into the twilight. Had Durban holed up to sulk, or was he lost? Would he be back tonight, or were they going to have to search for him in the morning? She pressed her palms to her lips to hold back a sigh. Sometimes it seemed like one worry leaked right into the next when it came to these children.

Jubal must have sensed her mood because he came for her, eased her back toward the firelight, and put a plate of supper in her hands. Ardith was just finishing her coffee when two riders loomed out of the darkness. One was tall and wore a shirt that shivered with fringe; the other was a sullen, half-grown boy.

Baird shot to his feet and was halfway across the compound before Cullen McKay could swing out of the saddle.

"I'm glad you're back," Baird said, bypassing McKay to address his son. "Your Aunt Ardith has been worried about you."

"I found him wandering the ridges out south of here," Cullen interjected. "That's damned rough country for a boy to be riding by himself."

Baird stiffened at the censure in the other man's tone.

Ardith approached them. "Good evening, Cullen. We certainly do appreciate you seeing Durban safely home."

Cullen dipped his head in acknowledgment. "The only reason he came back," he confided, "was so he could see his little brother."

"Then you'll be glad to know Khy's better," Baird said, speaking directly to his son again. "Why don't you get down from that horse and go look in on him?"

With that news, relief flickered across Durban's face, but he didn't move.

"Khy asked for you a little while ago," Ardith offered, easing nearer.

The boy looked down at her, his expression hopeful, but his eyes were still filled with uncertainty. "Did he really ask for me?"

Ardith nodded and stepped close enough to lay her hand on his pony's neck. "Go on. Go in and see him," she urged.

Durban shied a glance in his father's direction, then looked to McKay. Cullen gave an almost imperceptible nod, releasing Durban to jump down off his horse and run into the tent. That deference frightened Ardith more than she could say.

"I'm glad Khyber's better," McKay murmured, watching him go.

"We were worried about him this afternoon," Baird allowed.

His cousin's gaze swung back to Baird. "Durban says it's your fault the child got hurt."

Baird paled at the accusation, and Ardith did her best to intervene. "Khy sneaked away while he was with me. So I guess if you're assessing blame, it's my fault Khy was hurt."

"His horse got spooked, is all," Lem Spivey observed laconically from where he sat whittling by the fire. "The minute I saw that rabbit break cover, I knew the boy was in trouble."

"It could have happened to anyone," Matt Hastings said.

"Every cowboy gets dumped by a pony now and then," Bear Burton added, "and it's nobody's fault."

Ardith's heart went out in appreciation at hearing the hands defend their boss.

The cowboys' loyalty and the few moments their comments had taken allowed Baird to collect himself. "Like I said, McKay, I appreciate you seeing Durban back to camp tonight. But in future, I'll thank you not to interfere with me or my family."

McKay gave a snort of disdain. "Can I help it if Durban seeks me out? He's a good lad, bright and perceptive. He isn't likely to forget the way you treated his mother, or the kind of father you've been to the three of them."

Though his voice took on a forbidding tone, Ardith admired Baird's restraint. "What's between my son and me is no concern of yours, McKay. Now get back on your horse and get out of here before I forget my gratitude."

"Your kind never does know when to be grateful," Mc-Kay shot back as he sought his mount. Baird glared after him until McKay was out of sight.

Once he was gone, Ardith returned to the tent to see to Khy. He was curled up in a nest of blankets, looking tousled and fragile. Durban was sprawled on his own cot, asleep in his clothes. By the lantern's glow, Ardith could see that he'd been crying.

She glanced to where China was sitting beside Khy's

bed. "Thank you for looking after Khy. You've helped a lot today."

"He's my brother," China answered with a shrug, then cast a glance at the older boy. "Durban's really angry with Papa this time, isn't he?"

Ardith sighed. "I keep hoping they'll find a way to make their peace."

"Mama talked to Durban about Papa lots more than she did to Khy and me. I think she expected Durban to take Papa's place, to make up for Papa's shortcomings."

Ardith turned to face her niece more fully, her blood gone cold. "What do you mean?"

China shrugged again. "Oh, I don't know. She taught him games so she'd have a partner when she played cards with her friends. She had him read to her in the afternoons. She took him along in the carriage when she rode in Hyde Park."

Ariel had made a man of her son before his time, made him a courtier, a confidant. A pawn in her battle with her husband. How could Ariel have made such a shameless bid for her son's allegiance? *How could she have demanded so much for herself from her own child?*

Whether China realized how much she'd revealed about the interior of Ariel's relationships, Ardith could not guess. Yet she could see it all laid out, an insidious chess game with Ariel as the queen. She had been playing the game since childhood, using her allure to lay out her expectations, withholding love when her demands weren't met, showering affection on those who gave her what she wanted. Some men, wise men, saw through Ariel's facade, but Arthur Merritt never had. It was one of the reasons Ardith had fled to America.

Ariel had turned Durban against his father and rewarded him by letting him take his father's place. She had made Baird and his son into rivals, into enemies. She'd made it impossible for Durban to turn to his father now without betraying the memory of the mother who'd loved him so selfishly.

Not for the first time in her life, Ardith loathed her sister nearly as much as she loved her.

She was shaken by what China had revealed, but not enough to let the girl guess what she'd been thinking. "Matt's waiting out by the fire," she told her niece. "Go on and say goodnight to him. But remember, he has to be up even earlier than we do."

China did as she'd been bidden, and a few minutes later Ardith went to the head of the tent to check on them. China and Matt were sitting by the fire, nestled as close together as they could possibly be. The big, gangly boy had his arm draped around China's delicate shoulders, and he was smiling down at her as if she'd hung the moon. China's face was turned up to his, and they were laughing together, sharing something profoundly special. They seemed to glow as if lit from within, as if the affection they shared was almost luminous.

Ardith turned back into the tent, chiding herself for indulging such a fanciful turn of mind. Yet how lovely it must be to have someone to hold you and laugh with you and kiss you on such a perfect summer evening.

With a sigh for her far more solitary life, Ardith set herself to clearing away the clutter of the tumultuous day.

Not long after, she heard the low murmurs of Matt and China's voices from just beyond the tent flaps. She was aware of a few moments of silence while they indulged themselves in a goodnight kiss, then China came in and began preparing for bed.

Ardith knew she should do the same, but the strain of the day had left her tense and aching and longing for a bath. The mountain stream was ice-cold at the best of times, and it would be even colder at night. Still, she gathered up a towel and a fresh chemise and left the tent.

As near as she could tell, the men were all rolled in

their soogans and curled up by the fire. Having a few minutes' privacy after several weeks of communal living made the prospect of a late-night dip even more appealing.

She struck out toward the stream, and let herself absorb the quiet. The aspen leaves rustled like far-away laughter, and the wind hummed in the pines. Bullfrogs croaked somewhere down near the stream, and from off to the north came the lowing of cattle.

She had just reached the lacework of bushes at the top of the bank when a man loomed out of the darkness. She gave a squeak of apprehension and turned to run, but he closed his hands around her arms and pulled her to a stop.

"Ardith, it's Baird," he whispered.

The combination of their movements had sent her stumbling against him. In that instant she was overwhelmed by the imprint of his body on hers: his thighs lean and taut from hours in the saddle, his broad chest and hard-muscled belly, the solid strength and breadth of him. She noticed the scent of soap about him and realized he'd already had his bath.

"Goodness, you startled me," she gasped, righting herself. She pulled her towel and fresh chemise close against her chest, her sudden awareness of him unsettling.

"Is Khy all right?"

She wondered how many times he'd asked her that today. "He's fine," she reassured him. "He's asleep. So is Durban. China's with them."

He nodded, and she could sense the tension ease out of him. "Then I guess you had the same impulse I did," he said, a smile in his voice. "To wash away the smell of sickness."

That's exactly what had driven her, though she hadn't put the longing into words. She yearned to be fresh and clean again.

"I will warn you," he continued, "the water's cold."

"I think I'll take my chances," she answered and hurried past him. His voice stopped her a yard or two down the bank.

"You didn't come out here by yourself, did you?" he asked her, glancing back toward the camp as if he expected to see China trailing after her. "Did you at least think to bring a pistol?"

She hadn't brought the pistol. What good would a pistol do if she was covered with soapsuds and neck-deep in the stream?

"Do you want me to keep watch while you bathe?" he offered.

Ardith gave a snort of derision. "Give you license to spy on me, you mean?"

Even in the faint glimmer of moonlight, she caught the flash of his grin. "Of course I'd be tempted to look, but I'd restrain myself if you asked me to."

Warmth crept into Ardith's cheeks, and she thought he might be teasing her. Of course he might not care to watch, either. It wasn't as if she was graceful or beautiful. It wasn't as if she was Ariel.

But after what she'd learned about her sister tonight, she was glad—for the first time in her life—that she wasn't Ariel. It was a strange and very liberating notion.

Ardith tossed her head, deciding to tease Baird back. "And just how could I take the word of a scoundrel like you, if you promised not to peek at me?"

He hesitated, then took the words she'd spoken in jest and turned them serious. "Will you always consider me a scoundrel, Ardith?"

Something about the tone of his voice made confusion condense inside her chest. After what he'd done to her, what else was she to consider him? A man fighting through tragedies of his own? A man working to become a father to his children? A man who was trying to redeem himself at last?

Instead of answering, Ardith gestured to a rock at the head of the rise. "I'll give you the chance to prove just what kind of man you are. Sit right there and keep watch. And don't think I won't know if you've been peeking."

"You realize, Ardith," he pointed out with exaggerated patience, "that even if the moon were full, I wouldn't be able to see you down there in the shadows."

"Just sit where I tell you, all right?"

He harrumphed his acknowledgment and took his seat.

Ardith made her way down the bank feeling as if his eyes were burning holes in her. When she reached the edge of the stream she began to disrobe, removing her boots, her skirt and vest, unbuttoning her shirt and rolling down her stockings, loosening her demi-corset, and finally dropping her drawers. She paused before she stripped off her chemise.

Knowing Baird was at the top of the rise made her feel particularly exposed, especially naked. If he'd lied and he was watching her, she was about to expose her relentlessly imperfect self to him: the pillowy breasts she did her best to hide, her rounded hips and more-than-ample backside, the legs that seemed to go on forever. She was hardly the kind of woman Baird Northcross was used to seeing unclad.

Still, if she meant to bathe tonight she supposed she was safer with someone close at hand—even if he chose to peek at her. With an exasperated sniff, she jerked the chemise over her head and stepped into the creek.

The frigid water sluiced over her body. Her thighs rippled with goose-flesh. She moaned as she submerged herself.

"I told you it was cold," Baird called out.

Ardith jumped. It was damned disconcerting for him to address her when she had nothing on. "It's f-f-fine once you g-g-get used to it," she called back.

He laughed and a few moments later she saw a match

flare on the far side of the bushes. The sharp, pungent tang of tobacco tickled her nostrils. He was having one of the slim, dark cheroots Buck had sent up with the last batch of supplies, rewarding himself after a particularly trying day.

Well, at least it wasn't whiskey he'd rewarded himself with this time, she reflected and started to wash.

It had been a trying day for both of them. Though he'd turned Khy's nursing over to Jubal and her, having Baird there had made things easier. As much as he had been beside himself with worry, his presence had steadied her. He'd kept her focused on helping Khy and somehow kept her calm. She wasn't sure how he'd done that, but she was grateful. She hadn't felt nearly as frightened and alone as she had when Durban was sick on the train.

Just as she wasn't alone now. Baird was at the top of the rise, a dark presence standing guard. Or defiling her privacy.

The thought of him being so near made her hurry through her bath. The stunning cold seemed to make her more aware of the texture of her own flesh: smooth and sleek across her shoulders and down her arms, goose-bumpy along her ribs, almost velvety at the curve of her belly and between her thighs. Her nipples pearled and tingled as she rubbed the washcloth over them.

The night breeze chased fresh goose-flesh up her back as she emerged from the water. She dried herself haphazardly and shivered into her clothes. She stalked up the bank with her stockings and boots in hand. Baird was settled on the rock just where she'd left him.

"Did you look?" she demanded.

He lay his hand across his heart. "I give you my word as a gentleman—I didn't."

Ardith tried to ignore both the amusement in his tone and something that felt suspiciously like disappointment. She hated that he could turn her emotions like this, from black to white without so much as a mitigating shade of gray between them. Yet for all that he'd unsettled her, there was nothing for her to do but plop down beside him and put on her boots.

"What I have been doing," he went on, oblivious to her discomfort, "is trying to figure out what to do about Durban."

She looked up from where she was just tying the second lace. His shoulders were hunched and his fingers had plowed furrows in that thick, damp hair. It was all she could do to keep from smoothing it down again.

She wondered if she should share her insight about Ariel with him and decided Baird wasn't ready to hear anyone malign his wife. That perhaps he would never be ready to hear it.

"What Durban said this afternoon—" she began. "He was upset is all. He didn't mean it."

Baird's voice was taut. "Every bit of what he accused me of is true."

"Khy's getting hurt wasn't your fault," she tried again. "You *were* looking after him."

"Not carefully enough. I never seem to be careful enough."

The regrets were stalking him again tonight. He was thinking about Ariel, thinking about Bram. Thinking about all the things he could have done differently.

"Well, what is it you want for these children, Baird?" she asked him, determined to chase the specters away. "How careful do you mean to be with them? Are you going to wrap them up in cotton wool? Pull them in so close they won't have room to grow?"

Baird shook his head. "I can't help thinking that if I hadn't insisted the four of them share exile with me, Ariel would be alive, and the children would be safe."

He drew on his cheroot, then tossed it away in a trail of

sparks. "Do you know why I insisted Ariel and the children come to Wyoming?"

Ardith shook her head. She had never been able to imagine her sister, who had professed feeling bored and isolated at Heatherleigh, agreeing to come to Wyoming. But then, in spite of everything, Ariel had loved Baird; and of all his far-flung adventures, this was the only one he'd ever invited her to share.

"I asked them," he continued, his voice thick with disgust, "because I resented being dispatched to America. I was certain your father could prevail on my uncle to relent. I was willing to uproot my wife and children on the chance Northam would let me stay in England."

Ardith should have expected as much. Baird *had* always been willing to sacrifice anyone or anything to serve his needs. He'd sacrificed her so he could marry Ariel, hadn't he?

Yet Ardith wasn't nearly as outraged by the admission as she probably should have been. Perhaps it was because Baird understood what he'd done and seemed contrite, that he'd showed such concern when Khy was hurt, that Durban's accusations had wounded him.

"Well, I suppose Ariel might have miscarried the baby even if she'd stayed at Heatherleigh," she heard herself say.

Baird turned to look at her. "You blamed me for Ariel's death when you came out here."

Ardith shifted uncomfortably. "You were as responsible as she was, I suppose," she conceded. "And you do care about the children."

"Of course I care about them."

"I wasn't sure of that when we came here."

"Neither was I," he said so softly she wasn't sure he meant for her to hear. Still, his admission pleased her. It also moved her in a way Ardith wasn't sure she wanted to be moved.

She had always protected herself by believing the worst

of Baird, and surely his past behavior made him easy prey to such assumptions. But now she wondered if he might deserve better from her, deserve a second chance. Or perhaps she'd already given him that second chance. Perhaps that's what this was.

"You know, Ardith," he said, his tone a good deal lighter than before, "you're not at all the same girl I knew in England. Not at all the woman I thought you were when you came west."

"I'm not?" she asked, more than a little surprised that the trend of his thoughts so closely echoed hers.

"It was seeing your book that made me realize how much you've changed."

"My book?"

"I liked your book. I liked the story, and the illustrations were wonderful." Even in the half-light she could see the amazement in his eyes. "But what I didn't expect was to find such whimsy in you, Ardith, such gaiety and humor."

She could scarcely believe what she was hearing.

"I couldn't help being proud of you—seeing how clever you are, and what you'd accomplished all by yourself. Seeing the woman you've become reflected in those pages."

It seemed as if Baird might be giving her a second chance, as well. Drawn by the delight in his words, Ardith curled her hand around his arm and leaned closer. It was a simple enough gesture grounded in a growing acceptance that edged on friendship. She never meant it to be more than that.

Yet at her touch, some strange awareness fired up between them. Ardith became unaccountably conscious of the flex of his muscles beneath her fingertips and the warmth of his skin melting into her palm. She sensed his strength and bulk mere inches away, a proximity that hadn't seemed so overwhelming a moment before.

He turned to her, his eyes gone wide, his breath stuttering in his throat. "Ardith?" he whispered in a way that made her realize he knew what she was feeling because he felt it, too.

Every instinct clamored for her to pull her hand away and put as much distance as she could between them. Just being so near him turned her breathless, made her vulnerable.

"Ardith?" he whispered, less tentative now.

She stared at him, frozen and suddenly terrified.

He moved incrementally nearer, as if he saw how susceptible she was and didn't want to scare her off. His potency rolled over her, and she was awash in his clean, soapy scent. In his intensity and warmth, in the very essence of his masculinity.

He lowered his head.

Her heart fluttered in fear and anticipation. She didn't want this, *did she*?

His breath feathered against her face.

Her lips parted, needing to be touched.

His lips brushed over them, and she shuddered in response. He nibbled at the bow of her upper lip—slow, soft nips that left her gasping.

How sensitive mere flesh could be, she thought dizzily. How tingling and vulnerable, how responsive and defenseless.

He laved her lower lip, stroking the breadth of it with the tip of his tongue.

She whimpered against him, not wanting to feel what she was feeling, to want what she was wanting. Not knowing how to deny either him or herself.

He slid his hand around her waist and gathered her against him. He was broad and sinewy. He smelled of tobacco and wood smoke, of wind and night, of masculinity and peril.

His mouth sealed over hers, and his tongue brushed deeper—seeking hers, finding it, stroking fluid and soft.

He was all temptation and seduction; all conscience-blurring enticement; all slow, sweet ease.

A flush rose from the core of her, heating her skin, setting her cheeks and chest aflame. She knew she should resist the sensations Baird was evoking in her, but she couldn't help being coerced. She couldn't help wanting a few moments of helpless pleasure, a taste of longing, a hint of what reckless desire must be like.

His tongue probed deeper, courting hers, probing the sweet, silky cavern of her mouth. Her head fell back against his arm. A wave of fierce, unexpected longing rose in her. She was quaking inside, going pliable and soft, desperately yearning for every pleasure Baird Northcross could give her.

No one had ever kissed her like this. No one had made her feel so open and willing. So much like a woman. *But then, no one but Baird had ever kissed her.*

The thought shocked her, sobered her. It gave her the impetus she needed to wrench out of his arms. Ardith stumbled to her feet and stood there panting with lust and humiliation. Tears sprang to her eyes—tears Ardith prayed Baird wouldn't see.

"How could you do that?" she hissed at him, her voice trembling in spite of herself.

She thought for an instant that Baird was more than a little unsettled by the intensity between them. And then he spoke. "It was only a kiss, Ardith."

Only a kiss. The way he said it made her want to spit, to swipe at her mouth with the back of her hand.

"Something quite inconsequential," she prodded him.

"Well, yes," he said with a shake of his head. "Unless it meant more to you than that."

She didn't want to think what that kiss had meant to either of them, or the disparity that would come clear if she did.

She gathered up the soggy towel and chemise, and tried

to exert some kind of control over her face and breathing. Her lips felt smudged from his kisses. Her body was thrumming, as if blood was coursing through her veins like a river in flood.

She stiffened, taking refuge in excruciating propriety. "Very well, then," she said. "I appreciate you staying to see that no harm befell me as I bathed, but it was hardly necessary. Now, I bid you goodnight."

She turned on her heel and stalked in the direction of the campfire, relieved when Baird made no move to follow her. He stayed seated on the rock, and just before she passed out of earshot, she thought she heard him cursing.

*K*hy was better in the morning; it was Ardith who was sick at heart. When she thought about what had passed between Baird and her the night before, her face flushed and her breath seemed cinched up tight inside her ribs.

Even after the children were up and out of the tent, Ardith puttered around inside, loath to face their father. What could she say to him this morning? What could he say to her that wouldn't make things worse?

She sank down on her crisply made cot and buried her face in her hands. How could she have let Baird kiss her like that? How could she have kissed him back? No matter how much either of them had changed, no matter how things had altered between them, what they'd done was pure folly.

She should know better. She *did* know better.

But last night she'd touched him, he'd touched her, and nothing else had mattered. With his mouth whispering against hers, with her body bound to his, it hadn't seemed so wrong and mad and dangerous. *But, oh! In the light of day!*

"Ardith?" She jumped at the sound of Baird's voice from just outside the tent. "Ardith, are you in there?"

She stared at the half-open tent flaps, sick, hot dread flooding her chest.

"Ardith, are you all right?" Baird shoved his way inside and stood looking down at her. He seemed irritated with her, or worried. Or both.

"I—I was just s-sitting here trying to th-think—" She was appalled that she was stammering like a schoolgirl and couldn't seem to help herself. "I was trying to think how I was going to tell—tell the children I thought we—we should head back to the ranch."

She hadn't known she was going to say that until the words came out. Still, leaving seemed an inspired idea. Surely the children had had adequate time with their father these last three weeks.

Baird's face went perfectly still. "Is that what you want to do, go back to the ranch?"

Ardith scrambled to justify her decision. "I—I would feel a good deal better if we had a doctor look at Khy. He seems fine this morning, but since neither you nor I know much about treating children's ills—"

"I thought we did pretty well—with Jubal's guidance."

When she didn't seem to know what else to say, he came to his knees beside the cot. For a moment she thought he was going to take her hand. Instead he looked into her face, long and intently. "If this has anything to do with what happened down by the stream last night, let me assure you—"

Ardith stared at him, and even now the intensity in those lapis-dark eyes seemed to elicit ripples of excitement deep inside her. Even here where anyone could walk in on them, if Baird had bent toward her and brushed her mouth with his, she would have sighed with regret and kissed him back.

That flash of self-knowledge sent Ardith shooting to her feet, all but knocking Baird backwards.

"My decision to go back to the house has nothing at all

to do with that!" she denied hotly. "I'm worried about Khy."

"If you're concerned about Khy, of course you should have a doctor look at him," he told her, though his voice seemed tinged with regret. "But I've liked having you—having all of you—here. So don't rush off on my account."

Ardith couldn't help being pleased that he'd enjoyed the children, especially after everything they'd put him through.

"Do you think you'll be bringing them back?"

She saw the hopefulness in his face and smiled at him in spite of herself. "Perhaps."

Perhaps after she put some time and distance between Baird and herself. Perhaps once she felt less vulnerable. Perhaps when she'd had enough of the children's complaining and cajoling.

"Then we'll leave the tent set up. We need a wagon to transport most of these things, anyway. But if you mean to go, you'd better be about it. There's a storm brewing, and I don't want you getting caught in it halfway down the mountain."

Still, she couldn't leave without a final, private word to him. She caught his wrist and was unsettled all over again by the frisson of awareness that leaped between them.

"I just wanted you to know how much the children have liked being here with you," she said. She wished she could tell him how much she'd liked being in the mountains, how wondrous these weeks had been for her. They had been the most special time of her life, but it would never do to admit that to him.

Somehow Baird seemed to understand the words she would not allow herself to say. "I'm glad, Ardith," he told her softly. "I'm so glad."

With real regret Ardith relinquished her hold on him and led the way outside. She immediately saw that the sun was hanging like a burnished silver disk in a heavy sky, and the shadows it cast were gray and flat. The breeze had died, and for all the expanse of grassy meadow, the air wrapped close around them.

Ardith went to where the children were eating their breakfast. "I've decided we need to get back to the ranch. I want to have Khy looked at by a doctor—"

"But I feel fine this morning!" the boy protested.

He still looked a little pale to her, and Ardith decided she really *would* feel better once a doctor saw him.

"Will we be coming back?" China asked, looking wistfully across at Matt.

"Your aunt said she'd consider it," Baird answered. "But I'll feel better, too, once I know a doctor has looked Khy over."

Ardith sent him a grateful glance for siding with her in front of the children.

"I'd be glad to lead them down," Jubal offered. "I already got stew on for supper, and if someone stops by to stir it now and then, I'll be back in time to make biscuits. 'Sides, if that storm rolls in, we won't be dry enough to eat much."

After a flurry of packing, they mounted up. All but China. She lingered in Matt's embrace, looking up at him with her face alight. Matt smoothed her hair and brushed her cheek with one big hand. He bent and kissed her, there in front of her father and everyone.

As Matt helped China mount, Baird said his good-byes. His words to Durban were too quiet for Ardith to hear, but when he came to her and Khy, his son all but fell out of the saddle hugging his father. "We'll be back," she heard him promise.

"I hope you will," Baird told him.

He only smiled at Ardith by way of farewell, curled his hand around her booted ankle and gave it an intimate little squeeze. Awareness spiraled through her again, the memory of his kiss tingling on her mouth and the strength of his arms sheltering her. She could barely see for the vividness of the memory as she turned to follow Jubal.

The storm chased them all the way down the mountain, but the deluge didn't overtake them until they were almost back to the house. Myra hurried them all into hot baths and dry clothes, and served up soup for supper. They stood in the shelter of the back porch afterwards and looked out at the rain. The peaks where they had been only this morning were sheathed in clouds, deep impenetrable barriers that pulsed with light.

"I'm glad we came home," China said, turning back inside. "Thunder and lightning scare me."

The boys had both gone off to bed when someone came thumping up onto the porch and pounded at the door.

Ardith and China exchanged startled glances. Who could be out in weather such as this? Ardith took up her pistol and, with China on her heels, went to open the back door.

A rail-thin man stood shivering on the porch. His slicker was limp with wetness, and the brim of his Stetson straggled down in the front, all but hiding his face. When he snatched it off, he splattered water everywhere.

"Lem?" Ardith asked, her lips gone suddenly stiff. "Oh, Lem, is Baird all right?"

Lem wrung his hat in his two shaking hands. "Yes ma'am. He sent me down to tell you."

"Tell me what?" Ardith held her breath.

"There was an accident just after the storm blew in," Lem began, his pale eyes filling with tears. "I'm sorry to tell you, ma'am. Young Matt Hastings got struck by lightning."

Ardith felt the blood drain out of her face. "Is he—
Could you—"

"He's dead, ma'am. I'm sorry."

From behind her, Ardith heard a hopeless whimper of
disbelief, and as she turned, China slumped to the floor.

ELEVEN

Ardith looked up from where she was seated at the edge of her niece's bed when she heard the tread of boots across the porch.

"Do you think that's my papa?" China asked in a small, muffled voice, never raising her head from her tear-wet pillow.

Ardith stroked back a few tangled strands of the girl's damp hair. "I'll go see," she promised and climbed to her feet.

Baird was hanging his slicker on the coat rack when Ardith emerged from China's bedroom.

"Thank God you're here!" she whispered, hurrying toward him.

"Is China all right?" he asked and turned to her.

Ardith stopped and stared. "Are you?"

He was stoop-shouldered and haggard and soaking wet. His face was gray, and his eyes seemed as stark as the craters of the moon. Instinctively she reached for him.

He straightened as if every bone and sinew were protesting. "I'm fine."

Though she knew he was lying, she let it pass. She asked about Matt instead. "Lem said it was lightning that struck Matt down."

Baird nodded, but seemed too weary to form the words to tell her more.

She stepped closer to the man who just last night had been both her temptation and nemesis. Nearer to the man from whom she had sworn to keep her distance. She tightened her fingers around his arm, offering her strength, offering her comfort. Knowing full well that she must add to the burden he was carrying.

"China needs you."

Baird closed his eyes for a moment and nodded. "I knew she would. I wish I could have gotten here sooner, but I wanted to be the one to bring Matt home."

Grief burned in her throat. The tears Ardith had held inside for hours threatened to breach the rim of her lashes. "I'm glad you took such good care of him."

"My little girl loved him," he said simply. "It was the least I could do."

He looked toward the door to China's bed chamber. "Is she in there?"

Ardith inclined her head. "She's been waiting for you."

"As if I knew what to say to her."

His voice was as stark as his eyes, and she slid her arm around his waist, drawing him against her. She could feel the dampness of him through her clothes, sensed the marrow-deep weariness that made him bow his head over hers.

"She's your little girl," Ardith whispered. "Why don't you start out holding her?"

"Will that be enough?"

Ardith wasn't sure anything either of them could do would be enough. She had been patting and stroking and babbling platitudes for half the night, but China was inconsolable.

"You're her papa, Baird. She needs you with her."

She felt him nod against her hair. He straightened slowly. She could feel his fear and reticence in every movement, in the way he shifted back onto his heels, in the deliberate lift of his chest, in the way he relinquished the hand he'd lain against her back.

She saw the long, hard look he gave at the bottles of whiskey on the sideboard. She would hardly blame him if he took a good strong dose of whiskey to prepare himself for what lay ahead.

He made it to the door to China's bed chamber without so much as a drop. He knocked softly and wrapped his hand around the knob. He took a long, uneven breath and squared his shoulders. For a man who'd spent his life running from responsibility, opening that door and facing his daughter was an act of almost unimaginable courage.

She watched through a sheen of tears as he pushed the panel wide. Beyond the door, China lay sprawled on the bed like a broken angel. Her face was stained with fresh tears, and at the sight of her father, any pretense she'd made of bravery crumbled.

"Papa?" she said, her voice quaking.

"It's all right, sweetheart," Ardith heard Baird murmur as he stepped inside. "You'll be fine now. Papa's here."

It's all right. Good God, what was he saying? He couldn't make this right for his little girl. Matt Hastings was dead. The boy his daughter loved had been struck down violently, senselessly, and he had the audacity to tell her he could make things better.

What he wanted to do was hold her. He closed the door behind him and crossed to the bed. China lay pale and rumpled and limp, her tear-streaked face turned up to his.

He eased down beside her, braced his back against the

headboard, and gathered her into his lap. She sighed and curled against him like she used to when she was little, drawing up her knees and burying her face against his throat.

"How are you, baby girl?" he whispered.

He hadn't called her that in years, not since she'd stopped wearing pinafores and perching on his knee. The endearment brought her nestling, shifting against him, going heavier somehow. Not since the first time he'd held her had she felt so fragile in his arms.

He rested his cheek against her hair.

It took some time for her to get up the courage to ask. "Papa." He could tell she was trying to be strong, but her voice wavered anyway. "Is Matt—is Matt really dead?"

Baird saw that he was going to have to be the one to crush the last of her hope. The knowledge of what he must say to her made him hate himself. The ache at the base of his throat was like a collar of iron.

"I'm sorry, China. I'm so sorry, baby girl."

She breathed a soft cry, and he gathered her closer.

"It's not fair," she whispered around a sob. "It's just not fair."

"No, baby girl, it isn't fair. It isn't fair and I'd do anything in the world to change it, if I could."

She shuddered in his arms, weeping brokenly, then catching her breath and sobbing again. She clung to him, her slim body shivering with pain, and all he could do was hold her.

He cradled his shattered daughter in his hands, rocking her gently. He stroked her hair and her cheek and the turning of her shoulder. He crooned to her, odd bits of a lullaby he hadn't even known he remembered.

The wildness of her weeping gradually eased, and she lay against him. He felt her go still and did his best to steel himself for the things she would ask:

"Were you—" she finally murmured, her voice breathy and small, "—were you there, Papa, when it happened?"

He could tell she wanted the truth, and he could see no reason to lie to her. He tightened his arms around her before he spoke.

"I was riding beside Matt, not ten feet away. We were trying to hold the cattle, trying to keep them calm. I don't know why the lightning struck him instead of me."

He felt her nod and take a long, uneven breath.

"Was he—was he in any kind of—pain, Papa?" China asked, her voice clotted with tears.

Baird hugged her closer. "Not for a moment, China. He never knew what happened. He was singing to the cattle. You know how he did."

He felt her nod. "Kind of low, but pretty."

Baird could almost hear the melody in his head. "He was singing to the cattle, China, when the lightning came and got him. It happened in an instant. It just stopped his heart."

He could tell that she was crying softly again, and he pressed his cheek against her hair. "I'm sorry, little girl. I know how much Matt meant to you."

"I loved him, Papa," she declared on another sob. "He was so kind and good. He made me laugh. And he treated me as if I was something more than pretty."

More than pretty. Thoughts of Ariel skipped through Baird's mind. Had he ever given her that, made her feel as if there were more to who she was than her beauty, her allure? Had she ever wanted him to? Yet this simple, half-grown boy had given his daughter this very special gift.

"I made sure I was the one to bring him home. That's why it took me so long to get here, because I was taking care of Matt for you."

He could hear her swallow hard. "Thank you, Papa."

The words were almost his undoing. His throat closed;

his vision blurred. But it had been all he could really do for her.

"You're welcome," he managed to whisper.

"But, Papa—" From the tone of her voice, he knew what was coming, and tried to prepare himself.

"Why—why did this have to happen?" she asked, "Why did Matt have to die?"

He must have asked himself that a hundred times while he was bringing Matt back. He'd sought the answer in the hiss of the rain and the gusting of the wind. In the blackness of the night and the dark of his own soul. But he had no answer.

"I don't know why," he whispered. "No one could have done anything to prevent it. It was just Matt's time."

Baird wasn't sure if he was voicing the assurance for her or himself. He remembered how that spear of fire had burned out of the sky, like a finger pointing to one single man out on horseback in the rain. To Matt Hastings, a decent, innocent boy. Not to him.

She lay heavily against him, and Baird rocked her in his arms. He breathed the scent of her, half milk-fed child and half flower-bedecked woman. She was a life on the cusp, so tentative and delicate, so much in need of protection, so close to flying free.

"Oh, Papa," she breathed against his throat. "Promise you won't leave me."

The vehemence in her voice surprised him. He wrapped his arms even more closely around her. "No, China, no. I'm here with you. I'll stay with you as long as you need me."

"Oh, Papa. I'm so afraid."

"Afraid of what, sweetheart?"

She swallowed hard, then found the courage to speak. "First Mama died. Now Matt's gone, too. Aunt Ardith is going to leave for Concord." Her voice broke again. "Everyone I love goes away. Promise me you won't leave me,

Papa. Promise you won't go away and leave me here alone."

Baird closed his eyes, overwhelmed by what she'd asked. How could he give her that promise? How could he give her a promise no man on earth could keep?

Yet how much better had he faced the loss of the people he cared about? With Bram he'd drunk himself insensible for weeks and only gone home because he'd had no choice. When he'd found out about Ariel, he'd turned to drink again, and thrown himself into work here at the ranch.

The very notion of losing anyone else froze Baird's own heart. And in the face of his own terror, how could he refuse to give this promise to his grieving child?

He bound her to him, trying to reassure her with his own warmth and breadth and strength, with his own vitality. But he knew she needed to hear the words, knew he needed to make the promise and be willing to fight the world to keep it.

"I promise, baby girl," he vowed, his voice raw with conviction. "I swear I'll always be here to keep you safe."

He patted her and crooned to her. He offered a haven of security in his arms. He held her to him, comforting himself with her warmth, with the beat of life within her.

After a time, he felt her go lax with weariness. The grip on his shoulder eased. Her head drooped against his chest. When he was sure she was deeply asleep, he eased her down onto the bed and drew a blanket over her.

He stood over his eldest child, seeing her tear-smudged face and frail, sad mouth. With her pure, fresh beauty and moonbeam-colored hair, she looked so very much like Ariel. But she was stronger than her mother had been; he'd seen that tonight. Even in her grief, what she'd cared about was Matt. She'd cared about someone besides herself.

What would it have been like if Ariel had had a little of

her daughter's compassion when he went to her after Bram died?

He bent and stroked away the last of the drying tears from China's cheeks. He would have sold his soul to spare her this. He might have to sell his soul to keep the promise he had made to her. But could a daughter expect less of her father? Could a father promise less to his child?

Baird blew out the lantern beside the bed and the room plunged into darkness. He stood there listening to his daughter breathe, slow deep breaths punctuated by a few whispery sighs. For tonight China was safe; for tonight she was at peace.

Satisfied that he'd done everything he could, Baird eased out of the room.

Ardith heard the turn of the latch and glanced up at the clock on the mantel. It seemed as if she'd been waiting for hours, staring at the door of China's room and wondering if Baird had found a way to comfort his daughter.

He emerged at last, sagging like a man whose life had been bled away. Whatever had gone on in there had scoured deep, fresh lines between his brows and worn hollows in his cheeks.

Ardith got to her feet and went to him. "How is she?"

"She's asleep," he answered, his voice nearly as worn and faded as he looked.

"And she's all right?"

"She's as all right as she's likely to be for a while."

Ardith ducked her head in acknowledgment. Grief took time, weeks or months of thinking and missing and weeping. She wished she knew a way to spare her niece the pain of it.

"I'm so glad you were here when she needed you," Ardith told him. When he only nodded, she went on. "I've made some tea."

There was a tea-cozied pot and two porcelain cups on a tray at the end of the table. Baird cast a glance at the row of decanters and sighed. "Tea would be lovely."

As he eased into his place at the head of the table, Ardith fixed his cup. She nudged a plate of Myra's cookies in his direction. "Have you had anything to eat today? I could go to the kitchen for something more substantial if you want—"

Baird caught her arm and steered her into the chair at a right angle to his own. "It's all right, Ardith. Food isn't going to make this better."

She shivered a little when he took his hand away. She needed his touch. Needed it in a far different way than she had down by the stream when he'd drawn her into his arms and kissed her. She needed his warmth and his consolation, but she was afraid to ask more of a man wrung dry from giving to his daughter.

She reached for the tea instead of him and doctored her cup with sugar and cream. "Myra has been washing and getting Matt ready," she finally said. "He looked so young lying there, like a little boy who'd just fallen asleep."

Baird stared down into his tea and nodded.

She drew a breath, then continued. "I've sent Frank Barnes to see if there's anyone at Fort McKinney who could say a few words at the service tomorrow. I thought that grove of trees on the hill would be a proper place to bury him. Lem and Buck are going to dig the grave as soon as it's light."

Baird closed his eyes and ran his hands through his hair.

She stared at his bowed head and noticed a few gray strands woven through the waves of silky black. There wasn't much—not even enough to make him look dapper and distinguished—but Ardith noticed. It reminded her that he was not the raffish rogue he'd been at twenty-four.

Baird had changed. She'd tried so hard not to admit

that to herself, tried so hard not to admit that life had worn away his brashness, his thoughtlessness and arrogance. It was safer to pretend he was still the reckless youth who'd betrayed her than to acknowledge the man Baird Northcross had become. But the last of that illusion had died tonight, the moment he'd turned from hanging up his slicker and she'd seen his eyes.

She reached and stroked his tumbled hair.

He shuddered at her touch, and his voice was raw and low when he spoke. "Please tell me there is nothing I could have done to prevent Matt's death."

Her heartbeat fluttered and her fingers stilled. She should have known he'd blame himself.

"Of course there was nothing you could do! Matt was out in a thunderstorm doing his job. He knew the risks; all the men know them."

"I just keep trying to go back and rearrange what happened," he said without looking up, "as if by doing that I can make it come out differently."

"You were out there, too, weren't you?" When he shifted his shoulders in confirmation, she went on. "It could have been you. It could have been Lem, or Bear, or any of the other men."

"It should have been me." The words hung in the air like the last notes of an organ echoing through a vast cathedral.

She felt the heat come up in her face, took both his hands in hers, and waited. Waited until he looked up. His eyes, eyes that had always been the clear cobalt blue of prairie skies, were dark tonight. They were clouded with sorrow and weariness and resignation.

She held tight to his hands, feeling the shift of bones and tendons beneath her fingertips, the warmth of his flesh. "But it wasn't you," she told him fiercely. "It was Matt. It was just Matt's time."

In her mind she saw the boy's soft face, his wispy mustache, the peace on those half-formed features.

"It was just Matt's time," she said with fresh conviction.

She could see how much Baird wanted to believe her, how much he wanted to lay down the terrible burden of this responsibility. She held him tighter, willing him to accept the things he could not change and might never understand.

Finally, he let out his breath and nodded. Exhaustion lay on him like a pall. He turned his hand in hers and clung to her as if only she could give him sustenance.

"I'm afraid there's more," he said after a moment.

Fresh dread wove through her. "More?"

"I promised China . . ."

Ardith searched his face, trying to see beyond the darkness in his eyes. "What did you promise her?"

He let out his breath in a stream. "That after losing her mother and Matt, she'd never lose anyone else she cared about. That I'd keep the people she loved safe."

Ardith blinked at him. "Oh, Baird! How could you make her that kind of promise?"

His shoulders hunched; his fingers tightened. His gaze held hers. She could see the torment in him, see how hard he was trying to do what was best for his daughter.

"How could I refuse her? She's lost so much, and she's so afraid of losing everything."

Not seeing what he sought in her face, he released her hands and shoved to his feet. He took his empty cup to the sideboard and filled it to its gilded rim with whiskey. He downed half of the liquor in a single swallow, braced his hips against the cupboard, and stared at her.

"What would you have done?"

What indeed? How could any person who loved a child as much as this man loved his little girl deny her that security? She could see it wasn't arrogance that had driven him to give such a promise. It wasn't recklessness or lack of concern.

She came slowly to her feet and crossed her arms across her chest, confronting him. "What made you make that promise?"

He glared at her, not understanding what she wanted him to say. "I told you. China needed—"

"Why did you make that promise?" She wanted him to say the words, not so much because she needed the confirmation—she could see how he felt about these children—but because *he* did. Making him admit his feelings was the best gift she could give him to see him through the coming days.

"Because it tore me apart to see her so—"

"Why, Baird?"

There was an almost imperceptible softening in his face. He lowered his eyes as if he were ashamed for her to see the truth in them. "Because I love her."

"You love all of them, don't you?" she insisted softly.

"I'm their father, Ardith. I'm supposed to love—"

"Don't you?"

His gaze came back to her, so hot and fierce it took all her gumption to stand her ground. "I do love them," he told her. "Even Durban."

She nodded, warm, deep satisfaction settling inside her. "Loving them is a good thing."

"Is it?" he demanded almost angrily. "I've never done very well by the people I love."

"That was then. You're different now."

He glowered, afraid to believe her. "How do you know?"

She smiled, half to herself. "Because you promised China. Because you'll do everything in your power to live up to the children's expectations of you. And in the end, whether you fail or whether you succeed, you've given them something dearer by far."

"And what is that?"

She went to him without hesitation and curled her arms around his waist.

"Yourself."

She spread her palms against his back and gathered him in. He was broad and solid and still damp from being out in the storm. His arms came around her, too. He drew her against him.

As their bodies aligned, awareness tingled along her nerves. It hummed in her flesh, resonated at the core of her, a remnant of another time when they'd been together. But tonight it was a subtle thing, quiet, nurturing, a counterpoint for other more potent emotions.

Baird leaned into her, his head bowed, his muscles loosening. He rested his cheek against her hair.

They stood quiet for a very long time, sharing their warmth, listening to the steady rhythm of life beating in each of them, communing in a way that went well beyond words. Ardith closed her eyes and gave herself up to the unexpected succor of that simple contact, holding tight to Baird, touching him and being touched. They drifted, bound together.

At length Ardith stirred. "It's late," she murmured, her voice slurred and soft, almost as if she had been sleeping.

Baird eased back and blinked at her. He had been as caught up in the safety and companionship as she had been.

He shifted away, and she could see him trying to put some semblance of order to his world. "Let me help you take care of those things," he offered, gesturing to the teapot and cups at the end of the table.

Ardith shook her head. "They'll be fine where they are until morning. It's time we found our beds."

Both of them were worn beyond their endurance by the events of the day, and would be tested again on the morrow. But there was comfort here, something tangible and familiar, something unexpected and new.

He nodded in agreement. "I want to thank you—"

"There is no need."

"No, I need to thank you, Ardith, for taking such good care of China. For taking such good care of me. For making me see, well—" He hesitated and smiled at her. "—what you made me see."

She smiled back, warmed way down deep by his words. "Between the two of us, we'll get China through this. She's a strong girl."

"I know."

"Stronger than her mother was."

He smiled a little more. "I realized that myself tonight."

Baird touched her cheek, a caress so gentle that it might have been a veil of silk brushing over her skin. And then he turned toward the stairs.

In spite of herself, Ardith paused in the shadow of her own doorway to watch him. He wasn't the Baird Northcross she thought she knew. He had changed, or perhaps it was that she had come to see him differently. He was a man with fears and foibles and feelings far more complex and fragile than she had ever imagined he could harbor. He was a man, Ardith was forced to admit to herself, for whom she had come to care far too much.

*B*aird climbed the steps to the back porch of the ranch house and surveyed the gathering in the yard. For all his tender years, Matt Hastings had been a well-known and well-loved figure in the Powder River ranching community. Neighbors from far and wide had come to attend his funeral. Reverend Schneider, who had been overnighting at Fort McKinney, had conducted the service. Now everyone had gathered to fill their plates, lift a glass or two in

Matt's memory, and tell stories of a boy who had been mostly raised by the cowboys in one bunkhouse or another since his folks died ten years ago.

Baird sought China in the midst of the crowd and saw several of the neighbor women petting and consoling her. He searched out Khy and saw his son with three younger boys by the corral, showing them Little Paint. Durban stood with Cullen McKay. Something about the way Durban hung on his cousin's every word wrung Baird's insides.

He scanned the crowd for Ardith, hoping to catch her eye, knowing if he did she'd swoop down on Cullen and the boy and lure Durban away. But Ardith wasn't visiting with neighbors gathered at the end of the porch. She wasn't overseeing the long serving table set up outside the kitchen door. She wasn't anywhere in sight.

Baird shifted uncomfortably. His world felt a little out of balance without her there.

He wandered into the house wondering where she'd gone. It was cool and dim inside, peaceful and quiet. He was about to turn and leave when he heard a sound, soft and small, like the mewling of a kitten. It was muffled and indistinct, but it drew him toward the half-open door to Ardith's bedchamber.

Though he'd never been inside, he could have found it by the smell alone, the tang of linseed oil and turpentine. He pushed the door a little wider and saw a worktable filled with brushes and paints in front of the window. A half-finished painting was fastened to Ardith's drawing board.

He stepped inside. On his left was a scarred pine dresser with a ruffled cloth, painted china dishes of hairpins and doodads, vials of cologne, and an ivory-backed hair brush.

At the end of the room was a log-frame bed. Ardith was

seated at the edge, her dark head bowed and her body curled in tight upon itself.

At first he thought she was praying and didn't want to intrude. Then he heard that tiny, choking sound again, and he realized she was crying. He closed the door behind him and went to her. "Ardith?" he whispered.

She raised her head with a start, too quickly for her to wipe away the tears, too spontaneously for her to hide the anguish in her eyes.

He came and knelt beside her. He took her hands. The sorrow in her face sank into him.

"Oh, Ardith," he murmured and without another word he drew her against him. Without another word she came to him. He held her, broken and fragile in his hands—his brave, strong Ardith. "It's all right, love. You're safe with me."

As if she knew she was, Ardith curled against him. He splayed his hand against her back and circled gently. "It's all right, Ardith. Just let me hold you."

"I didn't mean to do this," she said, her voice muffled against his shirtfront. "I just felt so—so overwhelmed all at once."

She'd waited until no one needed her. "It's all right, sweetheart. You've been so strong for all of us."

God knows, she *had* been strong. Strong for the children when their mother died; for China when the news came down the mountain about Matt; for him last night. He didn't know what he'd have done without her.

"It was having everyone together—like a family."

They had become a family. Baird hadn't realized it, but that's how it felt. A family—he and the children and her, Buck and Myra and the cowboys—and that family had lost one of its own last night. They'd lose the rest at the end of the season.

And Ardith would lose the most. No wonder she was grieving.

He pulled her closer still and stroked her hair, feeling as helpless to change what was going to happen in two months time as he'd been last night, when Matt had died.

"I know," he whispered, rocking her a little. "I know."

There was something so right about the weight of her in his arms, the warm silk of her hair beneath his cheek. Something so gratifying about knowing he could give her this. It warmed him that she'd allow him to see her so vulnerable. He felt privileged that Ardith was trusting him with her tears.

She let him hold her for a good while longer, and finally shifted away. She swiped at her eyes with her fingers and sniffled. Baird offered her his handkerchief.

"I gave mine to China," she explained and blew her nose—not delicately, not in some ladylike sniffle. She blew her nose as if she was done with crying and meant to get on with living. Something about that made him smile.

"I didn't mean to do that," she apologized, and ducked her head. "I came in here so no one would see . . ."

"I'm glad I came upon you, then," Baird said. "I'm glad you let me help."

She gave him a watery smile.

Seeing that she was better, he pushed to his feet and stood for a moment looking down at her. She was marked by her bout of tears in the way fair-skinned women always were. Her nose was red, and her mouth had a blushed, smudgy look about it. He balanced this Ardith against the one she usually showed the world and savored the unexpected dichotomy.

He reached down and cupped her cheek, his thumb at her temple and his fingers rough along the soft curve of her jaw. She had fine, strong features, broad across the cheekbones and jaw, dark brows with a wry arch, a wide mouth. She was not a beauty by any means, but there was something compelling about her, something undeniably pleasing.

He tried to smooth the loops of her chignon and came up with several hairpins instead. They were warm from the heat of her body, heavy, and made of tortoiseshell.

He held them out to her. "You'll want to wash your face and tidy your hair before you come back outside."

She nodded and took the hairpins. "I want you to know how much I appreciate—"

He smiled at her and sketched the slightest bow. "I'm pleased to offer you this one small service, after all."

Sugar Creek Ranch
August 16, 1882

My Dear Gavin,

I regret to tell you that we are going through sad times here. We buried young Matt Hastings yesterday. I am certain I have mentioned him to you either in my accounts of the roundup, or as China's special friend. He was a fine young man, considerate, hard working, and quite hopelessly infatuated with China—as she was with him. He was struck by lightning while herding cattle. It is an occurrence, I am told, that is all too common.

China, of course, is devastated, and I am worried about her. This also reminds both her and the boys of how recently they lost their mother. Baird and I have agreed that it is important for both of us to be here at the ranch with them. That will necessitate him riding back and forth to the summer camp, and me staying on until mid-October. When they drive the stock to Cheyenne to be sold, I will in all likelihood accompany them, and catch the train east from there.

Once I'm settled again in Concord, I will have a good deal more time to dedicate to my books. I do thank you for your recent letter and your report on the con-

tinuing sale of "Abigail Goose Goes to Town." I can hardly believe that it has already gone into a third printing. Needless to say I am delighted by its early success.

Your devoted friend,
Ardith

TWELVE

$\mathcal{A}$rdith decided to make her announcement at supper. But before she could utter so much as a word, Khy began recounting his afternoon. He'd spent it stalking butterflies through the fields on the far side of the creek and had managed to snag several excellent specimens.

"Myra made a net for me from a looped-around branch and some stuff she called *cheesecloth*. Do they call it that because it has those holes in it?"

Durban glanced up from a copy of *Tale of Two Cities* he'd brought to the table in spite of Ardith's specific directions to the contrary. "Buck says Khy caught something called a Tiger Swallowtail and a Northern Blue."

"Things have such interesting names out here," China murmured half to herself. "Swallowtails and Waxwings and Fairy Slippers."

Ardith glanced up at her niece. In the several weeks since Matt's death China had been sleepwalking through her days, and Ardith didn't know how to waken her to the world again. In some ways Baird seemed almost as preoccupied tonight. He'd been more attentive to his children's needs since he'd brought Matt home, but seeing the weariness in his face Ardith wondered how much longer he could keep up the pace he'd set for himself with visits to the summer camp and his duties here.

Ardith took it upon herself to direct the meal, seeing that bowls and platters were passed, reminding the children to eat their vegetables, and admonishing Durban again about his book.

Myra had arrived with slices of pie and was pouring coffee when Ardith decided it was time to share her news. "I heard from Gavin today," she began, sliding his letter from her pocket.

"Gavin?" Baird asked, addressing her directly for the first time since they'd sat down.

"Gavin Rawlinson, my publisher," Ardith reminded him.

"I like Gavin," China put in. "He was nice to us when we were in Boston."

Baird's mouth narrowed with what could have been either disapproval or dyspepsia. Ardith chose to ignore him, and with a crinkle of pages, began to read:

My Very Dear Ardith.

I have marvelous news! Last evening an old friend of mine, Justin Daniels, stopped here at the office to pick me up on our way to a lecture on Goethe.

"Goethe?" Baird echoed with a hint of derision, as if only hopeless prigs attended lectures on Goethe.

Ardith scowled at him and kept on reading.

As you may know, Justin is an art dealer of some repute. While he was waiting for me, he leafed through the copy of "Abigail Goose Goes to Town" I had on the corner of my desk.

"Does this author ever paint anything but these quaint little animals?" he asked me. I assured him you did and showed him both your illustrated letters and the watercolor sketches you've been sending me. He seemed quite impressed. "This 'Auntie Ardith' has undeniable ability," he said. "But these western scenes are entirely unsuitable for a female to be painting. I'd show her work at the gallery, if she'd adopt a pseudonym so I could tell my patrons she's a man."

Ever since the mail had arrived this afternoon Ardith had been envisioning the children's exclamations of surprise and Baird's hearty congratulations. Instead Khy pushed the last limp string bean around on his plate. Durban sat absorbed in the perils of Sydney Carton and the Manettes. China blinked at her, completely missing the significance of what she'd said.

When Baird raised his head, Ardith's heart swelled with anticipation. "This art dealer wants you to sell your paintings under a man's name?"

Ardith battled the urge to curse with pure vexation.

"Well, I, for one, don't think it matters about the name!" Myra stepped into the breech, thumping the coffee pot down on the table for emphasis. "Just imagine! Ardith's paintings are going to be sold in Boston. Why, the next thing you know, the portrait she made of me will be hanging in a museum!"

Ardith flashed Myra a grateful smile. Trust another woman to understand how monumental this accomplishment was.

"What does he mean, 'adopt a pseudonym?'" China asked, just catching up to the conversation.

"It means your Aunt Ardith would have to pretend she was a man in order to sell her paintings," Baird answered in an aggrieved tone. "Which is patently absurd!"

Ardith blinked at him, mystified by his outrage on her

behalf. "That's what I thought at first," she answered as reasonably as she could. "But once I got used to the idea, I decided it wasn't so terrible."

"Well, take my word—once your patrons meet you at that gallery, they won't be fooled. You're too damn pretty to get by calling yourself by some man's name."

Pretty. The word rolled over her like high surf, leaving her reeling, exhilarated, and a little breathless. She'd been waiting sixteen years for Baird Northcross to think she was pretty. And he'd told her now—*now* when she needed something else from him entirely. It was all she could do to keep from kicking him under the table.

"I thought I would sign the paintings with my initials. I'd sign them as 'A. E. Merritt,'" she told him, "and let people draw their own conclusions."

"You should sign the paintings with your real name, and let that be the end of it!" Baird declared and pushed to his feet.

It would be the end of it, too—the end to a career she'd barely begun.

"While I thank you for your opinion, Baird," she answered, her voice frosty enough to condense on glass, "I'll do as I see fit in this."

"Fine, Ardith! Fine!" he shouted at her. "Do what you like! God knows, you've had a great deal of practice!" He stalked out the door.

The children stared after him owl-eyed, then turned to her. Until now she and Baird had managed to shield China and the boys from their disagreements, and Ardith couldn't think what to say to them.

"Aren't you going to cry?" Khy finally asked. "Mama always used to cry when Papa yelled at her. Then she'd throw things."

Durban elbowed his brother to silence.

"Of course I'm not going to cry," she assured them with far more conviction than she felt. "I save my tears for things that are important. Now, if you promise to take the plates and forks to the kitchen when you're done, you may have your pie out on the porch."

Given the opportunity to escape, all three children grabbed their desserts and scrambled for the door. Once they were gone Ardith drooped, sagging like muslin on a humid day. Only gradually did she realize Myra was standing over her, a sly smile on her lips. Myra had just seen her ambushed, complimented, and upbraided, and Ardith was mortified.

"Seems his lordship's got his dander up," Myra observed.

"I can't imagine what set him off."

"Oh, can't you now?" Myra flashed her a grin. "I'd say you just knocked that poor man's world off kilter again."

"This has nothing to do with Baird's world!" Ardith fumed. "This is about my paintings, my opportunities. My future."

"Oh?" There was something smug in Myra's smile. "Then why do you suppose he felt obliged to tell you you're pretty?"

Myra knew. Sick humiliation that started at Ardith's toes sluiced upward. Myra understood the way only another plain woman could what that word meant to her.

"It must be very satisfying to hear him say it," the older woman went on, "after all this time."

Fresh horror intensified the heat in Ardith's face. "How did you know?" she gasped. "Surely Baird didn't—"

"No, of course not." Myra pulled out a chair and lowered herself to the seat. "For whatever else his lordship's done, he's a gentleman. No. Buck heard Cullen McKay poking at him the night of the party—something about him running off with your sister when he was set to marry you."

Even at this late date, Ardith felt marked by the stain of what had happened years before.

"Is that why they were fighting?" she asked incredulously. Wouldn't *that* be the ultimate irony—Baird Northcross defending her honor?

Myra shrugged. "Buck didn't hear all of it."

Ardith knew there was no sense denying what had happened. "Baird and I were betrothed. He and Ariel ran off together the night before we were to be married."

"Is that why you left England?"

"I refused to stay and bear the scandal of being Baird Northcross's cast-off bride."

She could see both compassion and approval in Myra's face. "Yet you forgave your sister. You took in her children when she died and brought them to their father."

Ardith nodded her head. "Even after everything, I loved Ariel, but forgiving her took some time. She wrote me after Khy was born, and we made our peace. When Ariel died, I felt honor-bound to keep the promise I had made to her. And when I saw how aloof Baird was with the children when we arrived, I knew I couldn't just abandon them."

"He's better now."

"I know." During their stay at the summer camp, Baird had changed. He'd cradled Khy so tenderly when he was hurt. When Matt was killed, Baird had been the only one able to comfort China. He was still trying to make peace with Durban, no matter how hard the boy shoved him away. Up in those mountains, he'd become a father to these children, whether he wanted to be one or not.

"How are you going to manage by yourself when he takes the children back to England?"

The question made Ardith want to bury her face in her hands and weep. "I don't have any rights where the children are concerned," she answered, her voice raw with misery. "And I'd forfeit everything I've worked for if I followed them. In Massachusetts I have a position with my uncle. I have a publisher and books to write. And now there's this opportunity to have my paintings exhibited."

There was something else, too, something she wasn't sure enough about to discuss with anyone.

"And what about him?"

"Who?"

"His lordship. You forgave your sister for what they did. Have you forgiven him?"

"He hasn't asked me to."

Myra's smile was sly and knowing. "Yet you've come to care for him anyway."

Lying to Myra would be like lying to herself—an act of evasion and futility. Instead of answering, Ardith got to her feet. "Let me help you take these things into the kitchen."

Myra made a shooing motion. "Go drink your coffee on the porch and enjoy the breeze."

Ardith didn't argue. Between Baird's bluster and Myra's probing, she could use a little solitude. She picked up her cup, and found a place for herself on one of the benches that faced the mountains. Scattered above a darkening lavender landscape, the clouds glowed fierce, coppery pink; raging like live coals against the slowly encroaching night.

While she could still see, Ardith took out Gavin's letter and opened it to the second page.

Every day, my dear Ardith, I find my esteem for you growing. I don't know if you have changed in the months we've been apart, or if I have. I'm not sure if it is your absence, or the intimacy of communicating our thoughts and feelings in these pages that has made me so aware of you. I find you constantly in my thoughts. At night I lie awake here in Boston and try to imagine you lying awake there in Wyoming, thinking of me.

What I propose when you return is that we take some time for ourselves. I would like to show you my family's summer home. The shore is not so gay in the fall as it is in high summer, but there is a melancholy beauty about the dunes that pleases me.

Then, too, after your months in Wyoming, I will need to reintroduce you to culture. We will attend some concerts and the theatre. I want to make the time between us something wonderful.

Please give me some hope that these letters have affected you as they have affected me. I am most eagerly awaiting your reply.

> *Your affectionate friend,*
> *Gavin*

Ardith sat staring at the letter in her lap, much as she had this afternoon. She knew now that she hadn't mistaken Gavin's meaning; his feelings for her were deepening.

She curled her fingers around the page, wanting to be elated by what he'd written. She'd had a *tendre* for Gavin Rawlinson from the moment he spread her sketches across his desk and laughed out loud over her creatures' antics. He was witty and genteel and sophisticated, and just the touch of his hand had turned her warm inside. He'd sent a bright beam of light into her lonely spinster's life, given her hope and an income and a future. Now he was offering her even more.

But Baird said she was pretty. The words had such lovely resonance inside her head. Of course, other things mattered more: that Baird had held her when she cried, that he stayed with her when Khy was hurt. That he talked to her and argued with her and told her his secrets. Yet there was such satisfaction hearing those words on his lips—just this once.

"Isn't it too dark to be reading out here?" Ardith all but jumped out of her shoes at the sound of Baird's voice. He ambled toward her down the length of the porch. "Or are you committing that letter to memory?"

She jammed the pages into her pocket and scrambled to rearrange her hair, her expression. And especially her thoughts. She squared her shoulders and turned those errant thoughts to the question they had been so heatedly debating at dinner.

"Is it so hard for you to understand why I'm excited that one of Boston's most reputable art dealers is willing to show my work?" she challenged him.

Baird settled on the porch railing opposite her and crossed his arms. "I do understand," he told her reasonably, "and I'm pleased for you. I know recognition like this comes hard, especially for a woman. What bothers me, is that this dealer has asked you to change your name."

"I wouldn't be the first woman to deny her femininity for her art," Ardith argued. "Take George Eliot, for example."

"Mary Ann Evans, you mean."

"Would we have *Middlemarch* if she hadn't taken a masculine pseudonym?"

He frowned thoughtfully and curled his hands around the railing. "To my way of thinking, this gallery owner has asked you to negate part of what makes your paintings special."

"What do you mean?"

He shrugged a little self-consciously. "I think you have a vision of the west no man could see. Men see grass and timber and money to be made. You see history in the folds of these hills, emancipation in the breadth of the prairie. And the portraits you've been doing of Myra and the hands . . ."

"You think they're good?" she asked eagerly.

"I think they're exceptional. You seem to see beyond their faces somehow, into who they are. Those portraits

are your vision, Ardith. A woman's vision; not a man's."
He leaned back and laughed a little, seeming almost em-
barrassed by his own observations. "Does that make
sense?"

"In a way." His words warmed her, almost as if he saw
her paintings more clearly than she did herself. But life
had taught Ardith practicality. "As much as I appreciate
your reasoning, I still mean to sign my work as 'A. E.
Merritt.'"

"I never for a moment thought you'd take my advice,"
he replied with a wry twist to his mouth.

"And that's what had you so wrought-up at dinner?"

"Part of it." Though he lowered his head, Ardith saw
how grim he looked. "We've lost more of our cattle."

"Oh, Baird, what happened?" She rose and went to
lean against the railing beside him. Even the simple, consoling brush of her palm against his sleeve sent a strange
tingle dancing between them.

"They're just gone."

"It's not Indians or wolves this time?"

He shook his head. "Buck says he can never remember
so many cattle going missing in a single season."

Had Buck called it what it probably was?

Ardith hesitated, weighing her words, trying to see into
Baird's shadowed face. "Is someone rustling our cows?"

His shoulders tightened. "I'd like to tell you you've
been reading too many of your western novels."

"But you can't?" When he shook his head, she continued. "Are the other ranches having losses like ours?"

"No."

"Have they had trouble with wolves or Indians?"

"No."

She saw the stubborn cant of his jaw and knew he
wasn't willing to admit what seemed obvious to everyone
else. Still, she tried to make him. "Then isn't it time you

considered that Cullen McKay might be behind us losing cattle?"

Ardith felt the quiver of tension shoot through him. "It can't be Cullen."

"Why can't it?" She tried to keep her voice gentle. "Is it because he's Earl Northam's bastard son? Because he's got Northcross blood in his veins, and the Northcrosses never do anything dishonorable?"

"You know better than that." He cast her a glance beneath his lashes. "It's because we've been looking long and hard, and we still can't figure out what's happening to the cattle. We haven't found animals with fresh brands. We haven't caught anyone with a running iron. It's like those cows evaporate."

He pushed to his feet. "And we don't have any indication that Cullen's involved. Even if he was, how could I go to my uncle and ask him to excuse my failure because his son has been rustling Sugar Creek cattle?"

"So you mean to ignore what's happening and blame yourself!"

She was exasperated enough to get up and slam into the house except that Baird stopped her. He leaned closer, gripping the porch railing to her right and left, holding her in place.

"Why shouldn't I accept the blame? God knows I've never been called to account for half of what I've done."

She sensed a shift in his mood, one of those odd alterations in him that left her feeling confused and breathless.

Though he didn't move, he seemed suddenly nearer. His boots ruffled the hem of her skirt. She could smell the sun and dust and wind on him. She thought he might try to kiss her, and she knew she wouldn't shy away from him this time.

"Ardith," he said, his voice deep and serious. "I want to apologize."

"For what?"

"I want to accept the blame for what Ariel and I did to you."

Her stomach lurched. She said the first thing that came into her head. "You're a bit late doing that, aren't you?"

He nodded, refusing to back down. "More than a bit, I'm afraid; and I apologize for that, too."

In an instant, Ardith was flung back in time. She stood in the window at her father's London townhouse, the rain tracking down the windowpanes like the tears she refused to shed. She balled Baird's letter more tightly in her fist, clinging to the very thing that had torn her life apart. She'd tried to find some less devastating meaning in those carefully penned words, but Baird had been merciless in his clarity. He'd run off with her sister—proving once more that Ardith wasn't good enough.

"Ardith, I'm sorry."

From more than a decade away, Baird's voice reached her, calling her back to Wyoming, back to where cows lowed in the dark and the wind off the mountains was cool and scented with pine. Back to where the man who had wounded her so horribly was trying to make amends.

She stared at him, seeing the knot of concern between his eyebrows and the taut sincerity in the line of his mouth.

"When Ariel and I ran off," he murmured, his voice rough and low with regret, "we were in love and desperate to be together. We didn't think about how you would be hurt, how people would look at you afterwards. We didn't think about anything—or anyone—but ourselves."

Ardith felt the press of hot, angry tears at the backs of her eyes. "Would it have made a difference if you had?"

He stood over her, his shoulders hunched, his head bent close to hers. "I'd like to believe that if we'd tried, we could have found a better way—a more honorable way— to deal with the situation. What we did was thoughtless and contemptible. I'm so sorry you were the one who paid for our mistakes."

Ardith had never expected an apology from Baird, never dreamed he even understood the terrible pain he and Ariel had caused her.

"Why are you telling me this now?" she asked, her voice thready.

"Because you deserve the truth, and because I've finally managed to scrape together enough courage to face you with it. I'm sorry, Ardith. I'm sorry for everything we did, and everything that happened afterwards. And I'm especially sorry that it's taken me so long to see how badly I treated you."

She looked up into that shadowed face and saw the wild, beautiful youth he'd been—and the man he had become. Just tonight Myra had asked her if she'd forgiven him, and Ardith had said he hadn't asked her to.

He was asking now, and she was suddenly glad to have the question resolved between them. In truth, she'd begun to forgive him when she realized how much he'd loved Ariel and how truly he mourned her. A little more of her anger had melted away every time she'd seen him struggling to be a father to his children. The night he'd held and comforted China had loosened the last hard knots of her resentment.

It was time to let him know that she'd forgiven him. This had haunted both of them for far too long.

"I won't deny how desolate I was when you and Ariel ran off together. I'd always been second best in my father's eyes, and having you choose her over me reinforced everything he'd made me believe about myself. It made me feel betrayed—again."

"Is that why you left England?"

There had been more to it than that, and to be fair, she had to tell him all of it. "It's true that I didn't want to face the disappointment or the scandal, but I also knew that when you and Ariel returned from Scotland, father would welcome you back. I couldn't stay and be humiliated by seeing the two of you together day after day, so I packed my things and left.

"Uncle Franklin was kind enough to take me in for my mother's sake, and in the end, I can't say I regret the way things worked out. I wouldn't be the person I am if I hadn't left. I'd never have started painting or written books or gone out into the world. I'd never have come to the west."

She covered his broad, sun-browned hands with her own and looked up into his face. "It's all right, Baird," she whispered. "I'm glad you told me all of this, but I've gained far more than I lost. So don't feel sorry anymore."

She could see the gleam of emotion in his eyes. "Ardith, are you sure? You have every right in the world to tell me to go to the devil."

"Would you feel better if I did?" she asked him.

"No." He stepped back and gave a shaky laugh. "Well, maybe I would, but I'm glad you didn't."

"It's settled, then," she said and got to her feet.

He stopped her, catching her hand on her way to the door. "I really am glad about the paintings. I hope this A. E. Merritt sets the art world ablaze."

She grinned at him. "So do I," she said. "So do I."

THIRTEEN

Khy tore into the house just as Ardith and China were finishing breakfast. "There are *real live* Indians putting up a tepee down by the creek!" he reported.

"How do you know they're 'real live' Indians?" Ardith asked, somewhat unsettled by the news.

"I know because the man has feathers in his hat, and the woman is wearing war paint!"

Ardith and China exchanged startled glances. Except for a few cattle being appropriated for food, there hadn't been Indian trouble in this part of Wyoming for a number of years. Still, it seemed prudent to investigate.

"Who do you think these Indians are, Aunt Ardith?" China asked, more interested in their unexpected guests than she had been in anything since Matt was killed.

Ardith shook her head and wished that Baird was here instead of off at the summer camp. "I don't know, but let's go find out what's happening."

Myra was already down at the tepee when Ardith and the children arrived. She hastily made introductions. "Miss Ardith Merritt, I'd like you to meet Hunter

Jalbert," she began. "He was a scout at Fort Carr when Buck was in the army."

With undisguised curiosity Ardith stared up at the first western Indian she'd ever seen. He stood tall, well over six feet, and was muscular in that lean, graceful way horsemen often were. His face was dark-skinned and broad. He had high, molded cheekbones; dark eyes; and lines that bracketed the corners of his mouth, hinting that there was a sense of humor lurking inside him somewhere. Her gaze shifted to the feathers in his hatband, to the primitive amulet bound tight at his throat, and then to the long-bladed knife tucked in a beaded sheath he wore at his waist.

That must be his scalping knife! she thought and shifted a step away. As she did, Ardith caught a glimpse of Jalbert's expression. Experience and insight mingled with more than a little amusement. Hunter Jalbert knew exactly what she'd been thinking and was laughing at her! Ardith felt herself color up.

"How do you do?" she said, extending her hand and speaking in her most decorous tones.

Hunter Jalbert curled his broad palm around her fingers and answered in kind. "I'm so very pleased to make your acquaintance, Miss Merritt."

And then he grinned.

The heat in Ardith's cheeks intensified.

"Please allow me to introduce my children," Jalbert went on, putting her at ease a moment later. "This is Meggie," he indicated a golden-haired girl in her late teens. "And Andrew." Though he was darker than his sister, he was clearly not this man's son.

"This is Ben—" who was ten or so and the image of his father. "And our twins, Jess and William."

The twins were dark like Jalbert, but with eyes of a cool gray-green color, like the winter sea.

"This is my niece, China," Ardith responded, "and my nephew Khyber."

"They're both named for places so far away," Jalbert observed.

Ardith was a little startled that an Indian way out here in the wilds of Wyoming should be acquainted with world geography.

"Their father travels extensively," Ardith felt compelled to explain. *It's where he was when they were born.*

"Have you thanked Miss Merritt for granting us permission to spend a few nights on her land?"

Ardith turned to acknowledge the woman just emerging from the tepee and caught her breath. Khy had said the woman was wearing "war paint," but his description hadn't come close to preparing Ardith for Jalbert's wife.

The woman, with her ice-green eyes and gold-streaked hair, bore an intricate tattoo high on her left cheek. Dark blue lines radiated from the circle to form a star-burst design that nestled in the hollow below the bone. Yet what should have been a travesty on a woman as lovely as she enhanced her somehow, making her more compelling and exotic.

In an instant Ardith was fascinated not only by the tattoo, but by the woman herself. She needed to know how this woman had come to be marked, and where in a world bound by prejudice she'd found a place that accepted her beauty, her uniqueness.

"This is my wife, Cassandra," Hunter Jalbert said simply. "Cass, this is Ardith Merritt, and her charges, China and Khyber."

Cass Jalbert's chin came up, acknowledging them, daring them to react to the tattoo.

Ardith inclined her head and relied on the children's good manners to avoid embarrassment. "We are pleased to have all of you here with us, Mrs. Jalbert. I know Khy will enjoy having other boys to play with."

"I thank you for your welcome, Miss Merritt," Cassandra acknowledged. "I am looking forward to visiting some myself, especially since Myra has always been so good to us."

"I've never done anything much," Myra put in.

"Is there anything you need while you are here?" Ardith asked them.

"I thank you for your concern, but we're pretty well provisioned, at least as long as you don't mind my husband doing a bit of hunting."

"My brother-in-law likes hunting, too, though he is often too busy with the cattle these days to bring in much game."

"Then perhaps I can earn our keep while we are here," Jalbert offered.

"I could make wonderful things with a few elk steaks," Myra encouraged him.

"I'll see what I can do," he promised and headed toward the far corral, where a score of fine-looking horses were kicking up their heels. The Jalbert boys trailed after him, with Khy bobbing in their wake.

"Khy!" Ardith called out. "Khyber, I don't think—"

"Oh, let him go," Cass Jalbert told her. "Hunter likes children, and Andrew is used to looking after the younger boys."

"Khy can be quite a handful," Ardith warned her.

"No more than the twins, I assure you," Mrs. Jalbert said with a laugh. "I have just brewed up spicewood tea for Meggie and me. Would you all like to join us?"

Ardith immediately accepted. She had read about Indian tepees in her ten-penny dreadfuls, but had never expected to see one close up. She followed Myra through the deerskin door, noticing immediately that the interior of the conical structure was warm and dim. A small fire lay in a ring of stones at the center, and wisps of smoke trailed upward to escape through the gap where the poles came together at the top.

As Ardith took a seat on one of the low, blanket-padded cots, she was amazed by how colorful the lodge was inside. Tied to the poles on the lower half of the tent was a yard-deep inner flap painted and embroidered with intricate designs. Brightly decorated boxes made of leather were piled between the beds and must have held clothes and household articles.

Cass opened one of them and retrieved five tin mugs. She dipped tea from a pan steaming at the edge of the fire and served each of her guests.

Ardith tasted the brew and found it almost gingery.

"What is it that brings you here?" she asked after she had complimented her hostess on the tea.

"Selling horses," Mrs. Jalbert explained.

"Hunter's the best horse breeder and trainer north of the Platte," Myra put in.

"We fulfilled our contract with Fort McKinney yesterday," Cass went on. "We'll sell the rest of these horses to a man who hopes to start a stagecoach company north from Cheyenne."

Ardith nodded and sipped again. "How long do you expect to be staying with us?"

"No more than a few days. We appreciate Mr. North-cross allowing us to pasture our horses on our way south."

It might have been nicer if Baird had thought to mention giving the Jalberts permission to camp here, Ardith thought, though she was more than pleased with her new acquaintances. In truth, she could barely take her eyes off Cassandra Jalbert's face, the way the light played over her features, the strength of her brow and jaw, the contrast of vulnerability and sensuality in her well-shaped mouth. And of course there was the tattoo, enhancing her natural beauty, turning it pagan and romantic. More than anything, Ardith wanted to paint her.

"I was wondering, Mrs. Jalbert, if I might ask you a very impertinent question," Ardith began.

For an instant Cass Jalbert's expression froze, as if she were steeling herself for impending unpleasantness. "What is it?" she asked warily.

The other woman's discomfort made Ardith sorry she'd begun, yet she could hardly back away from the request she'd meant to make. "Please, Mrs. Jalbert, I have a certain skill as an artist, and I was hoping that while you are here, you would allow me to paint your portrait."

Cass started at the request, and then her pale eyes narrowed as if she were seeking the motives beyond the words. "Why would you want to do that?"

Ardith hesitated, realizing her answer could affect far more than whether Cass Jalbert agreed to sit for her. It would speak to the vulnerable core of this woman, speak to the dichotomy of what her life in the world outside her home and family must be like.

Ardith moistened her lips, suddenly needing to put into words a few half thought-out notions about the west and some of the observations Baird had made about her paintings.

"I think it takes a particular kind of woman to live out here," Ardith began carefully, "to love a western man, to live with him and make a home. I think that uniqueness is evident in the independence with which western women act, the way they carry themselves—and I think it is evident in their faces. I think women like you and Myra embody a kind of courage and strength of character that says something important about this frontier, about living in this time and place."

They were concepts she'd been rolling around in her head since that night on the porch, a string of observations that had suddenly been given a cohesive form. "I think it's something I could capture with brushes and paint, Mrs. Jalbert, and I would be honored if you'd agree to sit for me."

Ardith waited in silence for Cassandra's reply, and the woman eyed her consideringly. "So you paint?"

"Since I was a child."

"And are you any good at it?"

"She made a portrait of me," Myra spoke up, "and did a damn-fine job of it. There's an art dealer back in Boston who wants her work for his gallery, too."

Ardith flashed Myra a grateful smile. The older woman had expressed no real opinion about the small oil portrait when it was done, and she was glad to know Myra was pleased with how Ardith had depicted her.

"Could you teach someone to draw and paint if she was interested?"

"I've never taken students." Ardith looked at her in surprise. "Do you want to learn to paint?"

"Would you be able to judge another artist's work if you saw it? Could you tell if that person was good enough to warrant further study?"

"I could try," she answered cautiously.

Cassandra Jalbert nodded to where China and her daughter Meggie were seated side by side on one of the beds. "Show Miss Merritt your paintings, Meggie," she directed.

Meggie stared at her mother in horror and shook her head.

"Show her," Cass persisted.

Meggie shot her mother an imploring glance.

Ardith knew what the girl was feeling. Showing your work to a stranger was one of the worst moments in any artist's life. Ardith remembered the hot panic creeping up her throat as she'd watched Gavin leaf through her sketches that first time. She remembered how she had yearned for praise and expected derision.

"Why don't you let me see your sketches?" she coaxed gently.

Meggie stared, taking her measure, then turned and slid a dozen drawings and paintings from one of the leather folders.

Ardith went through them slowly, one by one. There were portraits of her family, several rugged landscapes, studies of individual plants and of the horses. The girl drew well, with a good eye for both detail and composition. Without instruction, she had mastered basic techniques and begun to improve on them. She used color with rare skill, and her work showed a sensitivity that went well beyond her years.

Ardith looked up at Meggie. Her hands were knotted demurely in her lap, though her eyes were alive with turmoil.

"These are wonderful," Ardith told her and reached out to touch her hand. "You have a great deal of natural talent. How did you learn to draw and paint so well?"

Meggie's face flushed; she lowered her lashes. "I practiced until I got things right."

"She takes after her father, my first husband," Cass Jalbert put in. "He began drawing when he was in officer training at West Point. After he came west he painted—"

Cassandra abruptly looked away, and Meggie, who must know what she was remembering, reached across and caught her mother's hand.

Ardith sensed the grief in them, things that were buried deep, regrets that had yet to be resolved. "Well, wherever she gets it from," Ardith broke in, "Meggie has a wonderful gift."

Still holding her daughter's hand, Cass Jalbert looked across at Ardith. "While we are here," she asked, "could you show her some things, give her lessons to make her drawing and painting better?"

Ardith considered what she could teach Meggie and how she could help her improve her work.

"If you agree," Cassandra Jalbert went on, ready to bargain away her comfort for what she wanted, "I'll sit for you. I'll let you paint my portrait in exchange for lessons for my daughter."

*T*here were all manner of strange people gathered on the back porch of the ranch house. As Baird approached, he could see Durban scowling across a chess board at a boy a few years older than he, and China giggling as she and a lovely, fair-haired girl struggled to untangle and roll a knotted skein of yarn. Ardith was seated on the steps turning the crank on some sort of barrel apparatus, as Myra and another woman offered suggestions and encouragement.

Khy noticed his arrival first, rounding the corner of the house with what appeared to be three Indian children on his heels.

"Papa! You're home!" Khy shouted and barrelled into Baird with enough force to rock him on his feet. "Aunt Ardith said you wouldn't be back until tomorrow or the next day."

"I got lonely," Baird admitted and stroked his son's wind-ruffled hair. "And who are these young gentlemen?"

"This is Ben, Jess, and William Jalbert. Or maybe it's William and Jess; I can't ever tell. They're camped in a tepee down by the creek."

Jalbert—the name jogged Baird's memory. Buck had asked if a horse trader he knew could stay a few nights on his way to Cheyenne. Baird had expected a single Frenchman and three or four horses, not a mixed-blood family and the good-sized herd he'd seen as he rode in. Still, as he approached the house, it was clear that the two families were getting on.

"What's all this?" he asked as he came nearer.

Ardith looked up and gave him a smile so broad and welcoming that it made him go warm all over.

"Oh, Baird, you're just in time! Myra's roasting a haunch of venison on a spit over a fire, and we're making ice cream."

"Is that what that contraption's for, making ice cream?" Baird liked ice cream, but never once in his life had he considered where it came from. "What flavor is it?"

"Vanilla," answered the woman squatting to Ardith's left.

As she turned to speak, he saw that a tattoo spread across her left cheek like a ruinous stain. He immediately averted his gaze, shocked that any woman should be so horribly disfigured.

"Let me introduce you to everyone," Ardith was saying, oblivious to his discomfort. "This is Cass Jalbert. Her husband, Hunter, is a friend of Buck's. They've stopped with a band of their horses on the way to Cheyenne."

Baird steeled himself and turned to the woman again. He could see by the wariness in her eyes that she had recognized his reaction, and Baird felt a flush of shame creep up his jaw.

"I'm pleased to meet you, Mrs. Jalbert," he answered formally. "I hope you're enjoying your stay with us."

She regarded him for one long moment, taking his measure, then inclined her head. "I'm very much enjoying my stay at the Sugar Creek, Mr. Northcross, as we all are."

"I see you met Ben and the twins," Ardith continued, struggling to crank the ice cream maker as she talked. "That's Meggie all tangled up with China in the yarn, and Andrew playing chess with Durban."

The children looked up and greeted him. They were a well-mannered and attractive lot, including the three younger boys, who were out in the yard teaching Khy to turn cartwheels.

"They've agreed to stay on a few extra days," Ardith informed him above the din of the younger children's laughter. "I'm going to paint Cassie's portrait."

"Perhaps you are," the woman put in—not as if she meant to refuse, but as if they enjoyed bickering over the matter.

"Sitting for the sketches wasn't so bad, now was it?"

Cass Jalbert lifted one delicate eyebrow in answer, and Ardith laughed. Something about the way everyone was getting on made Baird feel as if he was intruding.

Just then Myra pushed away from the railing, where she'd been supervising the ice cream making. "I guess I'd better go see how supper's coming. I expect we'll be eating in about an hour."

Ardith turned to Baird again. "I'm so glad you made it back in time for dinner."

Feeling a bit more a part of the group, Baird slung his saddlebags over the porch railing and squatted down beside her. "If you tell me what to do, I'll be happy to help with that."

"It's easy enough," Ardith answered, seeming more than willing to give up her job. "You need to keep the metal cylinder rotating while I put ice and salt down inside the barrel."

As she spoke, she sprinkled a handful of rock salt over the ice that had melted halfway down and added more from a second barrel that had been insulated with straw.

"Where did you get the ice?" Baird asked her, straining a little as he worked. It was a good deal harder to turn the crank on the ice cream maker than he'd expected.

"Cullen McKay brought it over from the Double T," she told him as she coiled and repinned her drooping hair. "One of their guests had something shipped in on ice from California."

"So they're having more of their investors visit, are they?"

Ardith lowered her voice. "Durban tells me he's seen Cullen showing a couple of them the Sugar Creek facilities, though McKay *has* had the decency to keep his distance from the house."

"He's hardly made a secret of the fact that the men backing him are looking to buy the Sugar Creek, and I don't see how I'm going to sell enough cattle this fall to keep it viable."

"You haven't had more cattle disappear, have you?"

He shook his head.

"You're doing the best you can," she said fiercely, inching nearer so the others wouldn't hear. "No one can expect more of you than that!"

He looked into her face, a mere handspan from his own, and was struck by the conviction in her eyes. It made him feel immeasurably better. Up this close, he could see how translucent her skin was, as delicate as porcelain, the color of cream; that her lashes were bristly and dark; that her irises seemed clear gray-green all the way to the bottom.

Whether the desire that came over him was based on those discoveries or on his appreciation of the faith she had in him, Baird could not say. All he knew was that crouched there beside her, he had an almost overwhelming impulse to curl his palms around the breadth of Ardith's jaw, draw her to him, and kiss her until neither of them could breathe.

But that was hardly something he could do with so many people looking on, and he focused his attention on the ice cream maker instead.

Ardith, who seemed as distracted as he was, put another handful of ice into the bucket and added salt.

"I suppose if Durban knows McKay has been showing

his investors around the Sugar Creek," Baird observed, "he and Cullen have been spending time together."

Ardith offered a delicate shrug. "I don't think there's any stopping them."

Baird's immediate inclination was to forbid Durban to spend time with McKay, but that would only breed further defiance. "I just wish Durban could see Cullen more clearly," he said on a sigh.

"I wonder," she began thoughtfully, scooping ice, "if some men aren't better for their contact with children who admire them."

Baird slid his gaze across to her, wondering if Ardith was talking about Cullen—or him. Was he a better man for the contact he'd had with his children? He imagined Ardith thought so, and he agreed. Before he could tell her that, Baird became aware of a dark, broad-featured man standing over them.

The fellow smiled and extended his hand. "Mr. Northcross, I'm Hunter Jalbert. I'd like to thank you for your generosity in giving me a place to pasture my horses and for extending your hospitality to my family."

Baird surrendered the crank of the ice cream maker to Ardith and rose to his feet. "It's Buck Johnson you have to thank."

"Your family has made us feel most welcome."

His family. Baird liked the way that sounded. It felt so good to be part of something. Part of a group of people who laughed and cried together, who argued and sulked and shouted at each other. Part of a group of people who welcomed him home at the end of the day.

"The children look as if they're getting on famously, and I understand Ardith means to paint a portrait of Cassandra."

A shadow crossed Jalbert's face, and Baird realized the man was afraid his wife would be hurt by Ardith painting her.

"Ardith is a very fine artist," he found himself reassuring Jalbert. "She's very careful how she approaches her subjects."

Baird had forgotten that Ardith was seated within earshot until she spoke. "If you think that, Baird, why haven't you let me sketch you?"

Baird glanced down at where she was sitting on the step with the ice cream maker clamped between her knees. The pure contrast of staid, proper Ardith in such an indelicate pose made him smile. "Well, if your portrait of Mrs. Jalbert is successful, perhaps I will."

Ardith grinned. "Don't worry. It will be wonderful."

Just then Myra came to the kitchen door. "I'm so glad to see you two big, husky fellows just standing there doing nothing. With so many of us all together, I figured we'd eat out here in the yard tonight, and I need someone to move the table."

Baird and Hunter ended up dragging the long, rock-heavy table from the mess room to the creek side of the house. Once Buck had carved the venison, they all gathered there together: he and Myra, Frank Barnes, Willy Martin, Bear Burton and the rest of the hands, the seven Jalberts, Baird and Ardith and the children. They passed around a platter overflowing with venison, crocks of beans, bread, sour cabbage, and Myra's pickles. They scooped ice cream for dessert, and the Jalbert children exclaimed over the unknown delicacy.

Lingering over a second cup of coffee, Baird sat back and watched them all. The younger children were flushed and grubby with play. Durban seemed less mad at the world than usual, and China was more animated than Baird had seen her since Matt Hastings's death. He also noticed how Buck had one arm draped possessively around Myra's broad shoulders, saw that Cass Jalbert was leaning back, secure against the wall of her husband's chest. Baird recognized the look she cast up at him. It was

one of adoration that transformed her ravaged face into
something unexpectedly beautiful.

The intensity of Cass's love for her husband and the
warmth in Buck and Myra's eyes gave Baird pause. Even
in their most fiercely passionate moments, he and Ariel
had never had the contentment and deep commitment he
saw in these people's faces.

It made Baird feel excluded again, somehow denied,
excruciatingly alone as he sat on the fringes of the older
couples' contentment. Halfway down the far side of the
table, he could see that Ardith was experiencing the same
sense of isolation. For an instant he caught her eye, and a
frisson of understanding flashed between them.

Then abruptly Ardith turned away. Before Baird could
reestablish contact, Hunter Jalbert came to his feet. "I'm
going to wander over and check the horses," he said.
"Want to see them, Northcross?"

There was pride in Jalbert's voice and Baird agreed.

As if that was a signal, everyone rose and began to carry
plates and bowls and platters back toward the kitchen.

Baird followed Hunter in the direction of the far paddock. He hadn't had a chance to do more than glance at
the horses when he rode in, and he had to admit that he
was curious.

He braced his elbows on the fence and watched as
Jalbert let himself in the gate to check the water trough.
He moved easily in among the animals. Several of the
horses came in to butt at Hunter's back or nuzzle his
shoulder. He patted them and stroked them, talking to
them in some low, melodious language Baird didn't understand. A beautiful little bay wickered, and Jalbert went
to check her right front foot.

"She stepped in a hole on our way here, so I've been
keeping an eye on her," Hunter explained as he latched
the paddock gate behind him.

"She's a beauty," Baird said admiringly.

Hunter took a place beside him at the fence and stood watching the animals grazing. "Buck tells me you've proven yourself quite a hand with horses since you've been here."

"Better with horses than with cows, I'm afraid." His self-effacing tone was sharper and more bitter than he'd intended.

Hunter's gaze swept over him. "Then why are you raising cattle?"

A very good question. He supposed he was doing it because cows were what he had. Because it was what his uncle expected. Because it had never occurred to him that he could be doing something else.

When Baird didn't answer, Hunter went on. "Buck says there are some grassy valleys tucked back in the hills that would make damned fine horse farms. If a man could manage to buy the land, and he did the training himself for the first few years, he could make a respectable living."

Baird understood what Jalbert was suggesting and couldn't have been more stunned if the man had proposed they ride to Cheyenne and rob the bank.

"Is that how you started out?" Baird managed to ask him.

Jalbert smiled either at the memory, or the pleasure of watching his horses run. "All I had when Cass and I began was a couple of saddle horses, and the mustangs I rounded up the following spring. It took damned hard work to build our ranch, but now I sell horses all over the territory. We'll never be rich, but Cass and I like what we do, like what we have. The children are healthy. We've built a new barn and added a wing to the house. The breeding stock gets better every year. From a humble beginning we've managed to put together everything we need to make us happy." Jalbert shrugged. "What more can a man ask of the world than that?"

What indeed? Baird reflected. Out here such things were

possible. Men with nothing struck it rich. Men with gumption manufactured opportunities. Men built ranches and families and lives on their own determination.

The possibilities piqued the edges of Baird's imagination. Could he really make a place for himself like the one Jalbert described? Was it too big a dream for someone like him—someone who'd failed and failed again?

He dismissed the notion with a shrug, but he couldn't quite banish the pinch of envy in his heart. "You're a lucky man, Jalbert. You have your ranch, a fine family, and a wife who loves you."

"No luckier than you could be."

Baird shook his head, and took more than a modicum of comfort in complacency. "I've never been lucky. Besides," he said, "I'll be taking the children back to England later this fall. I don't know if I'll ever get back out this way."

"And what about Ardith?"

Jalbert's question caught Baird hard.

What about Ardith? Truth to tell, he'd been thinking a great deal about Ardith—what losing contact with the children would mean to her. How desperately they'd miss her. What he would do without her prodding. God knows, she'd shoved him headlong into parenthood and showed him how empty his life would be without China's spontaneous hugs, Khy's mischief, and even Durban's scowls. Now he was coming to realize how empty it would be without Ardith herself.

"I only thought that because Ardith is so attached to the children and they to her . . ." Jalbert was saying.

Baird stepped back from the fence, a shiver of wariness chasing down his back. He needed suddenly to get away from the questions this man was asking, and the sharp discomfort of facing the answers.

"Ardith will be fine," Baird insisted. "The children will be fine. We've always known this was temporary."

Baird turned and stalked away, back to the barn to check on his own animals. But even as he carried water and scooped a few more oats into Dandy's box, the kind of life Jalbert described lingered in his mind like wisps of a lovely dream.

As she posed in the ornate, high-backed chair, Cassandra Jalbert began to speak in a quiet, almost cursory way about her past. "I was fifteen and on my way to Santa Fe with my family when the Kiowa attacked our wagon train."

Ardith paused, her paintbrush poised in midair, and stared at the woman whose likeness she'd been trying to capture for the last three days. They had spoken of many things as Ardith worked, sharing hours laced with the smell of turpentine and chamomile tea. But Cass had not spoken until now about the thing that had formed her, the thing that made her the woman she was.

"We tried to fight," Cass went on, memories scudding like clouds across the bright plane of her eyes, "but there were only a dozen men among us and half that many rifles. The Kiowa trapped us in a canyon and fired down from the walls until the wagons were on fire and my parents and my sisters lay dead."

In Ardith's imagination the scene took form: the boom of guns echoing from the canyon walls, the bite of gunpowder in her nostrils, and the heat of the burning wagons scalding her face. She was mesmerized, holding her breath, waiting for Cass to continue.

"As far as I knew then, only two of us survived the attack—the youngest girl from one of the other families and me. We were taken captive and dragged miles to the Kiowa village. I was stripped of everything that made me white and given to an Indian woman as her slave.

"I worked for her for several years. When the other girl

died, I tried to escape. I gathered what I could and I ran, but I was frightened and inexperienced at hiding my tracks. Within two days, the woman's husband found me. He beat me and took me back. It was then that she marked me—so I could never deny that I belonged to her. That I was her property."

Cass raised her hand to her cheek, her fingers skimming over the tattoo as if the pain and humiliation were fresh and new. Ardith shivered, awed by what Cass had endured, moved that this woman who shunned easy confidences had decided to trust her with the truth.

"What happened then?" Ardith murmured.

Cass's eyes were wide, focused on the past. "I was lost in a wager to a man of the Cheyenne. He traded me to the whites when he tired of me.

"It was then that I met Hunter. He was a scout for the army, and he befriended me from the beginning. He understood what it was to be caught between two worlds, to be watched with suspicion and hatred. And in the months I was with the army at Fort Carr, he came to care for me. And I for him."

Ardith sensed there was more to the story than what Cass had told her. A woman with a tattooed face would have been alienated from the soldiers sent west to fight the Indians. Her years of captivity would have made her a stranger in the world where she'd been born and raised. It must have taken immeasurable courage for Cass to make a life, to forge a future for herself. Yet judging from the adoration in her husband's eyes and the way her children revered her, Cass had done it and done it well.

Ardith waited for Cass to continue, to explain how all of that had transpired. When it became clear she had nothing more to say, Ardith spoke.

"Thank you for telling me what happened." Her voice was a little unsteady, giving the proof that Cass Jalbert seemed to need that Ardith had been moved by her story.

"I thought you should know," Cass said simply and settled back in the chair again.

She was extraordinary and compelling sitting there. The dark, turned wood and deep-blue shawl draped artfully behind her were the perfect foil for her sun-streaked hair and fair complexion. The way she turned her tattooed face into the light gave proof that she was not cowed by what had happened to her.

What Ardith had done to be deserving of this woman's confidences, she could not say. She had done her best to give form to the woman whose myth and mystery were written so plainly on her face, and yet she'd known there was something missing. Now that Cass had told her story, Ardith could see the fortitude that made this woman unique, the nobility of the struggle she'd endured. Ardith thought that at last she might be able to do Cassandra justice.

Ardith worked quickly after that, her senses humming, her face flushed with concentration, her skills honed sharper by what she'd heard. The changes she made in the nearly finished painting were subtle. She deepened the shadows at the corners of Cassandra's mouth, shifted the shading at the edge of her jaw, and added a crescent-shaped highlight on the point of her chin. She added nuances that deepened the subtext in what had been a painting of a strong and compelling woman.

The light streaming in the back windows of the ranch house had taken on a decidedly golden hue when Ardith stepped back from the portrait and set her brush and pallete aside.

"I think it is finished," she said with a sigh. "You may come and see it if you like."

Cass rose slowly and Ardith could see how much she dreaded viewing the finished painting. "I'm not sure I care to see myself as others see me," Cass said with a hollow laugh.

"I've captured what I wanted to," Ardith answered simply.

Cass came nearer in spite of herself and stood motionless, her shoulders hunched and her arms crossed protectively across her body. A full minute ticked by. Two minutes. Three. Ardith's hands began to sweat. The thudding of her heart seemed loud in the silence.

"Please, say *something*," she finally whispered.

"Is this the way you see me?" Cass asked.

Ardith turned and saw tears glistening on Cass's lashes.

"No! Oh, no!" Ardith moaned, horrified. "I'd hoped to paint you in a way that would make you proud of who you are, that would show the strength I see in you."

"But, Ardith," Cass said, her eyes swimming with tears. "You've made me beautiful!"

The words were filled with wonder, with hope and longing and delight. They were the words of a woman who had been given a vision of herself she had never thought to have, and was still wary of accepting the truth.

Cass reached out and caught Ardith's paint-smudged fingers in her own. "You made me beautiful—in spite of the mark on my face, in spite of everything!"

Emotion prickled in Ardith's throat, and she smiled through the sting of her own tears.

Cassie gave Ardith's hands a hard little squeeze, then spun toward the door. "I can't wait for Hunter to see what wonderful things you've done to me."

"I doubt he'll be surprised," Ardith answered, but Cass had already gone in search of her husband.

Ardith was washing out her brushes when the two of them returned. Cass led him directly to the portrait, then stood fidgeting as he considered it.

"But it's no more beautiful than you are," he whispered. He turned and touched his wife's face, tracing the lines of the tattoo with his fingertips. He smiled as if discovering the wonder of her anew, then lowered his head and kissed her. His mouth moved over hers slowly, lingeringly, with mingled tenderness and passion.

Just watching them together turned Ardith weak with longing.

When he raised his head, Cass looked soft, contented, and well-loved. Hunter smiled down at his wife, a hint of satisfaction hovering at the corners of his lips, and then he raised his gaze to Ardith.

"It's a wonderful portrait," he told her.

"I am pleased that Cass agreed to sit for me."

His reply was slow in coming. "I am, too."

With those three words Hunter revealed how long he'd hoped that Cass would discover what Ardith had helped her to see. Ardith beamed at him, delighted that for all her trials, Cass had found such a man to love her.

"Shall we ask her now?" Cassandra's question broke into Hunter's renewed contemplation of the portrait. He smiled a little and nodded.

"Ask me what?"

Cass cleared her throat. "As you have been able to see for yourself, Meggie has inherited her father's artistic ability. She very much wants to attend the Cowles Art School in Boston. Last winter she sent them samples of her work, and she has been accepted as a student.

"We've been reluctant to let her go," she went on. "She seems too young to go so far from home, and yet we want to give her a chance to make a life for herself. What we hoped was that when you go east, you would agree to take our Meggie with you."

Ardith looked at these two people, seeing the love and concern for their daughter in their eyes and feeling the weight of the trust they were putting in her. "Are you sure that's what you want, to send Meggie away?"

Cass slid a sidelong glance at her husband before she answered. "Meggie is different from our other children.

She wasn't born out here. She isn't connected to this life and this land the way the boys are. She is a young woman of rare accomplishments. She needs something more than we can give her. If you agree to take her with you, we will allow her to attend this school and see how she does."

Ardith could see how difficult this was for them and how worried they were about their daughter.

"Cowles is a well-run and well-respected academy," she hastened to assure them. "I know some of the teachers and have seen displays of the students' work. It seems like a good place for Meggie to begin her studies."

As Ardith spoke she could see both relief and regret in Cass and Hunter's faces. "Would you like me to keep an eye on her while she's in Boston?" Ardith asked.

She already suspected how empty she'd feel once Baird and the children returned to England, and how difficult it was going to be squeezing herself into her old life. Her time in the west had changed her, challenged her, and made her grow. She wasn't sure she'd fit in Boston anymore, but having Meggie there would help.

"I could see that Meggie gets enrolled in school and that she finds suitable lodgings," Ardith went on. There was a good deal more she could do, and Ardith was suddenly glad to have another child entrusted to her.

Hunter curled an arm around his wife and drew her close. "We'd be obliged if you would do that, Ardith," he said, his voice suddenly deep with emotion. He was no more sanguine about Meggie's leaving than her mother was.

It touched Ardith somehow, that this man had taken Meggie and Andrew, Cassandra's children by another man, and come to care so much for them.

She reached across and took both Cass and Hunter's hands in hers. "You needn't worry," she promised them. "I'll take very good care of Meggie."

Sugar Creek Ranch
September 6th, 1882

My dearest Gavin,

It seems that I am to have a young companion on my return trip to Boston. Her name is Meggie Jalbert, and she is the daughter of horse ranchers we have recently met. She has been accepted at Cowles Art School, and her parents have asked me to act as her chaperon while we are traveling.

Meggie is from a most interesting family, one that arrived on our property en route to Cheyenne and provided their own accommodations in the form of a buffalo skin tepee! Meggie's adopted father is a mixed-blood Arikara Indian, and her mother spent nine years as a captive of the Kiowa and Cheyenne. Their story is long and complex, one I will relate to you in its entirety when next we meet.

While they were here, I was privileged to paint an oil portrait of Meggie's mother. It is by far the strongest work I have done, and it has given me the idea to paint a series of portraits of western women. I have made arrangements for several of the ranch wives to sit for me, and I am currently painting one of the local Indian women. I can't say that I have ever felt a stronger attraction to a subject, and I am trying to make the most of my time here.

As my stay draws to a close, I find myself thinking of you with increasing frequency. Every letter you send reminds me of the attractions in Boston—not the least of which is spending time with you. I would delight in attending some of the entertainments you mentioned in your last letter, though at present I am not certain of the exact date of my arrival.

I miss you, too, and sense that we have much to

discuss when I return. I must close for now if this is to reach you in a timely fashion. Be assured that you are constantly in my thoughts.

Your very dear friend,
Ardith

FOURTEEN

$\mathscr{B}$aird sat at the edge of his log-post bed and stared fruitlessly into the dark. He hadn't slept through the night in weeks. No matter how hard he worked or how many hours he spent in the saddle, he would jerk awake in the dead of night with his brain on fire.

He knew from experience it was no use staying in bed. He scrubbed the grit from his eyes, and without bothering to light a lamp, located his trousers and a shirt. He padded barefoot down the stairs, seeking air, seeking space.

He prowled around the house and out onto the porch, finally settling on one of the benches. As if they were creatures of the night stalking nearer, the high peaks of the Big Horns gradually emerged from the blue-black darkness. Something about the weight and bulk of the mountains counterbalanced the responsibilities piling up on his shoulders. Their size and permanence made him feel as if his problems with the children and the ranch and the future were trifling things, things he could somehow resolve.

Finding a way to keep the Sugar Creek afloat was at the

heart of it. If he could round up seventeen hundred steers in the next two weeks, everything would be fine. But as near as he could figure, he was going to be short of that—more than three hundred head short—and he had no idea how to make up the disparity.

If he couldn't manage that, not only would the Sugar Creek and everyone on it be in jeopardy, but he'd be returning to London in disgrace for the second time in less than a year. He'd have failed his uncle and the stockholders and everyone here. He'd have failed his children—and himself.

For the first time in his life, Baird wanted things. He had ambitions of his own. Hunter Jalbert had planted a seed, talking to him about training and breeding horses. During the hours Baird had spent in the saddle between the ranch house and the summer camp, that seed had grown. He'd begun to dream about finding one of those lush little valleys back in the hills and building a horse ranch. He thought he could be happy—and maybe even successful—training and breeding horses like the Jalberts did. But it took money to start a ranch, money Baird wouldn't have unless he managed to get those seventeen hundred steers to market in Cheyenne.

He scrubbed his hands across his face and heaved a sigh. Small wonder he wasn't sleeping.

Just then, the door to the house snapped open. Baird started, jumping half out of his skin.

Ardith stepped onto the porch in an enveloping lawn nightdress and one of Myra's homespun shawls.

"What are you doing out here at this hour?" she whispered.

"What are you?" He wasn't sure he wanted her to know how accustomed he was to prowling around the house in the middle of the night.

"I thought Khy seemed a little feverish when I put him to bed, so I got up to check on him."

"Is he all right?"

"He's fine," she said with a smile, "and probably wouldn't appreciate me creeping into his bedroom in the dark."

Baird eased over on the bench. She accepted his invitation and snuffed the candle she was carrying so it wouldn't draw mosquitoes.

Still, the image of her lingered into the dark, one of a softer Ardith. An Ardith with sleep-smudged features and a shiny, dark braid trailing across her shoulder. He'd caught a glimpse of a delicate collarbone revealed by the neckline of her nightdress and noticed the sway of soft, full breasts shifting beneath the fabric. She smelled sweet and almost gingery, hardy and uncomplicated.

He remembered her scent from that night up in the mountains, remembered breathing her in, remembered holding her in his arms and kissing her. She'd amazed him with the uninhibited way she'd come to him, with the fire in her kiss. With the unexpected delight he'd found with her in his arms, and the hunger he'd carried around with him afterwards. That Ardith—of all women—should prove so pleasing and give him so much astonished him still. And yet the passion between them had seemed right, as natural as breathing.

Beside him, the woman herself stretched out her felt-slippered toes and turned to him. "So why *are* you sitting out here in the middle of the night?"

"I couldn't sleep."

"Are you worried about the ranch?" Trust Ardith to be direct.

"You keep the ledgers. Don't I have reason to be?" When she nodded, he went on. "Do *you* have any ideas about how I can deliver the profit the stockholders expect?"

"Find a couple hundred steers tucked away in a canyon somewhere?" she suggested. She studied him for one long moment. "All this has come to mean a great deal to you, hasn't it?"

"Beyond meeting my uncle's expectations, you mean? Beyond the ownership of the ranch and the cowboys' jobs?" He sighed, and when he went on his voice was deep and a little ragged.

"I don't want to lose what we've found out here. Even after all we've been through in these last few months with the children and the cows and the ranch, this has been a very special time—the best in my life—and I don't want to give it up. I want to stay out here. I like this country. I like what it seems to expect of me, and the man I am when I come close to meeting those expectations."

He knew she'd understand. She was as affected by this place as he was. It cut something loose in both of them.

"Do you have something in mind?" she asked him softly.

He held his breath, knowing he was about to divulge his most closely guarded secret. "I'd like to set up an operation like the Jalberts have."

"You want to raise horses?"

"And train them," he confirmed. At least she hadn't laughed at him. "Horses and hunting are all I know. If I started out working with mustangs the way Hunter did, maybe in time I could scrape together enough to buy some breeding stock. It would be hard work, but no harder than what I've been doing here."

It seemed right somehow to be talking about this with her. Ardith had ambitions of her own. She had discovered another part of herself since she'd come west. She'd found the courage to take her ideas and her talents and turn them into something wonderful.

He wanted to do that, too. Perhaps that affinity was what drew him to her, why her opinions mattered so much. He needed to know she believed he could succeed at this.

Ardith bobbed her head slowly, consideringly. "The way you broke the mustangs last spring seemed like magic. I wouldn't have believed anyone could do what you did with those animals unless I'd seen it myself. Do you think you could round up and train enough mustangs to make it pay?"

Baird shrugged, knowing he needed her practicality to help him make a plan. "I'd have far greater expenses than we have here. I'd need to buy and fence the land. Build a house and barn. Well-conditioned horses need grain as well as grass. We'd have to have equipment and some hands to keep things going while I did the training."

"What would you do about the children if you started your own ranch?"

He heard the concern in her voice, and he could just make out the fine, thin line between her brows.

I'd want to keep them here with me. I'd want to ask you to stay on with us, he almost said. But then, why should she stay? Ardith had a home, friends, and responsibilities back in Massachusetts. Beyond her affection for his children, he had nothing at all to offer her.

Unless he asked her to be his wife.

The thought astounded him, made him go hot and cold and achy inside. He'd never for a moment thought about marrying again. He hadn't wanted another wife. And even if he had, he would never have considered Ardith. She was his sister-in-law. In England marrying her wouldn't even be legal!

Yet while he was reproaching himself for thinking such things, unexpected images rose in his mind: of Ardith standing straight and resolute as she faced the mountain lion, of her hovering over Khy when he was ill, of how she'd given him the strength to go to China the night Matt Hastings died, of the pride in her eyes when she showed him the portrait she'd made of Cass Jalbert. What man wouldn't want a woman like her?

He found himself thinking of the way she looked tonight in that shapeless bed-gown and the lush, full figure that must lie beneath it. Of what it would be like to strip that gown away and take her to his bed. Of how her eyes would go smoky and dark when he made love to her.

The intensity of the visions made him unbearably aware of her beside him. He hadn't realized he'd come to think of Ardith quite that way.

"What about China and the boys?" Ardith asked him more insistently.

Baird blinked his imaginings away. "I'd want the children here with me, of course."

"Good," she said.

He let his breath out on a long, deep sigh. "But I don't think any of that is possible. In order for me to stay and start a ranch, I'd have to be taking a whole lot more steers to market than I'm going to. So I guess for all my lofty ambitions, I've failed again."

Never in his life had he hated that notion more than he did tonight, nor had he imagined that a crumbling dream could weigh so heavily on a man.

Ardith must have heard the resignation in his voice because she laced her hand through the crook of his arm. "It's wrong to blame yourself for this," she consoled him. "Just because you've decided to take responsibility for something, doesn't mean it's all your fault if things go wrong."

"Then who *should* I blame for being short of cattle?"

"Blame the winter snow or the summer heat," she told him softly. "Blame the Indians or the wolves. Blame the rustlers."

"The rustlers," he said. "The rustlers we've searched for and still can't find. The cows that disappear like they've dissolved in the rain."

"Blame anyone but yourself, Baird, because you've done your best."

"I've tried," he conceded.

She leaned a little nearer, the fullness of her breast brushing warm against him. "Even if this doesn't work out the way you hope, you mustn't let it change your mind about starting a ranch. We'll find some other way to make it work."

He turned to her, and even in the dimness, he could see the spark of conviction in her eyes. It drew him to her, close enough to feel the wash of her breath against his cheek, close enough for him to recognize the succor she was offering.

He hated to admit how worn and worried he was, how much he needed her tenderness. He slid one arm around her waist and gathered her against him.

She came, looking up at him with eyes that were wide and soft and a mouth that bowed gently, inviting his kiss. He lowered his head and took advantage of the solace she was offering.

She tasted of recent sleep, warm and wholesome and faintly dewy. It made him imagine what it would be like to turn on his pillow and find her beside him in the morning twilight. He could imagine kissing her awake and having her smile as he skimmed his hands over her night-warm flesh. He could imagine how she would turn to welcome him with rising desire and whispery sighs.

She was welcoming him now, her voice shivery as she whispered, "Baird. Oh, Baird."

He drank his name from her lips, seeking the warm, soft contours of her mouth; the sleek mysterious hollow of her throat; the grainy, sensual slide of her tongue against his. He wanted her, needed her with an intensity he had never in this world expected. How, in a few short months, could this woman have gone from a harridan to a temptress? From nemesis to confidante? How had she come to mean so much to him?

He raised his head and looked down at her almost as if

he needed to be sure it was Ardith in his arms, Ardith whose body flowed so naturally against his. Her face was luminous, soft with wonder, as if she were as amazed as he was by how right this seemed. He could feel her trembling against him.

Deep inside, he was trembling, too. "Ardith," he whispered, curling his hand around her breast. It more than filled his palm, full and lush and tempting. Awash in her femininity, his body stirred. "Ardith, I want you."

She went perfectly still beside him, staring up at him, barely breathing. With her bound so close, he could sense the brief, difficult struggle inside her. She wanted him, too. He knew it as surely as he knew his own name, yet she was afraid. And God knows she had every right to be. Certainly no one had hurt her the way he had; no man on earth had less to offer her. But he'd hoped—

Well, it didn't matter what he'd hoped. He suddenly knew that no matter what confidences they'd shared, no matter how much she'd given him already, he'd asked too much of her this time. He didn't begrudge her her need for security; he wanted her to be safe. Even from him. So when she shifted away, he let her go.

She scrambled to her feet and stood there tugging the shawl more tightly around her, collecting herself. *Becoming Ardith.* Becoming Ardith the way she always did when something frightened or unsettled her. He was just sorry it was him who'd made her feel that way.

"I'm sorry—" he began.

"Don't be sorry," she insisted. "You don't have anything to be sorry for—unless you give up on that ranch, unless you give up on yourself. There's far more inside you, Baird Northcross, than you know."

She turned in a rustle of homespun and lawn, and left him alone on the porch. He sat there staring into the dark, reliving the taste of her on his mouth; the flow of her sweet, lush flesh against him. And he realized that tonight it was Ardith Merritt and his unexpected need for her that was going to keep him sleepless until dawn.

Sugar Creek Ranch
September 11th, 1882

My Dearest Gavin,

I am writing to thank you for the extra copies you sent of "Abigail Goose Goes to Town." Each of the hands here on the ranch has requested a copy to remember me by, and after the incident in the summer camp I wrote you about, I simply can't refuse them.

Meggie Jalbert and I should be arriving in Boston about the middle of next month, and I must say I am eager to get her settled and enrolled in her art classes. I am so looking forward to introducing the two of you. She is such a bright young thing, and I know you will be as taken with her as I am.

If the sale of the Sugar Creek cattle goes well, Baird has decided to use his share of the proceeds to start a horse ranch of his own out here. Since he will doubtless be busy securing the land and overseeing construction of a house, I thought I might offer to return to Cheyenne and stay with the children while he gets things started.

Would you mind terribly, my dear Gavin, if I did that? I know it would mean forgoing some of the plans you and I have made, but I feel as if I owe this to Baird by way of thanks. He is the one who suggested that I start painting western subjects, and he has afforded me the opportunity to explore this magnificent country first-hand.

He has changed so much since I came west, becoming the kind of man and the kind of father I always hoped he would become. In light of that, I want to give him this chance to fulfill his dreams. I hope you will under-

*stand my reasons for making this offer, and be patient
with me for a little while longer.*

> *Your affectionate friend,*
> *Ardith*

"Randy can't just be gone!" Durban exclaimed, looking
up at his father from where he and Buck were squatting
together examining the shattered fence.

"I just don't see how that blasted bull could have
busted boards as thick as this," Johnson said, checking to
see if the ends had been cut. "I wouldn't have said any
animal was strong enough."

Baird stood silent, feeling like those fence rails were his
dreams, just so much scattered wreckage on the ground.

Until last night Randy the Bull had been right here in
the breeding paddock, quite happily doing his part to in-
crease the quantity and quality of the herd for seasons to
come. Now he was gone—just like the several hundred
other cows that had strayed or been killed or stolen in
these last months. Ardith would have to write Randy
down in her big ledger, make a record in black and white
of another loss, another of his failures.

Baird struggled with the weariness that rolled over him,
the sense of fatalism and desolation that had become all
too familiar. "We can track Randy, can't we, Buck?" Baird
finally asked.

Buck pushed up from his knees. "We can sure as hell
try."

"Khy loves Randy," Durban cried, running after them
as they went to the barn to saddle their horses. "We've got
to find him."

Baird would have preferred to leave the boy at the
ranch in case they ran into trouble, but Durban stuck to
them like a cocklebur. Since he'd learned to ride, Durban
had become far too fond of roaming, spending too much

time by himself—or with unsuitable companions. At least this way, Baird reasoned as they headed south, he'd know where his son was.

At first the big bull's trail was easy enough to follow, though the wide swathe of trampled grass seemed too straight to be made by an animal wandering by himself and too directly headed toward the Double T. Baird guided his horse along the track, wondering if Cullen McKay was fool enough, or arrogant enough, to take Randy directly to his ranch. Surely he knew the penalties for rustling. Or maybe Cullen thought Baird would care more about protecting the Northcross name than pressing charges.

Still, Baird was relieved when the trail shied off toward a line of bluffs that lay to the west. He hadn't wanted to have to accuse his cousin of something so reprehensible.

They'd ridden a whole lot closer to those bluffs and the mountains that mounded up behind them when they found what they were looking for—the clear print of an iron-shod hoof among Randy's tracks.

"I knew someone was leading him!" Buck exclaimed, squatting down on his haunches at the edge of a creek.

Durban didn't say much. He just chewed his lip and kept glancing off into the distance.

The ground turned rocky after they left the stream, making the tracks harder to see. Baird watched the bluffs drawing closer, and when they reached the base, the faint line of hoofprints wound in and out of the weathered outcroppings of wind-cut stone. Then abruptly the prints disappeared, leaving them face to face with a solid sweep of sandstone wall.

"Where the hell did he go?" Baird demanded, staring up the face of the wall, as if he expected Randy to be perched on top looking down at them.

"Damned if I know," Buck muttered and dismounted.

He walked a dozen yards one way and a dozen yards back, staring at the ground and looking for signs.

Baird should have joined him. Two pair of eyes were better than one, but he stayed in the saddle anyway. He stared out across acres of grassland, a sense of desolation weighing on him. Despite his fascination with this country, it seemed unbearably bleak today. Flat and lonely and barren beneath that wide, oppressive sky. Maybe Wyoming didn't hold the opportunities he thought it did. Maybe he'd been deluding himself when he'd decided he wanted to make a life out here. Maybe a man couldn't change enough to escape his failures.

The rhythmic squeak of leather intruded on his musings, and he looked across to where Durban sat on his horse a few feet away. The boy was bobbing in the saddle, rubbing his palms up and down against his thighs.

"Is something bothering you, son?" Baird asked him.

Durban jumped as if someone had jabbed him with spurs. "No!" he denied hotly. "Well, maybe. I—I just don't like this place."

A chill feathered the hair on the back of Baird's neck. He wasn't sure he liked it, either.

Just then, Buck came toward them, shaking his head. "I'll be damned if I know where that bull went. It's like he was plucked up by angels and set down somewhere else!"

In these last months Baird had come to rely on Buck's skills, his cow sense, his basic grasp of ranch finance, and his unerring instincts about the weather. It was hard to accept that the old foreman wasn't able to track Randy any further than this.

"You don't know where he went?"

The older man shrugged. "Maybe there's something here I just don't see."

Baird didn't see much either, but he eased his horse back along the base of the bluffs looking for anything

Buck could have missed. He couldn't find any sign of where Randy might have disappeared to, either.

"Let's ride back to where the trail is clearer," he suggested. "Maybe we'll see something if we look at things another way."

They were nearly back to the creek when a rider approached. None of them was surprised that it was Cullen McKay.

"Hullo," he hailed them, drawing his horse to a stop. "What brings you out this way?"

"Randy the Bull broke his fence last night," Durban answered. His words seemed almost a reproach, and Baird slid a long, speculative look in his son's direction.

"You've lost that fine Hereford bull you paid the sun and moon for a few months back?" McKay asked, sounding incredulous.

"Yeah, that's him," Buck confirmed. "We followed him as far as the bluffs, then lost his trail. *You* haven't seen him, have you, McKay?" Johnson's words stopped just short of an accusation.

"Can't say as I have."

"Are you *sure* you haven't seen him?" Durban's tone was taut, almost pleading.

"Well, no, son." Cullen shifted his gaze toward the boy, focusing on him in a way that made Baird nudge Dandy forward to shield his son from the chill in the other man's eyes. "What makes you think I've seen him?"

Durban ducked his head. "I just thought you might."

"I do think it's fine how you're out helping your father look," Cullen went on. "I know just how much he must appreciate you doing that."

Baird tightened up on Dandy's reins and put himself directly between Durban and McKay. He didn't understand the other man's animosity, but he wasn't about to let McKay direct it at his boy.

Cullen backed off a little and gave him a poisonous

smile. "So, in addition to this bull, I understand you've lost a lot of other stock this season."

Baird braced his forearm on his saddle horn and leaned toward McKay. "What makes you think that?"

Cullen gave an almost imperceptible shrug. "I hear people talk. I know Buck asked Thornton Watkins if he'd had trouble with wolves, and you talked to Frewen about losing stock to the Indians. I know what Ardith's told me. And Durban."

Baird suspected the boy had been carrying tales, but the confirmation surprised him anyway. He must have given his feelings away, because Cullen's eyes lit with satisfaction.

"It'll be a shame if you don't meet your quota," McKay continued. "You'll have to look me up at the Cheyenne Club when you get to town and let me know how you made out."

"The only quota you should be worrying about, McKay, is your own," Buck spoke up. "Now, we've got a bull to track, if you don't mind us doing that."

Cullen shrugged. "It's all free range, old man. Track him wherever you like. I'll ask my men if they've seen that bull of yours running loose, but I wouldn't expect to find him anytime soon."

McKay turned his horse toward the Double T and spurred away.

Buck sat scowling, watching him go. "Couldn't help bragging a little, could he?"

"Is that what he was doing?" Baird asked, feeling as if there had been something a good deal more insidious at work.

"He was bragging, all right," Buck answered with a nod. "Goddamned arrogant son of a bitch."

Durban didn't express an opinion on the matter. He just watched with apprehension as McKay rode out of sight.

FIFTEEN

Boston, Massachusetts
September 18th, 1882

My Very Dear Ardith,

*I read your letter of the eleventh with great disappoint-
ment and dismay. I find it nearly incomprehensible
that you would consider returning to that rough, unciv-
ilized place for the sake of a man who has repeatedly
taken advantage of your generosity. But my purpose in
writing this is not to disparage a man I have never met.
It is to broach a subject that has been close to my heart
for quite some time.*

*Surely, my dear Ardith, it has not escaped your no-
tice that in the course of the letters we have exchanged,
my feelings for you have altered. When you left Boston,
I considered you a dear friend and colleague; a delight-
ful companion for a lecture or an evening of theatre;
perhaps even a confidante. I have reason to believe that*

the admiration and respect I felt for you was reciprocated.

But now, after nearly five months of correspondence, I feel as if I have gained a more intimate understanding of your good nature, and my esteem for you has grown apace of it. I have been touched by the joys and sorrows you have seen fit to share with me, and I feel that they have bound us together at a level of communion I have rarely felt with anyone. Through the letters and our shared confidences, I have come to love you, dear Ardith, with all the passion in my heart.

It is because I have come to care for you so deeply that I am writing to ask you to be my wife. The letters we have exchanged have convinced me that you are the woman I have been seeking all my life, someone with whom I can share my thoughts, my ideals, and my love. Someone who appreciates the blessed closeness of family, and to whom beauty and culture are as vital as breathing. I want you here with me, Ardith, to be a part of my days and part of my nights. I want to hold you in my arms and never part from you. If you consent to marry me, I will shower you with my devotion for the rest of our days.

In the hope that you will give me the answer I seek, I am sending my grandmother's emerald as a betrothal ring. Please advise me of your willingness to wear it and be my bride. I look forward to meeting you at the railroad station three weeks hence, and welcoming you into my world and my life as my fiancée.

Let me tell you once more before I close how deeply I care for you, and how desperately I want you with me. I love you, Ardith, and I breathlessly await the assurance that you love and want me, too.

With my undying devotion,
Gavin

Ardith sank into the chair at the head of the long pine table, too breathless to think, too weak-kneed to stand. Phrases leaped out from the letter in her hands, saying that Gavin felt "bound to her," that he had come to love her "with all the passion in his heart." That he wanted to "shower her with devotion" for the rest of their days.

Oh, Lord! Dear Lord! This was what she'd yearned for all these years, the gossamer dream she'd woven from gallant kindnesses and warm half-smiles. Night after night she'd lain in that prim little bed in that prim little room at her uncle's house and imagined what it would be like to lie beside Gavin in the dark, to be enfolded in his arms, and taste his kisses.

Each time she prepared to go into Boston with her portfolio of sketches, she had looked into the mirror in the entry hall, adjusted her hat, and whispered to herself: "Perhaps today he will notice me. Perhaps today he will see me differently."

Now finally he had seen her as she had longed to be seen, and it was her words, not the cant of her bonnet, that made the difference.

She pressed her palms to her flaming cheeks. Gavin needed her, desired her as his wife. The thought of what that meant stole through her, how his mouth would crush down on hers; how his broad hands would stroke over her flesh; how his eyes of cobalt blue would hold her in thrall.

She blinked the image away, feeling oddly disoriented.

It was Gavin who wanted her—he had looked past the plainness of her face and the difference in their ages to the woman underneath. He had fallen in love with her thoughts and her words and her pictures. Gavin had come to want her for herself.

But exactly which self did Gavin want? Ardith suddenly wondered. Did he want the one who had saved herself from a mountain lion, or the one who could unerringly navigate the tangle of streets in downtown Boston? Did he want the Ardith who bathed in the creek or the one who could spontaneously translate the libretto of a Wagner opera? Did he want the woman who could run his house, hostess his salons and dinner parties, or the one who would lie every night for the rest of her life listening for the wind across the prairie? *Which one of those women did she want to be?*

She looked down at the box that had come with the letter.

"In the hope that you will give me the answer I seek," Gavin had written, "I am sending my grandmother's emerald as a betrothal ring." It was a lovely gift, thoughtful, romantic, cloaked in tradition, and bound to Boston as if by silken chains. It was not a token he had given lightly, nor one she could accept without considerable thought.

Still, she longed to see the ring, the treasure Gavin had offered up as a token of his love. She spread the layers of excelsior in the outer box and withdrew a small black velvet jeweler's case. Holding her breath, she lifted the lid.

Nestled inside on a bed of gleaming white satin was the most exquisite ring she had ever seen. The emerald was huge, square-cut, set in gold, and surrounded by seed-pearls. Ardith lifted the ring from its satin nest and might well have slipped it onto her finger if she hadn't heard the footsteps on the porch and the back door opening.

Needing time to consider Gavin's offer and all it meant, Ardith fumbled the ring back into its box and slid the velvet lid in place. China came up beside her before she had managed to tuck everything out of sight.

"Did you get a gift?" the girl asked, her eyes alight.

Ardith shook her head. "It's just something I asked Gavin to send to me."

"That *is* from Gavin, then?"

Ardith hesitated. "Yes."

"May I see what he sent you?"

Ardith jammed the velvet box back in among the curls

of wooden packaging. "It's nothing really," she assured her niece. "Nothing you'd be interested in. Nothing."

China gave her a long speculative glance. Knowing the girl's perceptiveness, Ardith did her best to divert her.

She gestured to another of the packages lying on the table. "There's something there for you from your grandfather."

China picked up the box and hefted it. "It's sweet of grandfather to think of us," China began, "but he doesn't seem to realize there's not much call out here for white kid gloves and hair ribbons. I think I'll let Khy open it; I like how excited he gets where there's something in the mail for him."

"What I was wondering," China went on, "was if you know how soon Hunter Jalbert will be bringing Meggie to the ranch?"

Ardith drew a breath, lightheaded with relief at having turned China's attention from Gavin's gift. She wanted to keep the news of his proposal to herself for a time.

"They'll be arriving any day now, I should think," she answered. "Your father has rounded up almost all the cattle he's taking to Cheyenne. The Jalberts know we'll be leaving a week after the herd, so they'll have Meggie here in plenty of time to go with us."

"And when we reach Cheyenne," China verified, "you and Meggie will be taking the train to Boston?"

At those simple words a wave of grief broke through Ardith, all but bringing her to her knees. Her chest ached with longing, and she had to tighten her fingers around the box Gavin had sent to still their trembling.

She had known for weeks that leaving was inevitable, that her time in Wyoming was coming to an end. She had known she was losing this small perfect piece of her life, this small perfect piece of herself. Why did China's simple words cast that loss in such sharp relief?

"If we're going to get Meggie enrolled in her classes,

we'll need to leave as soon as we get to Cheyenne," she said, trying to hide the depth of her regrets. "Once your papa has concluded his business, you'll all head for New York and take a steamship from there to England."

"I can hardly believe we're going back," China said on a sigh, "after everything that's happened."

Ardith curled an arm around China's shoulders and drew her close. "I know, sweetheart. I'm so proud of you for the grown-up way you've accepted Matt's death."

China snuggled against her, a child seeking reassurance, a half-grown woman with wisdom of her own. "I'll always love him, Aunt Ardith. But I know I have my life ahead of me."

Ardith drew China closer still. "I think caring for Matt, knowing how good and fine he was, will help you choose the right man for your husband when that time comes."

"He'll have to be someone special to be better than Matt," China said with a catch in her voice.

"Yes, he will." Ardith wrapped both arms around her niece and pressed a kiss into China's hair. "He'll be someone wonderful, someone who admires you and appreciates you. You'll recognize him when you find him because Matt taught you what to expect."

"Have you ever found a man like that, Aunt Ardith?" the girl asked her.

The question made Ardith look long and hard at her own life: at the woman she was and the woman she wanted to become.

Yes, she thought and glanced down at the box she'd received from Gavin just today. She thought of the beautiful ring tucked inside and the promise this wonderful man had asked her to make. She thought of Baird, who'd touched her heart and held her when she cried. Of Baird who had never asked Ardith anything and never would. Yes, she thought. *Oh, yes.*

She closed her eyes against the sting of tears.

• • •

*B*aird didn't make it back to the house until after the children were abed. Ardith had been sitting up sketching, wanting to tell him about Gavin's proposal before she mentioned it to anyone else. But when Baird finally dragged in, he looked so worn and preoccupied that Ardith decided to hold her peace.

"Have you had anything to eat?" she asked him as he sank into a chair at the end of the table.

When he shook his head, she bustled off to the kitchen and put the kettle on to boil. She fixed him a plate, slicing roast beef and bread, scooping out helpings of coleslaw and Myra's beans. She spooned canned peaches into a dish and sliced gingerbread to go with them.

Baird was asleep with his head on his arms when she got back, sprawled as if his bones were dissolving. She settled the tray of food on the table, and stood frowning down at him.

His lashes lay in the darkened hollows beneath his eyes. Concern for the ranch and the children had scored new lines into that beautiful face. She reached across and stroked his hair to awaken him, realizing that the thick, dark strands were damp, as if he'd taken time to bathe the smell of cows away before he came back to the house.

His eyes snapped open at her touch.

"I've made you something to eat," she said quietly, giving him a moment to realize where he was.

He straightened in the chair and looked at the tray before him. "I must have nodded off," he acknowledged with a vague half-smile.

"You must have," she agreed as she settled herself on the far side of the table.

He tucked into the food as if he hadn't eaten in days, and while he demolished the helpings of beef and bread and beans, Ardith sharpened her pencil and turned her sketchbook to a crisp, new page. She'd drawn portraits of each of the children, Buck and Myra and the hands, but she hadn't caught Baird's likeness yet. Her news could wait until she had.

For a moment she simply stared at him. The rhythm of her breathing slowed. A flush of concentration mounted in her cheeks. She compressed her lips and scrawled a few tentative lines across the page.

With the flick of her wrist she caught the shape of him, the angle of his shoulders and the tilt of his head. With firmer strokes she delineated the breadth of his brow; the shape of his nose; the high, broad slant of those sculpted cheekbones. She shaded the underside of his jaw, bringing the turning into sharp relief.

"Don't you need me to sit still for this?" he asked her.

The sound of his voice startled her. "You haven't time for me to do a proper sitting, and I'm determined to make sketches of everyone before I leave. I hope when we reach Cheyenne we can find a photographer to take all our pictures."

He turned his attention to the peaches and gingerbread. "I've been thinking about asking Durban to help us drive the herd to Cheyenne. He's been keeping up with the hands as if we were paying him. What do you think?"

Ardith lifted her pencil from the page as she considered it. She wondered if Baird knew the chance he was taking by suggesting this. Durban might just as well choose not to go, and she wondered how Baird would take it if he did.

"Buck and I will be there to keep an eye on him, and the hands will, too," he went on. "And with poor Matt gone, we could use the help."

"I think it would do Durban a world of good to go with you," Ardith answered carefully.

"You don't think I'd be expecting too much of him?"

She could see the uncertainty in his face: the hoping and the wishing and the dreading.

"I think you should ask a good deal more."

"He might refuse," Baird hedged.

"Maybe because you expect him to."

Baird was convinced he deserved his son's censure, but Ardith had begun to realize how much a part Ariel had played in causing the rift between them. Now if only Durban would give his father a chance, and Baird would stop blaming himself . . .

With a huff of frustration, Ardith spilled a new filigree of lines across the page. Baird's likeness was there; she had to capture the humanity.

And Baird seemed vastly human tonight. He made her want to soothe the creases of weariness and worry that wove across his brow, but she drew them instead. She shaded vulnerability into the corners of that sensual mouth instead, delineated the v of frustration that gathered between his eyes, instead.

She sensed an angry desolation about him. He wasn't going to have enough steers to meet his obligations in Cheyenne. He didn't have to tell her, Ardith knew, and she ached for what that shortfall was doing to him.

Baird shifted in his chair and reached for his mug of tea. "When you showed me the portrait you made of Cass Jalbert, I saw so much more to her than when I looked at her myself. It makes me wonder what I'll see when I look at the picture you're making of me."

She heard the fear in his voice and didn't know how to reassure him. Seeing beyond the subject was an instinctive thing, part perception, part emotion, and part magic.

"What is it you want to see?" she asked him instead.

Baird thought for a moment. "A far better man than I was when I came here. One who accepts responsibility and is aware of someone besides himself. A man who has ambitions of his own." He held her gaze with his. "I never believed that people could change," he said, his voice low, "but I think I have."

Ardith knew her heart was in her eyes. "You have changed," she told him, "and I'm so proud of the man you are becoming."

He retreated a little, sipping his tea. "You're implying I'm not finished yet."

Ardith's pencil danced, clarifying and refining. "I don't think anyone is ever finished. I think we are always in the process of becoming someone else."

"Are you, Ardith?" he asked her.

"Of course I am. Things happened today that changed me," she answered, wondering if he would detect the irony in her tone. "And tomorrow I may turn into someone else entirely."

She'd spent most of the afternoon thinking how she would tell Baird about Gavin's proposal, and she knew she would never have a better opportunity. But the words wouldn't come.

It wasn't as if Baird was going to object to her marrying Gavin. It wasn't as if he was going to offer her an alternative. Yet no matter how she tried, she couldn't seem to force the words up her throat.

She lowered her gaze to the portrait to hide her confusion, and realized she was pleased with what she'd done. She scrawled "A. E. Merritt" at the bottom of the page and came to her feet.

"Do you want to see the drawing?"

Now that the moment was upon him, Baird seemed reluctant. "You haven't shown me with cloven hooves and a pitchfork, have you?"

She held out the sketchbook, inviting him, challenging him to have a look.

His hand wavered a little as he reached for the pad of paper. He studied the drawing for a very long time. "Is this how you see me?" he asked her, looking up at where she'd come to stand beside his chair.

She could see the emotions gather at the backs of his eyes, dark and intense and disbelieving. She was suddenly afraid she'd hurt him.

"Don't—don't you like it?"

"You've made me look like some knight errant riding off to do battle against all odds."

She heard the accusation in his tone and looked down at the sketchbook again. She had drawn him as he was, more kind than inconsiderate, more caring than insensitive, more noble than contemptible. Less of a rakehell, and so much more of a man. She had portrayed both his vulnerability and his strength, the paradox she'd found in him. The things that drew her to him, and to the man he was becoming a little more each day.

"It's the way I see you."

She looked down into his face and realized he was afraid to believe in the good and strength and nobility she saw in him, though she could tell how desperately he wanted to. She wished she could convince him of his own worth, but that was something he had to discover for himself. Something he had to recognize in his children's eyes. Something he had to acknowledge in the deference the cowboys paid him. Something he had to allow himself to believe in.

All Ardith could offer was understanding, encouragement, and tenderness. She gave him that, reaching out to touch his cheek, trailing her fingertips along his jaw. She left a dark smudge in her wake, a comma-shaped curl of carbon that tracked from the corner of his eye to the corner of his lips.

In dismay she rummaged in her pocket for a handkerchief. "I'm afraid I've put a mark on you," she apologized.

Baird caught her wrist and held her still. "What you've done is put *your* mark on me."

Ardith stood there staring down at him, barely able to breathe. He had left his mark on her, too, once so long ago. Because of him her life had changed. Because of him she had discovered the best and the worst about herself. Because of him she'd realized what she wanted her life to become.

She wanted him to mark her again. Now. Tonight. Because of what this time with him had meant to her.

Not taking time to consider the consequences, Ardith bent her head and kissed him. She could tell she'd taken him by surprise. He stiffened a little, then raised his chin, opening his mouth beneath hers.

A wave of awareness moved between them.

Was it meant to be like this? Ardith wondered as spangles of delight glimmered through her. Was she supposed to like the taste of him so much, the sweet peachy spice that clung to him? Was she supposed to want to cup his face in her hands and hold him to her mouth? Did he like kissing her as much as she liked kissing him?

But then she thought he must, because his hands came around her waist; his fingers splayed, his thumbs brushing along the front of her blouse. The contact spread warmth up her ribs and along the underside of her breasts. It was a potent sensation, one she was already enjoying far too much.

Yet she braced her hands on the arms of his chair and leaned over him. He made an appreciative sound down deep in his throat, and she shivered at her own boldness.

The kiss gathered intensity.

He opened his mouth, inviting her to taste the soft inner margins of his lips. She did the same and felt the brush of his tongue against her. He made a languorous exploration, laving the bow of her mouth, slicking the wide, sensitive curve of her bottom lip. He slipped past her teeth to brush the tip of her tongue with his. It was a singular sensation, one that seemed to ripple to far more intimate places.

She bent nearer, discovering just how ripe and yielding that sensual mouth could be, how warm and enticing. Their tongues slid sinuously together.

He squeezed her waist, his hands riding upward along her corset stays, compressing her ribs, making it hard for her to get her breath. His hands rose higher until his thumbs traced the lower border of her breasts. Beneath her clothes her nipples tightened, the whisper-soft lawn of her chemise abrading them.

"Baird," she whispered against his mouth. "Oh, Baird."

She'd tried so hard to sate herself with drawing him, with detailing every turning and every hollow of his beautiful face, but drawing wasn't enough. Now she'd traced those lines on living flesh; she'd kissed his mouth. She'd sliced her fingers through the crisp, damp waves of his night-black hair, and still she wanted more.

She wanted him to make love to her.

She raised her head and looked down into his face. She could see the high flush of color beneath his sun-browned skin, hear the heightened tempo of his breathing.

"I want you to leave your mark on me," she whispered.

"What?"

"I want you to leave your mark on me." She wondered if she had the courage to say the rest of it, to tell him what she felt, what she wanted. She'd refused him that night on the porch, that night when her loss hadn't seemed so great, when their parting hadn't seemed so imminent. Or final.

She took a shaky breath. "I want you to make love to me."

His face went still. His eyes sought hers, his pupils wide with wariness.

"I want us to have tonight. I want you to touch me and

hold me and show me all the things I've never had the chance to learn."

"Ardith, are you sure?" There was incredulity in his tone and confusion—and eagerness. The wariness that had been in his eyes became concern. "What you're asking me isn't something to be undertaken lightly, Ardith, and I've hurt you so much already."

"Will you hurt me again?"

"No, of course not. Not if I can help it," he amended. "But making love with someone touches you, awakens your emotions. It makes you vulnerable in a very particular way—"

"Are you afraid of that?"

He hesitated before he answered her, and whatever stock he took of his own emotions surprised him. She could see it in his eyes. "No, I'm not afraid. It's too late to be afraid."

She wondered what he meant, but knew this was no time for questions. "I'm not afraid, either."

She straightened and held out her hand in invitation. He rose and took it, binding her fingers in his own. He let her lead him to her bedchamber, and he closed the door behind them.

She lit the lamp, but kept the wick turned low so that shadows softened the contours of the room. She stood at the foot of the bed, waiting. Now that they were here together she was not sure of what should happen next.

He went to her and cupped her face, searching her eyes for any hint of uncertainty. But Ardith was not uncertain. She wanted him, wanted this. For almost half her life she'd wanted it.

As if he were convinced, he lowered his head and kissed her. He held her to his mouth, sipping her in a way that made her lips tingle and her breath catch. She curled her hands around his waist, drawing him against her.

He fluttered kisses over her face, brushing her cheek,

the corner of her eye, her temples, and her brow. He bit her earlobe, sending shivers bursting through her.

He kissed the pale, vulnerable column of her throat. As her head fell back, he tightened his arms around her, holding her fast as a swirl of delight took hold of her. He nibbled lower until the high, starched collar of her riding blouse barred his way.

He settled her on her feet and raised his hands to the narrow black ribbon that threaded beneath the collar of her blouse. With a single motion he demolished the bow and sought the buttons down the front of her shirt. As he slipped them from their holes, his hands brushed warm against her.

When the crisp, tucked fabric was open to the waist, he kissed from the hollow at the base of her throat to the top of her chemise. The sensation of his mouth against that newly exposed flesh was shocking enough to make Ardith gasp.

He freed her cuffs and slipped the garment down her arms. "You're blushing, Ardith," he whispered.

"I know," she whispered back. "You make me want to blush for what I'm thinking, for what else I want you to do to me."

He gave a shaky laugh and draped a necklace of kisses around her throat. He lingered over a small sensitive spot in the hollow of her collarbone and paused at the apex of her shoulder. He nuzzled her nape, breathing against her skin in a way that sent shivers shooting the length of her back.

He worked his way through the layers of her clothes until she stood before him clad only in her lawn chemise. He looked down at her and smiled.

"I think I've been wanting to do this forever," he whispered. He began to strip the heavy tortoiseshell hairpins from her hair, letting them spatter onto the carpet of clothes beneath their feet and clatter onto the floor.

As he dropped them—three pins, four—Ardith felt her topknot slide. She shivered a little at the feel of his hands in her hair, at the unexpected intimacy of his touch. More pins fell—five pins, six.

The loops of her tightly bound hair unfurled across her shoulders and spilled down her back. They tumbled to her waist in a straight brown fall. Hers was thick, heavy hair, and it should have veiled her body from his view. Instead she felt more naked than before, as if she'd forfeited the last of her protection.

No man but a husband saw a woman with her hair hanging down, no man but a lover was granted this ultimate intimacy. By simply standing here in such disarray, she'd as much as told him that she loved him.

He must have seen the turmoil in her eyes because he paused, the last hairpin still in his hand. "Are you having second thoughts?"

Was she?

"No." She wanted this night with Baird, knowing she'd never have another.

He bent his head and kissed her. Gently, sweetly, with slow wondrous tenderness. He kissed her without touching her anywhere else; kissed her without tangling his hands in her hair, though she sensed how much he wanted to; kissed her as if they could stand here all night luxuriating in the simmering pleasure of his mouth on hers. She was loose-limbed and trembling when he was done.

"Good," he said, as if he knew very well what his kisses had done to her. "Take off your boots and stockings and get into bed."

She did as he had bidden her, then folded back the well-washed quilt that passed for a coverlet and tugged open the rough cotton sheets. She climbed between them.

He hung his gunbelt over the foot of the bed and took off his boots. "Have you ever seen a naked man before?"

Ardith flushed again. "They won't let women in anatomy classes at art schools," she told him, watching mesmerized as he made quick work of the buttons down the front of his blue-striped shirt. "I—I've drawn from castings, though, and viewed a good deal of Classical sculpture."

But none of the castings she'd drawn or the sculpture she'd seen had prepared her for the long, lean lines of Baird Northcross's body. His wide shoulders tapered toward his waist in a series of strong, angular planes. He had narrow hips and long, well-muscled legs. His flanks were hard with years of riding, and when he turned to blow out the lamp, she took careful note of the shape of his backside.

She wanted to remember every line of him, every flare and every hollow. His hair-roughened belly and chest, the broad v of his back, and the taut, ropy way his muscles moved beneath his skin. She wanted to draw him like this so she'd never forget, and knew she wouldn't have the chance.

Then the room went dark, and he came to her as a shadow gliding through the moonlight. When he reached the edge of the bed, she raised the covers in a silent invitation.

As he climbed in, the mattress dipped in his direction. When Ardith moved as if to scramble away, he pulled her against him.

"Ardith, love." The endearment melted through her like butter syrup. "I want to be close to you tonight, closer than any man has ever been. Is that all right?"

He was being kind to her, patient and considerate. Her eyes stung with tears and not trusting her voice, she nodded her consent.

"We're going to start with kissing." He sounded tender and instructive.

"I—I like kissing," she whispered back.

"I know you do." He proceeded to remind her just

how much she liked it. He started with small, soft kisses that drizzled like a summer shower over her forehead and cheeks, her throat and chest. He lingered over her lips, teasing her breathless with slow, gentle nibbles. He took her more deeply, making it the most natural thing in the world for her to kiss him back. He sought her tongue, stroking and darting away, teasing her just enough to make her chase him.

Kissing standing up was wonderful, but kissing lying down was better. Two people could get closer lying down. She liked the weight of him against her, the breadth of him that made even a woman of her generous proportions feel delicate and treasured.

She liked the way he bound her to him, as if no force on earth could tear her away. She liked the taste of him, the rhythm of his kisses, the way they flowed one into the next.

Kissing led to other things: hands that slid down from the small of her back to cup her buttocks, fingers that tangled in his hair, hips that nestled, legs that entwined, the friction of bodies rubbing together. Palms that swept up beneath the thin, rumpled fabric of her chemise to curl around her breasts.

"Oh!" Ardith breathed as a flurry of new sensations sped through her. "I didn't know you were going to do that." She was a little surprised at how much she liked the feel of his hand on her bare flesh.

"Neither did I. Do you mind that I did?"

Her face went hot again. "No."

"Would you mind if I took off your chemise?"

"N-n-no." It was gone in an instant, swooshed over her head and thrown away.

He pulled her against him length to length. The hair on his chest scuffed the sensitive skin of her breasts, their bellies bumped, their hips meshed. The thrust of his manhood slid unerringly between her legs.

"Oh," she said again, amazed how just the accidental brush of him kindled up such deep throbbing heat. She felt him smile in the midst of a kiss as if he knew exactly what she was feeling.

He sought her nipple with his thumb, circling and circling. She felt as if she were circling, too, dissolving into some vortex, going dizzy and languorous with something she was just coming to realize was desire.

He lowered his head and drew her nipple into his mouth, sucking gently. Ribbons of sensation unfurled to the farthest reaches of her body. Her throat went thick. Streamers of heat ran down her legs.

His hands spread against her skin, gathering up as much of her flesh as he could in his palms. And everywhere he touched he left a warm, rippling afterglow. It was as if the very pores of her skin had become luminous from the brush of his hands against them.

The glow sank deep into her flesh, deep into her belly and loins. Deep into her bones, warming her in a way she had never been warmed.

He skimmed her waist, the rise of her hip, the flare of her flanks. She could feel the rise and fall of his chest as he breathed, feel his shivery awareness of her, the needs that he was harboring.

It made her want to touch him, too, his face and hair, the breadth of his body, the strength of his limbs, but she didn't think she should surprise him by doing that.

"Do you mind if I touch you?"

"Indeed, Ardith," he said in a voice that seemed tinged with amusement, "I was hoping you would."

She filled her hands with him. With the width of his shoulders and the breadth of his back, with the dip of his spine and the rise of his hip. He rolled onto his back spreading himself before her in all his male splendor.

She rested one palm in the center of his chest and circled outward, the hair on his chest tickling her fingers.

She stroked his nipples more by accident than design and heard him catch his breath. She lingered over them, feeling the flesh bead up beneath her fingertips, teasing the nubs with her fingernails.

He stifled a moan deep in his throat. "You're going to be a veritable temptress, Ardith, once you get the hang of this."

She laughed and traced the high rigid arch of his ribs, the bones of his hips. His architecture; the very structure of him.

She slid her hands inward and down his belly where the hair grew thicker. His male parts lay only inches away.

"Is it all right if I touch you—there?"

"Touch my penis, you mean?" he asked her. His voice was deep. The amusement was gone.

"Well, yes," she agreed. "I won't hurt you, will I? I mean it seems so . . ."

"Large?" he offered, seeming amused all over again.

"Well, yes, that. But so—erect."

"It's supposed to be erect, Ardith. That's how it works best." When she didn't say anything else, he sighed. "Go ahead. Indulge your curiosity. I really won't mind."

"I wanted you to teach me," she said feeling faintly aggrieved.

"Yes, I know. I just didn't realize it was going to take quite so much forbearance on my part."

With a sniff she took her hand away.

With an imprecation he grabbed it back.

He fit her fingers around his shaft, then left her to discover what she wanted to know. His breathing seemed to grow a little unsteady as she explored the length of him, gliding her thumb up over the taut velvety cap. The tip was dewy to her touch, and he gave a little moan of pleasure.

He liked this.

The more she touched him, the more he liked it. The

more he liked what she was doing, the more she seemed to like doing it.

Intensity flowed between them like a current of heat, binding them together in some way she didn't fully understand. It gave them a strange equality, a strange interdependence that was pleasing in its complexity.

His eyes seemed to become dark hollows of yearning. His mouth bowed as he breathed. His face went heavy with sensuality—a word whose meaning she hadn't fully understood until now.

"I want to touch you," he whispered. His voice was low, his words both a request and a demand.

He shifted her onto her back and rolled half over her. He kissed her and kissed her and kissed her. He kissed her until she couldn't breathe, couldn't think, couldn't do anything but shiver beneath him.

He trailed his hand from her throat to her hip in a slow deliberate glide that left flutters of goose-flesh in its wake. He pressed his palm to the curls at the juncture of her legs.

Just the heat of it sent a swift dart of pleasure arcing to the core of her. With a gasp she rose against him.

He murmured as if he meant to soothe her, but the gentle circling motions he made against her most intimate flesh set off a tumble of new sensations. There was a rhythm to the way he moved, something primitive and oddly familiar.

She moaned and he drank deep, so deep of her pleasure. He touched her again and again—like an endlessly repeated request, a plea her body answered with shivers of wonder and gasps of delight.

His breathing was nearly as ragged as hers as he bent over her. "I want to love you, Ardith. Please let me love you."

She had never dreamed she'd hear those words on his lips and knew they couldn't mean to him what they meant to her. But tonight—just for tonight—she let herself pretend they did.

"Love me, Baird. Please, love me."

He came over her and into her, moving with a single gentle stroke. He came deep, so deep. She had never imagined she could be touched so deeply, never dreamed she could possess another soul as completely as she seemed to be possessing him.

Her body throbbed around him, the sensation part pain and part glorious elation. He began to move within her—slowly at first. Gently. Incrementally. Taking and giving back what seemed a greater gift with every delicious thrust. It was a gift that rose and expanded through her.

She looked up into his face, a face that was all arcs and shadows in the half-light. "Baird," she whispered as if she couldn't believe it was him making love to her. "Baird."

He lifted his hips, making her shiver with sensations so sweet they brought her near to weeping. He made those sensations sweeter still, easing her, nudging her toward higher and higher planes of pleasure with the escalating friction of their bodies.

She clung to him in the dark, the world contracting around them until there was only him in her universe. He was the source of her light, the source of her pleasure. The soul of her bliss.

She arched against him, her body craving his, needing him with a strange delicious frenzy. Delight danced along the surface of her skin. Restless expectation fluttered through her belly.

"Oh, Ardith, my love," Baird whispered.

She flowed against him. Deep at the core of her where their bodies joined, her expectation gave way to shattering fulfillment. Shivers of exquisite release rippled outward. They rose through her, shaking every perception she'd ever had of what loving was like.

Baird surged against her, his body pulsing as he tumbled with her into the maelstrom. They clung together, bound in a way that seemed both fleeting and eternal.

As the shivering ecstasy ebbed away, he drew her even more closely against him. He kissed her brow and temple and the corner of her mouth. His hands moved over her, stroking and savoring her, as if he couldn't bear for the loving to end any more than she could. But at length they drifted together, sighing, sated, and spent.

Ardith came to herself a good while later, sprawled half beneath Baird, feeling giddy and fluid, not quite sure where his body left off and hers began. It was a lovely feeling, hazy enough to keep the world at bay, imbued with breathless contentment. She never wanted to move again.

In truth she wouldn't have moved, except that Baird stirred against her. He mumbled a string of sleepy endearments, kissed her without even opening his eyes, and shifted so she lay safe in the curve of his body, his arms bound tight around her. Before she had so much as settled in, she heard his breathing deepen.

She knew how exhausted he was, knew all that lay ahead for him. Tomorrow was the last day of the roundup; the day after they'd leave for Cheyenne. Being able to number the days, count in hours the time they had left in this wild and wondrous place, tore the lovely cocoon of her contentment asunder.

Tears rose in her eyes and seeped silently down her cheeks. With the dawn she must put all this away, her memories of this night, her feelings for Baird. She must look to the future—a future that didn't include the man she had come to respect and care for so deeply.

She wasn't sorry she and Baird had made love; this had been the most wonderful night of her life. But it was over now, and she couldn't stop crying.

•   •   •

"*He* sent her what?" Baird demanded, wheeling toward China. She stood at the chuck wagon, drinking a cup of Jubal's coffee, having ridden out to the roundup ground where they were holding the steers they'd be taking to Cheyenne tomorrow.

"A ring," she confirmed. "An emerald ring, set with pearls."

"Did Ardith show it to you?"

"She tucked it away in one of those velvet jewelers' boxes when I came into the house. But I know what I saw."

Baird stared at her, dazed and stumbly and gone at the knees. He could barely force the words past the knot in his throat. "And you're sure it was Gavin Rawlinson who sent it?"

"That's what she said, and the postmark on the package was Boston."

He didn't even think to doubt China's information. She had that woman's sense about her, that way of knowing things no man could fathom. And if China took after her mother, she'd recognize expensive jewelry when she saw it.

He didn't take time to think things through. "Stay here," he told her, then grabbed up Dandy's reins and swung into the saddle.

The whole way to the house, his mind tumbled with impressions of the night before, of Ardith bending above him for that first kiss; of the way her breath had shuddered with nervousness and anticipation as he'd let down her hair; of how she had raised those pristine covers and welcomed him into her bed. The night had been filled with such wonder, touched by unexpected magic.

And now this.

Baird tied his horse to the porch railing and stormed into the house. "Ardith!" he shouted. "Ardith!"

The rooms were as silent and empty as they had been the day he arrived.

Where was that blasted woman, anyway? Out painting somewhere by herself, no doubt.

He understood her compulsion to do that. She was storing up as many memories of this country as she could before she went east. If he'd had half her skill, he'd have done that, too. But he needed to talk to her too much to have patience with her absence.

He turned on his heel and headed out to check Primrose's stall. He'd just gone down the steps when he caught a flash of color down by the creek. As he stalked toward it, he could see that Ardith was nestled in the shade at the top of the bank, her painting supplies piled up around her.

Relief went through him like a stiff wind across the prairie. At least he wasn't going to have to wait to ask her about Gavin.

She must have heard his boots whipping through the grass, because she swiped at her eyes and turned as he approached.

She looked impossibly prim this morning. Her blouse was buttoned all the way up her throat, and her hair was bound tight, with not so much as a strand out of place. She'd become calm, self-possessed Ardith again, except that her eyes were red from crying.

His heart twisted inside him.

He'd risen well before the sun and hadn't said so much as good-bye to her. After the night they spent together, he didn't know what to say. He'd wanted to kiss her awake and make her promises. But they would have been promises he couldn't keep, and he cared too much to lie to her.

Instead he'd slipped away. He wouldn't be here now if it weren't for China.

He stopped and stood looking down at her. "Just when did you intend to tell me about the ring?"

Ardith had the good grace to pale. "How—how did you find out?"

Fresh anger prickled up his spine. "China told me. She said it came in yesterday's mail. Has Rawlinson asked you to marry him?"

Ardith looked down at her paint-splotched hands. "Yes, he has."

Baird forced the question to his lips, determined to hear the whole of it. "And what do you mean to tell him?"

Surely she knew he would ask that, and yet she fumbled for an answer. "I—I'm tired of living as Uncle Franklin's poor relation. I'm tired of being alone. If the time I've spent here at the ranch with you and the children has convinced me of anything, it's that I want a home and a family of my own."

The breath he took burned all the way down. "Does that mean you're going to tell Rawlinson you'll marry him?"

He didn't want her marrying anyone else. In these last weeks he'd realized how much she meant to him. He didn't want to care so much, didn't want to feel like he'd be losing his soul if he let her go—but he did.

He couldn't face knowing some other man was going to argue with her, make plans with her, hear her most intimate thoughts and most devastating fears. He couldn't bear that some other man was going to share her laughter and hold her when she cried. The idea of some other man lying sated and entangled with her in the darkest hours of the night drove him half mad.

Clamping down tightly on his feelings, Baird squatted down beside her. "Are you going to marry Rawlinson?"

Ardith drew in her breath and expelled it on a sigh. "I expect I will."

"But if you meant to marry Gavin, what was last

night?" The words were torn from him at the forfeit of his pride.

"You know what last night was."

"I don't."

"You understood what we were doing as well as I did."

"I didn't understand anything," he insisted.

Her eyes sought his. Her gaze moved over him, caressing him in a way that made him ache. "Last night was our last chance," she whispered. "We were saying good-bye."

He could hear the anguish in her voice and knew how much her calm was costing her.

He didn't want to be calm. He wanted to shout at her and shake her and make her take back what she'd said. He wanted to grab her and kiss her until they burst into flame.

"You gave me your innocence," he whispered instead. "You gave me your virginity."

"I gave you myself."

She had given him not just her body, but her facile mind, her infinite tenderness, and her indomitable will. She had shown him her doubts and insecurities. She had offered up every attribute and every flaw. She had given him everything she was, to hold and cherish. *For this one night.*

Over these last months, he'd done the same, revealing his myriad of imperfections, his few trifling accomplishments, his fragile hopes, and his questionable virtues. Even knowing all that, she had bound him to her heart, made him feel as if he was worthy of the love she gave him. She had made him want to feel it every day of his life—yet he knew that was impossible.

Their world was crumbling. The chrysalis where they'd been safe, where each of them had grown strong, was turning to dust beneath his hands. Every breath he took brought that moment closer, and there was nothing he could do to stop it. He didn't know how he was going to bear what lay ahead.

She reached out and took his hand. When she spoke her voice was as frayed and fragile as ancient silk.

"You have your family, children who love you. You have the estate at Heatherleigh and your life back in England. You must let me go back to Boston and start again."

Her long, paint-stained fingers tightened around his hand. He turned his palm to hers and entwined their fingers. He wanted to hold her, to keep her with him.

"Last night was the most wonderful night of my life." She spoke so softly that the words were all but lost in the rustling of the grass around them. "I will carry the memory of what we gave each other for the rest of my days. But please, Baird, you must release me. You must let me tell Gavin that I'll marry him. You must let me build a future for myself."

Baird shivered, knowing what that meant. It meant she would raise her face for another man's kiss. It meant she would hold another man's baby in her arms. It meant that he must shield the hole she was tearing in his heart and let her go to someone else.

Did he have the nobility to do that? Was he able to say the words, to tell Ardith what he knew he must? She was asking him to give away the single thing he needed most.

He tightened his grip on her, relishing the warm, renewing brush of her flesh on his; reveling in the faint sensual awareness tingling between them.

His voice went thick with the effort it took to give her the chance she deserved. "No night in my life will ever mean as much to me as last night did. No woman, Ardith, will ever touch me the way you have. No one will ever aggravate and disturb me, or fill me with such joy and pride. You have shown me things inside myself I didn't know were there. You have made me want to be a better father to my children, to be a better man."

He could see the tears shimmering in her eyes, giving proof that her regret was every bit as deep and painful as his.

He drew in his breath knowing his next words would be the only benediction their love for each other was likely to have.

"Gavin is a supremely fortunate man to be able to spend his life with you. I hope that you and he will find real happiness together."

He brought her paint-stained fingers to his mouth and brushed a kiss across her knuckles. He held her hand a moment longer, soaking up her warmth, basking in her tenderness. Then he let her go.

He clambered to his feet and headed back to the house. He managed to stumble inside before his knees gave way. He braced his hands against the table and stood there hunched and fighting for breath. He had never felt so empty, so utterly lost.

It had taken everything he had to give Ardith the freedom she needed to make a life for herself. He was proud that he had done it, but how it tore at him to hold happiness in his grasp, then have to let it go.

He drew himself up again and found his way to Ardith's bedchamber. It was relentlessly neat, still rife with the smell of turpentine and linseed oil, and that clean, gingery scent that he had come to recognize as hers.

He moved to the bed and stroked his hand across the well-washed quilt, remembering how he had spilled Ardith down across it just last night. It filled him with a harsh, stark longing for this woman he could never kiss, never hold, never touch again.

He walked to the dresser. The glass that hung above it reflected back a man whose hollow eyes gave proof of all he'd forfeited in the name of love and honor.

Ardith's scant belongings were scattered across the top: her hairbrush and comb, a vial of scent, and a pile of frilly handkerchiefs. Mismatched saucers held several pair of earrings, buttons and coins, and her cache of tortoiseshell hairpins.

He curled his fingers around one of them, remembering how he'd slipped these pins from her hair one by one. He remembered how the soft, silky strands had tumbled around her, waving ever so slightly against her breasts and spilling down her back. He remembered how that glorious hair had spread around her as they made love and how it had trailed across his chest as he held her in the aftermath.

He smiled with the memory and curled his hand around one of the hairpins. He fancied that it still held the warmth of her, the essence of this tightly bound woman with her generous heart. Then, instead of putting the hairpin back, he tucked it away in the pocket of his trousers. It was the only piece of Ardith he dared keep.

He was just turning toward the back of the house where he'd left Dandy, when he heard a wagon rumble into the yard. It was Hunter Jalbert bringing Meggie to the house so she could accompany Ardith to Boston.

Baird stepped out onto the porch to welcome them just as Hunter helped his daughter down from the wagon. He held on to her a little longer than was necessary for her to get steadied on her feet and raised one hand to adjust her hat as if she were a far younger girl.

"Well, Miss Meggie," Baird addressed her, using a smile to hide his regrets. "Are you all set for your big adventure?"

Meggie beamed at him. "Indeed I am. Mother and I bought material and patterns when we were in Cheyenne, and we have been sewing clothes to take east with me ever since."

Hunter scowled and lowered the tailgate of the wagon with a bang and revealed a shiny, new leather-bound trunk. Baird went to offer help, but Jalbert nudged him away. He hefted the piece of luggage onto the porch and used the moment it took to compose himself.

"You're going to stay the night with us, aren't you, Hunter?" Baird asked, the offer of hospitality as much a part of life here in the west as the ceaseless wind.

"No," the older man answered gruffly. "I have business at Fort Laramie. I'm going to say good-bye to Meggie and see how far I can get before dark."

Baird could tell by Hunter's manner that he was no more at peace with sending his daughter off to Boston than Baird was going to be when it came to putting Ardith on the train.

He meant to give them a moment of privacy, but just then Ardith came rushing around the corner of the house.

"Meggie, Hunter, hello!" she greeted them, throwing her arms around Meggie in an extravagant hug. "Do come in. We'll get you something to eat and a place to bed down for the night. Then you can tell me all about Cass and the boys. You can't imagine how much all of us have missed you!"

"Cassie and the boys are fine," Hunter said, his dark face impassive. "They're seeing to the ranch while I came here. But because they're up there alone, I need to finish some business over east of here and get right back."

Before Ardith could try to dissuade him, Hunter opened his arms to his daughter. "Come hug me, Meggie girl, so I can get on my way."

Meggie went to him, and he folded her against him. "I know I'm not your real papa, Meggie, but no man could love a flesh and blood daughter more than I love you. No man could be any prouder of the woman you have become."

Jalbert's voice was low and quiet, but Baird heard the soft, deeply felt words of farewell. A knot swelled in his throat. One day he would have to let China go just the way Hunter was saying goodbye to Meggie.

Still, he had a little time, a few more years with China and the boys before they went out into the world on their own. Whatever else happened in his life, he meant to make the most of the time he had.

Ardith's shoulder brushed against him, as if she knew what he was feeling. Just the touch of her warmth, the realization that she was so attuned to his feelings, made him catch his breath. How was he going to get through his days and nights without her?

Beside the wagon, Meggie was hanging onto Hunter as if she never meant to let him go.

"No real papa could have been any better to me than you have been," she murmured. "I love you, Hunter, and I thank you for everything you've done for me. Take care of Mama and the boys while I'm away." He nodded, knocking the brim of her hat askew. "And take care of yourself."

They clung together for one moment longer, and then Hunter set his daughter away from him.

Ardith stepped up beside the girl and wrapped an arm around her shoulders as Hunter climbed up into the wagon seat.

Baird caught a glimpse of the set of his mouth and the sheen of tears in his eyes as he said his final farewell to her. "I love you, Meggie," he murmured, then whistled to the horses.

They stood and watched Hunter drive away: a girl on the cusp of womanhood, a woman who would lavish Meggie with the same care she had shown his three children. And Baird, who hoped for everyone's sake that he would manage his own good-byes with such quiet dignity.

SIXTEEN

$\mathcal{E}$veryone gathered early the next morning to see the men off to Cheyenne. Buck and Myra stood at one end of the porch with their arms around each other, as if they were going to be separated for a decade instead of a little more than a week. China and Meggie chattered with several of the hands about the wonders of Cheyenne, anticipating their own trip to the railhead. Durban was mounted up and all but bouncing with impatience.

Though Baird had been specifically waiting for Ardith to come out of the house, he took the opportunity to talk to Khy. "While I'm driving these cattle to market, I expect you to behave yourself. I want you to do what your Aunt Ardith tells you and try to stay out of trouble. If I hear you've been good, I'll buy you some of those lemon drops you fancy when you get to town."

He sounded just like a parent, Baird realized, more than a little appalled. When exactly had he started that?

"How come I can't help drive cattle, too?" Khy protested. "Durban is."

Baird hunkered down on his heels and looked at his

son. "You know how there are things that you've out-grown, like teething toys and last year's clothes?" Khy nodded noncommittally. "Well, there are also things you have to grow into. I'm afraid, Khy, this is one of them. I wouldn't be taking Durban with me except that he rides so well and has been so good about helping out."

Baird hoped Durban could overhear what he was say-ing. He hadn't been able to tell his son how proud he was that he'd overcome his aversion to horses and learned to ride. Or how pleased he was that the boy had made him-self so useful during the fall roundup.

But even the invitation to help drive the steers south hadn't broken through the wall of Durban's reserve. "I'll ride with you if you like," was all he'd said when Baird asked him.

Baird squeezed Khy's shoulder and smiled. "Do you understand why you can't come with us this time, son?"

"I hate being little!" Khy complained and scowled in a way Baird had seen in his own mirror.

He pulled the youngster into his arms. "Your time will come," he promised and got a reluctant hug for his trou-ble.

Just then Ardith breezed out onto the porch. Baird fol-lowed her with his eyes as she threaded her way to where Myra and Buck were standing together and saw her give a letter to the older man. Baird swung Khy up in his arms and ambled toward them.

". . . sure this gets mailed for me?" Ardith was saying as they came up. "It's very important."

Baird had no doubt the letter was to Gavin Rawlinson, but he peeked over her shoulder just to be sure. "I'll be happy to mail that," he offered.

Ardith started, then wheeled to face him. Her eyes were wide and bright—and oddly guilty. It was all the indica-tion he needed to guess what answer she'd given Rawlinson. When he saw the emerald and pearl ring on the third finger of her left hand, he went still inside.

"I—I appreciate you offering to mail the letter, Baird, really I do. But—but I know just how—how much you'll have on your mind when you get to—to Cheyenne," Ardith stammered.

"Why don't I just tuck it away in my jacket for safe-keeping, then," Buck offered, "so the boss won't have to remember to find the post office when we hit town?"

Baird scowled at the older man. How likely was he to forget what that letter entailed? Or that Ardith's future would be sealed once Buck posted it?

Regret grabbed him hard, and he wished with all his heart he had something to offer Ardith. How was he going to put her on the train knowing he'd never see her again? Knowing he was sending her off to marry another man?

Khy reached across, and Ardith took him into her arms.

He's getting too big for her to do that, Baird found himself thinking. The children were all getting so big, and he wasn't at all sure how he was going to manage them by himself.

He crossed to China and gave her a hug. "Good-bye, baby girl. I'll be seeing you in Cheyenne at the end of next week."

"You will be careful on the trail, Papa, won't you?" she admonished him, clinging a little tighter. "Remember what you promised."

He pressed his cheek to hers. "Don't worry, sweetheart. I remember."

He left China in Meggie's care and blessed the girl for her bright, sweet smile and knowing eyes. Her visit to the ranch had helped China get over Matt's death as much as anything could. It pleased Baird to know that Ardith would be looking after Meggie when they reached Boston.

Down at the foot of the steps, Ardith and Khy were saying their own good-byes. Her words to Durban were as full of admonitions as his to Khy had been. Khy's tone when he spoke to his brother was filled with grudging admiration.

Ardith had stepped back as if she were returning to the porch, when Durban reached out to her. "Aunt Ardith?" he said, then bit his lip. "There—there's something I've been meaning to ask you. There's a real pretty place up in the hills, and I—I was wondering if you'd paint it for me?"

Ardith's face immediately softened. Durban never asked for much, and Baird could see Ardith would have painted the sky bright green if he'd asked her to.

While Durban gave directions, Buck hugged his wife one final time. " 'Bout ready to start eating trail dust, boss?"

Ardith was still standing down among the horses when Baird gathered up Dandy's reins. He wanted just one minute alone with her. One minute to hold her, to feel her heat and her humanity.

Instead he touched her hand. "Take good care of China and Khy," he said, staring at her mouth, wanting to kiss her so much he was scarcely aware of anything else.

"I will. And you keep an eye on Durban," she warned him.

Baird laughed and shook his head, as much to clear the wanting from his thoughts as anything else. "Like as not, he'll keep an eye on me."

"Try—" she began and stopped herself. "Try to make the most of this time on the trail. Don't let things you can't do anything about spoil these days for you."

Did she mean not to waste this time with Durban? Not to let his own disappointments spoil his last weeks in Wyoming? Or was Ardith referring to her acceptance of Gavin Rawlinson's proposal?

"I won't," he assured her because he knew he should. He swung up into the saddle and followed Buck and the others toward where they'd pick up the herd. At the head of the rise to the south of the ranch, Baird paused and turned back.

Dawn was just breaking across the land, casting long gray shadows over miles of plains just quickening with gold. The rays of light crept up the mountains, casting their uneven faces in sharp relief, deepening the contrast between the rocks and the bristle of pines.

His eyes picked out the line of the creek high in the foothills and followed its course down toward the ranch. His gaze lingered on the treed hummock where they'd laid Matt Hastings to rest, and the field where Khy had hunted butterflies. He studied the raw, hardscrabble buildings nestled low against the earth: the corral where he'd worked the horses, the barn where he'd put up hay. A smile curled his mouth as he remembered Ardith making ice cream on the back steps of the house, and the dinner they'd had with the Jalberts.

This was the last time he would see this place, this country that had become so much a part of him. He wasn't sure how he was going to bear losing it, losing Ardith, losing the memories they'd made here. But there was no future for him in Wyoming.

At last, with great reluctance, he turned Dandy and galloped after the others.

*A*rdith nudged her horse up the long grassy slope.

"Now, just where did Durban say this valley was?" she muttered, as if Primrose had been listening the previous day when the boy had given directions. Because Durban had asked her to paint this place, she'd left Khy in China and Meggie's care and come all this way by herself. As she topped the rise, Ardith saw how the land fell away to the east, funneling sharply downhill. This entrance to the valley looked just the way Durban had described it, though he'd also mentioned another half-hidden passage at the opposite end. Sure she'd found what she was looking for, Ardith turned Primrose into the coulee and followed the scores of hoofprints.

The passage narrowed at the bottom to pass between two standing stones, then widened beyond it. Ardith drew rein and looked around. Striated walls of red and gold protected what must be a half-mile wide pelt of wavering grassland. A stand of pines swept part-way up the right-hand wall, a stream lined with cottonwoods burbled off to her left, and a golden wedge of aspens stood dead ahead. From there the canyon seemed to dog-leg south.

"I can see why he asked me to paint this," Ardith confided to Primrose and nudged the pony forward.

As she picked her way along the course of the stream, she noticed the large herd grazing in the deep, sweet grass. It surprised her that the steer nearest her bore the Sugar Creek brand, and she wondered if Baird and Buck had found this place when they were looking for stock. She spotted a second Sugar Creek steer and then a third. More than a little curious, Ardith left the shade of the trees and rode nearer. As she did, she realized all the cattle bore the Sugar Creek brand.

An odd, cold tingle worked its way up her back. What were these cattle doing here?

Before she could discern an answer, two cowboys came splashing across the stream not a hundred yards ahead of her. Ardith did her best to ease back into the trees, but they had seen her.

As they rode closer she could see they weren't like the hands on the Sugar Creek. They didn't look like the cowboys she'd met from other ranches, either. They were hard-faced men, unkempt and slovenly.

Her nerves jangled with alarm. *Just what had Durban gotten her into?*

Her first impulse was to flee, but Primrose was known

for his comfortable gait and lovely disposition, not his speed. She glanced into the canvas bag hanging from the saddle horn just to be sure her pistol was where she could reach it.

"You lost, ma'am?" the shorter man asked as he pulled up.

Ardith gave him her very best smile. "Not lost exactly. I'm looking for something to paint."

The men glanced at the things she had tied to her saddle, her paint box and drawing board. A pad of paper and some brushes stuck out of her canvas bag.

"You that Boston woman who makes pictures for books?"

"Yes, I am."

"I heard the boss talkin' about her," the first hand said.

"Don't make no difference who she is," the second man answered. "She don't belong here."

Ardith's throat went dry. "I didn't realize I was trespassing," she apologized, shifting away. "I'm sure I can find somewhere else to paint."

The taller man reached out and caught Primrose's near side rein. The horse snorted and shied.

"I think it best you come with us, ma'am, and we'll see what our foreman wants to do with you."

Panic rattled through her like a runaway freight train. She was alone with these men, miles from home, and there was no telling what they had in mind.

"There's no need for that," she insisted, grappling for control of Primrose's reins. "If you don't want me here, I'll just go."

The man acted as if he hadn't heard and turned down the valley, dragging her and Primrose in his wake.

Ardith stole a glance at the pistol in her sack, fighting down the urge to grab it and defend herself. She'd only have one chance to surprise them, and she had to figure out how to make the most of it.

As they led her beyond the dog-leg turn at the middle of the valley, Ardith saw there was a small, rough-hewn cabin on a rise at the far end. Several corrals had been built around back, and as they approached, Ardith noticed the big, broad-shouldered bull in the nearest one. Recognition was instantaneous.

It was Randy! These men had stolen Khy's bull, and she'd bet they had the rest of the Sugar Creek cattle, too!

Her head pounded as she tried to think, but all she could see was Durban bending over her, giving her directions. Durban asking her to paint this valley. Had he known there were rustlers here? And if he had, why in God's name hadn't he told his father instead of her? Baird would have known how to handle this. What had Durban expected *her* to do against men like these?

She glanced over her shoulder and realized she couldn't go back the way she'd come. She turned her attention to the canyon ahead, to a towering sweep of sandstone wall.

They were just starting up the rise toward the cabin, when Ardith noticed what looked like a deep, shadowed pleat in the rockface off to her left. Durban had said there was an entrance at this end of the valley, hadn't he? Could this be it?

Dear God, it had to be!

Ardith waited until they reached the cabin, waited until the man who'd had hold of Primrose's reins dismounted.

"Langley!" he shouted. "Langley, I got someone here you need to see."

The shorter man was just swinging out of the saddle when Ardith bent and gathered up both the reins. She kicked Primrose and pulled him sharply to the left. As if he knew what was at stake, the pony bolted.

Ardith bent low and urged her mount toward the dark, deep wrinkle in the rocks. She heard shouting and confusion behind her. When she glanced back, more rustlers were spilling out of the cabin. They'd be after her in seconds.

Ardith drove her horse relentlessly forward. Finding the passage was her only chance.

"Be there!" she whispered. "Please, be there!"

She was less than a dozen yards from the canyon wall when a tunnel opened up before her.

As she ducked inside, a gun popped and rock sheered away a foot above her head. After the brightness of the valley, the seam between the rocks seemed dark as midnight. The way was twisting and narrow. It turned sharply downhill. The ground was studded with pebbles and treacherous underfoot. Ardith kicked Primrose forward anyway.

She heard the men enter the twisting passageway. The sound of pursuit rolled up behind her, overtook her. It echoed in her ears. Ardith bent over Primrose's neck. *Dear Lord, how long can this passage be?*

They jogged once to the right and once to the left, then burst into the sunlight. Primrose picked up speed on the flat.

Ardith looked back just in time to see five men breach what seemed to be an impenetrable wall of rock behind her. Shots kicked up dirt to her right and left.

Ardith hung low on his neck and let Primrose run. When she looked back, two of the men had given up the chase, one had peeled away toward the southeast. The last two kept coming.

Ardith spurred Primrose for greater speed, knowing full well the horse was already giving her all he had. The next time she looked, only the taller man was following her.

His horse's strides were longer than hers, and he gained on her across the level ground. Ardith was sobbing for breath and Primrose's sides were bellowing when the rustler pulled up beside her and grabbed Primrose's bridle. The two horses danced around each other snorting and pawing. Ardith kicked at the rustler as he fought for control of the thrashing animals.

"You shouldn't have done that," he snarled and hit her.

The blow exploded along Ardith's jaw, all but knocking her out of the saddle. Her head reeled and her ears buzzed. She sagged forward and clung to Primrose, too stunned to resist.

Ardith didn't know how far they'd traveled back toward the canyon when she became aware of the bristle of horsehair beneath her cheek and grass swishing against Primrose's belly. All Ardith could think of as her head began to clear was that if she went back to that valley, she'd die there.

Fear shrilled through her. How she could escape? What could she use to defend herself? Then the handpiece of the Colt revolver in her artist's bag came into focus mere inches from her nose.

She blinked at it once, then curled her hand around the grip. She'd never realized a gun could feel so good in her hand—so heavy and cool, like confidence.

She sat up in the saddle and leveled the pistol at the rustler's back. "Drop those reins," she ordered him.

He glanced at her, and his jaw flapped open in surprise.

Ardith knew a moment's satisfaction before he turned in the saddle and made a grab for her pistol. He overpowered her in an instant and dragged her toward him. Up close she could smell his sweat and the reek of stale tobacco. She could see his slimy hair and the dirt ground into skin.

"Goddamned bitch," he breathed into her face.

Though he clung tight to her hand, Ardith lurched away. His grip tightened, grinding the delicate bones together, prying at her fingers with his broad, rough thumb. She fought him, rotating her wrist in his grip. She tilted the barrel of the gun up between their bodies and jerked away from him with all her strength.

The gun went off.

Her ears rang with the concussion. The sting of powder and singed clothing burned up her nose. The rustler's weight came full against her.

They toppled out of the saddle and landed hard. Ardith sprawled flat on her back with well over two hundred pounds of rustler on top of her. He crushed down on her, his weight grating against her hipbones and squashing her ribs. She fought for breath and dug in her heels, crab-crawling backward. Then, with a grunt of effort, she rolled the man off her.

As he flopped over onto his back, she saw blood spreading across his shirtfront. She scrambled to her feet and stood looking down at him.

She'd shot him! Dear God, she'd shot him.

Her knees and brain simultaneously turned to mush. Tears poured down her cheeks. Only when she lifted her hand to wipe them away a few moments later did she realize she was still clutching her pistol.

Ardith finally had the presence of mind to bend and relieve the man of his own revolver. Shoving both guns into the pockets of her riding skirt, she knelt beside him. She pressed one of her frilly handkerchiefs against his wound and felt for the pulse at his wrist. His heart was still beating. Beyond that, she didn't have the faintest idea what to do for him.

He moaned and stirred. "Miss?" he murmured weakly. "Miss?"

Ardith bent closer.

He opened his eyes and grabbed for her.

She leaped to her feet and backed away. "You aren't going to die, are you?" she asked almost resentfully.

He fought his way up to his elbow. "Ain't no woman made who can kill me," he sneered at her.

Ardith's brain cranked into action. She had to get out

of here before the other rustlers came looking for their friend.

She rushed to gather up Primrose's reins, then smacked the rustler's horse and set it running. By the time this man got to his feet and caught his pony, she'd be long gone from here.

She mounted up and headed east, leaving the man to see to himself. It took her awhile to realize where she was. She'd only been out this way once before, the night of the party at the Double T.

Though she knew she should ride for home, she turned Primrose south instead—toward where the herd was making its way to Cheyenne. Baird and Buck would know what to do about this. They'd have enough men with them to come and arrest the rustlers.

Even if she rode for the Sugar Creek, she couldn't mount a posse by herself.

Considering how far she'd come already, Baird and the herd couldn't be more than two or three hours ahead of her. If Primrose could keep up the pace, she should reach them just about dark.

*B*uck Johnson leaned back against the side of the chuck wagon and gestured with his mug of coffee. "Looks like a rider coming."

Baird shaded his eyes and peered off to the north. The horseman was coming at a run, his mount all but stumbling with exhaustion. At the sight, apprehension tuned up inside of him.

They'd just gotten the herd settled for the night, and after hours in the saddle Baird had been looking forward to stretching out the kinks, eating a hot meal, and snatching a few hours sleep. Whatever this was, it was bound to interfere with his plans.

Squinting a little harder, he made out that the rider was

hatless and tall, narrow through the shoulders—and wearing a skirt that flapped behind her as she rode.

"Dear God! It's Ardith!" He ran toward the edge of the campsite. Both he and Buck were waiting when she pulled her foam-flecked horse to a stop and all but tumbled out of the saddle.

"Ardith!" Baird cried. "For God's sake, what happened? Where are you hurt?"

"I'm all right," she gasped.

She didn't look all right. She was bruised and battered and covered with blood. He swept her up in his arms, shaking so hard he could hardly carry her.

"Look after Primrose," she called back to Buck.

"I got him," the foreman answered.

Baird set Ardith down by the fire so he could see where she'd been hurt. His hands trembled as he probed her clothes. Where the hell was all this blood coming from?

She caught his hand. "I'm all right, Baird. It's nothing. The blood's not mine."

He looked up at her and read the assurance in her eyes. But before he could catch his breath an even more horrible fear shot through him. "The children—"

"The children are fine." She tightened her fingers, reassuring him. "They're fine. They're back at the ranch."

He dragged her close anyway, needing the feel of her against him. His strong, solid Ardith seemed so fragile all at once. A dark bruise ran from her temple to her jaw. Her eye was ringed with purple, and one side of her lip was swollen to twice its size.

"Your face," he murmured, grazing his hand over her cheek. "Your poor face."

"I'm fine, Baird. Fine."

His flare of panic ebbed a little. Jubal arrived with his chest of medicines, made his own assessments, and began preparing a compress for Ardith's face.

Durban appeared suddenly out of the deepening dusk. "Aunt Ardith? What are you doing here?"

His features sagged with shock when he got a look at Ardith in the firelight.

"Your aunt says she's fine," Baird hastened to reassure him.

The boy dropped down on his knees and stared at her. "What—what happened?"

"I rode out this morning looking for something to paint," Ardith answered. Baird saw how intent she was, how focused on his son. "A pretty little valley someone told me about."

"Did—did you find it?"

"Oh, yes. The valley was lovely—except that it was filled to the brim with our missing cattle."

"Are you sure they were our cattle?" Baird murmured. Somehow he had never been quite able to believe the cattle were being stolen. If the herd was dwindling, it had to be because of something he'd done—or failed to do.

"I didn't check the brands on every one," she told him and pressed his hand. "But Randy was there."

"Randy!" Durban cried.

"Who had Randy?" Buck demanded, joining them by the fire.

"The passel of rustlers I discovered this afternoon."

Dear God! Baird tightened his hold on her. What had Ardith ridden into?

"Were—were there men in that valley?" Durban asked her.

Ardith answered with a nod.

"Hot damn!" Buck exclaimed. "I knew there were rustlers! I knew we couldn't have just *lost* so many cows. Did the rustlers see you?"

Ardith eased the compress Jubal had prepared against her cheek before she told them what happened.

As she spoke, Baird felt the tremors rattle through her

and could sense how she was fighting to hold herself together. The more he heard the more he wanted to gather her up in his arms and just hang on. Hold her so she'd know she was safe, so *he'd* know she was safe.

What he wanted was to find the men who'd hurt her and pound them into dust.

"I don't think they expected me to resist," she went on. "They weren't prepared when I turned Primrose and ran."

"Did they follow you?" Buck wanted to know.

More men had begun to gather at the fire, but Ardith seemed to be speaking only to Durban. "I knew I couldn't outrun them the length of the valley, so I took a chance on finding a way out down near the cabin."

"And did you?" the boy asked almost breathlessly.

Durban is as caught up in Ardith's story as he would be in one of her ten-penny dreadfuls, Baird thought, recognizing his anticipation in the set of his son's shoulders, in the way he rubbed his hands together. But this was no story. This was real life.

"How did you get away?" Buck wanted to know.

"The men chased me through the passage and out onto the flat. One by one they fell away—except that last man. He just kept coming. I knew I couldn't let him take me back to that valley . . ."

If they had, Ardith would have died there. Baird's stomach pitched every time he thought about what might have happened.

"So what did you do?" Jeff Mason demanded.

"I shot him," Ardith answered.

"You shot him!" Buck crowed in delight. The cowboys nudged each other, mumbling their approval.

Durban looked awestruck by what she'd done. "Did you really?"

Only Baird seemed to see what shooting that rustler had cost her. Her hands were shaking. Her eyes were wide and wet when she turned that pale, bruised face to him. She knew he'd understand. And God knows, he did.

"I didn't want to shoot him," she whispered.

"I know you didn't, love." He nodded and gathered her against him. "You only did what you had to do. I'm glad you got away from him."

He hoped she'd blown the bastard to kingdom come.

It warmed him, knowing he could give her this, these few moments of solace after all she'd given him. He felt her nestle against him. "Rest easy now," he murmured. "You're safe with me."

She swiped at her eyes and gave him a shaky smile. "He cussed me when I ran off his horse and left him there."

His hands moved over her. "I bet he did."

"Well, girl," Buck chuckled, "if that fellow was able to cuss at you, I doubt you did any permanent damage."

"I—I hope not." Ardith answered. He could see she was better now, more sure of herself, stronger.

"Do you suppose, Miss Ardith," Buck asked gently, "you could find your way back to that valley?"

Baird knew what the older man was thinking and shook his head. He didn't want Ardith going anywhere but back to the ranch where she'd be safe.

"It's right up in the foothills," Ardith said.

"We've had men riding through the foothills for weeks," the grizzled foreman said with some exasperation.

"It's out near the Double T."

"That's right where we lost Randy's trail," Durban cried.

Baird heard the distress in his son's voice and reached across to pat the boy's knee by way of reassurance. Durban shoved Baird's hand away, his eyes hot and shiny with tears.

"It'd be best to hit them at first light," Buck went on, already planning how they'd take the rustlers. "If they have a chance to clear out, we'll never get them."

Ardith sighed and clambered to her feet. "Then let me show you the passage into the canyon."

*B*aird heard the crush of someone moving toward them through the grass and grabbed his pistol.

Buck Johnson loomed out of the dark off to his left. "I took care of the guard," he reported, speaking softly in deference to the woman curled up asleep with her head in Baird's lap. "It's almost light. We'll be needing Ardith to show us how to get into that canyon."

Baird nodded, slid the Colt back into his holster and paused for a moment to stroke Ardith's unbound hair. He hated that she was here with them, hated that going after the rustlers might put her in danger. But at least they'd managed to leave Durban behind.

The boy had been determined to come, and neither he nor Buck had been able to talk sense into him. Finally Ardith had taken him aside, and whatever she'd said had convinced him, because when they'd ridden away last evening, Durban hadn't tried to follow.

As Buck moved off, Baird squeezed Ardith's shoulder, waking her as gently as he could. "It's time," he whispered.

Her eyes blinked open. She nodded and sat up. He could tell by the stutter in her breathing exactly when she realized where they were.

"It's going to be fine," he reassured her.

"Is it?"

His own fear trickled through him like melting ice. Seeing her ride into camp covered with blood had taken years off his life. He couldn't bear that she was ready to risk her safety again.

"All you have to do is show us how to get into the valley," he whispered and pulled her against him.

She clung to him in the swaying solitude of the high

grass as if he were something solid in a world adrift. He wanted to be that for her, wanted to offer her that kind of security, so he held her a few moments longer than he should.

By the time they joined the others and mounted their horses, the sky was lightening. They poked along the toes of the bluff, past deep-veined fissures and weathered outcroppings, through a field of boulders scattered like dice. Then, in a deep crease in the hillside, Ardith showed them a narrow, shadowed passageway.

Baird recognized the spot; they'd ridden right past it when they'd been searching for Randy.

Buck gave orders. "I'll head in first," he said, nodding at Jeff, Bear, Lem, and a young puncher named Wilcox. "Mr. Northcross will follow me, and Bear will bring up the rear. We'll move in slow and quiet, and hope they haven't posted a second guard. This is bound to be dangerous, so watch yourselves."

Baird caught Ardith's arm as they formed up. "You *are* staying here, aren't you?"

"I didn't promise that," was all she said.

Buck drew his pistol and nudged his pony into the dim world between the rocks. Baird fell in behind him and levered a cartridge into his Winchester. He'd never registered the cold finality of that sound, the snicking mechanical death knell of preparing a rifle to fire. A sick wave of terror ran through him.

He hadn't stopped to think about what he was doing here. He hadn't shot a gun since he'd killed the deer the day he arrived. He hadn't been able to shoot the mountain lion. How in God's name was he going to turn his rifle on the rustlers?

Still, he had to be here. These men had stolen his cattle. They had tried to undermine his ranch. They'd hurt Ardith. This was his fight. And if Buck and Bear and the others were willing to risk their lives to bring the rustlers to justice, he couldn't back down.

As they eased through the switchback chute between the rocks, sweat trickled down his ribs and ran into his eyes. The pounding of his heart seemed to reverberate from the walls of the twisting passage. Then, through the thin, gray twilight Baird saw the valley open up ahead of them.

Buck paused and gestured them across a narrow strip of meadow and into the trees off to the right. They seeped like wraiths through the wispy fog that blanketed the meadow. It was only as they were tying their horses that Baird realized Ardith was still with them. *He'd have sold his soul to have her anyplace else.*

He caught her arm and pulled her close against him. "Have you got your gun?"

She was whey-faced and breathing hard, but her hand was steady when she held up her pistol.

"Don't try anything heroic, all right?" he warned her.

She gave him a sudden, shaky grin. "Or you, either."

Not likely, Baird thought.

They worked their way up the canyon until they were crouched in a fall of timber opposite the cabin.

"Do you think they're in there?" Baird whispered.

"Smoke's coming up the stove pipe," Buck observed. "And there are ponies in the corral."

Baird could hear their horses wickering nervously. It wouldn't be long before the rustlers heard them, too.

"This is how we're going to do it," Buck whispered, drawing everyone close. "I'll take Lem and Bear and Jeff and sneak around back of that cabin. There's a privy out there, so I'm betting there's a back door, too.

"As soon as we're in place, I want you to draw the rustler's fire. As I recollect, Mr. Northcross, you're quite a shot. Can you break the windows and shoot some shingles off the roof?"

Baird inclined his head, wondering if he could.

"While you and Wilcox keep them busy out here, we'll come in around back." Buck looked at the ring of faces. "Everyone know what they're doing?"

The cowboys nodded.

"Boss," Buck said. "You start things off. And Miss Ardith?"

"Yes?"

"You keep your head down, all right?" Buck and his men crept away.

Once he'd made sure Ardith was tucked up tight in the crotch of the fallen log, Baird hunkered down beside her. He swiped the sweat from his eyes, and tightened his grip on the rifle to keep his hands from trembling.

Some sharpshooter, he thought and blew his breath in derision.

When he caught sight of the others in the rocks behind the cabin, Baird notched the rifle into his shoulder. He curled his finger around the trigger and aimed for the stovepipe protruding from the cabin roof.

It's a piece of tin, he told himself. *It's not alive. It's not an animal or a person. You can hit it.*

He fought to narrow his focus, get his breathing under control. Buck must be wondering why this was taking so long.

He sighted on the stovepipe and pulled the trigger. The report of the gun sent echoes booming up the canyon, but the stovepipe didn't so much as quiver. Baird mumbled a curse.

A head appeared and disappeared in the window of the cabin.

He felt Ardith's hand press tight against his back. "Try again," she whispered. Her voice was low and determined.

He pumped another cartridge into the chamber and tried not to hold himself so stiffly. He fired and this time the stovepipe pinged.

Relief tumbled through him. He gave a shivery sigh and shot out several windowpanes. He drilled a line across the roof, sending the wooden shingles hopping like keys on a piano.

The rustlers shot back. Wilcox took up firing, and Baird curled behind the fallen tree to reload.

Ardith was there an arm's length away. She didn't say a word, but he caught the glow in her eyes. She knew what doing even that much shooting had cost him.

Baird turned back to the cabin, feeling as if he could breathe again. He had fired several more rounds when he heard Buck and his men burst into the cabin.

The rustlers should have surrendered. Everything should have gone still. Instead the cabin erupted with gunfire. The rustlers weren't going to let themselves be taken. They were putting up a fight.

Wilcox must have realized that, too, because he suddenly vaulted the fallen log and took off running across the open ground toward the shack.

"Goddamned bloody fool!" Baird cursed, then leaped the log himself and pelted after him.

Guns kept popping in the cabin as they crossed the stream. Wilcox was ahead of Baird and starting up the rise, when one of the rustlers appeared in the window. He drew a bead on the young cowboy.

Baird yelled a warning and dove at Wilcox. He caught his shoulders and yanked him to the right just as the man in the window fired.

Dirt spattered up exactly where he and Wilcox had been an instant before.

The two of them slammed to the ground, rolling a few yards from sheer momentum. The firing inside the cabin continued a minute more, then silence fell.

The last gunshots had barely echoed away when Buck burst out the cabin door. "They're all dead," he announced, holstering his pistol.

Baird pushed up to his knees, spitting dirt. The singe of black powder hung heavy in the air. Wilcox sprawled a few feet away blinking in confusion but apparently unharmed—no thanks to his own rashness.

Baird had no sooner sat back on his heels when Ardith came racing toward him. "No heroics, I said!" she yelled at him.

"Sometimes I just can't help myself," he answered and burst out laughing.

Ardith slammed to a stop beside him. Her eyes went wide. "Are you hurt?" she demanded.

"Of course not."

"Then—then where's that blood coming from?"

Baird looked down at the bright red stain spreading down his shirtsleeve. He blinked at it; then realized it felt as if someone had laid a red-hot poker across his arm. He pushed open the rent in the fabric and looked inside.

"It's nothing, Ardith," he assured her and climbed to his feet.

"W-w-what do you mean it's n-n-nothing. You've been s-s-shot!"

"It's nothing, Ardith. Hardly more than a scratch."

"Why are you bleeding so much if it's only a scratch?"

"All it needs is bandaging."

"I think it needs a good deal more than that!" she shrilled at him and burst into tears.

Baird stood open-mouthed, watching something he never in this world imagined he'd see: unflappable, intrepid, clear-headed Ardith Merritt having hysterics.

Ardith was mortified. Not only had she burst into tears in front of the cowboys. Not only had she been useless when it came to helping Buck stitch up Baird's arm, but she'd had to excuse herself or faint dead away on the cabin floor. So here she sat on the steps outside, with her head tucked between her knees to keep from becoming a total disgrace.

It was an utterly ridiculous way to behave. Yet something about seeing Baird hurt left her feeling lost, so naked and defenseless. He was supposed to be strong and solid. He was supposed to be impervious and indestructible. She was furious that he wasn't—so furious she was quaking inside.

She couldn't bear that he might have been killed, couldn't bear that he was in there now having Buck patch him up, and she wasn't even able to help. She needed to be doing that. She needed to be doing something so she wouldn't have to acknowledge how much this foolish, dauntless, reckless man had come to mean to her.

She sucked in a lungful of crisp morning air and hoped it would revive her. She didn't want him seeing her all gone at the knees like this. It would make him realize how much she cared for him. It could make him think she loved him. And it wouldn't do for him to realize that, especially now. Especially when she'd just promised Gavin she'd marry him.

She wasn't in much better control of herself when Baird came out of the cabin and sat down heavily beside her.

"Damn you, Baird Northcross," she said from where she was still closely inspecting the toes of her boots, "for deciding to turn heroic at this late date!"

It didn't help that he had probably saved Wilcox's life.

She could feel him looking down at her. He lay his hand on her bowed back. "I'm sorry I upset you."

She let the warmth of his palm soak into her. "It was the most asinine thing I have ever seen you do!"

"I've been thinking that myself."

She heard a lilt of humor in his voice and glanced up to see if he was smiling. She saw the blood on his sleeve instead. Gray fuzzed the edges of her vision again. She dipped her head even lower.

"It's all right, Ardith," he told her. "It's all right now."

He rubbed slow, gentle circles on her back, patting a little like he did with the children. Only he had ever touched her like this, with such warmth and simple tenderness. She closed her eyes and gave herself to the contentment of that innocuous contact.

"I used to crave stories about the west," she confessed after a bit, still not daring to raise her head. "I read stories about cavalry charges and gunfights and cowboys shooting it out with rustlers. I was reading one of those to the children on the train."

"And I suppose they liked it." His voice was so calm and deep. It made her want to lie down somewhere and let it roll over her as if it were the summer sea.

"They did," she answered. "And so did I. Everyone in those stories was so fearless and romantic. And everything always came out right."

"It's fiction, Ardith," he told her gently.

"I know. But those stories lose their appeal when you see what can really happen."

He stroked her hair, combing his fingers through the mass straggling against her shoulders. "This turned out all right, too," he reassured her.

Tears scorched her downcast lashes.

His hand moved in her hair. "You're all right, Ardith. It's over now."

She drew a long, cool breath that tasted of sage and mountain meadows, and she knew he was right. The images of the gunfight with the rustlers had dimmed a little and with them the hard pinch of fear in her belly. She sat up slowly, shakily, and reached across to take his hand.

It was then she saw the stark disillusionment in his eyes. "Baird? What is it?"

He took a small, black leather book from his pocket. "We found this in the cabin."

She opened the pages, her hands trembling just a little. She stared at the dates, the columns of figures. "It's a tallybook."

"Cullen's tallybook. Buck says it looks like he's been keeping track of every cow he stole from us, every one they killed."

She leafed through the book again. McKay's name was on the flyleaf, and though it would take comparing these entries with Cullen's handwriting, Ardith didn't doubt he'd done this.

"It's like he kept that as a trophy, Ardith." Baird shook his head, his voice low and deep with disillusionment. "Like he wanted a record of how he'd cheated me, like he savored every cow he stole from us."

"I'm so sorry," she whispered, clasping his hand, feeling his fingers tighten. "I know you didn't want to believe that Cullen was involved with this."

"It makes things—difficult."

Just then Buck came striding up the rise. "The boys are almost done planting the fellows we shot. Then I figure I'd have them cut the steers out of this herd. We might as well add them to the ones we're going to sell."

Baird clambered to his feet. "Whatever you think."

"And I was wondering, Miss Ardith." Buck turned to her. "If you'll be needing an escort back to the ranch?"

Knowing he'd seen her at her worst only a few minutes before, Ardith heaved to her feet and tried to look like a woman who had regained possession of her faculties. "I'll be perfectly fine riding home alone," she assured him. In truth, she felt a good deal steadier than she expected. "By now everyone there will be frantic."

"Myra would've held things together."

Ardith gave Buck a grateful smile. "Of course she would. Still, I need to get back."

"If you could send Frank and a couple other hands over to pick up Randy and the rest of the cattle, it'd save us some time," Buck suggested.

"Of course I will."

Bear Burton brought her horse to her and stood waiting to help her mount up. Still, she couldn't leave without asking one question. "What are you going to do about Cullen McKay?"

"I don't know," Baird answered on a sigh. "He's a Northcross. He's *family*. How can I turn him in?"

The stark grief on his face and the ambivalence in his eyes made her want to be there to help him decide Cullen's fate, to keep him from doing something he might always regret. The children needed her home instead.

"McKay and the Double T drive headed out last week," Buck volunteered. "He'll be in Cheyenne when we get there."

In spite of Buck's words, Ardith knew this would be Baird's decision, his alone. One of the most difficult he'd have to make in his life.

"Baird?" she whispered and reached out to clutch his hand one last time. When he turned to her his eyes were vacant—the eyes of a man whose last illusions had been shattered and ground to dust. "Baird, please, don't do anything foolish in Cheyenne."

Baird nodded once, but he didn't promise her anything.

SEVENTEEN

They must have seen her coming. By the time Ardith had left her pony with Frank Barnes, China was racing toward her across the yard. She threw herself into Ardith's arms, while Khy, only a few steps behind, burst into tears.

Though she was tired down to the soles of her boots, Ardith scooped Khy up onto her hip and hugged him to her. At the feel of him hugging her back, her throat closed up and tears of her own rose in her eyes. She had never in her life been so glad to be home.

"Are you all right?" China demanded, dancing a little with agitation. "Where have you been? What happened to your face? Is that blood on you?"

Khy was holding on to her so tightly Ardith could barely get her breath. "I'm fine," she assured them, though her voice wavered just a little. "I had a little adventure, but now I'm home safe."

She continued toward the porch where Meggie and Myra were waiting. "I told them you'd be fine," Myra said, though Ardith could tell by the depth of her scowl that Myra had been as concerned for her as the children.

"Was your adventure with Indians?" Khy demanded. "Were there wild animals?"

"Well, no. But guess who I found?"

"Papa?" Khy guessed.

"Well, yes. I saw your papa."

"Is Papa all right?" China demanded, paling a little.

"Your papa's fine. Who I found was Randy."

"Randy the Bull?" Khy asked, his eyes going wide.

Ardith nodded. "I found Randy and the rest of our cattle. It seems we had rustlers, after all."

"Rustlers!" Khy exclaimed. "Like in that book?"

Not exactly.

"Well, sort of," she said instead. "But you're not to worry. Your papa and Buck took care of them. Frank and some of the men are going out now to bring Randy and the cattle home. Let's go into the house, and I'll tell you the rest."

"Would you like some tea?" Myra offered.

"More than nectar and ambrosia," Ardith answered. Trust Myra to know exactly what she needed.

Myra went scurrying ahead to put the kettle on, while Ardith shepherded everyone inside. She noticed how Meggie Jalbert slid her arm around China's waist, and Ardith was profoundly grateful that the older girl had been here when China needed her.

Once she had settled herself at the end of the table with Khy in her lap, Ardith began to explain. "I came upon the rustlers in a valley south of here while I was out looking for something to paint."

"Did the rustlers see you?" China asked. "Did they know you'd found where they were hiding?"

"Two of them did," she answered and fought to keep her voice from quavering. "There was a scuffle. That's how I got banged up, but Primrose and I managed to outrun them."

"Good old Primrose," Khy put in.

Ardith smiled and ruffled his hair. "Since I was pretty sure that most of the cattle were ours, I rode out after your father. Thank goodness they weren't any further south, or I never would have caught up to them."

"You were in their camp?" China questioned her.

Ardith nodded in answer. "Your papa and Buck decided that we should catch the rustlers. So this morning we rode out to their cabin and surprised them while they were asleep."

"And you're sure Papa is all right?" China persisted.

Ardith's stomach rolled as she remembered the blood on Baird's sleeve, and how shaken he'd been by finding proof of Cullen's betrayal.

"Right as rain," she assured them without a qualm. She glanced across at Myra, who'd just brought in her tea. "Everyone's perfectly fine."

The older woman gave her an appreciative nod for the assurance that Buck was all right, too. Still, Ardith had the feeling Myra would be questioning her more closely once they were alone.

"What this means," Ardith continued, "is that we will be leaving for Cheyenne tomorrow." She'd done a good deal of thinking riding back, and decided that she wanted to be in Cheyenne when Baird and the cattle arrived.

"Why are we going earlier?" China wanted to know.

So I can try to keep your papa from doing something foolish.

"I might need extra time in town in case there are legal things I have to attend to because I was the one who found the rustlers. And Meggie still has to be in Boston when her classes begin at the end of the month."

Seeming satisfied at last, China nodded her head.

"What I want you to do," Ardith went on, "is get your things together. Myra and I will be in to help you pack."

"I'll be glad to help China," Meggie offered. "Everything I have is already in my trunk."

Bless the girl. Ardith thought and gave Meggie an approving smile. The more she saw of Cass Jalbert's daughter, the better she liked her.

"Now if you'll get started, I'd like a few minutes to drink my tea and catch my breath. And Khy," Ardith said, holding him on her lap a moment longer, "we won't be packing anything *alive*, will we?"

Khy looked at her hopefully. "Not even the salamanders?"

"I'll help you put them back in the creek later," she promised before letting him go.

As the children hurried off to do as they'd been bidden, Ardith clambered to her feet and took the tea outside.

Myra followed her, and once they were well beyond China and Khy's hearing, the older woman fixed her with those sharp, dark eyes. "Now tell me what really happened."

Ardith did, and Myra listened without interrupting. When Ardith was done, she nodded. "You were right not to tell the children all of this, but I figured things hadn't gone quite as smoothly as you said."

Ardith shivered in spite of the sunlight and the warmth of the tea. Her fear for Baird was alive inside her—a sprawling, growing, breathing thing, feeding on her impatience. She was terrified of what could happen in Cheyenne.

"You love him, don't you?" Myra asked after a moment.

Ardith wasn't sure if she'd fallen in love with Baird when he admitted the truth about Bram, or when she'd seen how he was with China the night Matt died. She wasn't sure if it was recognizing the dreams in those sky-bright eyes, or the doubts Baird still harbored about himself. It had to do with the way he'd held her when she cried, how tender he'd been with her when they made love, and that he'd come to care for the children as much as she did. However it had happened, she'd had to stop denying how she felt this morning when Baird was wounded.

Ardith looked down at Gavin's betrothal ring and knew she could never act on what she felt. But surely it wouldn't hurt to say the words aloud just once—even if it wasn't to the man who'd earned the right to hear them.

"Yes, I love him," she admitted. "I love Baird with all my heart."

*C*heyenne appeared through a boiling film of dust just after midday. Though it wasn't more than a few hundred buildings, Baird recognized that it was an impressive place by prairie standards. Buck said the town had become the territorial capital as soon as the first few cabins were cobbled together, and that it was the major stockyard for several hundred miles around.

Baird paused at the edge of the range where the herd had been turned out to graze, wiped the sweat from his eyes, and took a swallow from his canteen. Buck had explained they'd hold the cattle here west of town while one of them rode in to negotiate the price they'd get for the herd. That price was based on a combination of the value of beef at the slaughterhouses in Chicago and the condition of an outfit's cattle. That's why they had taken their time on the drive, letting the animals graze so they'd arrive in prime condition.

Buck rode up just as he was putting away his canteen. "You coming to town with me to sell the cows?"

Baird knew once Buck and the stockman started dickering with numbers and prices, he'd never keep up, and he didn't want to make a fool of himself. The news wasn't going to be good in any case, and he'd just as soon hear it where he could wash down the bitter taste of failure with a shot of good whiskey.

Besides, he had other things to attend to in Cheyenne.

He shook his head. "You go on ahead. You're the one who knows how these negotiations work."

Buck regarded him, a speculative gleam in those wise gray eyes. "As wrought up as you have been about making your quotas, I figured you'd want to be with me."

Baird shifted in his saddle. "I've trusted you with so much else, I figure I can count on you to do what's best for us now."

Buck fingered his mustache. "You haven't got something else planned for this afternoon, have you?"

Baird shrugged a little; Buck saw through him like plate glass. "I thought I might see if I could find the Cheyenne Club."

The Cheyenne Club was where most of the big ranchers stayed when they were in town. It was reputed to have the atmosphere of a British men's club, except that it smelled of sagebrush and saddle leather instead of wind off the Thames.

Buck shook his head. "You going looking for trouble, son?"

"I'm going looking for Cullen McKay."

"What you need to find is the sheriff. Give him that tallybook you're carrying and let him take care of McKay."

Baird let out a long, deep sigh. "I've decided to handle this my own way."

"Because McKay's family, you mean? It don't seem like you two being family has done anything but make things worse."

Baird couldn't explain why he needed to talk to Cullen first. It had to do with feeling responsible for Bram and the tragic mistake that had taken his life. It had to do with his uncle sending him into exile in Wyoming, and him making peace with Ariel's death. But it had most to do with Ardith and the children, and the life they'd shared while they were here. With the memories he'd carry home with him afterward. He didn't want those memories sullied by regrets about Cullen McKay.

"I have to talk to him," Baird insisted. "But I suppose I should check on Durban before I leave."

The boy had been avoiding Baird more than usual since he and the hands had returned with the steers from the rustled herd. He'd tried to talk to Durban about what happened, but he bolted every time Baird mentioned Cullen's name. The affection Durban bore for McKay was also a part of the reason Baird was determined to confront his cousin privately.

Buck gestured with his hat brim toward the figures on the far perimeter of the herd, barely visible through the rising dust. "The boy was riding with Lem the last time I saw him."

Baird squinted through the haze. "Well, I guess Lem will keep an eye on him while I'm gone. I'd appreciate it if you'd bring him to the hotel later, if I'm not back."

Buck shook his head again, just so Baird would know he didn't approve. "Behave yourself while you're in town," Buck warned him.

"I'm doing what I think is best," Baird insisted. "Now, are you going to give me directions to the Cheyenne Club, or am I going to have to find it by myself?"

"*E*xcuse me," Ardith said to the florid-faced man behind the desk of the Wyoming House Hotel. "Can you give me directions to the Cheyenne Club?"

She and the children and Meggie and Myra had arrived half an hour earlier, travel-grimed and wind-blown after a wild, cross-country trip in an open wagon. With every turn of the wheels, the spark of impatience in her chest had burned a little brighter, flared a little hotter. Arriving in Cheyenne to find that Baird had not checked in gave

Ardith a modicum of breathing room. Still, she was determined to talk to Cullen McKay before Baird did.

The desk clerk looked her up and down. She had taken
time to wash and change her clothes and saw no reason for
him to eye her in such a manner.

"The Cheyenne Club?" she reminded him.

"There's no women 'lowed in there, 'cept by special
invitation, ma'am."

"Does that preclude you from telling me where it is?"
she asked in her most imperious Boston manner.

"Just thought I'd save you the walk, ma'am."

"Perhaps I crave a little exercise."

"You looking for anyone particular?"

Ardith glared at him, considering her options. Perhaps
the clerk was nosy; perhaps there was information to be
had from him. "I'm looking for Mr. Cullen McKay," she
volunteered.

"He sure enough is in town. He ate supper in our
dining room just last night. You want to send a note
'round to the club instead?"

"I don't want to send a note," Ardith enunciated,
smacking her palm on the counter for emphasis and leaning across at him. "I don't care if women aren't allowed. I
want you to tell me where the Cheyenne Club is, or bear
the consequences!"

The desk clerk gave her directions.

*B*aird heard the shouting the moment he opened the
Cheyenne Club's front door.

"I know what you've been doing! You've been rustling
our cattle!"

He recognized the voice instantly. *It was Durban.*

Baird crossed the foyer in three long strides and pushed
through a pair of plush velvet curtains into a room off to
his right. It was a parlor of some kind, though the furni-

ture seemed tossed about in disarray. The men did too. They stood like figures in a tableau, their actions suspended, their faces frozen with horror and fascination.

The only movement came from the center of the room where Durban stood over Cullen McKay, brandishing a pistol.

Cold slammed into Baird like lead shot. Dear God, what was Durban doing here? He was supposed to be back with the herd. He was supposed to be safe. *He shouldn't be confronting Cullen McKay; Baird had come to do that.*

Baird eased slowly to the right, shifting closer to where the man and boy were silhouetted against the light from a pair of etched-glass doors.

"You drove our cows down the mountain from the summer camp," Durban accused, the nose of the pistol he'd been given to carry on the trail drive wavering a little in his hand.

Cullen lifted his palms in conciliation. "Durban, son," he began, his voice intimate and cajoling. "You've made some kind of mistake. I never drove Sugar Creek cattle any—"

"You did! I followed you!" The boy's voice quavered. "I saw where you took them."

Baird moved a few feet nearer, taking care to step into his son's line of sight before he spoke. "Durban," he said, keeping his voice low and cool. "Put down that pistol, Durban. This isn't your fight."

The boy's gaze flickered to his father, then back to Cullen McKay. Though his expression was fierce and his hold on the pistol was steady again, Baird could see tear tracks down his son's face.

Baird stepped a little closer, speaking as if the boy were a skittish colt. "Give me that gun, son. I'm the one who has business with Mr. McKay. I don't need you handling my affairs."

Though he lowered the pistol, Durban held his ground. "He's been stealing our cattle!"

"I know, son," Baird said gently. "That's why I came. Just let me take care of this."

Baird caught the creek of a door being opened out in the foyer, heard the staccato beat of heels across the wooden floor. The portieres in the doorway rattled back on their rings.

"Oh my dear Lord!" he heard a woman whisper as she stepped up behind him. Ardith had arrived.

McKay eased to his feet and spread his hands, broadening his entreaty to the others in the room. "These are ridiculous accusations! Anyone who knows me knows I'd never steal cattle. This boy's made some kind of mistake, and his father is every bit as deluded."

All at once Baird realized who these men were. They were wealthy, hard-faced men, men of the cattle aristocracy. Cullen's peers. When he first came out here Baird might have aspired to be accepted among them, but not anymore.

"Leave the boy out of this, Cullen," Baird offered. "Come with me before someone gets hurt. Let's talk this out like gentlemen."

"I have nothing to say to you, Northcross," McKay declared. "This is all some kind of misunderstanding—"

"I found the valley," Baird said very softly. "I have the tallybook."

He saw the change in Cullen's face, the fear and desperation deepening the mottling of those already flushed features. "I never rustled cattle!"

"You did!" Durban cried, bringing his pistol to bear again. "I saw you!"

"Please, McKay." Baird moved closer. In another few steps he'd be able to ease the gun from Durban's hand. "Let's just go somewhere and talk about this quietly."

McKay seemed to realize how close Baird was. "I won't

go anywhere with you!" Cullen cried. In a blur of movement, McKay grabbed Durban's pistol and hauled the boy against him.

Baird dragged his own Colt from his holster and leveled it at the other man.

The men around the room scuffled backwards, getting out of the line of fire. Ardith seemed to be holding her ground just behind him.

McKay clamped one arm across Durban's chest and jammed the barrel of the gun against his temple. The boy went stiff in Cullen's grasp, his face crumpling with fear.

"Now let me tell you how I mean to do this," McKay instructed, backing toward the pair of tall French doors that led out onto the club's broad porch. "I'm going to take the boy outside. I'm going to grab the first horse I see. And if I'm not followed, Northcross, I'll dump your son at the edge of town. If anyone comes after me, I'll kill the boy."

Baird slid half a step closer. "Cullen, listen," he bargained. "It's not too late to end this peaceably. Put down the gun. Let Durban go. We can—"

McKay hauled Durban hard against his breastbone and pressed the gun barrel more tightly to Durban's head. "Don't come any closer, Northcross. I'll kill the boy. I swear I will. They're going to hang me, anyway."

Baird figured Cullen was two long strides from the double doors. He'd have to pause when he reached them, pause long enough to work the lock or use his weight to break it. When he did, Baird might have time for a single shot.

A single shot. Once he wouldn't have doubted his precision, his own skill. Once, before Bram died, he'd believed he couldn't miss. He didn't believe that anymore.

He straight-armed the pistol and brought his left hand up to steady it. "Let the boy go."

The moment went high-pitched and airless between

them. Sweat slid down Baird's throat. His muscles quivered, tension resonating at the core of him.

"Rot in hell," McKay said and dragged Durban back with him against the doors.

The boy hung in Cullen's grasp, his thin chest bellowing.

Baird could hear Ardith whispering—prayers, he hoped, because they needed them.

He had just enough of his hunter's instincts intact to pick his spot: the corner of his cousin's tweed lapel, six inches up and to the left of Durban's ear.

McKay pressed back against the center of the doors. The wood moaned softly. A seam of light streaked down the widening gap between them. With another shove Cullen would break the latch and step out onto the porch.

Baird's heart thudded like a cannonade. Panic shrieked in his head.

The French doors squeaked as wood and metal gave.

How in the name of God could he be sure enough of his aim to chance his boy's life? Then, like that day at the rustler's cabin, Ardith was there. Her touch came whispersoft against his back, her determination poured through him, giving him courage.

Just as Cullen began to turn, Baird fired.

The boom of the pistol filled the room, a huge, expanding, deafening sound. Smoke spiraled, acrid and black.

McKay lurched backwards.

Durban slipped down and away from his captor. Baird's heart stopped beating as his son dropped to the floor. Behind him he heard Ardith sobbing.

The doors slammed back beneath Cullen's weight, and he fell, sprawling out onto the boards of the covered porch.

"Durban!" Baird roared, anguish filling his heart as he started toward his son. "Oh, God, Durban!"

The boy pushed up from where he'd dropped to the floor and stumbled toward his father. He seemed unhurt and covered the scant distance between them in an instant.

He plowed into his father's chest. "I'm sorry," he moaned. "I'm so sorry. I'm sorry . . ."

Baird wrapped the boy against him so tight he wasn't sure how either of them could breathe. "It's all right, son," he gasped. "It's all right."

Durban pressed his face into his father's chest. Baird held him there, still clutching the smoking pistol in one hand as his other moved over his son. It came away wet—wet and red with Cullen's blood.

Oh God, his shot had been so close. He shivered convulsively, feverish and panting and terrified. *Dear God, so close.*

He burnished his son's back with the flat of his palm. He couldn't believe he was standing here holding Durban, couldn't believe his child was all right, couldn't believe what this boy had tried to do for him.

"You did well," he whispered. "So well. I'm proud of you for coming here. But it's over now; you're safe. Both of us are safe."

Ardith stepped nearer and gathered them in her arms, hugging and weeping. She bound them together just as she'd been doing from the start, loving them and holding them and making China and Khy and Durban and him into a family. He was so blessed she'd had the courage and the fortitude to do that. He leaned into them both, cherishing this moment when life was sweet, and the love he felt for Ardith and the children was sweeter still.

The men crept slowly out of the corners of the room. Some went to where Cullen sprawled motionless on the porch. Baird watched them bending over him.

He hadn't wanted this. He'd wanted to find a way to settle things quietly between his cousin and him. He'd wanted to preserve the Northcross honor; that's why he'd come. But the moment McKay threatened Durban, Baird had had no choice about what he must do.

He'd had to face McKay. And once he got to England he'd have to go to his uncle and tell him the truth about his bastard son, the cattle, and what had happened here. He'd have to make Northam understand what all this meant. Baird had the fortitude to face down his uncle now—now that he had found himself.

As he waited for some word about Cullen's condition, other men came to where he stood with his son and Ardith in his arms.

"Best damned shooting I've ever seen," one of them said.

"Sweet. Very sweet," another murmured and patted his shoulder.

"Never expected McKay to turn out to be a rustler. He seemed like such a gentleman," a third one mumbled.

"Has anyone gone to get a doctor?" Baird heard someone say.

"He's alive, then?" he asked.

"Of course he's alive," someone answered. "That shot passed through his shoulder neat as you please."

Baird holstered his pistol, feeling suddenly boneless with relief. Ardith tightened her arm around his back and leaned into him, half holding him up. She rubbed at him broad-palmed and none too gently, like she was warming a swimmer who'd just come out of the sea.

"Are you all right?" she whispered.

"I'm better now," he answered and let out his breath.

A small man in butler's livery breezed past them with a lawman in tow.

"What in hell's gone on here?" the sheriff blustered. "I'd have thought fellows in such a high-class establishment would know how to behave themselves."

Half a dozen voices rose to explain.

"May the three of us wait for you outside?" Ardith asked once the sheriff had a cursory explanation of what had happened.

The lawman looked her up and down, then nodded. "But don't go far. I'll be needing to question Mr. Northcross."

Ardith was just ushering Durban and Baird onto the front porch of the mansard-roofed mansion when the doctor bustled past them.

Once outside Baird braced his back against the railing and looked down at his boy. Durban's eyes had lost that glazed and hollow look, but he could still see the tremor in his son's hands and sense an odd, jittery energy about him.

Baird reached to smooth down his son's hair and saw the half-moon impression on his temple where Cullen had pressed the barrel of his pistol to Durban's head.

The shakes took Baird all over again. His pulse thudded against the turn of his jaw and his knees went wobbly. *If Cullen had pulled that trigger. If Durban had moved a moment too soon. If he . . .*

Ardith wrapped her arm around his waist and squeezed him hard enough to halt the thoughts flying wildly through his head. The feel of her pressed close against his side steadied him, made him realize how truly blessed he'd been to have her there when he needed her most.

He wrapped his arms around both her and Durban and felt complete. In these last months, he'd found his children waiting for him to be their father. He'd found Ardith—glorious, surprising Ardith—who had the courage to make him look at his life and the strength to help him change it. He'd found himself, in Khy's hugs, China's tears, and Ardith's kisses. He found the man he'd become reflected in Durban's eyes today. And for now—just these few minutes when he needed it so much—he wanted to hold on to all of that.

Long before he was ready to let her go, Ardith shifted away from him. By the set of her mouth, he could tell she had something on her mind.

"Durban," she began, laying her hand across the boy's shoulders. "Don't you think you have something to explain to your father?"

Color washed into his son's ashen cheeks. That shivery energy intensified. "I'm sorry," he began. "I'm sorry. So sorry. I didn't mean it. I wasn't sure—"

Baird stopped him with a hand on his arm. "Just tell me whatever this is, all right? We've had enough misunderstandings between us."

Durban straightened, and Baird glimpsed in his son's face the fine, strong man this boy would one day become. "Papa," Durban confessed, "I knew that Cullen was stealing our cattle."

Baird nodded. "Go on."

"I saw him rounding up some of our steers while we were up at the summer pasture."

Baird let out his breath, not sure if he should reprimand the boy or hear him out. "Why didn't you come to me then?" he finally asked him.

Durban dipped his head and looked across at Ardith beneath the shaggy drape of his hair.

She nodded to encourage him.

"The first time I caught Cullen stealing cows," Durban admitted, "was the day Khy got hurt. I was so mad at you then I couldn't tell you. I knew what Cullen was doing was wrong, but I—I thought you deserved whatever happened."

The child had punished his father in the only way he knew—by keeping his secret.

"I—I tried to talk to Cullen the day of Matt's funeral. I wanted to tell him I knew about him stealing cows and make him stop. But I didn't have a chance to be alone with him."

What would Cullen have done, Baird wondered, if he realized that Durban knew about the rustling? Would his boy have been safe or would Cullen have tried to silence him?

"I started following him after that. I found out where they were keeping the cattle. I almost told you the day we were looking for Randy, but I didn't know how. We were so close to the entrance of the valley . . ."

Not a hundred yards away, but neither he nor Buck had seen the passage. He remembered how jumpy Durban had been, how tight and restless. He wished he'd had the insight to recognize what that meant.

"So I told Aunt Ardith there was a place I wanted her to paint," Durban went on, "and I gave her directions."

Baird's head came up. "You what?"

Durban bowed his head, but made the admission anyway. "I told her about the valley."

Baird shoved to his feet. "Didn't you realize you put your Aunt Ardith in danger by doing that?" He could still see her riding into camp, so bruised and battered. Durban had very nearly gotten Ardith killed.

Durban's blue eyes clouded with tears. "I'm sorry. I—I didn't know there were men in the valley. I didn't mean to put her in danger."

"He didn't know how to tell you, Baird." Ardith stepped between them, fierce as a lioness protecting her cub. "He was afraid. You understand that, don't you? You've carried some secrets in your time."

He stared at her, knowing she meant about Bram's death, remembering how hard it had been to tell her all of that. Though he'd never forget what had happened in Burma, this time the images didn't flash through his head in all their vivid reality. They were softer, slightly blurred, like photographs left out too long in the sun. There was sadness and endless regret, but the horror seemed to be fading.

He settled back against the railing and let out his breath. "All right, son. Why don't you tell me the rest of it?"

Durban shrugged. "I wanted to go with you when you went after the rustlers, but Aunt Ardith said she'd tell. So when you came back shot, I figured that was my fault, too.

"The day we were looking for Randy I heard Cullen say he'd see you at the Cheyenne Club when we came to town. So I thought if I came to see him first"—Durban gulped and started to cry—"there wouldn't be any chance of you getting hurt again."

Baird pulled the boy against his chest, rocking him, holding him. Shaking his head in exasperation.

"I came because I wanted to get things settled." The boy's words were muffled against Baird's chest. "Because everything that happened after I found out about the rustling was my fault."

His fault. Baird understood his son's feelings of responsibility far too well. Baird had believed losing the cattle was his fault, that not making his uncle's quota was his fault. In some ways he still believed that, but he was learning to forgive himself for things he couldn't help.

"It's all right, son. I'm so proud of you for owning up to this, even prouder of you now than I was before." He couldn't think when he'd seen such courage or such gallantry in someone so young.

"But next time—" He tipped his son's face up to his and looked into his eyes. "—let me handle things, will you? I'm a lot more dependable now than I used to be."

He looked across at where Ardith was standing only a few feet away. There were tears on her cheeks and a glow of pride in her eyes. He pulled her into his arms again, and stood there holding her and holding his boy, and thinking he was the most fortunate of men to have been given all this.

That's how the sheriff found them when he came out onto the porch a good while later.

Baird straightened, his arm still looped around his son's shoulders, and faced the lawman. Ardith scrubbed the tears from her cheeks with one of her ridiculous handkerchiefs.

The sheriff was a bluff, businesslike man, with a chest the size of a puncheon barrel, and kindness in his eyes. "After talking to everyone inside I have a pretty good idea what happened. There won't be any charges lodged against you, Mr. Northcross. It isn't often I have so many upstanding citizens witness a shooting, and all of them ready to swear it was self-defense. I just have a few more questions I have to ask you."

"Will you need to speak to either my son or Miss Merritt?" Baird inquired.

"No sir, just you."

"But Pa," Durban began.

"No, Durban. It's up to me to settle this, not you. Now, can I count on you to see that your aunt gets safely back to our hotel? I've got some things to do here in town, but I'll join you as soon as I can."

"Sure, Pa. I'll see Aunt Ardith home," Durban answered and offered Ardith his arm as if he were far older than his years.

Ardith shot Baird an amused, if still slightly teary, glance as Durban led her down the steps. Baird watched them go, then shifted his attention to the sheriff.

"You've got a fine family there," the man commented.

"Yes, I do," Baird agreed. A very fine family, at least until he put Ardith on the train. He wondered again how he was going to give away something so precious.

"Now, about Mr. McKay?" the sheriff reminded him.

Baird nodded, turning his thoughts to the business at hand. "I saw the doctor go in. Does he think Cullen will recover?"

"It was a clean shot, and Mr. McKay is being well taken care of. The doctor did say there might be some damage to the nerves, that Mr. McKay might not regain full use of his arm, but it's too early to tell for sure. They've taken him to one of the rooms upstairs, and I'll be posting a guard."

"You've arrested him, then?"

"We don't take rustling lightly here, or endangering children, either. But, strictly speaking, the rustling is a territorial matter so I'll be giving them the information I've collected. They'll conduct their own investigation, and want a statement from whoever found the cattle."

"That would be Miss Merritt."

"And any evidence you might have of what he was doing?"

Baird sighed and withdrew the tallybook from his pocket. He'd hoped all this would come out differently.

"They'll probably want this," he said and told the sheriff everything.

"Once we verify the script," the lawman said when Baird had finished, "we'll have everything we need to prove the charges."

"What will happen to Cullen after that?"

The sheriff seemed to know what Baird was asking. "He's made his bed, sir, by rustling those cattle. But since they were all from your herd, I think if you have a word with the judge, he might be lenient."

"You mean McKay might go to prison instead of being sentenced to hang."

The sheriff adjusted his hat. "That's about the way I see it pulling together."

Baird felt weary all at once, with a bone-deep kind of exhaustion that came with shouldering responsibilities. Still, he straightened, shoving himself away from the porch railing. "Is there more you need to know, sheriff?"

The man shook his head.

"Then, if you don't mind, I have some cows to sell down at the stockyards. I'll be at the Wyoming House for the best part of a week if you need anything more."

"Mr. Northcross?"

Baird had started down the steps when the sheriff stopped him. "Yes?"

"This could have turned into something terrible, sir. I want to thank you for acting with restraint, and tell you you're either a damned fine shot or the luckiest man that ever lived."

"I'm the luckiest man that ever lived."

EIGHTEEN

*B*aird left the Cheyenne Club feeling like he held everything he'd ever wanted in his own two hands: Ardith, his boy, a sense of family, and his own lost honor. Even if the confrontation with Cullen McKay hadn't turned out the way he'd hoped, at least he'd had resolution.

Spotting Buck Johnson just coming out of the stockyard offices reminded Baird of the ranch and the sale of the cattle—and of how he'd failed again. It reminded him that in a few days time, he was going to have to open his hands and let go of everything that was precious to him, like it was one of Khy's damned butterflies.

He stood watching Buck make his way up the street, not sure he wanted to follow. He knew he'd tried when it came to running the ranch. He knew he'd done his best. But with Cullen undermining his every move, none of it had mattered. He'd accepted weeks ago that he wasn't going to meet the quotas his uncle had set for him or record the profits the shareholders expected. He didn't need Buck to tell him that. Still, he knew he should go after the older man.

Though dread lay heavy in his belly, Baird stalked along the wooden sidewalk in the direction Buck had gone. He caught up to him midway down the next block where the grizzled ranchman had paused to light one of his thin, dark cheroots. He turned as Baird approached.

"Did you sell our cows?" Baird greeted him.

Buck offered him one of his smokes. Baird accepted and lit the cigar, hoping the tobacco would take the edge off his anticipation.

"We got the beeves all counted and sold and driven into boxcars," Buck told him as they strode in the direction of the hotel.

"That went a good deal faster than I thought it would."

"They had a train headed out to Chicago this afternoon. I saw the opportunity, and I took it," Buck glanced over at him. "You wanted me to do that, didn't you?"

Baird gave a quick, jerky nod, wanting to hear the rest.

"I sent Jeff and Bear along to look after our beeves," the older man went on. "I gave the boys their wages, too. And a ticket back to Rock Creek in case they spend all their money on city women."

Baird did his best to smile. "That sounds fine."

His insides buzzed and sweat crept down his ribs as he tried to muster the courage to ask how much Buck got for the cattle. Even if they hadn't made the quotas, months of hard work came down to this. His self-sufficiency and the children's futures came down to this. It seemed so odd that he was going to learn something so monumental wandering down the street in a town thousands of miles from anyplace important.

He took a breath and forced the question up his throat. "So how did we do?"

One corner of Buck's mustache tilted as he fished a folded paper from the pocket of his jacket. "See for yourself."

Baird's hands trembled a little as he opened it. He paused in mid-stride to look down. His heartbeat stumbled.

Numbers! The paper was filled with numbers, notations in Buck's scrawled, uneven script. This meant more to him than any information he'd ever received in his life, and he couldn't make heads or tails of it.

Any goddamned fool should have known what this said, but Baird Northcross didn't. No wonder things had gone the way they had. He didn't deserve for them to go better.

He didn't even know if he should slap Buck on the back or hang his head in desolation. He slid a glance at the older man, trying to gauge what he expected.

"Giving the animals time to graze on the trail helped get that price," Buck was saying. "Matheson said our beeves were prime specimens, the best that passed through the stockyards all season."

"That's good," Baird answered, still studying the numbers. He couldn't bring himself to ask Buck about them, either. That would mean explaining his deficiencies, facing the shame. But he'd spent too much of his life making do not to know how to worm his way around this.

"Mind if I keep your notations?" he asked.

Buck shook his head. "Nah. I figured you'd need those for your report to the stockholders, anyway. The bank'll be transferring the funds into the Sugar Creek account first thing tomorrow."

Baird tucked the paper away, then reached across and clasped Buck's shoulder. "Thank you," he said, squeezing hard. "I wouldn't have been able to make my way on the Sugar Creek if it weren't for you. I didn't know the first thing about cattle when I came here. If we've had even a modicum of success, it's because you're such a damn fine foreman."

"Well," Buck ducked his head and chewed a little on

his cigar. "Well, you been a damn fast learner, son. You ain't afraid of working hard, and you've a feel for the land. You sure you won't be coming back for another season?"

That question was the highest compliment Buck could have paid him. Baird rode a swell of pride and ducked his head, mimicking Buck's movements, behaving in a way that never would have occurred to him in London.

"I don't know what's going to happen," he answered honestly. "What with having to think about the children—"

"Lord Almighty!" Buck stopped dead in his tracks. "I forgot to tell! Durban wasn't with the herd when I got back from seeing Matheson. No one seemed to know how long he'd been gone or where he went. As soon as we got the cattle into the railcars, I sent two of the men to look for him."

"It's all right," Baird reassured him. "Durban's with Ardith."

"The women are here, you mean?" Buck asked, his eyes brightening. It was clear he'd be glad to see his wife.

"They're at the hotel. I thought we'd all have dinner together tonight. Someplace where Myra doesn't have to do the cooking."

"She'll like that," Buck said, a grin breaking through his mustache. "So where'd Durban go?"

The image of Cullen holding the pistol to Durban's head flashed through Baird's mind. He felt the recoil of his Colt revolver against his palm and smelled the gunpowder. He remembered how Durban had clung to him afterwards, and how he'd clung to his son.

And to Ardith. *Dear God, how would he have gotten through that without Ardith?*

"Durban rode into Cheyenne to find Cullen McKay," he told Buck, a catch of pride in his voice.

"Well, damn me!" Johnson exclaimed. "You don't say. Did the boy find him? Did you?"

Buck steered Baird through the doors of the saloon they were passing and found a table in the corner. While they waited for their drinks, Baird told him the rest of it.

When he was done, Buck sipped at his whiskey and gave a sage nod. "It's what's right, son. There's no sense blaming yourself for something someone else done. It don't matter *why* McKay broke the law; he stole those cattle. And he threatened your boy, to boot. He deserves to face his punishment."

Baird toyed with his glass of whiskey and knew that Buck was right. He'd let himself feel responsible for this because of pranks he'd played on Cullen when they were boys. He'd excused Cullen's thievery because somewhere down deep he'd thought McKay deserved better than he'd got.

Baird refilled Buck's glass from the bottle at the center of the table. "I just didn't want it to turn out like this," he said. "I didn't want to shoot him. I'd hoped to protect his family, *my* family, from what he's done."

Buck drank down another inch of the amber-brown liquor. "Don't you think his father knows what kind of a man his son turned out to be? Don't you suppose Cullen ended up out here for a reason?"

"So did I," Baird acknowledged and sliced a glance at the other man. "His father sent me here because he wanted to watch me fail. But no matter how we made out with the cattle, no matter whether we made a profit or not, I didn't fail. This country gave me something to believe in. You taught me what I needed to know about the ranch. I had the children to keep me—honest. And Ardith . . ."

Baird's voice broke, and he looked down at his hands. He knew Buck could see how much he loved her, how much he regretted losing her. He didn't even try to hide his feelings, though he wasn't sure he could put into words what Ardith meant to him, how much she'd given him.

After a long moment filled with the tinkle of piano music and the clink of glasses, Buck cleared his throat. "Well, if Ardith means so much to you, just exactly what are you going to do about her?"

Baird shrugged, his throat too thick to speak. The misery of saying good-bye to Ardith and putting her on the train lay just ahead. She had become so much a part of the fabric of all their lives that he didn't know how he could rip out such a vital thread without their entire world unraveling.

He needed her so much. He would never have learned to be a father to his children except for her. He would never have become the man he was if she hadn't pushed and cajoled and believed in him. How was he going to find the words to tell her all of that before she left?

Baird swallowed down half the glass of whiskey and looked at Buck. "There's nothing I can do about Ardith. I don't have anything to offer her. Back in England it isn't even legal for me to marry her. Besides, she's going back east. She's agreed to marry that publisher of hers and she'd never break her word."

He heard the rasp of anguish in his own voice and knew that Buck must hear it, too.

"Well, no," the older cowboy said. "Strictly speaking, Ardith hasn't told him she'd marry him yet."

Baird's head came up. "What?"

Buck pulled the letter he was to have mailed for Ardith out of his pocket and laid it on the table between them. "I was just on my way to the post office when I met you. Why don't you be the one to put it in the mail for her?"

Baird looked down at the creamy envelope addressed in Ardith's flowing hand. He looked up at Buck.

Johnson's wise old eyes bored into him. He was smiling ever so slightly and fingering his mustache.

Baird didn't even pause to consider the consequences. He picked up the letter and tucked it away.

"I'll see you back at the hotel," he said and shoved to his feet.

*B*aird topped the stairs and had just started down the wide, carpeted hall of the Wyoming House Hotel when China and Meggie came out of a room on the right.

"Papa!" his daughter cried and hurried toward him. "I'm so glad to see you!"

She threw her arms around him and hugged him tight. "Aunt Ardith said you were fine, but I feel so much better now that I've seen you for myself," she murmured against his ear. "Who would have thought that Mr. McKay was a rustler, for goodness sake? I can't believe it even now."

Baird got a good look at China when she stepped back. She had on her city clothes, a fashionable bodice and slim, draped skirt in a wine-red shade, and a smart, narrow-brimmed hat. She looked years older here than she had at the ranch, and he wondered when she'd grown up so much.

"Where are you and Meggie going all by yourselves?" he asked her, acknowledging the Jalbert girl with a nod of his head. Meggie looked older here, too, and he found himself wondering if Hunter would be as bewildered by the change in his daughter as Baird was.

"We're meeting Myra downstairs," China told him. "We thought we'd get something for Aunt Ardith to remember us by."

Something to remember them by. As if Ardith was likely to forget. As if he was likely to forget the way Ardith was with his children. As if he was going to be able to bear it when she was gone.

"Meggie suggested jewelry of some kind," China went on. "And I think I quite agree with her."

It was a thoughtful, generous thing for them to do, and Baird gave China every bit of money in his pockets. He only wished there was more.

"You buy her something nice," he admonished them, his heart like lead inside him.

"Thank you for your contribution, Papa." China waved gaily and headed down the stairs.

He watched them go. Just when he'd begun to appreciate the wonder of all he had, his life was coming apart at the seams—and he didn't know how to prevent it.

He turned back down the hall and was trying to remember if the room number the desk clerk had given him was two thirty-two or two twenty-three, when he heard the clink of glass behind him.

Durban was coming carefully down the hall with two corked bottles of sarsaparilla in one hand and a sack of thick, doughy pretzels in the other. A smile spread across his face when he saw his father.

"How come you're standing in the hall, Pa? Our room's right here." Durban did his best to balance the bottles and bag against himself as he reached for the doorknob. "Aunt Ardith gave me money to go get sarsaparilla for Khy and me. I—I hope that's all right."

Baird reached for the latch. "Is Khy in with your Aunt Ardith now?"

Durban shook his head. "Aunt Ardith took a headache powder when we got back and wanted to lie down for a little while. I left Khy in our room."

"You left Khy alone?" Baird asked, trying not to sound accusatory.

"Oh, it's all right. Aunt Ardith gave him one of her leftover sketchbooks, and now all he wants to do is draw." Durban abruptly colored up as if he'd just realized who he was talking to so freely. "I—I think he draws lots better than China," he confided anyway.

Why hadn't someone thought of that sooner? Baird

wondered as they entered the room to find Khy cross-legged on the floor with the sketchbook in his lap. The boy climbed to his feet when he saw his father.

"Want to see what I've been making?"

Baird slung his saddlebags over the footboard of the big iron bed and hugged his younger son. He settled down to page through Khy's sketchbook. He recognized the wagon they'd driven to Cheyenne, a stream with pines on the opposite side, and a portrait of Myra which, in a childish way, was a very good likeness.

He ruffled Khy's already-ruffled hair, pleased to have this quiet moment with the boys. "These drawings are very good. You take after your Aunt Ardith, don't you?"

Khy beamed up at him, then accepted the bottle of sarsaparilla and the pretzels Durban had divided between them.

Baird begged a sheet of paper and a pencil and sat down at the little table. Buck's notations had been burning a hole in his pocket all the way back to the hotel. Now he had to find a way to make sense of them.

He worked over them and scratched things out. Worked and scratched things out again. He made tally marks at the top of the page. He counted on his fingers, but nothing helped. The longer he worked, the more mysterious the numbers became and the more frantic he was to learn what they could tell him.

He slammed back in his chair, and threw the pencil down on the table. Why was he like this, goddamnit? Why couldn't he see numbers the way other people saw them? Why was he so—

"What are you trying to do?" Durban asked, materializing at his elbow.

Heat ran up into Baird's cheeks.

"Nothing," he barked and covered the numbers with his hand.

"It's maths, isn't it?" the boy asked wisely.

Baird's face got even hotter. It was a hell of a thing for a father to have to admit to his son that he couldn't do the simplest sums.

"William Frederick isn't good at maths, either," Durban said, sounding sympathetic. "Sometimes Mr. Quinn, our tutor, lets me help William. Would you like me to help you, Papa?"

The tips of Baird's ears seemed hot enough to steam. How could he ask his eleven-year-old son for help? It was one more insult to heap on all the others this affliction had brought him.

Yet Durban sounded genuinely willing, and Baird wanted so much to know how close they'd come to their quota. He needed to know how badly he'd failed.

Baird let out his breath on a ragged sigh. "I'm trying to figure out how much money we made on the cattle Buck sold today. These are the numbers he gave me."

Durban sat down at the table and took up the pencil. Baird stood over him, shifting from foot to foot, going cold with sweat as he waited.

Durban finally wrote a sum at the bottom of the page. He checked it twice, and then sat staring.

"What is it? What did you get?" Baird asked, trying to brace himself.

Durban couldn't seem to take his eyes off the numbers. "Is this how much money they gave you for those cows?"

Baird's heart drummed hard against his ribs. He thought he'd steeled himself to hear this, but his palms were slick. "How much money?"

"Ninety-seven thousand dollars," Durban told him, still staring at the page. "Do we really have that much money, Papa? How much do you suppose that is in pounds?"

When he didn't answer, Durban looked up.

"Are you crying, Papa?" the boy asked, his eyes gone wide with incredulity. "Geez, Pa, why are you crying?"

• • •

*W*ith a sense of finality, Ardith threaded the last of her heavy hairpins into the smooth loops of her chignon. Tonight she would have dinner with the people who'd become so dear to her since she'd come west. Tomorrow she and Meggie would board the train for Boston. She was resigned to what must happen, and she refused to torture herself by putting off the inevitable.

After this afternoon's events—Baird's confrontation with Cullen McKay and Durban's reconciliation with his father—she had no reason to linger. She'd accomplished what she'd set out to do: Baird had come to love his children and would be the best father he could to them.

But, oh! How she would miss everyone here! She would miss Buck Johnson's slow, sly smile and Myra's homey wisdom. She despaired at leaving the children: China who was learning to laugh again, Khy who was showing signs of interest in her own beloved pencils and paints, and Durban who had turned a corner in his life this afternoon and would be a different boy because of it. And Baird.

Oh, God! Baird.

She couldn't help worrying about how he'd done with the sale of the cattle this afternoon. If only he'd made enough profit to meet the stockholders' expectations, if only he could go back to England with his head held high, she'd be able to leave for Boston with a peaceful heart. But if he'd failed . . .

Ardith swiped hastily at her eyes, glad that China and Meggie had already gone down to supper. No good could come of letting either of them see the depth of her regrets.

Her future was opening up before her; that's how she must look at things now. Far off in Boston, Gavin was waiting. He was a fine, decent man, the man she'd been so sure she wanted when she came west. She must school herself to be the very best wife she could to him. She must channel the deep affection she felt for him to make him happy. Still, she hated leaving the wild, windswept beauty of this place that had given her so much.

A sharp, impatient rap on the door of the hotel room startled her and made her realize she'd been dawdling. She leaned closer to the mirror, pinched color into her cheeks, and crossed the room to answer it.

Baird stood outside, so handsome he took her breath away. He flashed her his bright rogue's smile, a smile she hadn't seen in weeks. Something hot and reckless simmered in his eyes. She hoped this meant that things had gone well with the stockman this afternoon.

"You look lovely tonight, Ardith," he told her, and she could hear a note of real appreciation in his voice. "Are you ready?"

"Just let me get my reticule."

He leaned against the doorjamb freshly bathed and barbered, returned to his guise as a British gentleman. Yet, she had come to prefer him a little rough and unkempt, with his hair shaggy and long against his collar and his cheeks faintly sooty with a day-old growth of beard. That's how she thought of him now, as a western man, a man who'd proved his strength and heart.

"Buck and Myra have already taken everyone down to the dining room," she said as she stepped out into the hall. "They're waiting for us there."

"No, they're not."

She turned from locking the door. "What do you mean?"

He flashed that smile at her again, quick and a little impulsive. "I mean that Buck and Myra are looking after the children tonight. I wanted to have dinner with you myself."

Something about his mood unsettled her, made her wary. She tried to discern what it was, tipping her head as if listening to the strains of a song playing far in the distance.

"Why?" she asked.

He caught her hand and a frisson of energy danced between them. "Is it so hard to believe that I might want you to myself just once?"

Before she could answer, he led her past the head of the stairs to a door at the far end of the hall. He ushered her into a suite of rooms where a table was laid for supper in the parlor. Beyond it, through a set of double doors, stood a wide brass bed.

Ardith stopped just beyond the threshold. "I can't do this," she said.

He laid his hand at the back of her waist and eased her further into the room. Even that innocuous contact set something humming inside her.

"What can't you do?" he coaxed her. "Have supper with me?"

She turned to him and the power of his beauty and grace rolled over her, making the words so much harder to speak. "I can't go where this supper might lead me. I can't lie with you again."

He looked down at her for one long moment. His mouth narrowed, then smoothed again. "I have some things I need to discuss with you. Will you stay long enough for that?"

She battled her own instincts, wanting to stay but afraid her weaknesses would lead her to folly where he was concerned.

"All right," she finally agreed and went to settle herself in the single chair. She knotted her hands in her lap. "What is it you want to talk about?"

Instead of sitting at one end of the settee as she'd expected, Baird came to his knees beside her.

Her nerves jangled wildly in alarm at having him so close. It was all she could do to keep from reaching out to touch his face and smooth the few gray hairs that had begun to curl at his temple.

"I—I've been thinking about Hunter Jalbert," he began.

It wasn't what she had expected him to say. "Thinking about Hunter?"

"I have been thinking about what he said, about how I could start a horse ranch back in the hills behind the Sugar Creek. I have been thinking about what we talked about that night on the porch." She could see how the light shone in his eyes as he spoke about the ranch. "I've decided that raising horses and training them is really what I want to do."

"Then I think you should do it."

He took her hand. The warmth of his fingers linked with hers, the pressure of his thumb in the hollow of her palm sent tingles of warmth rippling up her arm. "I know it wouldn't be easy to stay in Wyoming and start again, and I'd want you with me if I did."

Ardith stiffened and withdrew her hand. "Oh, Baird, I can't—"

"I've got the money now—"

She caught her breath in surprise. "You do?"

"With the steers we recovered from the rustlers, not only have we met the stockholders' expectations—"

"You have?"

"We surpassed them!"

She leaped at him, throwing her arms around Baird's neck. She hugged him hard, feeling the joy in him, the strength and breadth of his body against her.

"Oh, Baird! That's wonderful! I'm so glad!"

He hugged her back. "We did it, Ardith. I can hardly believe it myself, but we did it!"

Ardith held on tight, blinking back tears. All his hard work and worry had paid off. He was going to be fine. He and the children were going to be fine.

"I'm so proud of you!" she whispered. "It means you accomplished what you set out to do! It means you succeeded!"

"What it means, Ardith, is that at great risk to yourself, you saved us. You saved all of us—the children, the Sugar Creek, all the hands. And me, Ardith. Especially me."

"You saved yourself. You worked harder than any man I've ever seen to accomplish this." She hugged him harder, and the tears she'd been trying not to shed spilled over. She clung to him, weeping freely at first, then fighting to get a grip on her emotions. But why should she be controlled in the face of such news as this? She wanted to laugh and dance—and weep if it pleased her. Baird had won; he'd conquered his doubts. He deserved this chance to start his life again.

"What this also means," he continued, "is that beyond my wages, I will receive a substantial portion of the proceeds. I mean to buy land with it and start that ranch."

She could see the fire spark up again in those fine, bright eyes; see the belief in himself that this had given him. It was the perfect ending for her stay out here: Baird settled and doing what he loved, and the children secure with their father.

"You buy that land!" she told him.

"I will! I'm going to stay right here in Wyoming—"

"Good."

"—where no damned English law can tell me who to love and who to marry."

Ardith's breath caught in her throat. "I beg your pardon?"

"It means I can ask you to marry me if I want to," he told her almost fiercely. "I couldn't do that when I thought we were going back to England—but I can do it now. Will you be my wife, Ardith? Will you marry me?"

She stared at him, going still inside. Baird was asking her to share his future, offering her a place in the lives of

the children she loved, and a home in this wild and glorious place. He was offering her everything she'd ever
wanted.

It was the most terrible moment in her whole life.

"Oh, Baird!" She looked up with her heart in her eyes.
"You have done me a wonderful honor by asking me to
marry you, but I—I've already committed myself to
Gavin. I've given my promise. I wrote him a letter telling
him I would—"

Baird dipped into the pocket of his coat and withdrew
the letter addressed to Gavin. He lay it in her lap.

"What—what does this mean?" she asked him.

He met her gaze without flinching. "Buck gave me
your letter to post, and I—well, for reasons of my own—I
haven't done that yet. Do you want me to?"

Ardith blinked at him. "I—I don't—"

"I love you, Ardith," he told her, his voice low and
deep and trembling with conviction. "I love you in a way I
never dreamed I could love anyone. I love you for the way
you've made me look at myself, and for what you've made
me see. I love you for the man you've helped me become.
Now I want to give you something back. I want to live
with you for the rest of our days and do everything in my
power to make you happy."

Ardith grappled with her own disbelief. She was
stunned by the choice he had given her.

He took out a small velvet box and set it in her lap atop
the letter she had written to Gavin.

For a moment she hesitated, simply looking down at
the letter and the box. Then, with trembling fingers she
raised the cover. A plain gold band gleamed in the lamp-
light.

"Oh, Baird," she breathed.

He pushed to his feet and paced away. "I can't give you
what Rawlinson can, Ardith. I can't give you fine jewels,
or fancy houses, or a refined and cultured life. All I can

give you is worry and hard work and three children who adore you. All I can give you is myself and a place in the west. But I love you, Ardith. I can give you that—and my ardor and my devotion and my hopes for the future."

She looked up at him, at this fine, strong man who had tried so hard and learned so much. At the compelling reality that had finally overshadowed all that had gone before. At the love of her life who was offering her everything he had to give.

The choice was there for her to make, marriage with a man who was everything she thought she'd wanted, or to a man who stirred her soul. She stared at the elegant emerald ring gleaming on her hand. She looked down at the box in her lap, at the plain gold band, and she knew which of them was right for the woman she had become.

With real sadness in her heart she worked the emerald ring down and off her finger.

She heard Baird catch his breath, but he didn't say a word.

She clasped it in her hand, thinking of Gavin, who had offered her this ring as a token of his love. Of Gavin who was kind and good, but who deserved far more than she would ever be able to give him.

Ardith put the letter she'd written on the table beside her chair, and with a long, lingering brush of her fingertips she set the ring on top of it. Then she looked up at Baird. Still clutching the velvet box, she rose and went to him.

He watched with pride and admiration in his eyes as she closed the distance between them. He enfolded her in his arms and drew her against him.

"I love you, Baird," she said, looking into his face. "I love that you have become the man I always believed you could be. I love that you have offered me your children to raise. I love that you trust me with them—"

"And my heart, Ardith. I trust you with my heart."

She smiled up at him. "I've given you my heart, too, Baird Northcross. And I'd be so proud to be your wife."

Baird bowed his head and kissed her, kissed her with all the tenderness and abandon any woman could want. She flowed against him, eager to hold him, eager for his touch, eager for the life they could have together.

He swept her up in his arms, carried her to the bed, and put her down on the soft, green coverlet. He drew the tortoiseshell pins from her hair, unwound the silken coil, and spread the heavy dark strands against the pillows. He worked the etched steel buttons down her bodice from their holes, then bent over her and kissed her.

His mouth moved on hers, tender and enticing, lingering in soft, exquisite explorations of the curve of her lips, the gentle bow, the corners of her mouth. He touched her face, his hand brushing over the fading bruise at the curve of her cheek. He smoothed back her loosened hair.

His eyes were warm and filled with tenderness. "Have I ever told you that your lips remind me of ripe, sweet raspberries?" he whispered, his breath tickling her skin, his hand curled over the mound of her breast. "And that your hair, your glorious hair, is the exact color of strong coffee? And your skin . . ."

"What about my skin?" Ardith whispered back, mesmerized by the poetry in his words and the adoration in his eyes. The love she'd never expected to see in them.

He smiled a little. "Your skin is like the most luscious Devonshire cream."

"It sounds as if you plan to eat me up."

He smiled a little more. "You're the most delicious, gloriously beautiful woman I've ever known. Of course I want to eat you up. I want to sip at you and nibble on you and kiss you in places and in ways you haven't even thought about yet. I want to make love to you and feel you melt beneath me."

He kissed her again, but this time the tenderness gave

way to stronger emotions, passions she had tasted only once before.

He sought her mouth, teasing her tongue with his, inciting her to answer in kind. And as her tongue rose to play with his he stroked her breast, circling her lawn-veiled nipple with the rough, callused pad of his thumb.

She stirred beneath his touch, fighting to catch her breath, moaning a little. He smiled against her mouth, teasing her with that slow, insistent friction. Delectable weakness spilled down her arms and legs.

He fluttered kisses over her brow and temple, her nose and eyelids, and the point of her chin. He lingered over the lobe of her ear, whispering wicked proposals between his kisses. A shiver of delight ran through her.

She drew him closer. She wanted him lying over her. She wanted to feel his weight, feel the heat of his chest and belly and legs sliding over her, feel the press of his desire against her thighs.

She wanted him naked. Her cheeks flamed with the sheer carnality of such a thought. Yet she turned her face against his throat and told him that.

Baird gave a quick, delighted laugh and eased her up to stand beside him at the side of the bed.

Nakedness was not an easy state for either of them to achieve. There was her tight-fitting bodice to slip down her arms. There were buttons on his coat and vest. He cursed over the hooks at the waistband of her narrow skirt, and the tapes that held the draping in place. She fumbled with the buttons on his trousers.

"Hurry," he whispered. "Hurry." But he was tangled up in the laces of her long ivory-busked corset a moment later.

He got distracted somehow, murmuring about the grace of her neck and shoulders and lavishing slow, sensual kisses over her delicate skin. But at last the offending object joined the rest of their clothing on the floor beside the bed.

Her chemise gave way, as did the soft well-washed fabric of her tucked-lace drawers, so that when he thrust back the covers on the bed and laid her down across the sheets she was very nearly naked.

Only her shoes and thigh-high stockings remained.

She knew she should feel ashamed to lie unclothed before a man, and yet for the first time in her life she was pleased with the full, soft turns of her own body, the lushness of her breasts, and the flare of her hips. She could see appreciation for every curve in his sky-dark eyes, see the need her femininity roused in him.

In that moment she came to believe that in Baird's eyes she was beautiful. It was a liberating notion, one she would dwell on when there were fewer and less fascinating things to divert her.

He let her watch as he stripped off the remainder of his clothes. The days of hard work had honed him well. As he bared himself to her, she traced the sleek, spare lines of his body with her eyes. Now she'd have the chance to draw him like this, capture the breadth of that powerful chest and the strength of his legs, the grace that was so much a part of him.

She told him that.

"Why, Miss Merritt, I never before suspected you had so many licentious ideas in that head of yours," he teased her.

"I've never before, Mr. Northcross," she shot back, "been so well and truly inspired."

He laughed again and finished removing her shoes. He left her knitted stockings in place and brushed his hands along the contours of her long legs. The sensation of his palms working slowly upward immersed her in sweet, seeping pleasure.

With gliding strokes he breached the boundary between the sheer black fabric of her hose and her pale, ripe flesh. The intimacy of that contrast was shocking, and set off a voluptuous tingling that swept from her scalp to her toes. She gasped with the sheer overwhelming delight of it.

Baird was smiling when he stretched out beside her, smiling as he splayed his hand at the juncture of her legs, smiling as he lowered his head to her breast and nibbled gently.

"You're delectable," he whispered, and it was Ardith's turn to laugh. It was a throaty, provocative sound that turned ragged and breathless as he drew her nipple into his mouth.

Fine filaments of pleasure crept through her, delicate glistening threads of delight: A flutter of the pulse at the base of her throat, a taut pearling of her nipples, a shimmer of sensation spilling down her spine, a fierce molten heat at the core of her.

As if he sensed what she was feeling, his fingers sought her most intimate flesh, gliding and pressing, inciting sweet chaos in her blood. She rose against him, tossing feverishly, whispering his name.

"Oh my dear, sweet, magnificent Ardith," he breathed, sounding a little feverish, too.

He licked a slow, juicy track from her breast to her mouth. He kissed her deeply, murmuring lovely, slurred, nonsensical endearments against her.

She turned to him. The hair on his chest and belly scoured her skin as she rubbed against him. His manhood brushed hot and tempting at the apex of her legs. With one sinuous motion she could have had him inside her, but she wanted to wait. She wanted time to touch him as he was touching her. Time to savor the deep, sweet pleasure of sensual beneficence.

She swept her hand along the warm, supple surface of his skin, her palm riding the long, lean contours of his body. The muscles in his back bunched and flexed, and she savored the way they slid beneath her hand. She trailed her fingers down his ribs, scaled his hip and moved down the taut slope of his belly.

Baird shivered and breathed her name as her hand encompassed him. She caught the rhythm it took to please him, a rhythm that was suddenly beating in her blood, her brain, in the substance of every cell. He moved with her as she kissed him, tasting the wanting on his mouth, the fervor on his tongue.

"Oh, Ardith, love," he breathed. "I need you."

"Yes. Yes," she whispered in answer. "I need you, too."

He rolled over her and made her his. For that moment it was as if the world stopped turning, as if nothing but the two of them existed in the wide, vast scope of earth and sky.

"I love you," he pledged.

"And I love you," she answered.

They held to the moment as long as they could, though fiercer needs were beckoning. They clung together for a few seconds more, until the lure of sensation became too compelling to resist.

The wildness took them, the frantic beat of life, the search for ultimate pleasure, the fiery celebration of their unity. It came in a rush, in a tumult of sensations sweeping over them. They held fast through the maelstrom, each caught by the flare of passion in the other's eyes, each bound by emotions that had been denied for far too long. They gave themselves up to something so bright and sweet that they cried out in mutual joy at the culmination and clung together as deep, sweet peace swept over them.

They lay tangled together for a very long time, joined and whole and sated. But at length Baird shifted onto his side, taking her with him and tucking her protectively in the bow of his arm. He lay quiet after that, stroking his fingers over her as if he would be content to contemplate the curve of her shoulder and the rise of her hip for the rest of their days.

Ardith curled against him, her leg across his hips and her head tucked into the curve of his shoulder. She was spent and dreamy and besotted by him. By them. By the wonder of what had passed between them. She had never thought she could be so happy.

Some miracle had happened in both their lives. After a long and lonely time, they had found this place, themselves, and each other. It was the love for the children that had brought them together—children who probably had no idea that she was about to marry their father.

She raised her head and kissed him. "Baird?"

He groaned with something that sounded like resignation. "I know that tone of voice."

"What tone of voice?"

He wrinkled his nose at her. An interesting expression, one she'd never seen on him before. "It's the tone of voice that means you're about to ask me to do something I won't want to do."

Ardith huffed a little and proceeded anyway. "I just wondered if you'd told the children about this. About asking me to marry you."

His face went serious, and he shook his head. "I didn't want to get their hopes up. Or mine, either."

"Don't you think we should?"

"Should what?"

"Tell them we're getting married?"

Something about the way he was touching her changed, the rhythm or the pressure or the intent. She couldn't say what, but it was making her heart beat a little faster, making her head a little light.

"Now?" He blinked at her sloe-eyed. "You want to get dressed and go tell them now?"

She could feel heat creep up her chest and into her

cheeks. She didn't know what he was doing to her exactly, but her blood had begun to hum.

"I thought we could . . ." Her voice sounded breathy even in her own ears.

"Well, we can, if you like."

His hand curled over her breast.

"Oh," she said. "Oh." She closed her eyes to concentrate on the pleasure of his touch. They weren't going anywhere.

"Someday you're going to have to teach me how to do this," she mumbled hazily.

"Oh, I will," he promised her. "And now, about the children?"

She was already aching for him to take her. "We'll tell them—" She paused on a sigh. "I think we'll have to tell them in the morning."

He laughed and kissed her.

EPILOGUE

*T*he matron with the magenta feathered hat lifted her lorgnette to get a better look. "I find this work quite shocking! Imagine, painting a woman with a tattoo on her face and calling it art!"

"Oh, but don't you find it fascinating?" her friend asked, drawing her peacock-patterned shawl a little closer around her shoulders. "What I mean is, she's a beautiful woman. Her hair and gown are lovely. Then there's that mark on her face—"

Through the crush to their left the gallery owner, Justin Daniels, was speaking to a group of Boston collectors. "We believe that A. E. Merritt has captured a truly unique perspective on the west. The paintings of western women suggest an attitude of strength and fearlessness and nobility that has never been expressed before. And her landscapes are exquisite; jewels, every one of them. The Boston Museum has already purchased several of the works for their collection. You could do far worse than to invest in such a promising—"

An aesthetic young man trailing a white silk scarf was

holding court in another corner of the crowded gallery. "There's no question that A. E. Merritt has broken new ground with these paintings," he was saying to a gaggle of fascinated art students. "They're bright and fresh, and while one may see the influence of Mary Cassatt in the portraits, Merritt has made her women partners with men in the settlement of western America. Take this woman for example—"

Baird Northcross stood in the center of the gallery, his youngest child asleep on his shoulder, listening to the comments being made around him and admiring his wife.

He smiled to himself. Ardith had painted nearly every day for the last two years preparing for tonight. She'd expanded the size of her canvases and worked in oil, her technique improving with every brush stroke. He was so proud of what she'd done and that she was getting the attention she deserved from the Boston collectors and critics.

Ardith stood out in this throng like an eagle in a nest of parakeets. She moved among them chatting, laughing, clasping the hands of old friends and new admirers. She had never looked more magnificent. Her sweeping bustled gown of bronze silk showed off her lush figure to perfection, and her face glowed with delight.

He just wished all the children were here to share Ardith's success, but China was in London with her grandfather, midway through her debut Season in society. She was just eighteen and so beautiful Baird had to catch his breath every time he looked at her. According to her letters, she had more beaus than any father cared to contemplate, yet she possessed a surprising maturity and undeniable sense—Ardith's gift to her, he supposed. Or Matt's.

Durban was back at the ranch in Wyoming, helping Buck and Myra run the place while he and Ardith were gone. And Khy—well, Khy was around somewhere—

probably up to his nose in trouble. He hadn't changed a lick since Ardith had brought the children west, except for his passion for drawing and painting.

Just then the baby raised her head, blinked sleepily at her surroundings, dismissed the whole of it with a sigh, and settled again. Baird rubbed her back and swayed with an expertise that bespoke months of practice.

"Mr. Merritt?"

Baird paused, amused to hear that he'd suddenly taken to using Ardith's name. When he turned, he found "Magenta Hat" addressing him. He'd heard the woman criticizing Cass Jalbert's portrait and had taken exception, though he knew for Ardith's sake he ought to be polite.

"Yes?"

"They tell me you're married to the artist, this A. E. Merritt, is that right?"

"Yes, ma'am, I am," he answered.

"And what do you think of a woman painting these kinds of pictures?"

Baird wondered why she wanted to know, or if she'd just come to bedevil him. "I think Ardith's paintings bring a special perspective to the west, a woman's perspective. What do you think?"

Baird could see he'd boxed her in and smiled to himself.

"I think *some* of them are quite—scenic. Is this really what the wild west looks like?"

Baird nodded, smiling outright. "There's nothing in the world to compare with the beauty out there in the mountains."

Going west had saved his life.

"They say you break horses in Wyoming?"

Not break exactly. Baird didn't believe in breaking horses, but he didn't expect Magenta Hat to understand the distinction.

"We have a ranch in the foothills of the Big Horn Mountains," he answered shortly.

After a couple of years of struggle when they'd lived on Ardith's earnings, they were beginning to turn a profit. With the breeding stock they'd bought from the Jalberts, next year promised to be even better.

"That's a pretty little girl," Peacock Shawl ventured, to cover the lengthening silence. "What's her name?"

Baird smiled again, this time with a father's pride. "Cheyenne," he answered.

"I hear," Magenta Hat spoke again, "that your children are all named for where you were when they were born. Were you in Cheyenne when the stork brought this one?"

He compressed his lips before he spoke, measuring out his words. "No, ma'am," he answered quietly. "It's where I was when she was conceived."

It was a moment before the meaning of his words dawned on the two dowagers. He waited, smiling politely.

Peacock Shawl caught the gist of them first and ruffled like a sparrow in the rain. Magenta Hat flushed a shade or two darker than her clothes.

"Well!" she huffed and spun away.

"Alienating my patrons, are you, dear?" Ardith asked, appearing at his elbow just in time to watch the two women elbow their way through the crush to the door.

"Not any more than they deserve."

"Oh, that's Mrs. Warburton," Justin Daniels observed, coming up behind them. "She has piles of money and never buys a thing. I think the only reason she comes to openings is the sherry."

Baird laughed and Cheyenne raised her head. She smiled at her mother, then nestled again.

He hadn't expected to like Daniels so much. He'd imagined the art dealer would be snobbish and oily. Instead the man was practical and shrewd, with a sense of humor that was as wicked as it was perceptive.

As the press in the gallery thinned, Gavin Rawlinson came to join them. He bussed Ardith's cheek and beamed at her. "It looks like tonight's an unmitigated success."

In spite of experiencing a twinge or two of jealousy when the man took liberties like this one, Baird liked Rawlinson, too. He would have been happier if Gavin wasn't quite so handsome, or as bright as a new-minted penny. Or still quite obviously in love with Baird's wife.

But when Rawlinson looked at Ardith like this, with tenderness and longing and deep regrets, Baird found he couldn't help feeling sorry for the man. He never had been entirely able to fathom why Ardith had chosen him over this paragon, but he'd be grateful until the day he died that she had.

Just then Meggie Jalbert joined the small group. "I've just ushered out the last of our patrons and locked the door," she reported to Justin Daniels. She'd been working at the gallery since she'd come to study in Boston and would have a small showing of her own paintings in the spring.

"Good!" Daniels said. "Now that the riffraff is gone, I can break out the champagne."

"Champagne?" Ardith echoed. "Have we done well enough to warrant champagne?"

"Indeed we have. I also have a copy of the review that will run in tomorrow morning's paper." Daniels withdrew several folded sheets from his pocket and began to quote. "They said your work was 'wondrously fresh.' They called your technique 'masterful,' and said you brought 'a woman's perspective, to the art of the west.'"

Baird beamed at her. "I guess that does warrant champagne."

"Oh, let me see!" Ardith begged and looked over the article while Justin uncorked the bottles of champagne. Baird read over her shoulder, his smile broadening with each line.

Ardith looked up at him when she was done. "I did it," she whispered.

"I'm not surprised." Yet he knew she needed these accolades to confirm what Baird had known from the start: that she and her art were something special.

Justin came around with a tray of glasses just as Khy wormed his way into the crook of Ardith's arm.

Baird shifted Cheyenne on his shoulder and raised his glass. "I'd like to make a toast," he said. "First, to friends, old and new. To Justin and the continued success of your gallery—and especially with my wife's work."

"Hear, hear!" Ardith said with a laugh.

"To Meggie, in anticipation of her own successes in the art world. And Gavin, whose friendship made so many things possible."

Ardith smiled her approval.

"And last, to my wife." Across the rim of the glass Baird met Ardith's rainwater-bright eyes. For an instant he simply smiled at her, so much in love with this woman he couldn't think. Then he cleared his throat.

"Do you remember, Ardith, the night you first got word that Justin was willing to represent your paintings?"

Ardith smiled at the memory.

"I told you then I hoped A. E. Merritt would set the art world ablaze."

"Yes."

He leaned across and kissed her. "Well, tonight, you have."

ABOUT THE AUTHOR

ELIZABETH GRAYSON was published for the first time in the fourth grade and had completed an historical novel by the time she was fifteen. COLOR OF THE WIND is her ninth published work, several of which were written under the pseudonym Elizabeth Kary. She holds degrees in education and has taught art in elementary schools and at the St. Louis Art Museum. She lives on the outskirts of the city with her advertising executive husband and tabby cat. Contact her at P.O.Box 260052, St. Louis, Missouri 63126 or by e-mail at egrayson@MVP.net

IRIS JOHANSEN

Teresa Medeiros

Breath of Magic
___56334-3 $5.99/$7.99 in Canada

Fairest of Them All
___56333-5 $5.99/$7.50 in Canada

Thief of Hearts
___56332-7 $5.99/$7.99 in Canada

A Whisper of Roses
___29408-3 $5.99/$7.99

Once an Angel
___29409-1 $5.99/$7.99

Heather and Velvet
___29407-5 $5.99/$7.50

Shadows and Lace
___57623-2 $5.99/$7.99

Touch of Enchantment
___57500-7 $5.99/$7.99

Nobody's Darling
___57501-5 $5.99/$7.99

Charming the Prince
___57502-3 $5.99/$8.99